# MORE OF *You*

## CONFESSIONS OF THE HEART

*A.L. Jackson*

*NEW YORK TIMES* BESTSELLING AUTHOR

A.L. Jackson
**www.aljacksonauthor.com**
Cover Design by RBA Designs
Photo by Wander Aguiar Photography.
Editing by AW Editing and Susan Staudinger
Formatting by Mesquite Business Services

Print ISBN: 978-1-946420-21-3
eBook ISBN: 978-1-946420-20-6

# MORE OF *You*

# More from A.L. Jackson

# prologue

## Faith

*R*ays of blinding light streaked through the moss-covered branches that stretched across the old dirt road like a living canopy.

It was a road we'd walked together what seemed like a thousand times.

It was our secret spot.

Our *sacred* spot.

He stared at me from where he stood five feet from me. Big hands stuffed in the pockets of his ripped jeans and guilt written on the lines of his perfect face.

"I don't care what anyone thinks." The words poured from my mouth, begging for him to hear.

To listen.

To finally, truly understand.

"I don't care what kind of trouble we're in. The only thing that matters to me is that you're standing right there in front of me."

Sadness crested his features. Face masculine and striking. Every time I looked at him, it twisted something deep inside me. My love for him was bigger—more important—than anything else in my small, little world.

But that was the thing when I looked at him.

I saw great things. A future spanning out in front of us that would go on forever.

But it was the expression he wore this afternoon that scattered the butterflies in a shock of fear and sent dread gushing in to take their place.

"It doesn't matter, Faith? How can you say that?" His voice was bitter and hard, every bit of disgust cast at himself.

I took a pleading step forward. "It doesn't. The only thing that matters is you and me."

He took a weary step back. It kicked up a plume of dust to hover around his old, worn shoes. "You matter, Faith. Who you are and who you're going to be matters. And I won't stand in the way of that any longer."

Tears burned my eyes. "No."

He shook his head. "I'm sorry. The last thing I ever wanted to do was hurt you, but that seems to be the only thing I can do. What happened last night is proof of that. It ends right now."

His broad shoulders heaved as he forced himself to turn around, bitterness and self-imposed rage coming from him in waves as he started up the road.

Panic filled my chest. A crushing force against my aching heart. I rushed for him. "Jace . . . please, don't do this. Don't leave me."

My fingertips brushed down his back. I swore that I could see the snap of energy crackle from the connection. The way it'd always been. This boy my fire.

I could feel his burn when he whirled around. A gasp raked from my lungs when he suddenly captured my face in both of his hands. Those eyes searched my face.

A tender memorization that contradicted everything about this hard boy.

My heart stampeded when he dipped down and took my

mouth.

His lips were soft and rough.

Possessive in their goodbye.

I knew that was what it was.

I could feel him taking pieces of me when he dropped his forehead against mine and breathed me in, his eyes squeezed tightly closed.

Pain radiated from him like the heat waves that held to the sticky, summer air.

He reached out and gripped me by both of the shoulders, pushing away from me as if he had to physically pry himself free.

Stripping and ripping and ruining.

The second he stepped back, I could feel the tear run through the center of me.

His gaze remained fixed on the ground when he reeled back around, his head dipped low because he couldn't bring himself to look at me as he went.

So, it was me who had to watch him go.

I couldn't stop staring as he trudged up the deserted lane. Spikes of sunlight slanted through the spindly branches, covering him in a golden, glittering light.

So bright he appeared unreal. Tall and strong and gorgeous in his rough, raw way.

An angel in tattered, demon's clothes.

He'd always viewed himself as the town pariah. The outcast. The *outlaw*.

Bringing trouble to everything he touched.

But that troubled boy was my shining star. He'd taught me to have *faith* that people were so much more than their exteriors and their reputations. Made me have *faith* that destinies weren't based on our circumstances but rather what we made of them.

In that moment, I had *faith* he'd come to his senses. Stop and turn around and realize we were always supposed to be together. No matter what.

But he didn't.

He just let the connection pull and pull and pull with each of his steps until my heart finally ripped under the strain of it.

3

It shredded me right in two.

That was the day Jace Jacobs walked out of my life.

And I swore I'd never be fool enough again to let him back in it . . .

# *one*

## Faith
### Ten Years Later

"*B*ailey?" I called from the top of the stairs. "Is that you?"

The old house was cast in darkness. Intermittent blips of lightning flashed at the windows as wind howled and whipped at the walls.

The foundation groaned and shook.

But I swore . . . I swore I'd heard a loud creak on the deserted side of the house when I'd made it to the top of the sweeping staircase.

Unease shivered through my senses, and I clung to the banister as I tried to orient myself.

To ground myself.

To latch on to sanity rather than the horror I'd been livin' for the last three months.

This old house had been my dream. Taking the neglected plantation and turning it into a bed and breakfast. Restoring it to its original beauty.

The gorgeous mansion was three sprawling stories of old-world charm and history. It was hidden on a secluded patch of land about ten minutes outside the small town where I'd grown up.

It was funny how dreams could shift into nightmares in the blink of an eye. How the comfort I'd found in this place could turn into this unbearable feeling of isolation and vulnerability.

"Hello, is anyone there?" My voice trembled as a fresh wave of fear rushed through my senses.

Even with the air conditioner doing its best to pump into the space, I could feel the sweat slick my back in the humid summer air, my breaths panted into the night as I peered into the darkened hallway to the right where I stood at the top of the stairs.

In this spot, the second floor split into two directions. There were four bedrooms to the right and four to the left.

Our rooms were to the left.

Was it my mind playing tricks on me that I'd heard something coming from off to the right?

The problem was, I no longer knew what was real. What was paranoia and what was a true threat.

My heart drummed, this erratic *boom, boom, boom* that thundered the walls as loud as the thunder that rumbled outside.

Heavy clouds hugged the old plantation while something like chills went skating across my flesh.

Silence echoed back.

But still, those spikes of awareness lifted the fine hairs at the nape of my neck.

"Who's there?" I called again, my voice cracking like a plea.

Nothing. Tears of frustration and helplessness built in my eyes. No doubt, my mind was conjuring things that just weren't there.

I was nothin' but a prisoner to shock and sorrow and a debilitating sort of fear.

I hadn't been able to sleep for more than a minute at a time for the past three months, and an anxious exhaustion had set in.

My body succumbing while my mind continued to race.

Pictures invaded my mind every time I attempted to close my eyes.

*Blood. Blood. So much blood.*

*His eyes so wide.*

*His body so still.*

I wasn't sure I would ever recover from the way Joseph had died, from the fact my husband had been murdered, my world rocked by grief and guilt and questions. I'd thought that moment was the lowest low. Rock bottom.

That was until the ominous notes had begun to show up, making demands of me that I didn't know how to meet.

I hadn't even been able to comprehend how terrifying things might become. How I'd begin to question everything I'd once thought I'd known.

I squeezed my eyes against the visions that assaulted me, shaking myself out of the spiral I was getting ready to stumble into and tried to convince myself everything was fine.

I had to get it together. Hold the splintering pieces together that were close to shattering.

The only thing left of me was dust and debris and desolation.

Except for one thing.

It was the one thing that got me out of bed every morning. The one thing that made me put one foot in front of the other. The one thing that forced me into believin' that one day, no matter how hard it was right then, everything would be okay.

Clutching my cell phone in my hand, I ignored the fear and turned left down the quieted hall. I gently pushed open the door that had remained open a crack.

A sliver of light lit up her angelic face, a little fist pressed to her chubby cheek, all those curls of wild, dark hair spilled out over her pillow where she slept safe and sound on the pink toddler bed.

My heart pressed at my ribs. The emotion so big I wondered how it didn't suffocate me.

My purpose.

My life.

The only reason hope still glowed within these walls.

Within me.

When everything felt impossible and wrong.

I edged across her floor and knelt at the side of her bed. My fingers gentled through the soft, soft locks of her hair.

In her arm was tucked the stuffed Beast doll that she'd found buried in my closet and had carried everywhere since, as if it were a lifeline that she didn't understand.

She sighed in her sleep, and I leaned up to kiss her cheek, whispering my love for what had to have been the millionth time that night.

It was almost a smile on my face when I pushed to my feet.

Then I froze because that feeling was back.

Something was amiss.

An ugly charge to the air that didn't have a thing to do with the storm.

Was I going crazy? Had it all finally become too much? Because I was sure it was footsteps I heard inching down the staircase.

Terror racing my veins, I struggled to breathe and inched for the door, ready to make a call for help, only to stop when I noticed the light on in the bathroom attached to Bailey's room.

Razors of fear scraped across my skin, and I edged that way, feeling like some kind of helpless, defenseless girl as I pushed out a shaking hand to nudge the door the rest of the way open.

Nothing but a fool who was afraid of the dark.

That had to be what this was. My imagination was finally getting the best of me.

Or maybe I was just afraid of the fact I was truly alone.

Then I gasped, hand flying to my mouth to stifle a scream.

The only sound in the bathroom was the constant *drip, drip, drip* coming from the tub faucet that was far too high for Bailey to reach.

Droplets steadily plopped into the water that filled the entire thing.

Floating facedown in it was one of Bailey's favorite dolls.

# *Two*

## Jace

"We just finished getting her statement."

I swallowed around the lump lodged in my throat as I stood on the sidewalk across the street from the police station, talking to Mack who was inside.

"How is she?" The words barely made it from between my lips.

He sighed on the other end of the line. "Not well, as you can imagine. Some asshole was definitely in that house. Slipped in and out with her barely noticing except for the fact she'd had the intuition that something was off. Pair that with the two letters she's received, and the poor girl is terrified."

Fury surged. So intense that I saw red.

I wanted to hunt someone down. Find them. End the threat. But every name I'd given Mack relating to Joseph had been a dead end.

So now I stood there like some piece-of-shit stalker, fighting the urge to pace like a lunatic or maybe bust through the station doors.

"What do I do?" I grated at the phone, at a loss. All the things I was aching to do might be frowned upon.

"You let me do my job. I could lose my badge for telling you any of this shit, so I need you to play it cool. Most of all, you need to give her space and time because you know she needs it. Deserves it. You can't come in like some kind of vigilante thinking you're going to set shit straight."

He might as well have not said a thing with the words that fell from my mouth. "I need to find this asshole."

He sighed. "It could be nothing more than kids playing a prank."

"You really believe that?" I bit out.

Frustration bled from him. "No, I don't. Gut tells me someone is trying to send a message. A warning. The question is why and what the fuck it has to do with Joseph's death."

I could hear him shuffling some papers in his office. "I am going to figure this out. I promise you that. But you need to give me the space to do it. I don't know why the hell I called you in the first place."

"You know why."

He sighed again.

Of course, he knew.

He really didn't have much of an option. There was too much history between us for him to keep me in the dark, even though he probably would have preferred to have left me hanging.

Out of his way so he could do his job.

But sometimes friendship and loyalty meant more than protocol.

The second Mack had called last night and told me the situation had escalated, there'd been nothing I could do.

I'd been in my car, a suitcase packed, the trip from Atlanta to Broadshire Rim made in three hours during the middle of the night. It was a small town twenty minutes outside of Charleston, and the one place I'd sworn to myself I'd never return to.

I hadn't even thought it through.

The consequences.

What it was going to do to me or how being around her again

was going to affect me.

The only thought I'd known was she was in trouble and I had to get to her.

Stop what should have been stopped a long time ago.

If only I could go back to that day and intervene. Make the right choice instead of the selfish, petulant one I had.

It had been one driven by bitterness and hatred.

One I'd regretted every single day since Mack had first called me and told me Joseph was gone.

Guilt clawed at my insides while this spot inside me screamed and groaned and demanded I cross the street, fly into the small police station, wrap her up, and take her away from here.

Was pretty sure that wasn't going to go over so well.

"Where are you, anyway?" Mack asked.

"Outside."

"Fuck . . . Jace . . . you can't do this."

"Watch me."

I ended the call and shoved my hands into my suit pockets, doing my best to keep my cool, trying to listen to all the warnings that Mack had made.

*Give her space.*

*We don't know what's happening.*

*It could just be punk kids playing a prank.*

Punk kids, my ass.

Main Street was busy, the rural town bustling with people as they went about their days, yet their pace somehow slowed.

It was like the entire population had gone back in time.

Stepped into an era that was simpler.

Small shops and stores and businesses were tucked in the old brick buildings that were fronted by large windows and colorful awnings. Trees grew high where they were sporadically placed in the cobblestone sidewalks, and some hugged the sides of the buildings, giving shade to the hot, heated summer day.

It was all mixed up with the familiar, distinct smell of the pluff mud in the marshes that sat back from the sea.

I caught a few curious glances. I'd been gone for so long and had changed so much that I doubted a whole lot of people would recognize me, but I stood out enough that I was sure they wondered what the hell I was doing there.

Yeah, join the fucking club.

Because I had no idea what the hell I was doing there, either.

Torturing myself, that was what.

The police station that hadn't been there when I left sat across the street, the two-story building tucked under a bunch of lush, green trees.

Cruisers and a couple of unmarked cars lined the curb and filled the parking lot to the side.

Sweat gathered at my nape, my body itchy.

Antsy.

I just needed to see her.

Know she was really okay.

But I guessed I really wasn't prepared for that happening. Wasn't prepared for a second to actually see her again.

My goddamned breath was gone when the door swung open and she fumbled out with her head dropped toward the ground. Her shoulders sagged and defeat lined her posture.

Her best friend, Courtney, was next to her, guiding Faith out with one hand on her lower back.

It didn't matter that ten years had passed or that a whole shitstorm had transpired during that time.

She was still the most gorgeous thing I'd ever seen.

Beauty.

Belief and purity and this innocence that made something crazy come unhinged inside me. It was overpowering, the need to get to her.

Protect her.

Worst was the way my body reacted.

The girl had always been so far out of my league it wasn't funny.

Better than me in every way.

Grace.

*Beauty.*

My guts clenched.

None of those things meant what I'd felt for her hadn't been real.

It'd just been stupid.

Just like right then.

Because a streak of possessiveness flew through my veins like a goddamned drug.

Energy crashed through the air.

A torrent of emotion.

Resonating.

Pulsating.

An echo of the past.

Chocolate hair fell down her back in silky waves, and I swore to God, I could feel the warmth radiating from her spirit, all this devastating goodness paired with a body that was meant for sin. All long legs and tempting curves.

*My sin.*

Taking her was exactly what that had been.

Since the first time I'd seen her, this girl had held the power to drop me straight to my knees.

So stunning that I went stupid.

Time hadn't had the power to alter that.

Because there was no stopping the lust that curled my guts with a need so intense I felt lightheaded.

Or maybe it was just the guilt that clotted the blood flow to my brain.

Sorrow clung to her like a disease.

I was responsible for that.

God. I was a bastard.

But I'd be a monster if I turned a blind eye. If I stayed in my cushy office back in Atlanta and pretended like none of this was going down.

I sucked down a breath and tried to steel my nerves.

I had a purpose.

A reason.

I just needed a motherfucking plan.

# *Three*

## Faith

*I* felt it.

Someone watching me from behind.

I should have been terrified of it after what had happened last night. I guessed in some way I was, but not in the way anyone might think.

I could feel it blazing from across the street. As if his stare was its own entity.

I should have known better than to look that way. But there was nothing I could have done, nothing that would have stopped me from shifting my gaze that direction.

Maybe I already knew what I would discover.

Knew who would be standing there like an apparition.

My mouth dropped open on a shocked gasp, the humid air gone, nothing but this blistering heat in its place.

My knees wobbled, and my hand shot out to the station wall to keep myself from falling.

My best friend Courtney was right there, always holding me up the way she did. She surged around to the front of me, brushing the hair back from my face.

"Are you okay? I know this is insane . . . crazy . . . what happened last night. But I promise you that no one is gonna let anything happen to you or Bailey. Do you understand?"

Of course, she'd mistaken my shock for fear, the dread coming off me in waves enough to pull me under.

And still, I couldn't find any words to correct her. I could only stare, the entirety of my attention locked on the man who stood directly across the street.

Energy crashed, like lashes of the sun.

Searing as the strikes hit my skin.

I swore that just his presence in this town had to have sucked every molecule from the atmosphere.

It left my lungs empty and starvin' for oxygen.

My chest stretched tight in pain.

This couldn't be happening.

How could he show up here? After all this time? After everything?

Courtney frantically searched my face before she finally realized my attention was pinned in horror on something across the street.

She looked over her shoulder. Shock hit her, too.

Anger rushed through her being, and she clamped down her hold on my arm. "Are you fucking kidding me?"

My insides curled and clenched in the most intense kind of pain.

Old, old love that shouldn't still exist.

All the hurt that went with it.

Every scar I'd prayed and prayed would heal.

I wasn't sure I could take any more.

"What the hell is he doing here?" Courtney seethed.

Her green eyes darted back to me where I was pressed against the station wall, praying the bricks might swallow me up and let me disappear.

Sympathy was written over every inch of her face.

I hated that every time she turned around she was having to

feel sorry for me.

"Stay right here, Faith. I'm going to take care of this."

I swallowed around the bile that'd lifted in my throat, and I buried the sting of old wounds that had been ripped wide open.

Raw and fresh and aching.

I refused to feel this way. Trapped by the simple fact he was there.

He didn't deserve it, and he was the last person I should be concerned about. The last person who deserved any of my thoughts or worries or questions.

I had real issues I had to deal with.

Disturbing, daunting issues.

Enough grief to keep me up for a thousand nights.

I grabbed Courtney's arm right before she went storming across the road. "Please. Don't. Just let it be."

She looked back at me, her stylish brown ponytail that was set high on her head swishing around her pretty face. "I'm not gonna stand here and pretend as if that asshole didn't show his face in this town. After all this time? After what happened? He has more nerve than anyone I know."

She exhaled a sound of fury and her own hurt and grief—grief for me—and glared back at Jace.

Jace Jacobs.

The man took a step out of the shadows where he'd hidden along the wall on the other side of the street.

Right into the sun.

Oh God.

I wished he'd have remained concealed. Stayed just wisps and vapor that didn't really exist. Wished with all my might that he wasn't looking at me like that.

As if he knew me.

Remembered me.

It didn't matter that he was at least a hundred feet away.

It felt as if he were standing right in front of me.

The rags he'd worn had been traded for a fitted, expensive suit. His once scruffy hair was short, styled in a sophisticated way around his unforgettable face, his beard short and trimmed and accentuating his strong jaw.

A shiver raced my spine and left a sticky, sick feeling that pooled in my gut.

A flash of that old, old love that I no longer could feel ricocheted in the depths of me. Through those dark, empty, vacant places.

It was a love I'd waited on for what had felt like forever before I'd given up and convinced myself that I had to move on before I lost myself totally.

Wholly.

I refused to call it settling.

I'd been happy. Content with a warm, comfortable love.

And there stood Jace, making me *uncomfortable* in his intense, potent way.

More gorgeous than he'd been. Taller and wider and older, and all of those things only made him that much more appealing.

Those eyes were fixated on me.

The color of a brand-new, shiny penny.

A coppered shimmer that ranged between red and brown and orange.

Familiar in a way I didn't want them to be.

They watched me as if they *knew* me. Full of something dangerous and possessive and alive.

Soft with lies of apology.

I felt pinned beneath them.

Trapped.

Courtney clenched her jaw. "What an asshole. Someone needs to put him in his place. And his place isn't here."

I tore myself from his gaze and looked at her. "It doesn't matter, Court. Let's just go. The only thing I want is to pick up my daughter and go home. I'm exhausted, and I just want to hold her, know she's okay."

I'd dropped her at my parents' house, the only place I felt secure enough to leave her before I'd come to the station.

They'd argued, wanted to be here for me.

I'd told them that the best thing they could do for me was watch my child, ensure she was safe, make her feel as if it were just any other day.

"Okay," Courtney relented. "Let's go get that sweet girl of yours and get you home."

She took me by the inside of my elbow and tucked me to her side, as if she could guard me from any bad things coming my way.

I could feel them all around me.

Getting closer.

Growing stronger.

Eyes watching.

Energy pulsing.

I struggled to keep my head bowed as I let Courtney guide me down the sidewalk toward her car, which was parked at the curb, our speed increasing with every step we took.

It gave me the sense that I was fleeing.

Running.

I guessed I should have known I could never run as fast and as far as him.

Because I could feel it.

The burst of hot energy that hit me from behind.

My heart stuttered a beat.

"Faith," he called, voice a gruff rumble of a plea.

My face pinched, and my legs went weak below me, my feet no longer able to carry me.

I wanted to jump into Courtney's car. Have her whisk me away to a secret place where no one could touch me.

Hurt me or my daughter.

Unable to stand beneath the intensity, I whirled around, the words already flying from my mouth as I did. "I don't have anything to say to you."

He stuffed his hands into his suit pant pockets. The man looked like some kind of distinguished model.

Polished and big city.

So different from the rough outcast I remembered, yet so much the same it hurt to look at him.

"What if I have something I need to say to you?"

Disbelief shook my head. "And what could you possibly have to say to me?"

Grief struck across his strong features, and despite the distance between us, I could see the way his thick throat rolled as he swallowed. His voice had only deepened when he spoke again, "I'm sorry about Joseph."

I choked over the incredulous sound that locked in my chest. I wasn't sure if it was laughter or a cry. "You're sorry?"

"I am. Incredibly."

I blinked. Long and hard. Before I forced my eyes to open and remain pinned on him. "You don't get to be sorry for me, Jace. You have no idea what I've been through. What I'm goin' through. Just . . . go back to where you came from. Go home."

I turned and started for Courtney's car. She returned her hand to my arm in a silent show of support, though I could feel her looking back at Jace from over her shoulder.

If looks could kill and all of that. Courtney could slay a man with a single glance of her razor-sharp eyes.

But Jace Jacobs was still standing, his words darts where they impaled my back. "I am home."

At his assertion, I stumbled a step and my hands clenched into fists. Somehow, I managed to force myself to keep walking.

A long time ago, he'd promised me I'd always be his home. That together, we were gonna build a castle.

And the man had never been anything but a liar.

# *four*

## Faith

*I* shot upright in bed, gasping through the remnants of the dream and the fear clouding the sanity of my mind. Again, I'd fallen into a restless sleep. Sucked down by the exhaustion, only to immediately jolt from sleep.

The sheets were tangled around my legs, sweat slickin' my back so that the thin fabric of my tank stuck to my skin.

I sucked in a staggered breath, trying to calm the terror that clanged like a thunder through my veins.

A constant thrum, thrum, thrum, that beat and bled and threatened everything that was important to me.

Blinking through the haze of night, I threw off the sheets and climbed to my shaky feet.

Maybe I should have given in and let either Courtney or my mama and daddy spend the night.

But I'd told them I couldn't be held prisoner in my own home.

That it wasn't right to uproot their lives, especially since Mack had promised he would have an officer driving by the plantation several times throughout the night, the entire squadron keeping a close eye on us.

Still, he'd warned me that I should be careful just in case.

Watchful.

Make sure all my doors were locked up tight.

As if I wasn't already jumping at every sound. Peering out the windows with each rustle of the trees and craning my ear every time the old house groaned. All the while, I'd be clutching my phone, at the ready to dial Mack if there was even a hint that someone might be trying to get inside.

It was just my luck that the old walls loved to moan all night long.

The hardest part was I had this overwhelming urge to take possession of my life. To pick up the shattered pieces and splice them back together. To find my strength in the midst of all the turmoil.

But how could I do that when I could feel danger lurking all around us? Dragging us into darkness when all I wanted was to reach for the light.

For safety and joy.

Heart still beating wild, my feet inched across the worn, hard planks of my bedroom floor, senses set to high alert.

Awareness prickled across my damp flesh.

But I wasn't afraid the way I'd been last night.

No, instead I was finding some sort of comfort in the disorder.

A fool who found security in the danger.

I edged toward the window that I'd already checked twice to make sure was locked. Off to the side of it, I pulled back the drape so I could peer into the night.

I sucked in a breath that didn't seem to have anywhere to go. My heart took off at a sprint, part of me filling right up with indignant fury.

How could he?

How could he?

Though there was a stupid part of me that was thankful someone was watchin' after us.

Gulping down the unease, I grabbed the short robe from

where it hung on the back of a chair and pulled it on, quickly tying the knot.

My door was wide open, the same as Bailey's so I could hear her if she needed me. I glanced into her room, my child again soundly asleep, unaware of the disturbance as I tiptoed across the creaking floors.

As quietly as I could, I moved down the sweeping, curved staircase, the house massive and dark.

Ominous at this time of night. Maybe it'd been all along.

Heart a thunder knocking at my ribs, I worked through the locks on the double doors, not even sure what it was that I was doing. Why I felt compelled to step out into the night.

Toward him when I should be running in tacklinthe opposite direction.

Away from the man who had destroyed me in a way that only he could. The only one who'd ever had the power to desolate me because he'd been the only one I'd ever completely given myself to.

And I hated it.

Hated that he still had that control.

The control to make me quiver and shake and question everything I thought I knew.

Pulling open the door, I stepped out onto the wrap-around porch, hugging the robe tighter around my body, wishing it was a thousand layers of protection.

A guard against my heart that beat a frenzy at the center of my chest.

Outside, the night was heavy, bugs trillin' in the massive trees that were hugged by the droning night. The ancient oaks lined the long, dirt drive, their branches covered in moss and stretched out like craggy arms to shelter the road.

I eased a step forward and lifted my chin in a stance of intimidation while, on the inside, I wasn't feeling close to brave.

I stared at the outline of the man who stood at the end of the tree-lined road.

As if he'd been there all along.

Waiting.

Squeezing my eyes closed, I wondered if I was hallucinating. Part of me praying that I was. That he'd never stepped foot back in this town.

When I opened them, there he was, moving forward, his steps slow yet somehow powerful and purposed.

He'd always moved that way.

His presence profound.

Hitting me with the force of a bolt of lightning. As if I were standing right at the edge of a moment that would change everything.

The first time I'd seen him, I was sure the boy was there to be revered, completely unattainable, shrouded in some kind of dark mystery, while the town called him trash.

They'd whispered that he wasn't worthy, when I'd known in my heart of hearts that he'd been worth everything.

Every risk.

Except right then, I was wishin' that I'd never taken it.

His intensity mounted and mounted with each step that he took.

Energy thrashed through the air, binding to the humidity.

My pulse went thready beneath the pressure, knees shaking as if I'd seen a ghost.

But that was what these walls had always held.

Ghosts and secrets and scandals.

I'd always been drawn to the beauty of it. Romanticizing this place. I guessed it'd been all too easy to fall in love under the shadow of it.

He stopped at the bottom of the five steps that led up to the porch.

Those hands stuffed in his pockets again. His hair that had been styled earlier had been tussled and mussed, no doubt the victim of those restless, big hands.

My breaths turned jagged as he stood there staring up at me, those eyes glinting beneath the moonlight.

His teeth clamped down on his lush bottom lip as he looked around the old, dilapidated plantation, expression intense, as if he were reaching out to caress a memory.

Rocking back on his heels, he tipped the potency of that gaze back up to me. "You always loved this place."

There was something there in his words.

Something wistful and sad.

It sent a stake of anger to pierce my heart.

*We loved this place*, I wanted to shout at him. Beg him. Because it didn't matter how many years separated us, the question still remained.

Why?

Why?

Why?

But asking would be wrong.

Misguided.

Nothing we shared in the past mattered anymore. And I hated that just him coming here could stoke even an ember.

My heart no longer belonged to him.

"What are you doing here, Jace?" A tremble rocked through the question.

He dropped his gaze to the ground, wary when he looked back at me. "I needed to check on you."

Bitter laughter rumbled out, all mixed up with the fear and sorrow and grief that lined the inside of me. It came rolling out in a rush of anger. "Check on me? I haven't seen you in ten years, and you needed to check on me at three in the mornin'?"

He blew out a sigh. "A lot has changed since then. I couldn't sleep, knowing you were here alone."

Gutting disbelief moved through me like a black, ugly storm. I'd always been the one who was the first to forgive.

But when it'd come to Jace, all of that had changed. The man had taken all the good and belief inside me and turned it into a mockery.

I couldn't believe he thought he had the right to stand there, in *that* spot, acting as if he cared.

"And none of those things have much to do with you, do they?"

He eyed me, words hard. "Don't they?"

"You gave up your place here, Jace. *You did.* You left, and you don't get to come back when you find it fit."

He flinched as if I was the one who was hurting him. As if he hadn't left me humiliated and broken. Like the *trash* I'd refused to let anyone convince me that he was.

I'd been the fool, and I wouldn't fall for his act again.

"Can't stop myself from being worried about you." His voice whispered on the wind, hitting me like knives against my skin.

"There's nothing for you to worry about."

He lifted a brow in challenge. "You sure about that?"

Looking off to the side, I bit my lip, realizing that Mack had most likely told Jace everything. I should have known I couldn't keep it private when Jace and Mack had been as close as brothers back in high school, and now Mack was the one leading the investigation.

Still, I couldn't stop the anger that slipped into my bloodstream at the thought of Jace being privy to any details of our lives.

I wanted to shut him out, put up every wall so he couldn't see inside.

It wasn't right for him to be afforded a view of my demolished heart.

It didn't matter how much I wanted to keep Jace out, the words were scraping free. "My husband was *murdered*. Murdered in cold blood."

*Cold blood.*

Is that what it'd been? It's what I'd believed in the beginning. When Mack had shown up at my door and delivered the news that they'd found Joseph shot outside the grocery store, I'd been devastated.

It didn't matter that the love I'd had for Joseph had been different than I'd ever imagined for the man I'd marry.

Ours had been a slow love. One that had grown out of friendship.

Joseph had been there for me when I'd needed a friend most. He'd picked me up after Jace had left me in pieces.

Losing Joseph that way had been a brutal blow.

A smack to the face.

Still, I'd been sure it'd been a cut and dry case of a man being in the wrong place at the wrong time.

But with each day that passed, I'd begun to question that. Began to question Joseph's innocence. Began to question whether he'd unknowingly set Bailey and me on a course of destruction.

Grief clutching my spirit, I plowed on, needing Jace to know he wasn't welcome. "You don't get to come here now and pretend like you care."

"He was my cousin, Faith. I have a right to know what's happening."

The fact they'd been family made my insides recoil.

My brows pinched in pain. "Do you? Do you really think you have the right? The right to show up here?"

He raked a hand through his hair, staring off into the distance, into the muggy breeze that rustled through the trees.

Finally, he turned back to me. "I know you hate me, Faith. You have every right to. You should hate me every bit as much as I hate myself, but that doesn't change the fact that I'm here. That I'm going to take care of you. Protect you. Whatever it takes."

If only I could hate him the way he assumed that I did.

I lifted a defiant chin. "The only thing I want from you is for you to leave."

His posture was hard, his eyes harder.

The man hazard and peril the way everyone had warned.

"That is not going to happen. You should know me better than that."

I moved for the door, pausing to look back at him from over my shoulder. "I thought I did know you."

Retreating inside, I slammed the door, closing off the connection.

Every part of me started shaking, my hands barely cooperating as I fumbled through the locks as if they might be strong enough to keep him out. My lungs squeezed with each battered breath, and my heart rioted at the center of my chest.

I couldn't let him in. Not ever again.

I sucked down a breath and turned for the stairs, climbing them quickly.

I stumbled to a stop three steps from the second-floor landing.

"Oh, sweetheart," I whispered into the darkness, my sweet, sweet girl rubbing a fist at her sleepy eye, and that torn, tattered Beast hooked under her right arm.

Just the sight of it nearly dropped me to my knees.

"Don't never *weave* me, Mommy."

Only three years old, she still dropped the L in every word she spoke, her mouth not quite ready to form the sound, the lilt of it always sending a fresh wave of affection crashing through me.

But it was her fear of abandonment, the loss that was haunting us both, that nearly destroyed me.

I swept her into my arms. Love and adoration and the strongest devotion pumped through me like a river. Growing stronger and deeper.

My heart no longer felt as if it was goin' to fail because I had my reason for living in my arms. My reason for fighting. My reason for surviving.

I pushed back the wild locks of her brown curls from her face and pressed a tender kiss to her forehead, murmuring against her baby-powder skin. "Never. Mommy would never leave you."

She wrapped her tiny arms around my neck, squeezing me tight, her lips against my cheek. "Oh-kay."

She yawned and snuggled tighter into my hold.

I hugged her closer and carried her toward my room. Part of me knew I was clinging to my daughter too tightly, feeding into her own fears of desertion and loss.

It was hard to stop when she felt like the only thing I had.

My very breath.

I set her on my bed, and she stared up at me as I took her in. Her pink cheeks were round and chubby, her lips full and red. Her dark eyes somehow grinned. "I *sweep* with you?"

"Yeah, baby, you can sleep with me."

The problem was, I didn't know who I was doing it for. Because I sighed out in relief when I snuggled up to her, pulling her chest to mine, our hearts beating in time.

In perfect sync.

"I love you, Bailey Button."

She giggled at her nickname and snuggled closer. "I's *wuv* you

27

the most," she murmured like a secret, her breaths quick to even out.

I held her in the darkness.

In the shadows.

I still couldn't believe someone had been in our house. That someone had invaded our sanctuary with the sole purpose to instill dread and fear. A terrorizing sort of manipulation.

My mind spun with the threat of the two letters that had been left. I'd found one sitting at the front door, and the other had been tucked in the mailbox at the road. The first had simply confused me.

*Joseph had something that was mine. I want it back.*

But it was the one that'd come last week that made me want to pack up my daughter and run. Hide us away until Mack found who was responsible.

*I know you have it. Joseph was a fool. I hope you're smarter than him. I'd hate to see you end up with the same fate.*

The problem was that I had no idea what the *it* was. What they were lookin' for and how I was supposed to deliver it. Didn't they know I'd give up anything for my child? To keep her safe? I just didn't understand.

I tucked Bailey tighter to my body, and I made the same promise to her that Jace had just made to me.

But mine was the truth.

One on which I'd live and die.

*I'm going to take care of you. Protect you. Whatever it takes.*

# five

## Jace

Good God.

It was hot.

The sun pounded down through the humid air, the moisture like liquid fire on my skin, a fucking sauna set to full blast that would never offer any relief.

I lifted the hem of my already drenched shirt, and I swiped the sweat from my brow before I moved back to my SUV and pulled more lumber off the luggage rack.

So maybe I'd had to get creative in order to get all this shit here.

But hell, growing up, my entire life had been about making do. So here I was.

I hoisted the stack of two-by-fours onto my shoulder and carried them to the pile of supplies I was making, eyeing the old house that was all but crumbling on its foundation.

Every plank on the porch was rotted, paint peeling from the walls, and pieces of the third-story roof were caving in on one side.

The place was a gorgeous disaster.

The rambling plantation was teeming with history and charm, all of its potential hidden by a layer of rot.

*Beauty.*

I saw it right there, simmering in the sagging heat waves and begging for reprieve.

My spirit clutched.

A painful, blissful pinch.

Just about every good memory I had was of this place. Of course, it was the keeper of my worst one, too.

It had been her dream.

*Our* dream.

A dream that was falling down around her.

Dangerous.

As dangerous as the ghosts that lurked in the shadows. As dangerous as the bastards who wanted to cause her harm.

Every step fraught with peril.

*Fucking Joseph.*

It felt like another sin to still be pissed at him, but I couldn't help it. What the hell had he been thinking?

Only about himself, obviously.

I dumped the stack of wood, and it clattered onto the growing pile. The sound of it crashing to the ground ricocheted through the bated morning.

Subtlety had never exactly been my strong suit.

I went back to my car to gather the rest of the tools I'd picked up at the hardware store this morning.

At the hatch of my SUV, I blinked at the unopened boxes I'd stuffed inside. An electric saw, sander, hammers and nails, paint and stain, a ton of shit I hadn't used in years.

So out of practice, so far away from the world I'd built for myself, I wasn't even sure where to start building this one.

Of course, Faith wasn't either.

Because when I popped my head back out, still bent over with my hands pressed to the tail end of my car, she was on the porch, glaring at me.

If she wasn't so damned sweet, that single look might have

taken me out.

Wouldn't have been necessary when I was already getting the wind knocked out of me.

Not when Faith had that little girl hooked protectively on her hip. The kid had her head tucked under Faith's chin and her thumb in her mouth as she stared out at me with the same color and depth as Faith's knowing eyes.

It brought a lump the size of the boulder up to lodge itself in my throat.

I tried to swallow around it.

The anguish and awe and fucking jealousy.

Impossible.

Instead, I blinked and tried to pretend like it didn't hurt so damned bad.

Faith stood on the porch looking like some kind of maternal angel holding her perfect match, light all around her, the girl glowing that glow that had always made me feel like I was sinking my fingers into something good.

She covered her little girl's ear with her hand, her words seething from between pursed lips. "What the hell do you think you're doing, Jace Jacobs?"

I hauled a heavy box out of the back of my car. "What does it look like I'm doing?"

"Trespassin'."

Low, disbelieving laughter made its way around that lump in my throat. "Trespassing, huh?"

"You are on my land after I asked you not to be."

"You want to call the police? Go for it. I'm sure Mack would love to pay a visit."

So maybe my tone was antagonistic, but she needed to know I wasn't backing down.

Frustration billowed from her, her attention darting from the pile of wood I was making, to my face, and then to my chest before she jerked it away, gulping for something to say.

She hugged her little girl tighter, her words turning to a whispered plea. "I told you, you don't get to do this."

"What, help you?"

*Protect you?*

A huff of air puffed from that delicious mouth. Incredulous. Breaking with the day.

I was nothing but a fool because I wanted to get lost in that sound. In her voice and her need and her despair.

Take every bit of it away.

Fill the spaces that'd gone bad with something good.

Bitterness pounded at my ribs.

That was kind of hard to do when I didn't have anything good to offer.

Except this.

Maybe for once, I could do something that would make a difference in a positive direction.

For her.

Maybe even for Joseph.

I just prayed he wasn't looking down and hoping I'd have a slip up with the saw and cut right through an artery rather than the wood.

"You know this isn't about you helping me."

"That's exactly what this is about, Faith. I'm here to help you."

*I'm here to protect you. Take care of you until I get you out of this mess. God knows, if I wasn't such a selfish bastard, I might have been able to stop it from happening in the first place.*

Moving back toward the steps, I dumped the huge box that held the saw and table onto the ground before wiping more sweat away.

I could feel her. The emotion that came from her, like it was pinned to the air, caught up in the stagnant heat waves with nowhere to go.

"I don't want your pity," she finally whispered. There was no missing the grief coming through on the words or the way they cracked with the sob she was trying to hold back.

Funny, considering it was me who'd never wanted this girl to pity me.

She was the one who'd made me strive to be better.

Change my situation.

Made me see I didn't have to be another victim of

circumstance.

I dropped my gaze to the ground, hands on my hips, my chest heaving.

Knowing I wasn't equipped to handle this.

What I felt and what she was going through.

The impact of her grief and my regret colliding might send the rest of the house crashing to the ground.

I had to suck it up and lock that shit down. Remember why I was there.

Standing at the base of the steps, I looked up at her. Her little girl had pried her head free of her mother's chin, her eyes wary and curious as she peered out at me.

A tremor rolled through my chest.

I tore my attention from the little girl and turned it on Faith, which wasn't exactly helping matters, either.

My eyes narrowed in emphasis, praying she'd get it. "Pity you? I don't pity you, Faith. Does it kill me that you're going through this? Am I worried about you? Do I want to go on a mission to track down whoever is threatening you? Do I wish I could fix it? Yes. But there's a big difference between the two."

Those chocolate eyes swam with moisture, and she hiked her little girl up who was sliding down her body, running her hand over the back of her head.

I wasn't entirely sure which of them she was comforting, the two of them clinging to the other, each the other's support.

"You can't say those things to me."

I stepped onto the bottom step, hand clenching the railing to keep myself from getting any closer. From rushing the rest of the way onto the porch and pulling her against me.

Was surprised the rickety wood didn't bust in two from the force.

Because my muscles flexed and contracted and tightened.

Body roaring. Demanding I make a claim.

*Mine.*

She'd always been mine.

"I'm only speaking the truth."

The little girl popped her thumb from her mouth, grinning up at her mom. "The truth is good, Mommy. Always, always tell the truth."

Her tiny voice nearly bowled me over, the little thing dropping all her L's. It sent her voice into this sweet, innocent drawl.

Guilt blazed a path through my insides. Hurt lining the middle of it. My head trying to shut the little girl out, ignore her, *hate her* like the bastard I was while my spirit threatened something I couldn't allow it to feel.

"We're barely making it, Jace. Barely surviving. I can't have you here making things harder on us." Somehow there was an apology in her voice, as if she were the one who should feel ashamed.

"And the only thing I'm here for is to lighten some of that load."

Stupidly, I took another step up, getting closer to her and that little girl who sent a tumble of fear sliding beneath the surface of my skin. "Please, Faith. Let me help you. Let me be here until Mack figures out who is doing this."

She blinked, turning her head away. It was almost like she couldn't keep looking at me and hold her ground. "It feels too complicated. Everything's twisted and mixed in a way it never should have been."

Knives.

I felt them slicing right through the center of my chest.

She'd always been so honest. So damned, brutally honest.

Wearing that beautiful heart on her sleeve.

And I'd been the asshole who'd reached out and plucked it free.

Smashed it in the palm of my hand.

I'd known it then.

I knew it still.

"I've made a lot of mistakes in my life, but coming here, helping you . . . helping her?" I gestured with my chin toward her child. "It's not one of them."

What was I doing? Saying?

But I couldn't stop it. The worry that bound up inside me.

"Jace." Faith blinked a bunch of times, bouncing the little girl like she was an infant, like she was trying with all her might to keep her emotions at bay. But tears streaked from her eyes and raced down her cheeks.

Fuck.

I was a fool.

Because I reached out and caught one. Remembering the way it'd felt when I'd had that same soft skin of her cheek pressed to my bare chest, the girl running her fingers over my abdomen as she'd dreamed her dreams, her voice a whisper in the darkness.

"Let me help you," I murmured, my thumb lingering on her skin for a beat too long. "Please."

Helping her with the house was an easy excuse to get close to her. A way to be around to look out for her.

But there was something about the thought of fixing this place up that felt like I was making amends. Atoning for a sin.

She flinched under the touch, backing away a step to put some space between us.

She looked away again.

But I could feel it.

Her wavering. Giving.

She'd returned to bouncing and squeezing the chubby thing in her arms when she swung those eyes back to me. "All this hurts, Jace."

"I'm not here to hurt you."

She'd been hurt enough.

"You have your own life. Your career. You don't need to be wasting time here."

*I have nothing.*

I didn't say it. I just sent her a grin. The one that had always gotten me what I'd wanted from her.

So maybe I'd resorted to playing dirty.

"It's my company, Faith. I get to say when I come and when I go. When I work and when I don't."

And I was staying. No one was going to get close to her. Hurt her. I'd die before that happened, just as gladly as I'd put the asshole in the ground.

"Jace . . . this is insane."

"No, it's not. It's logical."

She frowned at me, some of the strain draining from her tone, and for the first time, lightness made its way in. "Logical?"

"Yup."

She arched a brow, almost playful in her reasoning. "Like showing up here at the break of dawn with a bunch of construction supplies strapped to the roof of a brand-new Porsche? That kind of logical?"

I roughed a hand over the top of my head, chuckling under my breath. "Uh . . . yeah . . . just like that."

"Sounds reckless to me." All the playfulness had vanished.

"I'll try to be careful."

Those words climbed to the space between us as if they were alive. A promise and a threat.

I hesitated and then I dealt the lowest blow I could go. "You've always dreamed of getting this house into working order so you could turn it into a business. I can do that for you. And if you don't want me to do it for you, at least let me do it for her. This place isn't safe in the state it is in right now."

It wasn't safe all around.

Not the place or the people or the threats that remained.

I pushed my foot against the loose board beneath me to prove my point. "I'm willing to bet the entire place is falling down around you. And you know it would be good to have an extra set of eyes around here."

No doubt, I wouldn't be her first choice for the job. That didn't mean I wasn't the one who was meant for it.

Her little girl grinned like my helping repair the house was the best idea she'd ever heard. "Every'fing's broke, Mommy."

Faith looked at me like I'd punched her in the gut, her attention sweeping to the child who was blinking up at her like she was trying to talk her into the same thing.

Faith pushed out a frustrated sigh, her voice going hard. "Fine. You can fix this porch. That's it. Then you need to be on your way."

# *six*

## Faith

*He'd try to be careful?*

Good Lord, what had I gotten myself into? I pressed both palms to my face, scrubbing hard before I dragged my fingers back through my hair as I peered out the big window to the porch he was working on.

The man was bent over the portable table saw, dragging a pencil down a plank as if he'd spent the last ten years putting things back together rather than sending them crashing to the ground in a heap of rubble.

That was the way he'd left me.

Rubble.

It was Joseph who'd picked up those shattered pieces. Dusted me off.

Held me up when I didn't know how to stand. Maybe at the beginning it'd felt wrong to fall for Jace's cousin, and God knew, it wasn't something that happened overnight.

I wasn't struck by the brush of his hand.

Jace had been a thunderbolt.

Joseph had been my comfort after the storm. A friend who'd been there for me until he'd grown into something more.

My gaze moved to the living room floor where Bailey was on the rug, attempting to stack a big blue block on a small red one and rambling to herself as if she could verbally coax it into balancing.

My ribs squeezed against the swell of love that engulfed me.

So powerful.

The child was the center of my heart. Given to me right smack dab in the middle of two tragedies.

A reminder that there was a bigger purpose to my life.

More than the two brittle, battered pieces of my heart that had been shredded and scattered between two men.

I thanked God that she could sit there as if it were any other day. As if three months ago, we hadn't lost Joseph. As if two nights ago, someone hadn't been in our house, filling me with a fear unlike anything I'd ever felt before.

My cell rumbled on the end table next to the couch.

I nearly jumped through the roof.

"Phone, Mommy!" Bailey shouted so loud I would have heard her even if I had been upstairs.

"Thanks, Button," I rushed, scrambling that direction, thankful for the distraction. My hands were shaking when I picked it up, not exactly sure what I was going to say when I saw the name on the caller ID.

My voice was a frail fumble as I pressed my phone to my ear. "Hey, Courtney."

"Hey, I hadn't heard from you this morning, and I wanted to check on you. Are you okay?"

How was I supposed to answer that?

Because I wasn't okay.

I didn't know if I was ever going to be.

"I'm doing the best that I can," I answered.

Her worry was palpable, floating through the line in the slow breath she inhaled. Finally, she said, "I don't like this . . . you bein' there alone."

With the heel of my hand pressed to my eye, I almost laughed, though there wasn't a single thing funny about it.

The last thing I'd ever wanted was to be alone here, either.

Now . . . now I wasn't. I was surrounded by the presence of the man I'd never wanted to see again, and somehow couldn't help but find comfort in his return.

Oh, were those the most dangerous sort of thoughts I could ever entertain.

Banging struck up from outside, the walls shaking with the telltale sounds of a man at work.

It made something inside me tumble, old instincts right there, threatening to surface.

Courtney mistook my quietness for something else entirely. "I bet you didn't sleep a wink last night, did you?"

Courtney instantly shifted into her take-charge demeanor. "That's it. I'm gonna pack a bag and come stay with you two until Mack makes an arrest. It probably isn't helping that Jace showed up in town. It's a miracle you haven't lost your mind. You need someone there with you."

Oh, I had half lost my mind, all right.

My stomach in knots, and my heart doing these stuttered, scattered jumps.

Finally, I pulled myself from the stupor. "You aren't goin' to do anything of the sort. You have Felix. There is no way I'm going to ask you to leave behind your new boyfriend to come stay with me. That's not right, and you know it."

"It's not like we're livin' together."

My brow lifted. "You might as well be."

"I do have to admit that I don't mind the man spending the night. He's ridiculous in bed. It shouldn't even be legal, the things he does to me. He does this thing with his tongue—"

"La, la, la, la, la."

I might as well have shoved my fingers in my ears like I used to do when we were thirteen. The woman had no filter, and if she'd been given one, she'd have long since ripped it off. No topic was ever off-limits with her.

"What? Don't tell me you don't want all the details."

"I don't want *all* the details," I deadpanned.

The girl had been giving me all the information I could do without for all my life. She was lucky I wasn't scarred from some of the stories she'd told.

"Hey, I'm just tryin' to give you the *good stuff* since you've been dealing with so much bad."

"I think I can do without your *good*."

More banging echoed from outside, and there was nothing I could do to stop myself from inching back to the window, pressing my palm to my forehead, and wondering if I had some sort of a fever.

The saw suddenly made a high-pitched squeal as it came to life, the blade spinning, screaming as the teeth tore through a piece of wood.

Like some kind of sick, twisted voyeur, I peered out, watching him. Head dipped down, Jace guided the piece of wood through, his attention rapt on the job he was doing.

Meticulous.

*Careful.*

"What's that sound?" Courtney asked, so quickly I could almost see the lines twisting on her brow.

Crap.

This was so not goin' to go over well. Hell, it wasn't going over well with me.

The saw trailed off before it struck right back up again.

I still wasn't saying anything, just staring out the window like a fool.

"Faith, are you there?"

"Yes," I finally managed.

"Tell me what's going on."

"Jace is here." It tumbled out like a confession.

She sucked in a breath. Anger and mortification. "Tell me you still have that shotgun."

"Courtney." I couldn't help but chastise her.

"What did your daddy tell you that thing was for? Intruders. And that man is an intruder."

"He's not any danger."

"Really?" she challenged.

"Not in the way you mean."

"No, Faith, he's a danger in exactly the way I mean."

My head dropped. "I know." I breathed the words through the strain.

"What the hell is he doin' there?" she hissed.

"Fixin' my porch," I hissed right back.

"Holy Mary," she wheezed. "It's worse than I thought."

I groaned. "Tell me what to do."

"Um . . . hello . . . that is a no-brainer, Faith. Kick him to the curb."

"He said he's just here to help."

The problem was, I needed it.

God, I needed the help.

By some miracle, Joseph had gotten the money together to buy this place when it'd gone into foreclosure four years ago. We'd had every intention of fixing it up, investing in it until it provided a return.

Owning this house was something I'd dreamed of for all of forever, since the day my mama and I had gone for a walk when I was seven and I fell in love with the place.

With the mystery.

The beauty and the history.

The only thing I'd ever wanted was to make this place a destination, nothing but welcoming rooms and smiling faces and meals I'd prepared shared in the expansive formal dining room.

In reality, it was nothing but a burden. Dangerous, just as Jace had said.

But more than that? Jace had been right with the quiet implication he'd uttered, when he'd tilted his head in emphasis and said I could use an extra set of eyes around here.

Being out here alone had left me vulnerable.

"Help?" Her tone was sharp.

"That was what he said."

"Oh, I'm sure he'd gladly *help* get you right out of your panties."

I gasped, whirling around, covering up my phone like it might shield Bailey from what Courtney had said, because I was pretty sure she'd issued it on a loudspeaker.

Bailey was on her knees, babbling out a made-up song.

I jerked back around, my voice a barely there whisper, shoulders curling down as I hunkered over the phone. "What is wrong with you?"

"You know me well enough to know I'm not gonna tiptoe, Faith Avery. I'm gonna call it as I see it, and I *saw* the way he was looking at you yesterday. That man's a wolf who is bound to eat you up."

Hurt balled up in my belly, so big I could feel it pushing at my heart. "No, Courtney. He's not. The only way he could hurt me again is if I let him. Besides, I'm *married*."

She sighed a painfully elongated sigh, as if she wanted to be there to hug me when she let go of the reminder. "No, honey, you're not."

Sorrow.

It swelled like a flood.

Deep. Dark. Suffocating.

I dropped my face into my free hand, trying to keep it together.

I wasn't a weak woman. I'd never been. So why did it seem like every time I turned around, I was falling apart?

I choked back a cry before it broke just a little.

"Hey," she whispered, "I'm not tryin' to be hard on you. You're free to make any decisions you want. If you want Jace to help out, and he means it? Then fine. I just want you to be careful. You and Jace have a whole lot of history, and a whole lot of it isn't the good kind. But you have to know, the only thing I really want is for you to be happy. You deserve it more than anyone I know."

My voice was thin. "I'm not ready for that kind of talk. I'm not sure I'm ever gonna be. It's too soon."

"You will be, Faith. Maybe not today. Maybe not in a year. But someday, you will be. Someday, it won't hurt so badly and all of this suffering is going to be behind you, and that giving heart of yours is gonna be ready. And whoever you choose to love is gonna be one lucky man. All I'm asking is to make sure he's worth it. That he deserves it."

Her voice shifted into a tease. "And for the love of God, make sure he's a good man—both in his heart and in bed—because this time, I'm liable to hunt the man down and chop off his dick if he doesn't take good care of you. Apparently, that's frowned upon. Just ask Mack."

It should have been impossible, but choppy laughter made its way out of me. Courtney just had that way about her. No matter the circumstances, she always found a way to make me smile.

"You're insane. I never, ever should have told you about that. Remind me never to share a bottle of wine with you. Things come out that you're bound to use against me."

It was all a soft tease.

I was nothing but grateful that she'd always been there for me, even when she was saying things that made me turn bright red.

"Um, yes you should have. If you can't talk to me about these things, who else are you going to talk to? You don't have to be ashamed of it."

For a second, we both giggled, until she trailed off, and silence filled the space between us.

It seemed as if maybe she were giving me time to catch up. That was the crazy thing. Time was always marching on. I could feel it pushing one part of me forward, while the other part felt forever chained to the past.

I just wasn't entirely sure exactly where I'd gotten trapped.

"And you don't have to be ashamed if that man is stirring up feelings in you, Faith. I know you, and I know what you're thinking. He was your first love. Your *life* love, which is why I'd gladly maim that pretty face if he's up to no good."

"He left me, Court."

A hammer striking a nail rang through the air, a *pound, pound, pound* that rattled the walls.

"Sounds to me like he's back."

# seven

## Faith
## Sixteen Years Old

The door to the office banged open. Faith startled where she was

tucked in the back corner behind a tall metal filing cabinet all by herself, sorting the pile of reports the school secretary, Ms. Minks, had left for her to file during her TA hour.

Rustling echoed from up front, a disorder in the air, and she carefully peeked around the edge of the cabinet.

Mr. Flores had ahold of a boy's elbow, trying to lead him inside. Face obscured by a flop of tawny hair, the boy flailed and tried to yank his arm away. "Don't touch me," the defiant voice said.

Faith's heart started thrumming faster, a rash of discomfort prickling her senses. She didn't know whether to continue hiding or step out and shout that she was there. Reveal herself since she was feeling like an intruder.

Mr. Flores grumbled in frustration. "If you'd do what you were asked, I wouldn't have to. You were told to go to the office, and I found you in the boy's restroom. I don't know about where you came from, but that's not how things are done around here. Now, I want you in Mr. Dagon's office."

"I didn't do anything."

"Yeah? Well, Mitch said he saw you swipe the sandwich from his tray. At this school, we respect each other, including their possessions. I'd suggest you learn that quickly, or things won't go so smoothly for you around here."

And Mitch was a complete asshole, Faith thought, but that didn't mean he deserved to have his lunch stolen.

She hadn't seen them yet, but the two brothers and their cousin had just moved into their neighborhood on the outskirts of the city and had been the talk of the entire town.

*Rebellious.*

*Trouble.*

*Trash.*

She'd heard all those words thrown around.

Whispers about a junkie mother who'd moved them into an abandoned trailer down on Hyde street.

Faith's mama and daddy had always taught her to be kind. Not to judge people for what they looked like or for the rumors that flew through the neighborhood.

To ignore the old ladies whispering everyone's business as if it were the fifties and they were still wearing pink curlers in their hair.

She'd been raised to believe you never knew what was really underneath, what someone was going through, or the reality of their situation.

Admittedly, she was caught off guard when her daddy had pulled her aside yesterday afternoon and warned her to give those boys a wide berth, telling her he didn't want her anywhere near them and that they couldn't be trusted.

Fear tingled across her nape and skittered down her spine as the boy struggled with Mr. Flores again.

It was the strangest sensation.

One she had never experienced before.

Right then, she thought she might understand where her daddy was coming from

There was something that vibrated through the air that she

could taste.

An omen.

A premonition.

Heck, it was probably just basic intuition.

Some boys were just trouble.

Bad to the very bone. That expression hadn't been made up for nothing.

"I told you, I didn't do nothin'." The boy spat the words at the junior English teacher, yanking his arm free.

"Tell it to Mr. Dagon."

Alarm flapped at her ribs. She'd stepped into the middle of something she didn't want to be witness to. She should cover her ears to shield herself from it all because it sure wasn't any of her business.

She just couldn't resist this burning curiosity that clawed at her insides. Unfamiliar and somehow urgent. She held her breath, trying to remain unseen as she peeked out around the cabinet again.

Then she sucked in a staggered breath.

The most piercing eyes she'd ever seen stared back at her. As if he'd known she was there all along.

Those eyes held her hostage.

Scary in their severity.

They were almost red. Orange maybe. Like an apple and an apricot had been crushed together, then whipped up in a blender with a full container of bronze glitter dumped in.

Striking and shiny and . . . and . . . and . . .

*Angry.*

Oh, the boy looked angry.

Raging mad as he tried to tug away from Mr. Flores, who'd latched on to him again. Every bitter action of the boy was lined with a stunning sort of sadness that Faith could feel feeding the vibrating hostility in the room.

That fear in her chest expanded, her pulse a thug, thug, thug.

It felt as if time had been stopped as the boy glared back at her.

As if he were issuing her a challenge.

To judge him, too.

Hate him the way the rest of the world did.

She found she couldn't look away from him.

His jaw harsh and sharp, nose defined, his lips almost too full for the narrow oval of his face.

His shoulders were wide while the rest of him was almost gangly, as if he were just waiting to grow into the aggression that wrapped him just as tightly as his tattered, dingy shirt.

A shiver rolled through her, head to toe.

He was beautiful.

Terrifyingly beautiful.

As if looking at him alone should have come with a warning.

No wonder her daddy had given her one.

Mr. Flores jostled him. "Please don't make this harder than it needs to be."

"Harder than it needs to be?" The boy scoffed, tearing his attention from Faith as if he hadn't even noticed her gaping from there in the corner. "You don't know anything about things being *hard*."

"I don't need to hear any excuses for your actions because there's none for stealing from another student. Now move it."

Incredulous laughter snorted from his nose. "Whatever. You're all the same. Every town. Every city. Every asshole."

"Watch your mouth."

Footsteps scuffled along the floor, and the principal's door slammed.

Faith held back, trying not to eavesdrop through the thin walls as she continued to file her papers. But she could hear every word they said as if they were amplified in her ear.

"Did you take it?"

"No."

"Mitch says you did."

"Do I look like I give a shit what Mitch said?"

The squeak of a rocking chair. "You know the consequence for stealing, don't you, son? We expel kids for that around here."

"Go ahead. Wouldn't be the first time."

Mr. Dagon sighed a rough sound. "I'm just trying to help you here. Confess what you did, apologize, and I'll give you a second chance. I know you've had it rough."

The boy huffed. "You don't know anything. None of you do. Don't pretend like you give a crap about us."

There was so much anger in his words. Faith was sure that kind of anger had to physically hurt. She squeezed her eyes shut, wishing she could shield herself from having to listen to it.

From feeling it.

Experiencing it.

Because right then, she was sure she could. She could feel that ragged boy's pain. It was breaking on every lash of his tongue.

More squeaking of the office chair, and Faith's nerves gathered right at the base of her throat. She shouldn't have kept listening, but she felt desperate . . . desperate to know what would happen next.

The principal sighed. "Fine. I'm going to give you the benefit of the doubt. This one time. But the next time you end up in my office, I'm not going to go so easy on you."

She barely made out the sound of surprise, the boy's voice so quiet when he said, "Thank you, sir."

She thought she could physically feel the anger drain from the space.

A breath taken.

A break given.

She was shaking when the boy appeared in the doorway again. His face was contorted in a way that twisted her up on the inside. Agony and regret. Grief and guilt.

So much guilt.

As if he thought he were dirty.

She could feel it—the shame radiating off him.

He lurched to a stop when he saw her, as frozen as she was before he jerked away and his expression morphed into one of pride and indifference.

She was pretty sure it was the fakest demonstration she'd ever seen.

He blew out the door. The heavy glass and metal banged shut behind him.

She didn't even know what in the world she thought she was

doing as she haphazardly shoved the rest of the files into the drawer, feeling frantic as she gathered her things and flew out the door behind him five minutes before she was supposed to leave.

He was already gone when she raced out into the deserted outdoor courtyard, fifth period still in session.

The enclosed area was lined by classrooms, and a bunch of concrete tables took up the grassy space in the middle.

She exhaled heavily, air puffing into her bangs on a sigh of defeat and frustration. It was stupid, anyway, chasing him out there.

She slung her backpack over her shoulder and started for the restroom, figuring she probably should soak up the sweat that had gathered on her brow before the bell rang and she headed to her next class.

She trudged up the narrow walkway and started to turn the corner, only to stumble a step when she heard the quieted voices coming from the backside of the building.

Holding her breath, she inched that way, pressing her back to the brick wall as she was hit with another rush of that fear.

That warning fluttering through her insides as if it were carried on wings, which was kind of funny, considering there was no chance she could turn away.

She felt drawn.

Compelled.

Curious in a way that wrapped her heart in a bow of despair.

She peeked around the corner.

The boy was there with another who looked almost identical to him.

Only maybe a little bit younger.

The younger boy was stuffing that sandwich in his mouth and crying at the same time, groaning as he devoured it, as if it'd been weeks since he'd eaten.

Everything inside her clenched in sympathy as the pieces snapped together.

That was the same second the older boy snapped those copper eyes her direction.

Shackling her to the spot.

Glaring with that same hatred and shame. Darkening with the dare. Sure she was going to run and tell.

Her ribs clamped down painfully, and she blinked at him, wishing her mouth would work, knowing she wouldn't know what to say anyway.

## Jace

"You went over there after I told you to lie low?" Mack scowled at me as he slammed a stack of papers onto the desk and flung himself into the chair beside me where we were meeting at Ian's office.

My brother Ian laughed and rocked back in his executive rocker, taking a pull from the tumbler he'd just poured a finger of whiskey into. "You didn't actually think he was going to listen to you, did you?"

I shot a glare at my brother. *Thanks a lot, asshole. Thought we always had the other's back?*

Ian's brown hair was styled impeccably, face clean-shaven, sleeves of his button-down rolled up his forearms, exposing the ink he normally kept hidden beneath his suit.

My brother, who was just eleven months younger than me, was a dichotomy of rough and smooth. Sharp tongue and charming words. He could be the guy next door if it weren't for that quiet layer of intimidation that was scary as fuck.

I guessed he'd learned from the best.

"And you knew this how?" I asked, voice dry as I sipped from my own glass of whiskey, looking from Ian back to Mack.

"My job is to know who's going onto her property, wouldn't you think?" Mack demanded.

I gave a short shrug. "Didn't come here to sit on my damned hands."

"I'm pretty sure Jace here has all kinds of good ideas for his hands." This from Ian, that punk.

"I'm helping her with the house. No secret the place has become a fucking shithole. Falling down around her. Plus, I can keep an eye on things. It's a win-win."

I said it like it didn't matter all that much.

Like going there in the middle of the night last night hadn't been one of the hardest things I'd ever done. And still, it'd felt like instinct. Breathing. So goddamned natural there was no place else I could have gone.

I'd basically stuck around all night, leaving only long enough to go pick up the supplies I'd needed.

"A win-win for who?" Mack raised a brow.

"Her. You. That kid." Nearly choked on the last.

"And what about you?" Concern had made its way into Mack's voice.

"Doesn't matter what I feel. Owe them."

I deserved every punishment and penalty coming my way.

"That so?"

No doubt, Mack worried I was going to go over the deep end. Get myself into trouble and drag him right into it with me.

"Yup."

Mack shook his head, and Ian laughed under his breath, words cynical. "Well, aren't you a regular humanitarian. You should start a charity in your name."

He took another sip, muttering under his breath, "God knows, you've been giving all your dough to lowlifes for all these years."

A growl clanged in my chest. "Don't," I warned.

When my brother and I had moved into town during my senior year in high school, we'd met Mack, who'd been drawn to us. It was like he'd seen the same thing in himself reflected back. My best friend had seen as much trouble as Ian and I had growing up, begging and fighting to survive.

Mack had pulled himself out of the poverty. Out of the depravity. Worked his ass off until he had *detective* tacked to the front of his name, wanting to change the world he'd come from.

Ian and I had harnessed all that bitterness and anger from our youth, too. Made something of ourselves.

Though we'd done it differently.

Against every odd, I'd clawed my fucking way to the top, building an empire so no one could ever hurt us again, doing everything I had to do in order to put my brother through school so his life wouldn't be set to repeat.

So he could have something better.

When we were kids, we'd made dumpster diving a family sport, scrounging whatever food we could steal or find.

Lucky to have a roof over our heads, even though the places were infested with rats and littered with garbage and our mother was a fucking waste, rotting away with all that poison leaking into her veins.

Ian had been the one who'd found our mother when she'd finally taken it too far. When her body had finally given up after the years of abuse she'd put it through.

Even though he'd never admit it, I knew he was scarred from it in ways I could never comprehend.

Ian's eyes glinted, my brother rocking back in his massive chair like he owned the goddamned world. "No need to get all up in arms. Talking about myself, brother."

Sighing, I scrubbed a palm at my face. "Don't do that, Ian."

"What, tell the truth? There's no bullshit between us, remember? You, me, and Mack—we tell it straight, and I'm telling you right now that you're getting yourself involved in something you aren't going to be able to dig yourself out of."

"She's worth it."

"Or maybe you're *worth* it. Maybe it's time you came back here where you belong."

"You know better than that."

"Do I? You were always different with her. Changing your

tune, singing a different song from the one you'd been singing to me since I was a little kid."

But that was the way it'd always been with Faith, hadn't it? She'd always made me feel like I was two different people.

A fucking king in pauper's clothes.

Like her touch could calm the beast that raged inside me. Quiet the storm that had roiled and thrashed and threatened to take us out.

Or maybe when I'd been around her, I'd become an entirely different person altogether.

A better person.

That was what had gotten us here to begin with. My dragging her into our sordid world when I'd known better all along.

After everything, there was no chance I could sit back in Atlanta, where I'd built something for myself, putting my brother through school.

The one thing he'd ever wanted was to be an attorney.

Watching him attain it had felt like my own victory.

After everything, seeing him survive was the only thing that had mattered.

Ian sat forward in his chair, both elbows on the desk, drink held between his fingers, swinging back and forth like a well bucket. The etched glass caught the glittering rays of light that filtered in through the window from over his shoulder.

"I know you want to take care of her, Jace, but we all know you're asking for trouble."

There had always been something about Faith that had set Ian on edge, like he was fearful of losing me if I gave myself to her.

In the end, I guessed it was a worry that hadn't been that far off base.

Dark laughter rumbled free. "Haven't I always asked for trouble?"

"Yeah. And every single time it was for the sake of someone else. You've always stepped into the middle of things to take care of some leech who didn't appreciate you. Who didn't have the first clue as to what you were actually sacrificing for them. When are you going to start watching out for yourself?"

My face pinched in anger. "You think Faith would actually take advantage of me?"

Ian sighed. "Not what I said, and you know it. Only leeches I was talking about were me and that piece of shit who has you in deep again. Asshole just keeps taking, even from the grave. How many times did you get yourself into hot water doing something for him? For me? And Faith is neck deep in that mess. You get any closer, and she's going to drown you."

His head angled to the side, like he actually thought he might be able to talk me into walking away from her.

From him.

Like I'd ever take back the things I'd sacrificed for both of them.

"I'm your older brother. You were mine to look out for."

A hot puff of hatred spouted from his nose before he drained the rest of the whiskey from the glass. His voice was twisted in hostility as he slammed it back down onto the wood.

"No . . . that pathetic bitch who was supposed to be our mother was supposed to look out for me. For us. And instead of getting to be a kid, you basically had to spend your days wiping my nose and making sure I didn't fucking starve."

Uneasiness moved through me. That was the thing about Ian. He'd been pissed growing up.

Mean. Miserable. Nasty.

Lashing out at the cruelty of the world every chance he got.

He was still a vicious fucker. There was a darkness inside him that scared me sometimes. Made me worry that, one day, he would take his bitterness too far.

But with me? He didn't hesitate to lay it out. Make himself vulnerable by admitting the position we'd been in.

"You think I regret taking care of you? You're my brother. I love you. Simple as that."

Concern blazed in the depths of his eyes just as a taunt slid off his tongue. "So, does that mean you still love her, then?"

Emotion gripped me in all the wrong places. My damned heart threatening to beat out of my chest. It made me want to do a little of that *lashing* out.

But I'd gotten him mixed up in this, I couldn't very well get pissed that he had questions about my intentions.

"Would like to know the answer to that myself," Mack added, fingers tugging at his jeans, directing all that pent-up, radiating fury at the fabric.

I was supposed to be able to handle coming back here.

I thought I had it all under control.

A plan.

But finding her standing on her porch in the middle of the night had made it hard to think of any other reason than her.

Loving her.

Holding her.

Protecting her.

The girl was so goddamned perfect, it had nearly made me forget why I was there in the first place.

*Beauty.*

That was what she was.

Soft and sweet. So pretty and fierce in her stoic, wistful way. Like she could take on an army just standing there with the wind whipping through her hair.

She was the one who'd filled me with the belief that I could change my world.

She'd made me believe in something bigger. In something *better.*

Hadn't mattered what I'd started to believe. I'd ended up in the same place anyway.

Without her.

Fucking destroyed.

It'd been a tough lesson for a lovesick, teenaged kid to learn.

How to protect himself.

How to build up the steel bars necessary to make it through this tortuous life.

How to keep the assholes waiting around every corner from eating him alive.

But sometimes I wondered if I would have ever found the determination to build the empire I had without the memory of her words.

Without the way she'd looked at me like I was something different from what the rest of the world had seen.

I'd left here this wrecked, battered kid, crushed in a way I'd never expected, and somehow, I'd found the grit to push through and to take my little brother with me.

Like somewhere inside me, I knew how *much* it fucking mattered.

Maybe I'd just wanted to prove to all the pricks around here that they were wrong.

Or fuck . . . maybe I'd wanted to prove to her that she was right.

I took a steeling gulp of the liquid fire, eye trained on the floor in front of me, voice grating over the words. "Will always love her. Doesn't change anything though, now, does it?"

"Seems to me that everything has changed," Ian said, rocking back in his chair, eyeing me from across the expanse of his massive desk.

The guy was so intimidating and successful, that just sitting there, looking at how he oozed power, I couldn't help but feel fucking proud.

Fucking proud that he'd made it. That we'd run it together and survived. Didn't mean I didn't still worry.

For his heart and his spirit.

The guy so damned cold I was wondering when he'd finally freeze everyone out.

"Won't touch her, if that's what you're getting at."

"No?" Ian challenged.

"No way in hell."

It didn't matter how much I might want to.

Twisted humor snaked its way across Ian's face. "What? You have some kind of moral dilemma now?"

"What . . . like her being our dead cousin's widow? Is that the *moral dilemma* you're talking about?" I bit out, anger and revulsion pulsing through my veins.

"Funny how Joseph didn't have a problem climbing into her bed after you'd been there."

I fisted my hand on my thigh, trying to keep my cool. Knowing this was just Ian's way.

Laying it out.

Not worried that he was poking the beast.

Or maybe that was exactly what he wanted to do.

I sucked in a shattered breath, cool slipping fast. "Some things just turn out the way they're supposed to," I grated.

"Is that right?" His voice was incredulous. Almost mocking.

Leaning forward, I dropped my elbows to my knees and my attention to the ground again, trying to keep my anger under control. I could feel it slipping, seeping from my pores.

"Never deserved her."

Ian slammed his palm down on his desk. "Bullshit. I'm thinking it was the other way around."

Startled, my head jerked up.

He pointed at me. "You saved my fucking life, time and again. I don't care what happened in the past or what you've had to do. The only thing that matters is who you are. You're the best guy I know . . . and the fact you think you don't deserve to be happy? That's every kind of wrong, Jace. Faith would be lucky to have you."

He scraped a flustered hand through his hair, hidden emotion bleeding free. "Shit . . . I know you love her, man. But I'm not willing to lose you over her again."

"It's too late, anyway. There's too much history between the two of us."

Too much hurt.

Too many lies.

"Why's that?"

"She hates me."

And she only stood to hate me more when she found out what I'd done.

"Bullshit," he said again. This time quieter, tone shifting in emphasis. "That girl has loved you since the day she first saw you."

"Not so sure about that."

I mean, God, she'd been married to Joseph before I could even explain to her why I had to go in the first place. If she'd loved me so much, how could she have done that?

Hooked up with him?

I hated not knowing, but I was pretty damned sure I couldn't handle knowing, either.

Ian huffed a frustrated sound. "You're an idiot, brother. You want to be miserable your whole goddamned life?"

Pointedly, I glanced up at him. "Guess I'd be in good company, wouldn't I?"

"Fuck you, man. I'm as happy as can be." He lifted his arms out to his sides, gesturing around him, like his expensive suit and expensive furnishings in his corner office was the giver of joy.

I knew better.

Firsthand.

But money sure as hell made things easier, and I'd gladly give up every dime of mine to make up for what I'd done. Make her life *easier*, too.

"Think Faith has had enough of being yanked around, yeah?" Mack almost challenged, glaring between the two of us. "Why don't we focus on whoever this fucker is rather than quibbling over who deserves what, because I'm pretty sure what both of you deserve is to get your asses handed to you."

I sighed and then chuckled. "Why don't you tell us how you feel, man?"

He nearly rolled his eyes. "Want me to profess my love to the two of you? Keep dreamin'."

"Oh, come on, Mack, know you've been dreaming of me," Ian baited.

"Dreaming of squeezing the life out of you."

"Ouch." Ian threw his hand over his heart, so overdramatic that this time I was the one rolling my eyes. "You wound me, Mack. Wound me."

"Keep it up, and I will," Mack razzed.

I blew out a sigh, needing to get back on course, and I gestured to the reports Mack had brought with him. "Did you guys find anything?"

Mack rubbed a hand over the flop of hair on top of his head. "Nothing inside. Nothing out of place other than the tub. No fingerprints. Just one goddamned footprint out front. Size eleven and a half. Boot that could belong to a thousand people."

Fear clamped down on my chest.

Heavy and hard.

Fury building into its own beat. Something that felt outside my heart. Bigger than me.

"Seems to me, we hunt down every asshole within a hundred-mile radius who wears a size eleven and a half."

"Ah . . . guess that clears my name. Size thirteen, bitches." Ian smirked, the smug bastard.

I cut him a glare.

Mack clapped me on the knee. "*You* aren't going to do anything except fix that porch and call me if you see anything out of the ordinary."

Mack pushed to his towering, hulking height. "Keep on the straight and narrow. Think you know well enough that you can't afford to find yourself handcuffed in the back of a cruiser again. We clear?"

He didn't wait for an answer. He just rapped a fist on the wall as he strode out the door.

# nine

## Jace

*A* rush of anxiousness rolled down my spine as I knocked on the front door, trying to keep my cool.

Wasn't like I hadn't spent the entire night staking out the front of her house. She'd been tucked safely inside, behind closed doors, which had made it a whole ton of a lot easier to focus on why I was there.

All those reasons scattered in the wind when the front door whipped open.

It took everything I had not to stumble back. I should have been prepared. It wasn't like it was the first time I'd seen her since I'd gotten back. But every single time, it nearly knocked me from my feet.

My attention darted down to her bare legs. My heart slammed against my ribs. Faith was wearing nothing but a flimsy pair of tiny pajama bottoms and a white tank top.

Then my heart froze when my attention landed on the little girl who peeked out from between her mother's long, slender legs. She stood behind Faith, holding the outside of her mom's legs and was peering at me as if through the bars on a cage.

Faith this fortress in front of her.

Protective and perfect.

My insides tangled.

Yeah. That little thing was going to be a problem. It wasn't like I hadn't known they'd had a kid. But, fuck, seeing it was a whole different ball game.

Like that impossible piece of hope inside me had been written on a scrap of paper. Kept hidden away. And was then ripped up and torn to shreds.

I pinned a smile onto my face, hoping it didn't come off as too fake, and lifted the two one-gallon paint cans up at my sides. "Stain or white?"

Not that I needed the answer yet.

I just needed a reason to talk to her.

See her face.

Honestly, I was weeks away from being ready to paint anything.

Yesterday, I'd managed to get a few solid planks secured between the front door and steps.

They'd have to be fully ripped out and replaced when I got to this section, but for the time being, someone could leave the house without the worry of falling and breaking their neck.

A frown pulled across Faith's pretty face, and her gaze swept across the porch to the small patch off to the left where I'd started to pull out the old planks.

Her attention came back to me, worry on her brow. "You didn't make it very far yesterday."

I laughed out a feigned sound of offense. "Trying to get rid of me already?"

Chocolate eyes narrowed, and her full lips pursed, glistening in the sun, tendrils of hair sweeping down over her slender shoulders while the rest of it was piled in a restless mess on the top of her head.

Lust was such a bitch.

It came on at the most inopportune times.

Like when I was standing there with her little girl peeking out from behind her mother's legs like the tiny thing was there to do the protecting rather than the other way around.

God. I was a sick fuck.

But this woman just about did me in.

She always had.

I gulped it down.

Pretended like my dick wasn't straining in my jeans.

Pretended I didn't wish I was waking up with those legs wrapped around me rather than alternating between spending the night sitting in the front seat of my car and pacing the property.

"You said you were gonna patch the porch."

A smirk pulled at the corner of my mouth. "No, I didn't, Faith. I said I was going to *fix* the porch. The entire thing needs to be replaced. Top and bottom."

Her eyes widened and her lips parted in shock.

My guts twisted.

I thought that each time I saw her, it might get easier, that I'd be able to lock down the need racing inside me.

And the only thing happening was those thoughts were coming stronger.

Urges and ideas filling my mind.

Taking her. That body and her mind and that heart that was supposed to be mine.

She crossed her arms over her chest. "That's two levels of porch that wrap around the entire house."

"I never said I wasn't up for the challenge."

Worry flooded her tone. "That will cost thousands and thousands of dollars, Jace."

"So what?"

She took a floundering step forward. Like she was struck with a sudden bolt of anger. "So what? So what?" Her hands fisted at her sides.

Her little girl was still clinging to the backs of her legs. She came forward with the movement like she was an extension of her mother.

Faith's voice lowered in an emphatic hiss. "So, I don't have any money to pay for that, that's what."

"Didn't ask you for any."

"I'm no beggar."

Yeah, well I was going to be in about five seconds if she didn't stop worrying at that plump bottom lip with her teeth.

"Never said you were."

"Jace."

I stepped back, shaking my head. "This isn't up for discussion, Faith. I told you I was going to fix your porch. You accepted. You can't take that back now."

Redness climbed to her face, something like shame and embarrassment written there. "It's just . . . so much time. So much money. I don't understand why you want to do this for me."

Had she forgotten everything she'd done for me? The kindness she'd shown me when everyone else walked by and kicked me like I was a dog?

Couldn't keep the softness from infiltrating my tone. "I want to do it."

Something tender moved through her features. Something so familiar that it punched me in the gut.

"It's going to be okay, Faith. It is."

Her eyes pinched, and I cleared my throat. "Now . . . white or stain?" I asked, lifting the containers in each hand, because I needed to step back, get the hell away from her before I leaned in closer.

Ran my nose along the soft slope of her delicate neck.

Her little girl poked her head through her mother's legs, hands clinging to the backs of her knees, the child grinning like crazy through a veil of soft brown curls. "Pink!"

Faith ran her fingers through the little girl's hair. "I don't think pink is the best color for outside, Bailey Anne."

*Bailey Anne.*

The air jetted from my lungs.

Agony.

My body rocked forward, slammed by the shock, every cell constricting with excruciating pain.

Obliterating.

"Pink is the best *cowar* always," she said, drawing out the words in a strait shot of sweetness.

I blinked and tried to see through the memories that were nothing but torment ringing in my ear.

Focus on what the little girl was saying rather than feeling like Faith hadn't just driven a knife into my back.

Shit.

This was not good.

Not what I expected.

Definitely not what I signed up for.

"I want a room that's *aww* pink." She was peeking out again, acting shy while also staring at me, clearly trying to figure me out.

"Is that so?" I manage to ask around the thickness in my throat.

"*Wif* unicorns because they're magic." She whispered the last word like it was a secret. Chocolate eyes, just as genuine as Faith's, widened at me in guileless awe. Like she was wondering if I believed in it, too.

Sadness slammed me so hard it nearly bowled me over. It got mixed up with this overwhelming feeling of possession. Of protection.

I was going to make sure these two were safe. No matter the cost. Even if being here was gutting me.

Faith would hate me in the end, but she'd always been worth the sacrifice. That hadn't changed.

"How about we save the pink for your room then?" I offered.

It came out a promise. The stupidest thing I could say.

Because her smile went brilliant, filled with a mouthful of tiny teeth.

"Oh-kay." She craned her head to peer up at her mother's face, her words an amazed whisper. "He said he make my room pink, Mommy."

Faith gulped, staring at me like I'd punched her.

Apparently, both of us were getting the fuck beat out of us.

Blow after blow.

But it was the wounds inflicted that couldn't be seen that always scarred the worst.

I wanted to erase hers.

Soothe them and keep them.

Take them on as my own.

Just as I felt the scars written on me growing thicker.

"Jace—"

I knew what she was getting ready to say. I shook my head to cut her off and held the cans up higher, both of them swinging from the handles. "White or stain?"

She glowered at me, but there was something different in the depths of her gaze. Something close to amusement. An old kind of understanding.

The slightest smile pulled at her mouth. "Seems to me like you'd already know the answer to that."

Satisfaction welled in my chest, and I laughed out a surprised sound, shocked Faith would give me that inch.

"Now, if you'll excuse us, I need to shower."

She leaned down and swept her little girl into her arms, spinning on her heel, and heading back through the door without another word.

Her daughter peeked back at me from over her mom's shoulder, shy but still curious.

*Bailey.*

I gulped and then jerked when the door slammed shut, jarring me out of my stupidity.

# Ten

## Faith

The old pipes squealed as I shut off the showerhead. It sent the steamy bathroom into silence.

A dense, vacant kind of silence.

I peeked my head out from behind the shower curtain. "Bailey?" I called.

More of that silence echoed back.

Instantly, the paranoia set in. The horrible feeling that someone might be lurking, lying in wait.

I hated it.

I knew I was letting my mind run wild. But how could I not?

Still, it couldn't have been five seconds ago when I'd glanced out to make sure she was still playing on the carpet in my bedroom, right outside the open bathroom door.

It was her spot while I showered. One she knew she wasn't supposed to leave.

Her pile of toys was still there, a Barbie and a book and her favorite blocks scattered all over the floor.

Unease rippled, and I swallowed around the alarm that bleeped from somewhere deep in my consciousness.

"Bailey," I called again, a little louder this time, panic rising to the surface.

Nothing.

Throat closing up, I squeezed my eyes and tried to refuse the instant fear that wanted to suffocate me.

Bleed me dry.

I hurried out of the shower, not taking the time to towel off before I grabbed my robe from where it was hanging on the wall and shrugged into it, tying the belt as I headed out my bedroom door.

I went straight for Bailey's room.

The door was open.

She wasn't there.

More of that unease slithered across my flesh. Scenarios I didn't want to see flashing through my mind like a horror story.

But Jace was just outside. My rational mind told me that Bailey had only gone exploring.

That didn't sit all that well with me, either. The trouble she could get herself into.

This house?

It was huge.

Which was why I tried to keep her corralled. It had been much easier when she'd been younger and the play gates kept her restricted. But it had started to get more and more difficult to keep her in one area.

She was curious and inquisitive. Smart in a way that made me incredibly proud and scared me a little too. The child so intuitive.

That also meant sometimes she wandered, roaming the house and playing through the little worlds that were so vivid in her head.

It hadn't worried me so much until those notes had started coming. Until someone had been in our home.

I backed out of her room. "Bailey," I called down the rambling hall, my voice bouncing off the wooden floorboards.

No answer.

Quickly, I started to search through the second-floor rooms where we were staying until the third-floor rooms were renovated.

Eventually, the third floor would serve as our own, personal living space and the second floor would be guest rooms.

If that ever happened.

Each step I took incited something frantic in me as I searched under beds and old furniture and behind curtains.

She wasn't there.

Dread crawled across my still wet skin.

I was fighting tears when I got to the end of the hall and stepped over the baby gate that was supposed to keep her contained on this end of the house. Quickly, I searched the rooms on the other side of the hall.

It was just as quiet.

Flying back out, I took the third story steps to the top floor where she wasn't allowed to be, shouting out her name.

"Bailey? Where are you, Button? Please come out. This isn't a good game."

It was dim and dark up there, sunlight barely breaking through the thick curtains that covered the windows, a thick coat of dust covering every surface.

The top floor had hardly been touched since we'd moved in, the area one large space and crammed full of the old furniture that had been left there from more than a century ago.

In a frenzy, I rushed through it, searching.

Desperation took over.

My blood running thick, pulse thumping in my ears and slogging through my veins as I raced back down the third-story steps.

I took the staircase for the bottom floor, and my limbs started to shake as I moved through the living room, the office, the parlor, the formal dining room.

I shouted her name.

Over and over.

It echoed back.

Dread spiraled through me, my soul screaming out, no.

No.

Not my baby. I wouldn't let anyone hurt her.

By the time I made it to the huge, country kitchen set at the very back of the house on the first floor, I was completely devoid of breath.

Sure someone had found their way back in.

Then I saw the back door was wide open, and a whole different type of fear took over. The thought of her wandering off. Getting lost or worse.

"Oh my God."

I ran through it and into the sunshine that blazed down from the blue, blue sky, already suffocating in its heat.

"Bailey!" I shouted.

I ran down the porch steps and onto the back lawn.

"Bailey!" It'd shifted into a scream. Dread and terror and every fear I'd ever had slammed me.

Full force.

My thoughts streaked from the idea of someone taking her, hurting her, and went directly to the stream that ran at the back of the land, just on the other side of the thicket of trees that rose like a hedge around the property.

Terrified she'd wandered that direction. It was her favorite place to play, where she begged me to take her every day.

I flew that way, my bare feet pounding across the lawn, my robe flapping open as I hit a sprint, gasps raking from my lungs. "Bailey! Bailey!"

My voice echoed through the heavens, rushing through the leaves.

A howling plea.

"Faith!" His voice hit me like protection, and I spun around. Jace was sprinting around the side of the house. "What's happening?"

"Bailey . . . I . . . I can't find her. Oh my God, my baby."

Those copper eyes flamed, and he flew around me, going directly for the path that led for the stream as if he'd had the very same thought as me.

"Bailey!" he shouted. His gruff voice reverberated back, held in the arms of the dense trees.

I started after him, only to freeze when the tiny voice hit me from behind.

"Mommy?"

I was trembling when I turned around.

Bailey was off to the right on the other side of the porch. Clinging to a red beach bucket that she played with in her sandpit, which was on that side of the house.

A cry raked from my throat. "Bailey."

I staggered that way, and she started to round the porch.

I started running for her.

"Mommy?"

I scooped her up, knocking the full bucket from her hold, and crushed her against me.

Feeling her weight. The steady beat of her heart.

I dropped to my knees while holding her.

The adrenaline drained, and the terror that had bottled inside me burst.

Sobs ripped free.

Coming all the way from my soul.

And I realized how close I was to cracking. The pressure too much.

Little fingers were in my hair. "You cry, Mommy?"

"Button . . . Mommy was so scared. You're not supposed to go outside by yourself." The words were so clogged in my throat that I doubted she could even understand what I was saying.

*You aren't supposed to go outside by yourself.*

*It's dangerous.*

*You aren't allowed to leave me.*

I felt the presence fall over us.

A shadow.

His intensity so thick I choked over that, too.

I hugged Bailey closer to me, refusing to look up, refusing to let her go. Her scent filled my senses.

Baby powder and lilacs and life.

My world.

That presence lowered to a knee, and I felt his fingers in my hair, brushing it back from my face. "Faith, sweetheart, it's okay."

My head shook frantically.

It wasn't okay.

Nothing was okay.

"Come here," he murmured. One of those masculine arms slipped around my waist.

So foreign and so familiar.

I gasped at the contact.

"I *sowwee*. I need dirt, Mommy. Don't be sad."

I squeezed Bailey tighter. "You scared me, baby. You can't do that."

She burrowed her head deeper into me, her little breaths coming out on the skin of my throat, her chubby fingers clinging to the lapel of the thin robe.

As if she could suddenly feel my terror.

"Let's get you two inside." Jace's voice was rough when it fell on my ear.

He didn't try to pry her from my arms—I wouldn't have let him if he'd tried. He just helped me to stand with Bailey still wrapped around my neck.

The man lifted me from the ground with the arm he had around my waist, his other hand set protectively on Bailey's back.

"She's fine, Faith," he murmured, his voice as thick as the sun I could feel burning against my skin, my hair sopping wet, my body suddenly feeling overwhelmed by the pressure of the muggy air.

My knees shook, threatened to give.

"She's fine."

The problem was that I wasn't.

I wasn't sure I was ever gonna be.

"You have her. You have her," he quietly encouraged. He guided me up the rickety porch steps at the back of the house.

Steps that needed replacin', too. Everything falling apart around me.

*Everything.*

And I had no idea how we were goin' to survive. How we were going to make it past all of this.

Tears streaked down my face, and I dropped my head as I let him lead us back through the still gaping door.

Numbly, I moved through the massive kitchen, the one room that had already been fully renovated. My feet shuffled down the hall toward the front of the house.

All the while, Bailey continued to cling to me, probably feeling a little of her own fear, too.

The child was smart enough to realize she'd disobeyed; though, I knew she hadn't realized what she'd done would elicit the reaction it had.

Too young and innocent to realize the danger she'd put herself in.

Too young to understand the threat and danger that loomed like the darkest shadow over our home.

I couldn't make it any farther than the antique sofa that rested in the middle of the main living space. I sank onto it, still holding her, breathing her in.

My limbs began to shake. Trembles jerking through my muscles, a stutter at my very soul.

Bailey rested her cheek on my hammering heart. As if she were trying to soothe it.

Jace dropped to his knees in front of us.

I didn't want to look at him.

Didn't want to see the judgment on his face when he saw what a mess I was.

When he realized I didn't know how to handle all of this on my own.

Those copper eyes stared back. Somehow hard and tender at the same time.

He set his hand on my bare knee. A jolt of hot energy blasted through my body. I squeezed my eyes against it.

"She's safe," he murmured. "She's safe."

"I safe, Mommy," Bailey whispered, so quietly. Her little fingers fumbled over my chin like an apology.

Images flashed.

The pictures of Joseph that I'd demanded of Mack.

Demanding that he *show* me, because I'd refused to believe what had happened to him was real until I saw it with my own eyes.

My mind flashed with the warning of those notes.

The doll floatin' in the tub.

All the questions.
All the fear.
And I didn't know if I would ever truly feel safe again.

# eleven

## Jace

The shrill sound of the drill digging through wood echoed through the kitchen. My hand was cinched tight where I held the power tool, teeth gritted, my shoulder turned as I bore down.

All I could feel was the sticky apprehension that clawed at the walls.

Clawed at my insides.

The drill hit, burrowing out the spot, and I set the drill aside and began to install the hardware high up toward the top of the door where it'd be out of reach of curious fingers.

I'd already taken the same care on the other two doors that led outside.

Unease rumbled through my consciousness.

No one was getting inside here.

Not on my watch.

Problem was, I'd never get the chance to erase what was at the heart of it.

What dimmed those chocolate eyes to a murky, black

desperation.

What marked her in scars that would never heal.

*I did this.*

Guilt screamed through my mind, and my shoulders tensed when I heard the floorboards squeak behind me.

I finished securing the last screw into place and then bolted the lock at the top, making sure it worked, metal screeching against metal as I slid it home.

I could feel Faith watching as I did. Her presence crawling across the floor and climbing my legs.

Sinking in.

The way she always had.

Carefully, I shifted a fraction, enough so I could peer back at her.

She'd come to a stop in the kitchen entryway. Wearing fitted jeans and a long-sleeved tee. Her hair dry and tied back into a ponytail.

A goddamned vision.

Angelic.

*Beauty.*

Filling me with the kind of awe that made me want to drop to my knees and sing.

Or maybe confess all my sins.

She looked between me and the new lock that had been installed. Sorrowful gratitude moved through her expression.

I gave an uncomfortable shrug.

"No one's getting in or out of here without you knowing," I promised.

I mean, fuck, I couldn't handle it. That overbearing feeling again.

Whatever the hell it was I'd felt when I'd come around the corner of her house and realized Faith was searching for her daughter.

The fury that had laced my blood, a burst of rage combusting with desperation.

At first, I'd been intent on hunting some fucker down, then I'd seen where Faith's mind had gone—to the stream at the back of the land—the threat of that much more realistic than the idea that someone had slipped by me when I'd been working out front.

I wasn't supposed to feel this way about Faith's kid.

About *Joseph's* kid.

Wasn't supposed to care.

The fact she even existed felt like a cruel joke.

And there the little girl was, getting under my skin. Grin after tiny grin.

At the beginning, it'd been easy to use her as an excuse to protect Faith.

And as I'd secured those fucking locks, the only thing I could think about was the lengths I'd go to in order to make sure she was safe.

Kept protected from this ugly mess that had nothing to do with her.

"I did the rest of the doors downstairs as well. I'm going to secure the windows upstairs and the doors leading to the upper porch. You don't have to worry."

Right.

Like a few new deadbolts would strip away the fear I could see lining her features. But it sure made me feel a whole hell of a lot better.

"Going to call for a security system to be installed, too."

"Jace—"

"Don't say it's not necessary," I cut in, "because you and I both know it is."

She gave a wary nod of agreement. "Thank you," she whispered, clutching at a monitor that had a speaker and a screen.

I was thinking it was a shame it didn't have a record mode on it so we could push rewind. Go back a few days ago, stop this bullshit, erase what was written on Faith's face.

"She asleep?" I asked.

Faith gave a jerky nod. "Yeah. I think I scared her."

Tossing the screwdriver into the toolbox, I leaned back against the counter, crossing my arms over my chest and an ankle over the other.

You know . . . making myself right at damned home.

"She probably needed to know how badly that scared *you*, Faith. Don't think you should shield her from that."

Awesome.

Now I was giving parenting advice, too.

But this shit was serious.

Faith gulped over a little sound and wandered farther into the kitchen.

Every step brought her closer to where I was.

The girl filling the air.

She pulled out a chair at the round table that was situated close to the bank of windows that overlooked the back patio and lawn. She sank onto it like she didn't have any energy left.

I moved over to the coffee pot, poured her a cup, spooned a ton of sugar into it, and then dumped a bunch of creamer in, too. If I knew her at all, that would be the way she would take her coffee.

I edged back across the floor, my heavy footsteps thudding on the floorboards.

It was like every step I took moved that energy around, pushing it higher, making it flare.

Faith was sucking in a bunch of short breaths by the time I'd crossed the small distance and set the cup down in front of her. "I thought you might need that."

Warily, those eyes darted toward me.

Genuine and real.

"You don't need to take care of me."

I sank to a knee in front of her. Her chair was angled out to the side, and it was right that second when I realized the girl was too fucking close.

That I was in her space.

Breathing her air.

But I couldn't help it, reaching out and brushing back the long piece of dark, dark hair that had fallen from the tie and down around her face.

"Maybe you don't need help, Faith, maybe you can handle this all on your own, but I wish you would let me, anyway."

She choked out a pained sound. "Who am I kidding, Jace? I

can't even take care of my daughter."

I frowned, rearing back an inch to take in the expression on her face.

Defeat.

"Don't say that. I may not have anything good to compare it to, but I know just by looking at the two of you that you are exactly what that little girl needs."

Tears brimmed in her eyes. I wanted to make them stop falling. Dry them up. Kiss them away.

"She's my entire world, Jace. My entire world. But sometimes, I don't know how I'm gonna hold my world together. It feels like it's crumbling at the seams, and no matter what I do, there is nothing I can do to patch it back together."

She sniffled, blinked, her eyes darting around the kitchen like she was taking in the whole house. "I wasn't supposed to have to do all of this alone. Joseph . . ."

His name was a blow all on its own.

Like she'd conjured his spirit into the dense, heavy space. Unease slicked across my skin. Tingling and hot.

What would he think if he knew I was here?

Her tongue darted out to wet her dry lips. "He was supposed to help me with all of this. We were supposed to be partners. And now . . . now . . ."

She blinked some more, exhaling in despair and resignation. "Maybe I should just sell it. Give it up. God knows I don't have the money to fix it up anyway. And with everything that's happening, I'm not sure I can handle all of this. I'm not sure I want to stay here alone."

"Don't say that, Faith. This place was your dream."

I wanted to reach out and grab her by the shoulders.

Shake her.

Shout it.

Claim it.

*Our dream.*

Sadness poured from her as she stared at me, her head angled slightly to the side. "Some dreams change, don't they?"

*No. Never.*

At least mine had been haunting me for all of forever.

Glancing away, I took in the immaculate kitchen. By my estimate, it was the only part of the house that had been fully renovated.

It boasted massive, top-of-the-line appliances and rustic, white stone countertops, a huge worker's island in the middle with an old-style pot rack hanging low from overhead.

A bit country and a lot chic.

But I thought the centerpiece of it all was where we were, at the huge round dining table that sat at least twenty people, tucked in the curved bank of windows that took up the whole back wall.

It overlooked the back porch and expansive lawn that rolled down a sloping embankment toward a copse of trees.

Right toward that babbling creek.

After what just happened, I was half inclined to fill the fucker up with rocks and sand.

Blot it out.

I roughed a hand through my hair, knowing I was digging, pushing in a way I shouldn't. But I didn't know how to stop.

I'd hopped on a train that would lead me straight to my destruction. But fuck, I guessed I'd been heading there all along. The only thing that counted now was doing a little good until I got there.

"There's no money left?" I hedged, voice gravel. But I already knew the answer to that, didn't I?

Her eyes squeezed shut, and she warred with what to tell me. When that chocolate sea fluttered open, I swore they were going to drown me.

Take me in.

Hold me under.

"No, Jace. There's no money left. I thought . . ."

Confusion wound through her, and she stared at the wall over my shoulder with her brow pinched. Like it might hold the answer she was searching for.

"I thought we had plenty, and then when . . ."

She twisted her fingers together on her lap. I had the urge to haul her onto mine.

Fuck.

She peeked down at me, embarrassment lighting her cheeks. "When I went to make arrangements for the funeral, there was nothing there. The accounts had gone dry. I had to borrow from my parents to even give him a service."

She looked out through the glittering windows, her voice getting lost in the room, so quiet when she whispered, "When it first happened, I couldn't help but keep thinkin', if I just hadn't have sent him that day. I'd forgotten the milk, and he had to go back. If I'd just done that one thing differently, if I hadn't been in such a hurry earlier that day, he'd still be here."

Was that what he had really deluded her into believing?

That he was the good guy?

That he was in the wrong place at the wrong time?

The victim of some mindless robbery?

If he had gone fifteen minutes earlier or later, he wouldn't have stumbled down the wrong path?

Didn't she know he'd gone running down that path a long time ago?

It didn't matter what time he'd gone. Where he'd gone. They would have found him.

My guts clenched.

Shit.

I didn't know what was worse, her going on thinking that or me telling her the truth.

Shame had taken hold of her when she looked back at me. "Now, I don't have any idea what to believe. I'm so confused . . . so scared. It wasn't as if we had a perfect marriage."

I flinched.

Not sure I could handle her even talking about it.

Still, I stayed silent, allowing her to continue even though the picture of them together made me want to stab a hot poker into my eye.

"But I at least thought he cared about us enough that he wouldn't do anything that would harm us."

As if she bore the blame, she looked down. "But after everything? The things that have been happening around us? I can't help but question who he really was. And I hate that . . . hate questioning a man who isn't even here to defend himself. Who isn't here to explain. And . . . and . . . the only thing I have left of him is waiting on his life insurance policy to come through."

Once she admitted it, urgency started to pour from her mouth. "How pathetic is that? His worth is now wrapped up in the little he left behind. What kind of person does that make me, Jace? Fighting for money I never even wanted? But I don't know what else to do. It's the only way I could ever get this place turned and profitable. With the case bein' unsolved, it's going to be tied up for a while, and we don't have anything left. I've . . . ."

She choked on the last, her head dropping between her shoulders. Like she needed to hide the expression on her face. "God, I shouldn't be tellin' you any of this."

I reached out and took her by the chin. "Hey, look at me."

Warily, she met my gaze.

I felt the weight of it strike right at the middle of me.

"What it makes you is strong. It makes you a fighter. It makes you a good mother who wants to take care of her child. It makes you brave. That's the kind of person it makes you."

The corner of her mouth trembled. "I just wish I could go back to that day and change it all."

"You couldn't, Faith."

It was the truth.

There was nothing she could have done.

Changing it had been on *me*.

Silence moved around us. Comforting waves that ebbed and flowed, receding to reveal the hurt and gaping wounds oozing from underneath.

"Let me take care of you." The words grated from my tongue.

She blinked at me. "Why did you really come here, Jace? After all this time? After all these years? What is it you want?"

*You.*

"I need to be here. I tri—"

The confession locked in my throat, and I swallowed hard, forcing it out between the constriction I could feel baring down on every cell in my body.

"I tried to stay away. But I couldn't. Not knowing what's happening. Not knowing what you've been through."

Not knowing just how fucking deep Joseph had gotten. Not knowing the lengths those assholes might go to. I was getting a better and better idea of what that might be.

Protectiveness swelled.

An anger so intense I saw black curled through my muscles.

I could feel it, a wire tripping somewhere inside me, one of those pieces I'd been trying to keep contained, held back, ripped free.

No way in hell was I backing down from this. No way in hell was I walking away from her.

"I'm moving in."

She reared back. "What?"

"You heard what I said."

A heated anger rushed in to take over the helplessness. "Well, I thought I did . . . and what I think I just heard you say was you're movin' in here, and that's not goin' to happen."

"You need someone here to look after you. Besides . . . there are what? Eight rooms here? You will hardly notice me, and someone needs to be here to watch over things."

"And you think that job lands on you?" It was all a rushed horror as she pushed back her chair and stumbled to her feet.

Energy flashed.

So intense my chest tightened.

Painfully.

Protectiveness pulsing out. Filling everything.

"I think that's exactly what it is."

Harsh, hoarse laughter rocked from her, and she was biting at her lip like she wanted to bite back her words.

"You are the last person I want movin' in here. I already told you, all of this is too hard. It feels too complicated. It's hard enough you bein' outside. You want to take up the inside, too?"

I edged closer, breathing in all that intensity.

Taking it on as my own.

Standing next to the girl felt like inhaling life.

Did she think this wasn't going to be brutal for me, too?

My voice quieted, though it was hard as stone. "You aren't safe here. You're scared. You can't deny that."

I edged closer, and she edged back. She hit the wall behind her. She was so close.

So damned close I wanted to take one step closer and feel all of her. What it was like to be against that skin.

Her words were so rough she could barely force them out. "Then I'll call my daddy to come and stay."

My fingers were back to toying with a lock of her hair, my head angled to the side. "Let me take care of you, Faith. Let me be the one."

"Jace—"

"Please . . . let me do this for you. I'm your family, whether you like it or not."

"This is a terrible idea," she whispered. Like it was her last plea.

"It might be the only good one I've ever had."

# twelve

## Faith

"What am I gonna do?" I flew into the small realtor's office like I was running from a rabid skunk.

Basically, that was what I was doing. It was the only way I'd been able to get away from him, the overbearing man not even wanting me to go into town to get groceries without him tagging along.

I'd barely convinced him I had to remain standing. Continue living. Besides, it wasn't like Mack wasn't watching my every move. There was a cruiser sitting right outside to prove it.

And God, I was grateful for it. The fact that this town had rallied around me. The hardest part was the fact there was a reason for them to have to do it.

Courtney's attention flew up from where it'd been buried in the laptop on her desk, her voice all sorts of wry. "I might be brilliant, but I'm not psychic, so you're gonna have to clarify."

Rolling my eyes, I plopped down onto one of the chairs on the opposite side of her desk, blowing out the biggest breath from my lungs. "Jace Jacobs."

Her face pinched into a sour expression.

Apparently, she didn't need any more clarification than that.

"What'd that dog do now?"

"Oh, you know, nothing much . . . he was just there when I couldn't find Bailey this morning and freaked out. I mean, really freaked out, Court. I started shouting and screaming and carrying on, but it turned out she was just fine. Of course, while I was getting her to take a nap, he went and fixed up all the locks in the entire house so no one can get in or out, and then he turned right around and told me he was moving in so he can watch over us. That's what."

It all left me on a rush of incredulity.

A tumble of confusion and frustration and this niggle of need that I sure didn't want to feel.

Her eyebrows lifted for the ceiling. "Excuse me?"

"You need me to repeat it?"

"Just rewind to that part where you said something about him movin' in." She spun her index finger in the air.

"That's right." I hugged my purse to my chest as if the thing might be a shield. "He said he's moving in."

Chin angling away, she laughed a short sound. As short as the shake of her head. "You've got to be shittin' me. That man has a lot of balls, doesn't he?"

That was what I was worried about.

She swung her green eyes back toward me. "So, what'd you tell him?"

"What do you think I told him? I told him no chance in hell."

"And how'd he take it?"

The vigor in my voice faded out, and I started fiddling with the strap of my purse. "He said he'd be back with his things later. That man just doesn't take no for an answer."

A low chuckle rumbled from her.

Why was she grinnin'?

"Oh, you're in so much trouble, Faith Avery."

I frowned at her. "What's that supposed to mean?"

"You know full well that man would take *no* for an answer if you really meant it. He knows you better than anyone."

I jarred back with her statement. "He doesn't know me."

"Really?"

Shit.

I gnawed at my bottom lip.

"See?" she said, as if that was my answer.

"I just . . . what if something really would have happened to Bailey? What if she really had been in danger? It'd be nice to have someone else there, looking out for us."

"And the man looks pretty *nice*, too."

"Courtney," I chastised.

"Faith," she shot back.

"Where is Button?" she asked.

"She went to the park with my mama. I'm trying to keep things as normal as possible through all of this."

Courtney nodded and then didn't say anything for a second, clearly chewing on her thoughts as she worked her jaw.

"Come on, Faith," she finally broached. "Are you really gonna sit there and pretend you two didn't have all sorts of unfinished business when he left?"

"Oh, I think he finished me off just fine the first time around."

"Did you ever really blame him?"

Offense churned in my blood. "Of course, I blamed him. He left me."

"Didn't you ever think he might be doin' it *for* you?"

Unease rippled in with that offense. Courtney never did hesitate to put me on the spot.

She just loved playing devil's advocate.

"It didn't matter why he left. The only thing that mattered was he did."

She grabbed the pen that was on her planner and thumped the end of it against the thick paper. "I'm not saying what he did was right. I've just always wondered if he might have had reasons for it."

"I thought you hated the man?"

"Oh, I hate him plenty for the fact he hurt you. Doesn't mean I didn't see the same things in him that you did."

I pushed out a heavy sigh. "Well, none of that matters now, does it? I think it's plenty clear the only reason he's back is out of obligation to Joseph."

As if I could handle anything else, anyway.

"He didn't even come back for his funeral. He's feelin' guilty, that's all."

"Maybe."

She thumped her pen again before she rocked forward and settled her forearms on the desk. "The question you need to ask yourself is if you're willing to accept his help and how that might make you feel."

Anxiously, I tapped my toes on the floor, and I looked out the windows into the blinding light.

Warily, I looked back at my best friend. "Is it wrong that it might feel good to have someone there? I really feel like I might lose it, Court. That I can't keep juggling all this sorrow and worry and fear and remain standing on my own two feet. I'm scared." The last was a whispered plea.

Understanding climbed to the features of her pretty face. "No, Faith. It's not wrong that you feel more comfortable with someone there. Not at all."

What worried me was it felt like more than that. I was worried the reason it felt *good* was the fact it was him.

I pulled my thumb to my mouth and chewed at the nail. "What's the town gonna say if I let him do this?"

"When have you ever worried what the town had to say about him?"

"Things are different now."

"You're right. They're different, and everyone here knows you're gonna have to move on with your life. Whether that's today or tomorrow or five years down the road, you're gonna have to move on. And you know my offer still stands. You want me to come stay with you, and I'm there."

Her eyes narrowed in speculation. "Though it seems like you're gettin' all kinds of tempting offers. It has to be a bear to choose."

She hiked a nonchalant shoulder. "I mean, Jace is no ninja like me, but I'm sure he could hold his own."

There she went again, making me smile when it should be impossible.

"You're terrifying," I told her.

She grinned. "Deadly."

I jumped when the glass door flew open.

Felix loped in, all casual smiles as his massive body filled up the doorway.

He was a new officer on the Broadshire Rim force. He and Courtney had met just a few weeks ago when he'd come by to check up on me at the plantation while Courtney was visiting.

Their attraction had been instant.

"Felix, baby, what are you doing here?" Courtney asked, her eyes raking over him as if he'd just dropped by to offer himself up for lunch.

With the way they were looking at each other, I was pretty sure that was the case.

"What, I can't drop by to see my girl when I'm missing her?"

"Oh, you can *drop by* any time."

How the hell Courtney managed to make talk about dropping by sound dirty, I didn't know.

He rounded the desk and dropped a kiss to her forehead as he handed her a keyring. "Also, I came by to drop these off. I found them in my car."

Courtney gasped. "Ah, my hero. I was looking all over for those. I was wondering where I'd left them."

"You'd lose your head if it wasn't attached to your neck," I told her.

"What are you talkin' about, Faith? I lost my head a long time ago."

I grinned.

Felix tore his hungry gaze from her and turned it on me.

"How's Faith, today?" he asked.

"She was just leaving," I said, sparing Courtney a knowing glance. "I apparently have *company* coming to stay."

My best friend laughed a salacious sound. "What, you don't want to stick around?"

I was already on my feet, waving them off. "Um . . . no but

thank you."

Felix frowned, the cop in him immediately on edge. "Who?"

A lump formed in my throat. "Jace . . . an old . . . friend."

God, I didn't even know what to call him.

An old lover?

My dead husband's cousin?

Yeah, neither of those things sounded all that right.

He frowned. "Are you sure that's a good idea? If you aren't feeling safe out there, you should stay with Courtney or your parents."

I should take him up on the suggestion.

But I was shaking my head, hating the idea of some monster chasing me out of my house. "I think what's done is done."

"All right . . . just . . . be safe, okay?" he said.

"I will. I promise."

I pushed open the door to the bright, bright summer light.

Laughter rippled from behind me. "Don't do anything I wouldn't do," Courtney called before her voice dropped to a whisper meant only for Felix.

"I won't do *anything* you would do," I hollered back, managing a grin as I stepped out onto the sidewalk. Sun bright and warm, I lifted my face to the blue sky as I headed down the walk to the side of the building where I'd parked.

Doug, an officer who I often saw driving by my house, was the one who was sitting at the curb.

I gave him a little wave as I opened my car door, and he returned a grin and playful salute before he pulled from the curb.

I sank down into the driver's seat, hit with a rush of gratefulness that people were watchin' over us.

Then I thought of Jace. Packing his things. Coming back to me. And I wondered if it was guilt that sloshed through my senses when I thought of him, the small shot of comfort injected into my veins at the thought of him bein' around.

Shaking it off, I shifted my car into reverse and glanced out the rear-window, attention catching on what was sitting in Bailey's car seat.

A rose.

Not just any rose.

One of the one's from my garden.

A lavender rose.

Terror raced, a drum in my heart that made it difficult to see. Difficult to breathe.

I rammed on the brakes and threw it back into park, hands shaking like crazy as I reached back and grabbed it, the little slip of paper that had been left under it.

*Time's running out. I want it, and I want it now. For your sake, I hope you're smarter than him.*

# *thirteen*

## Faith
## Sixteen Years Old

*A* rowdy clatter of voices lifted in the cafeteria. It was always about fifteen decibels too loud in the big, open room. The linoleum floors like a loudspeaker set to high, tossing the noise higher and higher, as if each one had to climb on top of the other to be heard.

In the middle of it, Faith was trembling her way through the line, filling her tray to the brim and looking over her shoulder as if she were on some sort of covert mission.

She paid for the food and sucked in a breath, her feet quaking in her shoes as she looked for the courage to take the long way to the table where she always sat with her friends.

Dropping her head as if it might conceal her, she hugged the wall at the far end of the room. Slowly, she cut between two long tables, her heart rate spiking with each step she took.

She was sure her approach was louder than the din that blasted her ears. Sure that everyone was watching.

She felt like an intruder as she slinked down to the farthest end where students sat sporadically.

A few alone.

A few together.

The nerds and the outcasts, the troublemakers and the friendless, which was just sad in itself.

She was shaking like a leaf.

Heart hammering.

Throat dry.

She edged up behind the boys. This time, four were in their group.

Mack, who'd lived in the area for all of forever, and the three new students the town had been going on about.

Only now she knew their names.

Ian.

Joseph.

And Jace.

*Jace.*

That terrifyingly beautiful boy who was tucked against the long table, acting as if he were too cool for the tray that he'd pushed off to the side.

He'd edged it toward his brother. His brother who was again shoveling food into his mouth as if he didn't know when he'd get the chance to eat again, their cousin doing the same.

Faith sucked for air. She swore the only thing she did was breathe in his anger and hostility.

But she continued, determined, the little bit of courage and hope she felt was the only thing that allowed her to be able to grab the extra sandwich and milk she'd purchased.

She slowed just enough to discreetly set them on the table beside him as she passed.

Her arm brushed his shoulder.

His spine stiffened.

Her knees turned to goo.

*Oh goodness.*

She faltered a step and squeezed her eyes closed against that same sensation she'd experienced for the first time yesterday in the office.

Though this time, it almost felt like a welcome memory. As if she were aching to feel it again. She inhaled it. Kept it.

Her feet were barely able to keep her standing, but she knew she had to keep moving. That she couldn't stop to wait and see what he would say.

She made it to the end of the table and beelined it for hers, panting from nearly sprinting the rest of the way over as she slid into her spot.

Her tray clattered to the table in front of her.

Courtney, who was sitting directly across from her, looked at Faith as if she'd gone crazy. "Did you get lost or something?"

Faith widened her eyes at her, telling her to mind her own business. "Just tellin' a friend hi, is all."

Courtney's gaze flew the direction Faith had been.

*Crap.*

That'd been the wrong thing to say.

Even though she wasn't looking that way, Faith could feel hard, hard eyes glaring back. She swore that they held the power to shoot fire. Heat seared across her flesh.

She shifted in her seat.

Courtney kept looking between her and the direction Faith had just come from.

"Stop it," Faith hissed, angling her head at Courtney.

Courtney looked back at her, worry on her face. "What are you up to, Faith Avery?"

"I'm not up to anything."

"Sure looks like you're up to something to me."

"Stop it, you're bein' ridiculous."

Courtney frowned but was quick to get distracted by Keegan, who sat next to her.

Faith tried to eat her lunch, but she found she could only pick at her food, still too off balance because of the stare she could feel burning into her back from across the room.

Finally, she couldn't take it anymore.

"I have some studying I need to do for my math test seventh period. I'm gonna head to the library."

Courtney jerked her attention back to her. "You barely even ate."

Faith shoved what she could into her mouth before she stood. "There."

She walked across the cafeteria and was quick to toss her tray into the dirty bin and race out the door, her head dropped between her shoulders.

She didn't know why she was feeling so uncomfortable. As if she'd done something wrong when she'd only been trying to do something right.

Something nice.

But she guessed she understood it better when she was standing out in the courtyard and she felt the presence press against her from behind.

That hot, blazing hostility.

Shockwaves of heat and hatred.

Yet, it was chills that flashed across her skin when he leaned in closer, the boy so much taller than she was, casting her in shadow, his breath brushing across the shell of her ear. "What the fuck do you think you're doin'?"

Shivers rolled, and her heart sped. She fumbled with her backpack strap. "I don't know what you mean."

He laughed a hard sound. "Really. So that sandwich and milk just up and appeared at my table. Like magic."

She dropped her head forward, giving, because it was stupid to deny it. "I just thought you might be hungry."

A scraping sound came from his throat, sliding over her like a threat she somehow wanted to hold.

To turn around and see what it might look like coming from his mouth.

"Mind your own damn business. I don't need your pity or anyone else's. I can take care of myself."

She frowned, her teeth clamping in refusal, her courage flaring as she peeked at him over her shoulder.

He was right there.

The sharp lines and curves of his handsome face so close she could hike up onto her toes and press her nose to them. Feel them.

Skin to skin. "Maybe I was just tryin' to be nice."

"Maybe you're puttin' your nose where it shouldn't be."

A flush rushed to her cheeks. She couldn't help but wonder if he'd known what she'd just been thinkin', how she was imagining what it might feel like to trace his features.

For him to trace hers.

To breathe him in like she was achin' to do.

A shudder flashed.

What was wrong with her?

She spun all the way around and took a step back, lifting her chin in a show of defiance, needing to put some space between them. "Maybe you shouldn't be such a jerk."

His brows lifted, which only made those copper eyes appear bigger. Like they might gobble her up.

"And maybe you shouldn't be such a little priss."

Offense dropped her jaw. "I'm not a priss."

"No?" he challenged.

She straightened her shoulders. "No."

His eyes moved down her body, over her summer dress, which was hardly as scandalous as half the girls around here got away with wearing.

But her shoulders were bare, the bit of her exposed chest heating with a blush as his gaze traveled over her body.

She was right.

Those eyes could devour her.

She gulped, only for her mouth to run dry when he brought his stare back to hers.

"Looks like it to me," he said, but his voice had gone somewhere else.

Deeper and darker.

Faith shook. "I need to get to the library."

He laughed a disbelieving sound and took his own step back, as if he needed the space, too.

Or maybe she just repulsed him.

But when he looked at her again, there was something sad in his eyes. "Go on. Good girls like you don't need to be hanging around with boys like me."

Unsure if it was meant to be an insult or a compliment, Faith dropped her gaze to her feet, hiked her backpack up higher on her shoulder, and started up the sidewalk.

She didn't know whether to be embarrassed or angry.

She really was just trying to be nice.

She'd almost made it around the building when he called out to her. "Faith."

A quiver rolled through her. Like the piercing of an arrow.

She didn't really know why it was so impactful that he knew her name. Why it made her feel the way it did, as if she'd just stumbled onto the missing piece of her life.

She slowly turned around to face him.

He was running his hand nervously through his unruly hair.

"Thank you," he said roughly, nodding slowly, as if he were having to process the fact that he'd even said it.

"You're welcome," she answered, full of honesty.

He rocked a little, as agitated as a summer storm coming in the distance.

Faith's spirit thrashed, sure that was exactly what he was.

# *fourteen*

## Faith

Mack had just left a few minutes before. He'd assured me they'd amp up the security before he'd told me almost reluctantly that it was a good idea that Jace was moving in.

Was it?

Because I was trembling like mad as I ripped the sheets off the bed.

It wasn't as if they'd been used since I'd changed them a few weeks ago, but I needed to do something with my hands.

Quickly, I put on the fresh sheets, hands trembling as I tucked them into the mattress.

This was such a terrible idea.

I mean, seriously, Jace Jacobs was staying here. In the room right next to mine.

So stupid.

The hardest part was knowing it would be stupid to turn him away.

To disregard what he was offering.

I gave myself a sharp shake of my head as I dragged the comforter toward the massive headboard, thinking of how my dreams undulated like a flag blown in the wind.

Twisting this way and that, my hopes rising and falling and whipping and howling.

When we'd lost Joseph, they had gone straight to the backburner, *someday* drifting farther and farther away.

It was hard to admit it, but because of Jace's generosity, that *someday* felt as if it'd gotten one day closer.

His promise to watch over us and start working on the house while he was here was the kind of proposal only a fool would refuse.

Of course, I'd had to sell my soul to the devil to make that happen.

I just prayed Joseph wouldn't think it wrong. That he wasn't somewhere, caught between heaven and hell, judging the choices I was making now.

Squeezing my eyes closed, I lifted my face toward the ceiling, and whispered, "I'm doing my best."

Would he understand that?

And had he done his best?

My heart clenched with the thought, and I let myself get lost in the memories as I went to the antique dresser to dust it.

I'd felt as if I'd won the lottery when Joseph had come home on that night a few months before Bailey was born and gave me the news that he'd purchased this house.

I'd been awed and humbled and grateful beyond measure that he'd worked so hard to give me something he knew I'd wanted so desperately.

One of the best things about the house was that it'd come with the furnishings. Every room was fully furnished, the ornate, handmade pieces that had been left behind by the previous owners teeming with history and charm, perfect accents already in place.

At one point, this room had been painted a dark blue, though it'd faded and chipped.

The wallpaper, which someone had to have put up sometime in the seventies, was peeling, and the worn wooden floors were in dire need of a good sanding and staining.

But other than that, it was in fairly good shape, which was the reason I'd picked it.

Well, that and as I'd nervously flitted from room to room, trying to picture where in the world I was supposed to put the man, my child had claimed, "*Bwew* is for boys. This room, Mommy."

It'd been decided.

Now, I was questioning how in the world I'd agreed to let him stay in the room right next to mine.

That was nothing but a disaster waiting to happen.

I tipped the polish onto the rag and began to wipe down the aged, darkened wood, every stroke brightening the dresser to a gleaming sheen.

I quickly wiped down the bronze handles and tugged open the drawers to make sure they weren't providing shelter to a dust bunny or two.

I made it through the top row and started on the lower, only to pause in surprise after I'd tugged one open.

Inside was a key.

An old, ornate, antique key.

But it was the thick piece of parchment paper folded in half underneath that sent nerves skittering across my flesh.

I could have sworn I'd been through these drawers before and this hadn't been here. Was sure this wasn't a relic left from centuries ago to tease us with a love that once was.

It was funny how it almost felt that way, though. As if I were reaching out to touch something in the distance.

Something lost.

A whisper of a memory.

My pulse beat a sluggish cadence of sorrow as I pulled the note free.

Our anniversary had only been a week away, and I was bettin' he'd hidden this here.

I sank onto my bottom on the rug, hands shaking as I opened the note.

The words were drawn in pencil, sharp and choppy, the blocky handwriting one I would never forget. My heart fisted in my chest.

*Faith,*

*The first time I saw you, I wanted you. I guessed I'd always chased after the things that weren't mine. I'm so sorry for that. But I don't regret it.*

*Do you remember the day we got married? Look at that picture, Faith. Look at me. It was the most honest day of my life. But even that honesty was tainted because you never really belonged to me.*

*I could never regret you. The only thing I wish is that I'd done it all differently.*

*Look at that picture, Faith. What you see there, it's the truth.*

*Joseph*

Uncertainty flooded into my broken heart, a river of it gushing in to fill the cracks and crevices, carving out a canyon of questions and confusion.

I'd never belonged to him?

What was he saying?

Frantic, I flipped the sheet over, looking for something else. For something more. Needing to know what it was he was trying to say.

But that was all that he'd left me.

I wanted to cling to the letter as if it offered some sort of comfort.

But there was something about the words that felt like a warning. As if something sickly crawled from the page and sank through my flesh, filling my consciousness with dread.

As if he were warning of what was to come.

Did he know he was gonna be taken from us? Did he know he was leaving Bailey and me in danger? Had he done something to make it that way?

Is that why he said I'd never really belonged to him?

Grief fisting my heart, I sat on the floor, having no idea what direction to go. So lost, I felt disoriented.

My spirit quivered within its confines, and I forced myself to shake off the thoughts that felt like some kind of morbid betrayal.

That was right when I heard the sound of a car engine turn up the drive.

I told myself to get it together. The last thing I needed was for Jace to find me this way.

Pushing to my feet, I edged toward the window and peered through the drape.

That fancy black Porsche pulled to a stop in the round drive.

I rushed into my bedroom next door, where I shoved the key and note into a drawer, finding the barest comfort in the fact Joseph had left behind a relic that he knew would speak to me.

An old key.

As if maybe he too had once wanted to be able to unlock a different world. One different than he'd been living. I was just terrified to know what kind of world he'd actually been involved in.

I edged back into the hall and popped my head into Bailey's room where she was playing quietly on the floor. "I'm just going to let Jace in, Button. I'll be right downstairs if you need me."

"Oh-kay, Mommy," she drawled, not even looking up from her dolls and blocks.

I bounded downstairs, not sure why I was running right toward the disturbance that rumbled in from out front.

But there I was, working through the locks, including the new one up high that he'd added, in a rush to open the door.

Once I had, though, I forced myself to slow as I stepped onto the porch, the breath leaving me without me giving it permission to.

Slowly, I moved over the unstained temporary boards, just watching as Jace stepped out of his car and rounded to the back to the hatch that slowly lifted.

He leaned forward and then pulled out a suitcase and a small overnight bag.

Emotion stretched tight. Tugging at all those places that I'd so long ago forgotten about.

The hope I'd had for this boy.

The belief that one day, things would be better.

"You did good for yourself, Jace," I found myself calling, voice soft though filled with pride, wondering why I couldn't stop myself from saying it.

Offering it.

But there were some things that were too important to ignore. It didn't matter that the cost of him attaining them had been him leaving me behind.

An even softer huff left his nose as he pushed a button on his key and the hatch began to lower. He watched it go, not looking my way until it was secure. "I seem to remember someone telling me that I would if I wanted it badly enough."

A chill of something flashed across my skin, cool in the muggy evening. I rushed my palms up my arms as if it might stand the chance to chase away the unease.

"I used to believe we could achieve anything if we wanted it badly enough. That we could close our eyes, and if we imagined it fiercely enough, we could will it to be," I murmured, not even sure he could hear.

Jace started up the walk, slowly taking the porch steps, those coppery eyes on me. He leaned in when he got to me, his tone coarse. "It'd kill me if you stopped."

He hesitated there. An inch away. Filling my senses.

Cloves and expensive leather and need.

I blinked, cleared my throat, tucked a strand of hair that'd gotten loose behind my ear. "Come on, I'll show you to your room."

Jace followed me inside.

I went right for the grand staircase, which was the centerpiece of the entire house. My hand slipped up the railing, holding tighter and tighter as we edged upward, his presence expanding with each step that we took.

If I let him, he'd fill this house. Take over everything.

I had to be careful. Guard myself from harboring the idea that this was anything but temporary.

Hitting the landing, we went left, and I stepped over the baby gate that blocked the end of the hall.

Jace chuckled a rumbly sound. "We might need to add a few extra inches to the top of that gate."

I released an affectionate sigh. "She seems to figure things out when she needs to."

"That's because she knows she *can*, just like her mother."

His words were fueled with his own belief, and my footsteps slowed until I was no longer moving, just standing two steps ahead of him facing away in the narrow hall. "Her mother's older now, and she's learned the hard way that's not always the case."

He was suddenly right there, so close he might as well have been touching me, his heart beating so loud I could feel the pound of it at my back. "Maybe she needs someone to remind her."

My eyes slammed closed.

As if it could stop the wave of emotions from slamming me, so overwhelming, they almost knocked me from my feet.

Belief enveloped me, a shroud of the words we'd shared when we'd snuck out to meet in the middle of the night.

As if he'd captured them in the palms of his hands when I'd given them to him, carried them through all the years, and then softly blew them back my direction at the exact moment I needed them.

I cleared the roughness from my throat, shook myself off, and forced myself to keep moving. I stopped at the first door on the right and pushed it open.

Turning to face him, I stepped off to the side and gestured inside.

"This is you."

He stood in the hall, unmoving, staring at me with all that potency. So big and enthralling. That mystery I'd always wanted to discover, his gaze almost too much to take.

He pointed to the room directly across from it. "Huh, I would have been sure it was that one."

A sharp wheeze filled my lungs at the forwardness of his words.

Presumptuous and brash and cruel.

It was a room I'd scarcely been able to force myself into in all the years I'd owned this home.

I was suddenly assaulted by images that I'd tucked way down deep inside.

Of that night.

Our bodies in the shadows, a twist in the moonlight. Before the sun had broken and we'd lost everything.

Heat burned on my cheeks. "Jace. You can't do that. Say things like that."

"Why?"

Was that anger in the word?

As if it had been my fault?

As if I hadn't begged him to stay?

"It's not fair . . . you coming into my home and stirring up ghosts."

His face pinched with frustration and remorse.

Severe and dark.

"You think I can come here and not think of it? Not think of you?"

I could feel the anger pulling across my features. "You did perfectly fine the last ten years."

He flew forward a step, stealing my breath. "Is that what you think? That I was fine?"

My lungs squeezed, and my heart stampeded, the man in my face, eyes overpowering, soul shattering.

"Fuck." He cursed so low that I could barely hear it before prying himself away and releasing me from the hold of his stare.

I lurched forward as if I'd been freed from an invisible force that'd held me pinned.

Strain radiated from him, and he moved into the room I'd prepared for him. I hovered at the doorway, watching him as he set his suitcase on the bench and let the strap of his bag slide from his shoulder.

Standing there? I didn't have the first clue what the hell I was supposed to do.

How I was gonna deal with this kind of devastating presence in my home.

Day after day.

I jolted when the pound of tiny footsteps echoed from behind. Bailey suddenly squeezed past my legs. She scrambled right passed me and onto his bed before I had the chance to stop her.

"Bailey," I scolded, starting for her.

I hadn't even made it two steps when my little girl had jumped to her feet, singing, "One, two, three," as she bounced, not even hesitating for a second before she leapt for Jace, who watched her with wide, shocked eyes.

My stomach nearly sank right to the floor, figuring that was exactly where she was gonna end up.

Right on the floor.

But Jace . . .

He snatched her from the air as if he'd been planning to do it all along.

Reflexively. Catching her in his arms.

"Whoa," he said, a rough chuckle leaving him as he looked between the two of us in something between discomfort and awe. "Looks to me like someone really is a daredevil."

Bailey was beaming at him, hungry for attention. "I jump high."

"Really high. But next time, you need to give me a little warning, yeah?"

I finally shook myself out of the stupor and went for my daughter. "Bailey, you can't just come in here like that."

And she sure shouldn't be jumping into his arms.

"She's fine," he said as if he was in some kind of pain as he awkwardly held her. Though he didn't seem to be all that inclined to set her down. "I'm the one invading your home."

Yeah, and I wondered if it weren't an ambush.

"She needs to know boundaries, Jace," I told him, a spit of anger making its way into my tone, because he sure didn't have the right to tell me how to raise my daughter.

Or maybe it was the unsettling feeling of relief that he was there to catch her that worried me most of all.

That he was here, and for the first time in three months, I truly felt safe.

He nodded slowly. Almost sadly. "Okay."

He set her onto her tiny feet, his fingertips sweeping through the very back of her curly hair.

I blinked through the burn that abruptly stung my eyes, my emotions everywhere. "I'm sorry. I'm just . . . I'm not used to anyone being here."

"You don't have to apologize to me, Faith. I get it. I keep pushing past the boundaries I should know better than to push against."

From his stare, I could see clearly what he was referencing, referring to the tension that had bound the walls back out in the hall as he'd taken us back to that day—to that moment—all those years ago.

Unable to keep standing under his gaze, I stretched my hand out for Bailey. "Come on, Button. It's time for bed."

She swung her attention up to Jace. "Can you read me story?"

There was so much hope behind it that I nearly dropped to my knees.

Jace didn't seem too steady, either, his attention swiveling between the two of us as if he were begging for help.

For direction.

"Bailey, honey, Mommy will read you a story."

"But I's want him to." It was all a sweet plea as she peered up at him with that eager smile.

"It's fine," Jace said, looking at me as if he were asking for permission.

"Jace." I guessed I'd regressed to begging it. Because I no longer knew where I stood.

He shook his head. "It's fine," he said again, this time resolute.

And I was terrified that it wasn't ever going to be.

# fifteen

## Jace

What the fuck was I doing? I felt like I was being led to the execution block. Or maybe I was standing at heaven's door.

Because my heart rustled out an extra beat when the little girl looked up at me like I was some kind of hero.

This just from my agreeing to read her a story.

Headful of dark, dark curls and a smile so big I felt the magnitude of it like a swift kick to the gut.

*Bailey.*

I gulped as my spirit twisted around that name, the kid trotting along at my side with her tiny hand wrapped in mine, wearing this pajama set with unicorns printed all over the front.

She kept looking up at me.

Chocolate eyes so big and curious.

"I *wike* stories," she told me, all kinds of eager.

"You do, huh?"

"Yep. You *wike* 'em?"

Unease moved through me. "Uh, sure I do."

How the hell had I ended up having a conversation with this kid like it was the most natural thing in the world?

Okay, not natural.

Because my damn heart felt like it was going to bang its way right out of my chest when she led me into her room.

She released my hand and ran straight for her tiny bed and hopped into it, grinning back at me.

But it was what was sitting on it that staggered my steps. Made me feel like the floor had been ripped right the hell out from under me.

Fucking falling.

Nothing below to catch me.

Ratty and worn, one of the arms hanging by a thread.

It was that cheap, stuffed Beast doll.

It was sitting right there on top of her bed.

My heart was back in my throat, doing stupid, stupid things.

She reached out and grabbed it like she felt my reaction to it.

Because she was hugging that damned doll to her chest, her teeth biting her bottom lip the same way her mother had always done.

Like she felt bad she was looking all the way to the center of me but didn't know how to stop herself.

"You *wike* my room?"

She studied me. Wary and shy. Sweet and intrigued.

God, this kid really was getting under my skin. I was an idiot for letting her get there.

I glanced around, trying to find something to put my attention on rather than her.

"Yeah," I managed to tell her through the clot of emotion in my throat.

But it didn't matter how desperately I was trying to find a different focus.

Here was this kid that wasn't more than a baby.

On her knees on her mattress.

Waiting on me.

"You paint it *aww* pink?"

She gazed at me like I might be her savior.

Her cheeks were about three times too big for her small face, rosy, almost chapped against her pale skin, her hair a mess of curls.

I had to wonder if her mom didn't call her Button because of her nose.

The kid was adorable, so damned sweet as she waited.

But there was something deeper about her. Something that made me feel like she knew more than any little girl her age should.

I knelt down at the side of her bed. "If it's okay with your mom, someday, I will. I think we need to get the porch fixed first."

She grinned wider. "Oh-kay."

Like that explanation totally satisfied her. Her mind innocent enough that she didn't have to consider the fact that I wasn't going to be there that long.

That her mother hated me. That she was going to hate me more when she found out what I'd done.

"You *wike* unicorns?" she suddenly asked. "I's want a story about unicorns. The magic kind. Good magic, not bad," she said, all too seriously. "Bad's bad."

I almost laughed.

Of course, she did. The proof of it was painted all over the front of her shirt.

Shit.

What did I think I was doing? Coming here like this?

I hadn't exactly thought this through, had I?

Definitely hadn't even begun to ponder what it might be like being here and having all of this rubbed in my nose like a fucking tease.

My life back in Atlanta had been nothing but long, grueling days taking over companies, building some back up and selling others, building and destroying and building, over and over, going after every fucking dollar I could make.

When that left me empty, my nights were wasted on expensive bottles of scotch and any nameless, willing bodies I could find, fucking myself into oblivion.

Like it might hold the power to erase what I'd left behind.

The proof of it was huddled right there, grinning up at me like I might be a *good guy*. Someone she could trust.

Not the pathetic piece of shit who was responsible for getting her and her mother into this situation.

Not that Joseph hadn't done a bang-up job of getting them there, himself.

"All right then, no bad magic. Just good magic. Do you have a book like that?"

Warily, I glanced around, catching Faith who was standing at the doorway like this was causing her as much grief as it was causing me.

I ripped my attention from her and turned it back on the little girl. She was frowning at me. "No, silly."

There she went what that adorable drawl, dropping the 'l's', looking at me like I was crazy. "You tells the story in your head."

Right.

Okay.

I gulped all the uncertainties down and made up the most ridiculous story I could conjure.

One about five magic unicorns who protected a little girl. A little girl who wandered and got lost.

About how scared the unicorns were that they couldn't find her.

So what if I hid a message right in the middle of it.

She'd scared the hell out of both of us today.

I wanted to beg her never to do it again.

But it was what Mack had called and told me about this afternoon that left me vibrating with barely contained rage.

The need to hunt some fucker down barely controlled.

Someone had been in Faith's car. Left another threat.

Right out in the fucking open.

The only thing I wanted to do was stop this. It made me feel worthless that I didn't even know where to start.

The only thing I could do was be here.

A soft giggle filtered from Bailey, something like belief in her gaze where she had her head angled to the side, staring back as I let the story fall from my tongue.

"You a magic unicorn?" she asked me like she'd plucked that message right out of the story. "You gonna *sway aww* the bad dragons?"

A clusterfuck of emotions ripped at me from all sides.

"I'm going to try," I told her.

I still wasn't sure how to deal with them, but I knew I had to push through. Deal with *this*, with *this* feeling, until I knew they were safe.

I owed them that.

I owed them everything.

I could feel Faith behind us.

Watching us.

Could feel the torment radiating from her.

I wanted to stand. Go to her. Tell her everything was going to be okay.

That I was going to take care of them both.

"You better get to sleep now," I told Bailey, agitation swelling.

She climbed down under the covers. "You be here in the morning?"

"Yeah, I'll be here in the morning."

"You make me breakfast?"

God, this kid.

Deeper and deeper.

"Sure."

"Pop Tarties?" It was all eager, hopeful question, like she was wondering if I could even manage that, or maybe she was just like I'd been as a kid, stealing every sweet I could find.

I locked the direction of that thought down fast.

Mock offense had me dropping my mouth wide open. "What? You don't think I can cook you a real breakfast?"

Her head shook, letting me know my cooking skills were definitely being called into question. "Grampa says toasters are made for men."

The second she mentioned him, old hatred ripped through my veins.

Spite and animosity.

A bolt of a memory that cut through me like a bullet. A slap of words that had stung like a bitch.

*"Stay away from her? You hear me?"* His face had been contorted

in disgust. *"You aren't worthy of her, and I won't stand aside and let you get her dirty."*

I wasn't that pathetic kid anymore. But it sure as hell wasn't like I was any better.

Cringing, I shook the memory off, mentally scraping it from where it'd been etched like a scar into my skin. I wasn't going there. I had a better use for the bitterness that remained.

Besides, could I have blamed Faith's father? I hadn't done anything but prove him right.

"Well, I don't know that much about your grandpa, but this guy right here has had to take care of himself for a long, long time. I know my way around the kitchen."

"You gonna take care of me?" she asked, all bright and shining anticipation.

I gulped around the impact of it. Like she just trusted me to. Without question.

"I'm going to try to," I mumbled, knowing I was a damned fool. Such a damned fool. "God knows, I'm trying."

I muttered the last.

"How abouts eggs and bacons?" she offered. "And *owange* juice?" Her face lit up in unfound glee.

Yeah. Like I was going to reject that.

I ruffled my fingers through her hair, trying to ignore the tug at my spirit. "Yeah, sweet one, you can have whatever you want."

Her eyes went wide, but her voice tipped to a whisper. "And a cookie?"

Oh shit.

I'd walked right into that one.

"Maybe after you eat all your breakfast."

"Deal," she drawled in that sweet way.

God, this kid was going to do me in.

Tentative footsteps edged up from behind, and I forced myself to standing, my gaze tangling with Faith's for a beat.

Tension and need and pain.

I tore my attention away and looked back at her daughter. "Goodnight, Bailey."

"Nights," she said, and I backed away, into the darkness.

Doing my best to run from the light.

Maybe Joseph was still playing the puppeteer, after all. Pulling these fucked-up strings and dangling what he'd had in my face.

All the while laughing his ass off from somewhere on the other side.

One last begrudging kick to the gut as he reminded me what was his.

What he'd taken from me.

Because watching Faith kneel at the side of her bed? Run her hands through that little girl's hair? Whisper her love?

I'd never felt as if I had less than right then.

Destitute.

Penniless.

Impoverished in a way that hollowed me out.

# sixteen

## Faith

*I* kissed my daughter's forehead, fighting with all of me against

the sorrow I'd felt at seeing Jace with her that way.

Fighting against the way she was lookin' at him.

As if he might be the sun.

As if he might be there to fill a little of that void that echoed through these walls.

It was all so hard to ignore as she hugged that Beast doll tighter. Her security blanket.

I tried with all my might to ignore it, to forget the night he'd given it to me and focus on the day when she'd found it buried under a pile of old clothes in the back of my closet.

I lifted the sheets, and she snuggled in. I ran my fingers through her soft, soft hair.

My mind was still spinning with the tale Jace had spun for her. As if he already knew her. The man telling her the type of sweet fantasy she loved so much.

One where everything was good and right and bad never

prevailed.

I wanted it to be the truth.

So badly, I wanted it to be the truth.

But the reality was that we lived in an evil world.

One where hearts got broken and our dreams got smashed.

Ones where daddies sometimes didn't come home after they'd promised they'd be right back.

I stayed there with her, needing the space, the time with her.

The distance from Jace.

I knew him being here was going to be hard. I'd just had no idea how much.

Bailey finally fell asleep while I just knelt there, and I leaned up, kissed her forehead, and then ran my nose along the softness of her cheek.

Heart pressing full.

So full.

So perfect.

"Good night, Bailey Button."

God knew, she was the hook that kept everything together.

Slowly, I climbed to my feet, quiet as I moved across the floor.

A shiver of awareness skated over me the closer I got to the door.

I should have known.

Jace was standing on the other side of the hall, his back pressed to the wall as if he'd been listening all along.

I froze in the hazy shadows the old house had fallen into, his profile still strong in the suggestion of night.

"I'm sorry about earlier," he said, though I could see him flinch, the jerk of his muscles in his arms. "About that room."

Hurt fisted my heart at the thought of what he'd implied about the room that he'd thought should be his.

I shoved it down, said, "It's okay."

I got stuck there, staring out at him, wishing I didn't find comfort in the fact he was there. Wishing it didn't feel as if he was supposed to be. These walls forever echoing with his presence.

With the remnants of his ghost.

I'd ignored it for so long. Pretended I couldn't hear his

whispers trapped in the grain of the wood.

"She's beautiful, Faith."

Emotion swam.

Old love that tried to claw out of the rubble of demolished dreams.

"She's the best thing I have ever been given."

"You named her Bailey," he murmured, hurt and regret wound with the pained taunt.

"I guess some dreams don't die, after all, do they?" I whispered.

His lips twisted, and he cast his face toward the floor. "And sometimes those dreams are stolen from us."

I had the urge to move across the hall, force him to look at me, and demand he tell me what he was really thinking, what he was really feeling. To demand to know how he could have walked away from me the way he had.

But I couldn't regret our history. My direction ripped out from under me before I was set on another.

My daughter at its end.

I'd never, ever wish for that to turn out differently.

"I think I'm going to call it a night," I forced myself to say before I did something stupid. "There's a casserole in the refrigerator you can heat up if you'd like something to eat. Make yourself at home."

It was only eight, but I wasn't prepared for this. For the moments when he would actually be *here* and not just working.

Telling the man to make himself at home was a foolish statement in and of itself.

I knew I needed some space. Time to think and clear out the muddle of thoughts clouding my brain.

"Yeah," he agreed, pushing off the wall and heading for his room.

He paused at the doorway and peered back out. "I'm going to hire a few guys to help me work on the house, Faith. I might be able to do it myself, but Bailey would probably be grown by then, and I'm thinking that's not exactly what you had in mind."

There was a sadness mixed in with the amusement he tried to

inject into his tone, and there was a really stupid part of me that wanted to tell him that was fine, he could stay for as long as it took.

There I was again, playing the fool.

"I'll never be able to fully repay you, Jace, for doin' this for me. For doin' it for Bailey. For being here for us."

There was no question some of this was about the money. After all, it was what made the world go round.

It might not buy happiness, but it sure was the solution to some dire situations.

But it was more than that. He'd returned, put a hold on his own life to come here and make sure ours was safe.

Whatever the reason, I couldn't find anger in that anymore.

He offered a short nod. "The only repayment I need is that one day I might see a real smile on your face."

He rapped his knuckles on the doorframe after he said it, not giving me a chance to respond before he disappeared inside the room, quick to snap the door shut behind him.

Leaving me staring there at the vacant space.

Space that had never felt so alive.

# seventeen

## Faith
## Sixteen Years Old

"Can I get this, too?" Faith asked, grabbing a Snickers bar from the display.

Her mama glanced up from where she was scrolling through her shopping list for the hundredth time and double-checking to make sure she'd gotten everything.

Faith swore that it didn't matter how many times she checked, every time they got home, they'd forgotten something, and her mama would have to turn right around and send her back to the store.

"Just as long as you don't ruin your dinner," her mama said.

Faith all but rolled her eyes. "I'm almost seventeen, Mama, not four. I don't think you have to tell me not to ruin my dinner."

The belt moved forward, and Faith grabbed a divider, tossing the candy bar onto it, and she began to load the contents of their cart onto the belt.

"Just because you're almost grown doesn't mean you're not my baby," her mama shot back. "It's my job to warn you of all the dangerous things in this world. The pitfalls of chocolate bars included."

Faith fought the affected smile that pulled at her mouth. Her parents were the best.

Courtney would have loved to pretend her parents didn't exist, but Faith hadn't ever reached that stage where she felt as if her parents were dumb or embarrassing.

She guessed she should be embarrassed that she spent more time with them than anyone else.

"Well, I'll be sure to save it for after then. Daddy is grillin' my favorite, after all." Faith waved the package of sirloin toward her mama before she set it onto the belt and continued to unload the rest of the groceries.

Veggies and rice and potatoes.

Eggs and bacon for the mornin'.

All the makings for a fresh-baked apple pie.

No wonder she stuck around.

"I swear you bribe me through food to make sure I'm home to study every night, don't you?" Faith teased.

Her mama grinned. "Every mother has her ways," she told her, leaning down to grab the gallon of milk she'd placed under the cart. "Yours happens to be through your stomach."

"I thought that was Daddy?" Faith tossed out, laughing lightly.

"Like father, like daughter."

"Oh lord, don't tell me I'm gonna end up chained to a ratty old recliner watching sports every night."

Her mama chuckled. "God forbid."

The customer in front of them paid and walked away, and her mama moved around Faith to push the cart the rest of the way through to the bagging station.

Faith distracted herself with the garbage magazines that lined the racks.

Apparently, Angelina and Jen were fighting it out for the covers the way they always did, another child star had turned into an addict, and there was some poor waitress getting slammed for having the audacity to date a celebrity.

She didn't believe a word of it, but she reached out to grab one anyway, only for her hand to freeze midair when she heard the low voice from off to the side.

"Would you like your milk in a bag, ma'am?"

She swore, she could hear the creak in her neck as she slowly shifted her head that direction.

A sizzle of intrigue and a shot of that terror slipped through her insides as she looked that way to find Jace Jacobs bagging their groceries.

That terrifyingly beautiful boy with those copper eyes that uneasily flickered between her and her mama before they dropped down, only to dart up again for the flash of a second.

As if he didn't know where to look.

And Faith? Faith just stared.

"Oh, no bag, thank you. We can manage just fine."

"Yes, ma'am," he mumbled.

Those intense eyes stole a quick, furtive glance at Faith before they dropped back down in discomfort.

He started to work a little more quickly, tossing all their stuff inside as if just touching it made him self-conscious or uneasy, the barest hint of that hostility coming out with the way he worked.

His arms straining.

Muscles flexing.

Faith suddenly realized all the little luxuries he was piling high in those bags. And she wondered if he was hungry. If he hated her for flaunting it, literally right under his nose.

But she was sure there was something more to it. Something different that shot between them, as if he were hooking her with something unseen with every glance that he stole.

Something that made her heart flutter and her skin go sticky with sweat. Right underneath the air conditioning vent that was pumping freezing cold air.

She could feel her mama's gaze bouncing between the two of them, and something sly rode to her mouth when she fully set her attention on Faith for a beat.

Warily, Jace placed the bags into the cart.

Her mama swung her attention back to him. "Well, you are a

strong young man, aren't you?'

Faith cringed.

She took it all back.

She was totally, one hundred percent embarrassed of her mama. What did she think she was doing?

"Uh . . ." Jace stammered, roughing one of those hands through his hair before he quickly said, "Have a nice day."

Then he was off, moving to the next checker's line and quickly filling those bags, though Faith could feel his secreted glimpses, that fire hitting her from behind as she all but dragged her mama out the door and into the blistering heat.

"What is wrong with you, Mama?" she scolded.

"What?" she defended, completely innocent. "I was makin' a simple observation, that's all."

The trunk to their Camry popped open, and Faith started tossing the bags inside. "That he's strong? That's just . . . so weird and wrong and gross. You can't say things like that."

"Not the observation I was talking about."

A frown pulled to her brow as she paused to look up at her mama, who was gazing down at her, some kind of strange smile lighting her face.

That was when Faith felt it again.

That feeling that she couldn't put a finger on.

Something that made her sweat and shake and her stomach do funny things. Her mama looked over Faith's shoulder, and Faith couldn't help but do the same and follow her line of sight.

Jace was pushing a cart for an elderly woman who was parked in a handicap spot. He opened the driver's door for her and helped her inside before he went to the back to load her groceries into the trunk.

Faith's throat suddenly felt too tight.

Damned South Carolina heat.

He looked their way. Longer this time. Those eyes glittering beneath the sun as he leaned over the back of the woman's trunk, his head angled to peer their way.

"That boy likes you, that's the observation I was making."

Faith's attention snapped back to her mother. "He does not."

"And you like him."

"Mama," Faith defended, slamming their trunk shut. "I do not."

"Liar."

"You know, sometimes I think you're the child and I'm the parent."

Her mother softened, some kind of lesson weaving its way into her voice. "That's because you never let yourself have any fun. You're too busy studying and watching sports with your dad."

A tease curved into the last.

"Mama," Faith huffed again, not even denying it.

She looked back that way to the place where Jace had been, but he was already back inside the store.

Something heavy filled her chest.

"He's trouble, Mama," she whispered.

Faith could feel the truth of it tremble all around her.

Her mama reached out and touched her chin. "Maybe. Or maybe he's just trying to figure out how to survive, just like the rest of us."

"I need to get back home to study for finals," Faith said, slipping off the side of Courtney's bed and into her sandals.

Her best friend looked up from where she was on her stomach flipping through one of the same trashy magazines Faith had been looking at earlier, except this one was giving them all kinds of sex tips.

With the way Faith had blushed through the torture of Courtney reading them aloud, she was pretty sure she was never gonna need them, but Courtney was intent on trying a couple of them out on her boyfriend that night.

It was definitely Faith's cue to get the hell out of there.

"But you just got here," Courtney whined.

"Two hours ago. And we have finals all next week. I need to

close out this year strong."

Courtney pouted. "You're no fun. It's Friday. Stay and go to the party with me."

"I have to get home. Daddy is grillin' steaks tonight. Besides, I don't need to be within a ten-mile radius if you're planning that." Faith pointed at the drawing on the magazine, nose curled in mock disgust.

Courtney laughed. "You're such a prude. I swear, you should have been born in the fifties . . . or, better yet, the eighteen fifties with the way you're so obsessed with all that old crap."

"Crap? Bite your tongue, woman."

"Oh, I'll be biting something, all right."

"Ewww."

Just ewww.

"I'm out of here," Faith said, dipping down to smack a kiss to Courtney's cheek. "Be good," she told her.

"Never."

"That's what I'm worried about."

Faith slung her backpack onto her shoulder, leaving Courtney with a small wave as she headed out of her bedroom and down the hall.

"Bye, Jenny!" she called from the kitchen to Courtney's mother, who was watching television in the living room.

"Bye, sweetheart. You sure you don't want a ride home?"

"Nah, I'm good."

She didn't pause as she ducked out of the screen door and onto the back porch, quick to take the trail that led behind the neighborhood, behind a bunch of trees, and dumped her out right on the old dirt road.

The area was pretty much deserted. Hardly a soul coming down this way.

Which was probably the reason she was so drawn to it.

She lifted her face toward the blazing rays of sun that poured out of the late afternoon sky, letting her eyes drift closed as she rambled down the road, feet shuffling through the pebbles that'd worked their way out of the packed dirt.

She was grinning when she dropped her gaze back down, her

step lighter as she started walking, swaying a bit, twirling once.

She loved this time of year, the tease of summer break hanging in the distance. The thought of dipping her toes into the ocean and afternoons spent reading under a big tree.

Birds flitted overhead, the air salty, tinged with the sea.

She came to a stop at the end of the drive that led to the old house, which was the real reason she liked to walk home this way.

Well, if you wanted to call it a house.

It was a mansion, worn down as it was.

A relic from another era, tucked back in the thickest, most gorgeous line of moss-covered oaks.

There was something haunting about it, the way the massive, spindly trees closed out the light and hugged the plantation as if ghosts from the past hissed and swished like phantoms through the branches.

Standing like a hedge of protection that lined the property.

"What are you doing?"

She nearly jumped out of her skin when the low voice hit her from out of nowhere, breathing over her from behind. A rush of chills skated her heated flesh.

She whirled around, her hand pressed to her hammering heart.

"What are *you* doin' here?" she demanded, words ragged pants from her lungs. He'd scared her half to death.

That terrifyingly beautiful boy cocked his head. It almost looked like a challenge.

Her stomach dipped.

Oh goodness, why'd he have to look that way?

Like temptation and sin.

Like she wanted to dip her fingers right in and experience exactly what that might taste like.

"Walking home." He tucked his big hands into the pockets of his pants. "Don't you know that this road leads to nowhere?"

She couldn't tell if it was amusement or venom that fell from his tongue, and she was instantly picturing the dead end about a half mile up and the handful of old, rusted trailers dotted on the half-acre of overgrown land.

The shock at finding him there drained from her, though now

she itched, part of her having a good mind to go running for safety down the opposite direction of the road.

The other part of her was pinned to the spot, enraptured by those eyes that were watching her.

"What are *you* doing here?" he finally asked again because when she looked at the situation, she was the one who was out of place.

"I just . . ." Her teeth gnawed at her bottom lip. God, he was gonna think she was stupid.

His brow furrowed in curiosity, and she saw something there that had her opening her mouth and letting her dumb little dreams come pouring out. "I always walk home from Courtney's this way. I like to look at that house."

He peered over her shoulder, down that tunnel of trees that seemed to lead to another dimension. As if you could step right into another time. "You call that a house?"

A shock of nervous laughter ripped from her. "I was just thinkin' the same thing." She turned a little, wonder gliding into her tone. "It's amazing, isn't it?"

"Yeah. A little scary. My cousin Joseph said it's haunted." She thought it was laughter that glided across his face when he said the last, trying to get a rise out of her.

She slowly turned to look at it. "I think that's what I like most about it. It's like it just got left out here. Forgotten. I can only imagine the stories those walls could tell."

He moved to stand at her side. "No one lives there?"

"No one has been there for a long time, though there was a family who used to come and stay for a bit in the summers. Guess they still own it, but the mother passed, so they haven't been around in a long time. Heard a rumor they're gettin' behind on the taxes."

They stood there in the silence. The boy standing at her side as if he might appreciate the beauty as much as she did. Faith was sure she'd never been so uncomfortably comfortable.

Maybe too comfortable because she was suddenly murmuring, "One day, I'm gonna own this house. Fix it up. Make it something spectacular. A hotel. A bed and breakfast, maybe. I don't know."

He looked over at her. The threat of a tease wound up at one side of his mouth, twisting up her heart at the same time. "Why would you want to go and ruin the mystery by fixing it up and chasing away all the ghosts?"

She felt the smile slide to her lips. "Oh, I'll let them stay."

He laughed a low sound. It was quiet, but somehow, it still managed to shake the ground. "Of course, you will."

Then he reached out and snatched her hand.

Fire flashed up her arm, this time so intense she couldn't help but gasp out a shocked sound at the feel of it, his hand so big and warm where it was wrapped around hers.

"Come on, let's see if we can see any of those ghosts."

He started hauling her down the narrow drive, the trees hugging them from both sides, branches rustling and waving in the hot, summer wind.

Alive.

A low whistle coming from their leaves.

"Jace, what are you doin'?"

"Chasing ghosts."

"That's a bad idea. We aren't supposed to go up there."

He looked at her from over his shoulder, his face so gorgeous, eyes so bright. "What, are you scared?"

*Terrified.*

"No."

"Then hurry up."

"I'm wearing sandals."

She shrieked when he suddenly spun around and hoisted her up and tossed her onto his back.

Her legs wrapped around his waist as if she'd done it a million times before, and her arms held fast to his neck.

His hands clasped around the outsides of her thighs.

Oh goodness.

Her stomach twisted and pitched, and she bounced all over as he raced up the deserted driveway.

"Jace."

"Don't you trust me?"

*No. Not at all.*

He ducked down a fraction, laughing as he ran, something

carefree winding with the whispers uttered from the trees.

Faith held on for dear life, sure she was in some sort of mortal danger, because this boy was the only thing she could breathe.

Her nose to the flesh of his neck, his deeply tanned skin a kiss of summer.

She didn't want to let go when they got to the base of the magnificent wraparound porch that was held up by massive pillars, but finally, she slipped down his back and onto her feet.

"Whoa," he said, awe striking him the same way as it did her.

"Told you."

He stretched out his hand, taking hers again, his movements slowing as he carefully led them up the whitewashed steps that moaned from disuse.

Silently, she followed him to the window that sat off to the side of the door, and they both pressed their faces to the glass, their hands cupped around their eyes so they could peer inside.

It was like looking into the set of a movie. Antique furniture and ornate rugs and a staircase that may as well have been taken right out of *Gone with the Wind.*

Not that it was her favorite book and movie, or anything.

"Must be nice," Jace suddenly whispered, an edge of that hostility winding back into his tone as he peeled himself away from the window.

Faith did the same, squinting as she peered at him through the rays of sun that slanted onto the porch, fingers of light that rustled through his tawny hair. "What must be nice?"

"Come on, Faith, look at all that stuff. And someone just *left it.* Like they have too much to even give a shit that they left all of this here. Hardly seems fair, does it?"

She blinked at him, unable to keep up with his moods. They seemed to shift as quickly as the swing of the pendulum on the massive grandfather clock that rested against the far wall inside.

Her voice was soft but strained with emphasis. "I don't know anything about these people, Jace. I don't know how hard they work or what they were given or what their situations are. Just like I don't know all that much about your situation, but I'm not gonna make assumptions based on that, either."

He laughed.

A biting sound that pinched her skin.

"Oh, give it a rest, Faith. You know all you need to know about me."

He stepped back, the planks groaning beneath him, his arms stretched out to the sides as if he were daring her to look inside him.

He was wearing a black-collared shirt, the same kind every employee at the grocery store had to wear.

But his black pants?

She could see where they'd been patched and mended and were a smidge too short for his long legs, and the soles of his black shoes were peeling up at the toes.

His clothes were a bit tattered.

His hair a bit too long.

But none of those things were what she saw.

The only thing she could recognize was a face that was far too striking.

"The only thing I know is I can't stop looking at you. Can't stop thinking about you." Her words scraped from her throat like a confession.

Instantly, she wished she could take them back because they exposed her in a way that she wished they wouldn't.

Because his expression almost looked disgusted . . . almost horrified by what she had said.

Her gaze fell away, to the ground at the base of the steps. "God, I'm stupid."

Her knees wobbled when his fingers were suddenly on her chin, urging her to look back his way. Those copper eyes searched hers, squinting as they hunted her face, looking for a secret she didn't know she possessed.

Her mouth went dry, and her heart hammered in the space between them.

So hard.

So fast.

She could hardly breathe.

"Stupid? What you are is innocent and sweet. So pretty that I can't even think straight. You are *beauty* looking back at me."

Her tongue darted out to wet her lips as a swarm of butterflies breached her stomach and flitted through her entire body. Tickling beneath the surface of her skin.

His face pinched. "You're a good girl, Faith. I can tell."

Embarrassment had her teeth clamping down painfully on her bottom lip. What he meant was her inexperience was showing, seeping through her flesh the same way those butterflies that were climbing right through did.

She really was stupid.

"Don't do that," he softly chided. His thumb moved to her lip that was tucked between her teeth, setting it free.

The skin tingled from his touch.

"Do what?" she whispered, her eyes wide and unsure.

"Make me want to kiss you."

Faith moaned.

Just from him saying it.

From the feeling that gripped her everywhere, something heavy at her heart and throbbing at her center.

"Fuck," he said, inhaling sharply, as if he'd felt it.

Her reaction to him.

She couldn't stop it.

The rush of need that flooded her senses.

She couldn't stop the way she wanted to lean forward and fall right inside.

Get lost in this boy.

"Faith," he muttered. A warning and a question. Half a second later, those big hands landed on her neck, gliding up to tangle in her hair.

She gasped at the onslaught of sensation brought on by his touch.

But she wasn't prepared. She wasn't even close to being prepared for the way she would feel when his mouth slanted over hers.

His lips rough and smooth as they pressed against hers.

Slowly at first.

Giving and taking.

Testing and tasting.

Those butterflies shivered.

He edged her back until she was pinned against the wall of the house.

He pressed himself against her as he deepened the kiss, and she could feel him harden, every inch, his penis pressing against her belly.

*Oh God*, she almost whimpered, nearly losing it when his tongue darted out and tangled with hers.

Wet and demanding and full of heat.

Lightheadedness swept through her head. Through her heart.

Those butterflies took flight, lighting from her skin.

Flapping all around them as he kissed her.

Sweetly and somehow desperately.

A kaleidoscope of color filled her mind. Touched her spirit. Her hands were shaking when they searched the lines and curves of his face, touching him, exploring him, making their way into his soft, soft hair.

Feeling his shoulders.

Fluttering down his chest.

He gasped out a strained sound, rocking away when the only thing in the world she wanted was for him to get closer.

Touch her in places she'd never wanted to be touched before.

She shivered, and he set both of his hands on her face, holding her by the cheeks, pants tearing from his lungs as he carefully peeled himself back.

He swallowed hard, leaning away only far enough to be able to peer at her face. "Fuck . . . I can't believe I just did that. I'm sorry."

Her fingers came up to feel the heat that blistered her lips, awed as she brushed them across the sensitive skin. Then she turned and did the same to his, her fingertips grazing across his flesh, his mouth swollen and red.

"Don't tell me you're sorry. Just tell me you'll do it again."

Disbelief filled his slow smile.

Her heart ached, a crater of bliss and need carved out at the center of her, filling full with that same feeling she'd never felt before until the day this boy had banged into the school office and barged right into her life.

Right then, she was sure she'd been waiting for him all along.

He fluttered his fingertips across her face, her brow and her cheek and over her lips. "You're so damned pretty. I don't have pretty things in my life, Faith."

She heard the pained warning flow out with the words.

She peered up at him, staggered by the intensity in his eyes. "That's funny, since you're the most beautiful thing I've ever seen."

"You saw what my life is like."

She knew what he was referring to. The office and behind the bathroom. Again in the cafeteria.

She frowned up at him. "And you think that makes you a bad person? That I'd like you less?"

He blinked and his tone filled with the same hardness he'd used on her when he'd backed her up against the wall in the school courtyard. "There's an ugly spot inside me, Faith. I will do anything, whatever it takes, to take care of my brother and my cousin. They don't have anyone else."

She glanced away into the thick foliage that separated the house and the old trailers down by the river.

"And what about your mama?" she chanced, peeking back at him, knowing she was crossing into a territory where he wouldn't want her to go.

But she didn't want the rumors. She wanted the truth. She wanted to know this boy.

"My *mama* doesn't give a fuck about us, so I don't give a fuck about her."

She nodded slowly. Resolute as she lifted her chin and said, "Okay then, we don't give a fuck about your mama."

She met those roiling eyes, praying he'd see in hers that she was with him. For him. That she didn't care about his situation. The only thing she cared about was him.

He laughed out a strained sound. "You are something else, you know that?"

"Fine, go on and call me weird just like everyone else."

He chuckled and then sighed before rushing a hand through

his hair and shifting in indecision. Then he reached his hand out for her. "Can I walk you home?"

Faith slipped her hand into his, leaned into his side, and let him lead her back down the steps and down the drive.

And she knew right then she'd follow him anywhere.

## eighteen

### Jace

*I* jerked my head up from where I was lying facedown on the

pillow, the bed like freaking paradise, or maybe it was where the bed was that made it feel that way.

Either way, I'd been out cold.

I hugged the pillow to my chest as I lifted my head and squinted against the harsh rays of early sunlight that streaked in through the cracks in the drapes.

I searched into the early morning light that awakened the stilled room.

Motes tossed in a frenzy, the tiny particles floating before they'd quickly shift, stirred by the charged atmosphere.

My eyes narrowed farther, trying to figure out what it was that'd shocked me from sleep when everything was so damned quiet.

Instantly on edge.

Ready to go toe to toe. Blow to blow. Bullet to bullet. Whatever it took.

Then those dark, dark curls crested the edge of the mattress.
*Bailey.*

"Breakfast," she said, peeking up over the mattress and
grinning wide. She was looking at me. All kinds of hopeful that I
would hop out of bed to feed her.

She flashed me a row full of tiny teeth. "You promise."

Pushing out a slow sigh, I rubbed a hand over my face to chase
away the fatigue, laughing lightly.

And this was how a man was wrapped around a little girl's
finger.

I'd bet Bailey could write a book on it.

I rolled to the opposite side of the bed and quickly dragged on
the jeans I'd left on the floor.

I buttoned them, raked both my hands through my tangled
hair, and started around the end of the bed.

The wood groaned as I moved that way, and I craned my head
to peer around the opposite side to where Bailey was still on her
knees on the floor, just sitting there, waiting for me.

Carefully, I reached down and picked her up from under her
arms.

She giggled the softest sound, her arms stretching out for me.

I held her out away from me. Unsure of exactly where to go
from there. Like I was fearful of bringing her closer.

I was.

Fuck, I was.

Because when I pulled her against my chest, my heart started
beating faster.

"Let's get you something to eat." I kept my voice low so Faith
could sleep in, sure she hadn't been afforded that luxury in too
long a time.

I carried Bailey down the hall, angling a bit as I stepped over
the baby gate, her eyes going wide in some kind of adorable guilt
when I did.

"Yeah, you aren't supposed to be crawling over that yourself,
are you, you little stinker?"

She scrunched up her nose. "Stinker?"

Low, rumbly laughter rambled around in my chest. "What, you

aren't a stinker?"

Wide-eyed, she shook her head, her voice that sweet drawl. "I's take a bath."

That chuckle grew warm. "I guess you aren't a stinker then. My mistake."

"*Aww* of us make mistakes," she told me, completely serious and resolute, like she held the secret of life and needed me to know.

"Some of us more than others," I muttered under my breath.

It was the truth.

The realization hit me.

Because I could feel it.

Light. Blazing and blinding. It bounced through the room, ricocheting from the walls. Wasn't entirely sure where it started and where it ended, though I knew both Bailey and Faith were its source.

It was like it was feeding from the two of them, amplifying with each pass.

I didn't know if I was the lucky bastard who got caught in the middle of it, got to taste it for the barest second, or if it was going to leave me blinded and scarred in the end.

But it was that second that I knew it.

It didn't matter that she was Joseph's kid. That she represented every goddamned thing I'd ever wanted and was the fruition of what I could never have.

I'd protect her the same.

Just like I was going to protect her mother.

With all I had.

With whatever it took.

# nineteen

## Jace
## Seventeen Years Old

*J*ace didn't look back as he slipped out of the tiny, rusted trailer and into the night.

It wasn't like he wanted to see.

His mama's door sitting half open, all that shit lying on her nightstand, her passed out beside some asshole Jace was itching to grab by the hair and drag outside.

Give him a good beatdown. Watch the blood drip from his mouth and his nose as he promised he'd never come around again.

This guy was different from most of the guys his mama suckered in. Wearing nice clothes and rolling up in a shiny car.

That kind of pissed Jace off, too.

He swallowed it, bit it back, because he had more important things to focus on.

Under the light of the moon, he jogged up the path from the trailer, hitting the dirt road, increasing his pace until he stood right in front of the tree-lined drive.

The night was quiet. Super still. The leaves barely rustling where they stretched across the road. Surely, the small whispers they hissed were the ghosts Faith loved to dream about.

Standing in the middle of the road, Jace shoved his hands into his pockets and just . . . waited.

He was early by twenty minutes, but he couldn't lay around and pretend to sleep in that trailer for one more second when he knew he had something *good* to look forward to.

He rocked back on his heels, tipped his head back, and looked to the stars.

Anxious.

Excited.

And somehow feeling guilty that he'd convinced her to do this.

It really hadn't taken all that much. It wasn't like they hadn't been sneaking off to meet here almost every day after school. It was just the first time they'd decided to do it in the middle of the night.

He felt it the second she stumbled out of the thicket of trees up the road, coming from where she was spending the night with her best friend.

His attention immediately jerked that way, his breath hitching at the base of his throat when he saw her.

All chocolate hair and chocolate eyes and everything sweet.

A rumble clattered through his body.

Shaking him up.

Making him feel like he'd stolen into a place he didn't belong but would pretend that he did forever if it meant he got to stay.

For a beat, they just stared across the space. Both of them frozen.

But then she started running.

Running below the blanket of the night, a milky glow all around her, looking exactly like that angel Jace knew her to be.

Two feet away, she threw herself at him, jumping into his arms.

He wrapped her tight, hugged her close, breathed her in as he spun her around.

God.

She smelled delicious. Vanilla and roses. Felt so right.

He could feel the force of his smile as he held her.

"You came," he whispered into the still, still night.

Carefully, he set her back onto her feet but didn't let her get far. He reached out to snatch her delicate hand so he could thread their fingers together.

She was all red blushes and shy grins when she peeked up at him. "Of course, I came. I told you I would."

His fingers followed the tremble in her throat as she stared up at him. At the sound she made, he was sure his heart pounded harder than it ever had, and there was nothing he could do.

He drove his fingers into the long locks of her hair, savoring the flash of need in those chocolate eyes before he dipped down and kissed her hard.

Possessively.

Her nails dug into his shoulders as her tongue swept against his. That feeling burned between them.

Something big and profound.

Like he'd somehow gotten lucky enough to stumble into the place where he was meant to be all along.

He got the sense that he'd been made to stand right there with her in his arms.

Unease tickled at his spirit.

God, he wished he were different.

That he had something better to offer her.

That he'd be the kind of guy she would be proud to bring home.

She sighed against his lips, and he swallowed the sound. Tucked it deep.

Reluctantly, he pulled away and dropped a quick kiss to her forehead. Then he reached out and grabbed her by the hand. "Come on before I maul you right here on the road."

She grinned one of those shy smiles, their hands swinging between them as they started down the gravel lane toward the house. "Hmm . . . I like the sound of that."

A surprised laugh jetted from Jace's lungs, but the words came out deep and low. "You'd better watch what you say, Faith. I'm liable to take you up on that."

She spun out ahead of him, walking backward, the girl so damned pretty his insides twisted up like a bow. "You act like I'm scared of you."

"You should be," he warned her.

She laughed, this light, tinkling sound, her voice a tease. "You just wish you were scary. I know you better than that, Jace Jacobs."

"Do you?" he teased back. Still, a clot of discomfort fisted in his chest. She had no idea the kind of life he'd had to live.

She'd had a good life. A good home. The way it was supposed to be.

He hated to drag her into his world. But there was something about her that made this feel unavoidable.

Inevitable.

He doubted he could keep away from her if he tried.

Mossy branches stretched overhead. Glints of moonlight broke through the leaves and shone on her face. Warmth radiated out. Her smile genuine and real.

Filled with belief.

Goodness and grace.

He wanted to reach out. Dip his fingers into the well of her sweet mouth and take some for himself.

Taste what it felt like to be that good. That pure. To be blameless and without shame.

A blush crept to her cheeks. "Why are you always lookin' at me that way?"

"Because you're so damned pretty that I can't look any other way." They'd made it to the deserted plantation, and he was backing her up the stairs and pressing her against the wall.

Time and time again, they seemed to end up right there.

They might as well have carved their initials in the splintering wall. Right inside the flaking paint.

That redness deepened on her flesh. Heat and fire.

He pinned himself against her, his hands planted above her head as he rocked against her. Taking more than he should.

She whimpered. "Jace."

He kissed her. Deep and long and with everything he hoped one day he might be able to give her. Showing her how much he wanted to be good enough for her.

He cupped her face in his hands, this girl so precious, so delicate he was kind of terrified to touch her but never wanted to stop.

Especially when he ground himself against her. Almost delirious when he thought what it might be like to be inside her. Taking her.

Shit.

He was getting carried away.

And he couldn't.

Not with her.

He had to be careful.

He gathered himself and forced himself to take a step back.

A needy, desperate sigh seeped from her mouth, though there was something confused and scared mixed up in it, too.

That sound alone nearly wrecked him.

Trying to compose himself, he took her hand and led her down the side steps to the patch of grass off to the side of the massive house.

Right to the garden of lavender and pink roses that grew like their own forest.

He stood in the middle of them.

Surrounded by beauty.

He shivered when fingers ran down his back. Slowly, he turned around to face her. Her expression was confused, eyes rich and dark, her lips still swollen from his kiss.

His chest clenched.

God. She didn't get it. How perfect she was.

"Why do you always do that?" she finally whispered into the stilled night.

"Do what?" he asked just as quietly.

She almost smiled. "Treat me like you're gonna break me."

He reached out and played with an errant strand of hair at the side of her face, his head tilting to the side and the words coming so low.

"Because I'm afraid that I might." He stared at her, his brows pinched. "Don't you see it, Faith? You're a *good girl.* I knew it the first time I saw you. And I'm not a good guy. I'm going nowhere, and you've got your whole life ahead of you."

"What if I want to spend that life with you?" That was the way she always was. Honest. Her pretty heart tacked right on her sleeve. Hiding nothing.

His spirit thrashed, and he wanted to wrap her up.

Maybe run away with her.

Hide from all the bullshit in his life.

The way the people in this stupid town looked at him.

The way his mama talked to him.

The way the men through the years had beaten him, and when he'd started to fight back, had turned to beating his brother and his cousin instead.

The anger it'd bred inside him, not to mention all the things he'd had to do to survive those things.

He was terrified that the only thing he'd ever amount to was the title of trash.

It was grief that flooded from his mouth. "I'm not sure I'll ever be good enough for you. I won't ever be able to take care of you the way you deserve to be."

"Who says?" she challenged.

He laughed a bitter sound. "Everyone."

She turned away and lightly ran her fingertips over the petals of a rose. "Do you want to know why I love this rose garden so much?"

He was behind her, her hair a dark river that tumbled down her back.

She glanced back at him. "Because someone planted them and then left them to die. I bet they wilted good when whoever used to care for them left them to fend for themselves. Forgotten. But they fought through all of that, grew stronger in the midst of it, and now they flourish. Now, they're probably the most beautiful thing on this whole property."

She turned around to face him, her voice fierce and soft. "It doesn't matter what anyone says, Jace. It's what you believe. What you see in yourself. If you want it badly enough, you can have it. If you work hard enough? Fight for it? You're going to come out stronger on the other side."

Her brow pinched. "I see that in you. See how great you are. I can see all the amazin' things you can achieve. It's all right there, waitin' for you to accept it."

A feeling swept him.

Something so intense.

So full.

*Love.*

It was the most powerful, scariest emotion a person could experience.

It crawled all over him. Seeping into the crevices and the cracks.

He set his palm on her jaw. "You make me feel like maybe I can."

Sending her a soft smile, he grabbed the small pocketknife he carried from his back pocket and stepped around her, cutting one of the roses at the base of its stem.

He rolled it between his fingers, could feel the weight of her gaze burning at the side of his face.

"I think you're all wrong, Faith. You are the most beautiful thing in this place. I look at these flowers, and I think of you. Maybe it's you who believed in them enough, you willed them to grow."

Her teeth raked across her bottom lip, so much affection in her voice that Jace shook. "Would that be such a bad thing? Everyone needs someone to believe in them."

Her face pinched, and the confession came out. "I love you, Jace. I believe in you. I trust you. Maybe that's the only thing that matters."

He nearly crumbled at her feet.

"You are beauty, Faith."

The epitome of it.

Inside and out.

He couldn't help the bitterness from filling his tone. "And I'm exactly like that beast in that story. Everyone saw she was too good for him, and he fell in love with her anyway."

Soft laughter rippled from between her lips. "What are you

talkin' about? You're the most gorgeous boy I've ever seen. You walk the school halls, and every girl you pass swoons."

He took her hand, pressed her palm to his thundering chest. "All my ugly is on the inside."

"No . . . you just don't see yourself for who you are."

"Or maybe you're just seeing what you want to see."

She let her gaze sweep off to the side, to the house that sat like a massive shadow covering them. "Well, I guess it's a good thing we have this haunted castle to keep us company, then."

He wrapped an arm around her waist and tucked her close, swaying her around in the moonlight. She chewed at her lip, peeking up at him, something playful on her face.

"You think you aren't goin' anywhere, Jace Jacobs? Well, I'm not goin' anywhere, either. I'm goin' to stay right here in this very spot. I told you one day I was going to own this place."

He brushed back the hair that'd fallen in her face, cupping her by the cheek, the anger and fear that had lined his voice turning light. "You gonna let me stay right here with you?"

"Mm-hmm." Something shy and sweet took hold of her expression. "You and me. We'll buy this place. Fix it up together. Run it together. Make something of it while we make something of ourselves."

He spun them around, hugging her closer, their hearts beating in time as he joked, "Beauty and the beast and their haunted castle?"

"That's right . . . except this castle is gonna be a bed and breakfast," she said all cute and resolute.

Dreams. That was the thing about them. It didn't matter if they were impossible or not. And Jace? He wanted to dream with her.

Chase it with her.

"What if I scare all the guests away?" he teased.

"Never . . . you're too good to look at. I'm pretty sure once the word gets around, you're going to be what brings in the crowds. At least the ladies."

He shook his head. "We're going to have to save a couple of those rooms for my brother and my cousin."

"That's just fine. They're your family. And I like them. They're sweet."

*Sweet.*

Yeah, right.

Jace smiled, though there was a ripple of possessiveness behind it. "Joseph has a crush on you."

Faith swatted at him. "Oh, he does not."

"You really are blind, aren't you?" There was a smile at the corner of his mouth, nothing hard in the words.

"If seeing this place as ours is blind, then so be it."

"Hmm . . ." he mused. "Beauty's Bed and Breakfast. Come stay at the BBB."

A small giggle rippled up Faith's throat. "For someone who thinks he's so tough, that is the cheesiest thing I've ever heard."

"What?" His mouth dropped open in feigned offense. "You don't like it? Come on, Faith. This has to happen."

She giggled a little more, a blush rushing to her face, her teeth tucking her bottom lip in a tight clamp.

And Jace let himself dream. What it might be like to get to stay there with her.

Forever.

The mood shifted around them, that intensity, the powerful energy he felt every time he was around her gliding through the damp, humid air.

He stared down at her as she tipped her face up to look at him, the moon all around her.

He touched her face. "Beauty," he murmured.

A wistful smile played around Faith's mouth. "Beast."

Jace couldn't take it any longer.

He took her mouth.

Her lips so soft.

Her tongue so sweet.

And they danced and they kissed and he let his arms roam down her sides.

Over her breasts.

Faith moaned and shuddered.

And he laid her down on the grass, hovering over her, wanting to sink inside.

But knowing he had to be careful.

That he didn't want to taint beauty. Not when it had finally been offered into the protection of his hand.

Faith looked up at him.

Those eyes so trusting.

Jace let himself lay down over her, molding his body to hers, his kisses deep as he rocked against her.

Faith kicked her head back, gasping for air, and Jace kissed down the column of her neck.

Delicate fingers found their way into his hair. "Why's it you feel so good? Just like this, our clothes still on?"

The threat of a smile pulled at one side of Jace's mouth, and he moved to whisper in her ear. "Maybe that's because we really do belong together."

"Jace," she whimpered, and the only thing Jace wanted was to love her. Hold her. Take care of her.

He kissed her softly. Tenderly. And he sucked in a breath when he let his hand slide under her dress.

She tensed, whispered, "Be careful with me, Jace."

He dipped down, murmured at her lips. "Always."

He touched her.

Carefully.

Holding himself in restraint because he refused to hurt this girl. Ruin her in any way.

Her fingers dug into his shoulders when she came apart, and he captured her mouth, captured her cries.

And he knew that he'd always hold her high.

"Oh my gosh, look." Faith grinned up at him where her hand was wrapped up in his, the other pointed at the stuffed Belle and Beast dolls strung up over the ridiculous carnival game that was set up so no one could win. "There we are," she teased, squeezing his hand.

He grinned right back, loving that she was at his side. Out in the open. That she wanted to claim him every bit as much as he wanted to claim her.

He hauled her toward it. "I guess I'll have to win it, won't I?"

Faith giggled. "Um . . . those games are impossible."

"I thought you told me if you wanted something badly enough, believed in it enough, you could have it?"

Her brows lifted, a sweet blush on her cheeks, affection on her face. "I do like the sound of that."

He was grinning when he stepped up and pulled the five dollars out of his pocket. So maybe he should be saving it. Buying something to eat for his brother and cousin, but if he ever wanted to be good enough for Faith, he had to step out, believe that he could, just like she'd said.

The carnie gave him the balls. He had three chances to knock all the pins down.

He took one ball, closed his eyes, and didn't even open them as he sent the ball sailing.

He just believed.

He heard a crash and a clatter, and then Faith was clapping beside him, jumping up and down, and shouting, "Oh, my goodness, Jace. You did it! You did it!"

Jace's eyes popped open, and he was grinning, and then he was kissing her hard right in the middle of the fair.

"Which one do you want?" the carnie asked.

Faith looked him straight on. "I want the Beast."

## Faith

*I* peeled my eyes open against the grogginess still pulling me

under. Banging echoed from somewhere outside, the clatter of noises and the lift of voices dragging me from a deep sleep.

It was funny how now that Jace had been staying with us for the last three weeks, the only thing I'd wanted to do was sleep.

It was as if my body and soul were catching up. Given reprieve in the safety that his presence afforded, the months of sleepless nights soothed away as if I were being rocked in the security of his arms.

During that time, I'd grown accustomed to the sound of him getting to work each morning.

But this morning?

Something had changed.

A riot of energy sizzled through the rays of light, as if they were rising with the sun.

Scrubbing a hand over my face to break away the sleepiness, I rolled out of bed and moved for the window. I pulled back the drapes and peered out.

What in the world?

There had to be ten cars parked in front of the house.

I quickly dressed and raced downstairs, jerking open the front door only to stumble in my steps when I saw what was happening.

"Well, if it isn't Sleeping Beauty," Courtney said as she lifted her head and cocked a teasing, accusing eye at me from where she was on her knees on the porch, ripping out a plank.

"Hi?" That single word cracked in my throat like a question while I slowly scanned the area. Almost the entire front porch had been ripped out, all thanks to an army of family and friends who had shown up.

Courtney and Felix.

Mack and a few other guys I recognized from the station.

My cousins, Tyler and Shane.

My heart tumbled a little when my gaze moved off to the left where I saw Ian, Jace's brother, unloading a bunch of supplies from the bed of a truck.

He'd never exactly been my biggest fan. He'd watched me with suspicion as if he thought I might be the one to pluck his brother from his grasp. As if I might steal him away.

As if Ian could ever, for a single second, become *less* important to Jace.

I wondered if he knew that was impossible. Jace would have done absolutely anything to provide for him.

Protect him.

It made me wonder what their relationship had been like over the past ten years.

That time was an empty gap between us. During those years, I'd been sure I'd never really known Jace at all, the boy I'd thought I'd spent my life with nothing but callous and cruel when he'd walked away.

But I wasn't so blind and broken not to realize that the two of them had their own histories written in that time.

No doubt, enduring their own hardships, even if on the outside, it looked as if the two of them had risen to the top without any effort at all.

I was pretty sure the lines creased into the corners of Jace's eyes contradicted that impression. The strain etched there. Years of worry and his own grief.

Was it wrong that I wondered its source? That I even cared at all?

But each day, I only cared more.

Because I could feel Jace's torment.

Could feel it radiating through the walls, seemingly becoming greater with each day that passed and we still had no new clues or answers.

It was hard, coming to terms with the fact the boy I'd fallen for, so fast and hard all those years ago, might be right there, standing in front of me.

Hidden behind that same harsh exterior he'd worn then. It terrified me that I was sure I could still see beneath those fortified layers. That I could stretch my hand out, sink my fingers into that kind, kind heart, know him from the inside out.

It sure didn't help the confusion that the man was kneeling in front of my daughter and securing a tiny, children's work-belt around her waist.

Bailey was clearly buzzin' with excitement that she got to help. Oh goodness.

My hand went to my throat, the emotion coming too fast. It was amazing that I didn't crumble beneath the pressure of them all.

Sorrow and affection and a million reservations.

I tore my attention from them and looked back at my best friend. At least she was safe.

"What's going on?"

Courtney smirked. "What does it look like? We're out here working our tails off while you're upstairs sleeping half the day away. A little help would be nice."

Felix laughed beside her, giving a shove to her shoulder and teasing, "Such a ball buster."

Her grin grew, taunting him, "You have no idea."

His brows lifted, and his voice dropped. "Oh, I think I do."

"Mornin', Faith," Mack called as he tossed some old, rotted wood onto the growing pile.

He'd checked in with me often, coming by to ensure we felt safe, and made sure other officers were driving by, constantly surveilling the property.

But standing there this morning? He was nothing but an old friend. Someone who cared about me and my daughter.

"Mornin'," I managed through the awe, trying to catch up to what was happening outside my home, as I realized why they were there.

They all knew I needed the help. That I was feelin' so alone and helpless and scared.

And they'd all shown up here to help me. To be here in the surest show of support.

Gratefulness surged, filling my insides like a buoy. A promise that they weren't going to let me drown.

I looked at Mack. "Who put you all up to this?"

Mack laughed as if it were a ridiculous question.

Instinctively, my attention traveled back to Jace, who'd pushed to his feet. The man was wearing a tight white tee and a pair of tattered jeans that teased my mind into thinking wicked things.

It didn't matter how guilty those thoughts made me feel. How wrong they might be.

I couldn't stop them.

The attraction that flared in the bright morning light. The energy that flashed when he cast those eyes in my direction.

Standing there as if he owned the place.

Looking better than any man had the right to.

For the last three weeks, he'd been taking stock.

Making lists of what needed to be achieved and the different projects that needed to be tackled.

Not to mention the fact that he paced, watching out the windows, continually ready to step in and protect Bailey and me if anything threatened us.

Sometimes I wondered if he had manifested from the walls. As if he'd been there all along, waiting to be awakened, summoned back into existence.

There to tease and taunt me with ideas I couldn't keep out of my mind.

He started my way.

The air shivered.

The ground shook.

Oh goodness.

I was gettin' in deep. Feeling things I shouldn't.

Couldn't.

My mind continually traipsing through the memories of what we'd once been and what we'd once hoped to be, stirring them up, tendrils of them trying to crawl up through the dirt where they'd been buried and take root.

Blossom.

Just like those roses that had once been forgotten but had come to flourish.

But that was an impossibility.

As he approached, Jace sent me the softest smile, and still, somehow, it was lined with the fierceness of the man.

A quiver took to my entire body.

Impossible, I tried to remind myself.

Right?

God, I just didn't know anything anymore.

I shook myself off and returned the easiest smile I could manage with nerves whipping through me as strong as a tree trying to stand its ground in the middle of a hurricane.

"Tell me you didn't drag everyone I know here before dawn to make them work all Saturday."

No doubt he was responsible.

"Now why would I go and do something like that?"

Something playful pulled at the corner of Jace's mouth, something soft that I'd seen coming from him more often over the last week.

Something that twisted through me, made a place inside me glow that should have been forever dimmed.

Bailey's eyes went wide when she finally noticed me. She raced to catch up to him and then started to trot along at his side. "Surprise, Mommy! We *pwans* the whole big secret. Jace said we a team."

Emotion crashed in my chest. "This is quite the surprise,

Button."

"You *wike* it?" she asked. "We gonna fix *evwy'fing.*" She threw her arms up, bouncing a step.

"Yeah, Button, I like it."

Loved it so much.

Only I wasn't looking at her when I said it because it was getting harder and harder to look away from the man standing in front of me.

"How'd he manage to put you up to this?" I asked as I situated a bunch of glasses on the tray next to a pitcher full of fresh lemonade.

Courtney took the knife she was using to cut the watermelon and used it to slide all the diced pieces into a bowl, cutting me a glance as she did.

"Um . . . didn't take a whole lot of convincin' considering all of this is for you and Button. I mean . . . all of those cards and flowers you got after Joseph died?"

She studied me. "How many people said to let them know what they could do to help you? But if anyone knew you, they would have known you weren't gonna ask for a thing. You needed someone who would step in and actually take action. Someone who saw a need and could figure out a way to make it happen."

I peeked out the big window off the kitchen where everyone was starting to gather.

My breath left me when Jace, Ian, and Mack rounded the corner and climbed the rickety porch steps.

They had peeled their drenched shirts from their bodies, sweat gathered across their heated skin, and all three of them looked like a little taste of sin.

My stomach tightened.

But Jace . . . Jace looked like the ultimate temptation. Everything I'd ever wanted and should have known better than to take.

All hard, packed muscle on his towering body, chest so wide, his flat abdomen carved and cut and making my mouth water a little bit.

Oh, had the man grown into his tall, gangly frame.

God, the sun had to be putting me into a swoon.

That was it.

Courtney pinched my forearm, shocking me out of the stupor. "What are you lookin' at, Faith?" she singsonged.

I swatted at her. "Nothin'."

Her brows lifted. "Oh really?"

"Really."

She spun her finger around my face. "Somebody is tellin' lies. It's written all over you. I know where that mind of yours went. I bet you're thinking about running your hands all over that delicious skin, aren't you? Giving it a little lick? I wonder what else you're thinkin' about lickin'."

There was nothing but suggestion in her tone.

Redness rushed all over me, heat climbing my neck and landing on my cheeks.

"Courtney, I swear to goodness, you are ruthless." She could give Jace a run for his money with all the *trouble* she was glad to provoke.

She let her salacious gaze travel out the window. "What? Even I have to admit that is one fine-specimen of a man. Now tell me if he's given you something a little fun over the last few weeks he's been here."

I choked out a sound of disbelief. I shouldn't be surprised. This was Courtney I was dealing with. But even after knowing her for over twenty years, she still managed to shock me with the things that came out of her mouth.

"Show me yours, and I'll show you mine." She hiked a not-so-innocent shoulder. "Felix does rock my world. Now you'd better start fessin' up on the details of what's going on between you two, because I know it's something. I can't believe you've left me in the dark. That's not cool, Faith Avery, after all, I tell you all my dirty little secrets."

I started to fill an ice bucket. "Who said I wanted to hear all your dirty little secrets? You usually leave me feeling like I need to pour bleach into my ears. And there is nothin' going on. He's watching out for Bailey and me. That's it."

Why'd that sound like a lie?

"Right . . . the man is staying under the same roof? Him looking the way he does and you all smokin' hot and sexy? All that unresolved history built up between you two? I bet you are absolutely killing him."

She clucked. "Hell, I bet the only thing filling up that big head of his is the image of him sneaking into your room and doing all kinds of dirty things. I just wonder how long it's gonna be until he actually does it."

Visions slammed me.

What that would be like.

Jace over me.

Our bodies drenched in sweat.

The expression he'd wear on his face.

Heat flashed.

Too much.

Overwhelming.

Courtney grinned. "Or maybe you've already done it."

I forced a scowl onto my face. "I hate you, you know that?"

"Pssh . . . hate me? You love me. Who else is gonna tell you like it is?"

"Stop it. We're just friends and you know it."

Her smile was somehow soft and wry and brimming with sympathy. "Cut the crap, Faith. *Friends* is not what you call what's going on between you two. There's so much friction and energy radiating from the two of you that you're about to make the entire house go *boom*."

"You know I'm not ready for that," I whispered, an emphatic plea. "I don't understand why you keep pushing me that direction. My heart doesn't have room for any more breakin'."

What kind of horrible person did it make me that I was having these thoughts at all? The feeling rushing me every time Jace stepped into the room.

Attraction and desire.

Part of it made me feel dirty. The other part of me was sure I couldn't stop it if my life depended on it.

I guessed that probably stemmed from the fact that's the way loving Jace had once felt.

As if my life depended on it.

Courtney reached out and fiddled with a loose strand of my hair, her expression encouraging. "I think you're ready for more than you're willing to admit. I think you're so much stronger than you think. And I think maybe that amazing heart of yours is ready for something good after it's been dealt so much bad."

Good?

A gust of air left my lungs, my heart and spirit at odds with what she'd said. "Jace is dangerous," I told her, barely able to free it from my tongue. "That beast is liable to wipe me out flat."

She swung her attention back out the window.

Jace was leaned casually against the railing, chatting with his brother as he wiped the sweat from his forehead. His profile so striking, so dominant and commanding as he stood there, that it was borderline painful for me to look away from it.

It didn't matter if he was wearing ratty jeans or a suit.

He appeared as if the world couldn't touch him. Only because he owned it.

But, oh God, could I feel him touching me from across the space. His presence these tendrils that wrapped around me, held me hostage, sank right in.

Taking root.

Through the window, those coppery eyes flashed my direction.

A tremble rumbled through the walls.

"And what if that's exactly what you need? A beast to watch over you. His strength to hold you up."

Guilt lined my throat. "It's not right."

She shook her head. "Love's not about right or wrong, just like grief isn't about counting days. Love is about being given a gift. Sometimes when we least expect it. Usually when we need it most."

My lips pursed tightly in refusal. "Love? He doesn't love me."

She grabbed the bowl of watermelon, a grin threatening at her mouth. "You just go on tellin' yourself that."

I scowled at her. "I thought you didn't want Jace anywhere around me."

Another shrug. "Maybe I changed my mind."

"And why would you go and do that?"

She looked out the window. "Only a man who really gives a shit shows up in the middle of a tragedy. Assholes? They like it nice and easy. They tuck tail and run the second things get rough. It's the ones who really care who stick around."

"It was way easier when you were hatin' on him," I muttered quietly, barely a breath, pretty much talking to myself.

"Hatin' is always easier than lovin', isn't it?" she said right before she pushed open the door and stepped out onto the porch.

No.

She was totally wrong.

Because loving Jace Jacobs had always felt like the easiest thing in the world. Right up until that love was taken away.

# twenty-one

## Jace

"And here I had to come out of the ocean buck naked in front of half the high school." Mack glared at Ian, who was rocked back in one of the patio chairs, all smug the way he always was.

"Hey, warned you if you told Delaney I was crushing on her, you were going to regret it."

Somehow, we'd started tossing out stories from back in high school while we sat under the shade of the porch. Tyler and Shane had taken off, so it was just a few of us left.

The mood had gone light.

That didn't mean that energy wasn't billowing from her.

Floating through the atmosphere.

Clouds at the edge of heaven. Maybe right in her hands.

I tried to pretend I wasn't all wrapped up in the way she felt sitting two feet away from me and watched as Mack gave a shrug with one of his hulking shoulders. "Turns out, it worked in my favor, anyway. Maddie didn't seem to mind all that much."

"Ewww." Courtney laughed and smacked at her thigh. "You

would go for Maddie, Mack. You were such a dirty bird back in high school."

Mack grinned and drained the rest of his lemonade as he looked at her. "Was?" He winked at her. "Besides, what was so wrong with Maddie?"

There was a smirk riding around his mouth, his beard twitching as he kept himself from laughing.

"Uh, how about the fact she went around braggin' about every boy she sacked. She might as well have been a football player."

Mack scoffed. "I think you were just jealous those linebackers weren't trying to take you down."

Courtney shot him a glare. "I'll have you know I could have had anyone on that team. I just liked the boys I dated . . . a little more seasoned."

Mack squinted with the accusation, the cop in him always right at the surface. "You mean you were jail bait? Not cool, Courtney, not cool."

Courtney laughed. "I'll never tell. Besides, why are you always tryin' to find a good excuse to arrest me?"

"Uh, because you're nothin' but trouble." It was purely a tease.

A grin pulled up at the corner of Felix's mouth, and he ran his fingers over Courtney's arm. "Trouble maker, huh? Do I need to get my cuffs out?"

"I have been a bad girl."

I could feel the flush coming from Faith beside me, the way she was looking at the porch floor and fighting a grin, peeking up at her best friend.

Satisfaction tightened my chest.

It felt like with each day that passed, I got to watch her come farther out of her shell.

Heal a little more. Even with the possible threat looming over her head, the girl was blossoming again.

Like her spirit had been fed, wilted petals coming alive.

Comfortable in her own skin, in her own home, while her little girl ran and twirled and danced on the lawn. Not a care in the world since she was off living in all her make-believe ones.

That was the only thing I wanted for them.

For them to feel like they could live without fear. Without Faith having to constantly watch over her shoulder.

"So, birthday party next weekend for Mack," Ian said, grinning at Mack who probably would prefer to let the milestone pass him right on by. Unnoticed.

As if any of us were going to let him forget.

"That's right. It's the big one. Thirty."

I grinned at Mack, who was rubbing his fingers through his beard and grinning as he sat there in his own comfort.

"Getting up there, man," I told him.

Mack scoffed. "Hardly. Just another day as far as I'm concerned. Besides, the rest of you assholes aren't far behind me." He pointed around the circle of us.

"Don't worry, Mack, we'll all be there to help you cross over to the other side," Felix said, lifting his lemonade as if it were a shot.

"Can't wait," Mack said, response dry, though there was a smirk behind it.

Everyone seemed to trail off and settle into the rest, a light breeze blowing across the back lawn from the stream at the back, the little bit of cool welcomed after we'd been baking under the rays of the sun for the last six hours.

"Made pretty good progress this morning," Ian finally said, voice faraway, like he was somewhere in his mind calculating how long it was going to take to get this place whipped into shape.

Fucking forever, that was how long. The porch was barely scratching the surface.

"Going to need to hire a crew," I said, looking toward the peeling paint on the porch overhead.

"Know some guys," Felix said. "I did a bunch of construction in the past. I could get you in touch with some guys who could help you out."

I sat forward. "Really?"

"Sure."

I glanced at Faith, who sent me one of those wistful, sad smiles.

Like she still couldn't understand why I wanted to do any of this for her.

Why she deserved it.

When the girl deserved the entire world to be placed at her feet.

Everything I possessed.

I bit those thoughts back, my mind and heart going a direction it couldn't go. I cleared my throat and broke the connection, swinging my attention back to Felix. "That would be great. If you want to get everyone together Monday morning."

"Absolutely."

Faith suddenly shot up. "Where's Bailey?"

In a second flat, both Mack and I were on our feet, heading down the porch steps.

That feeling swept over me. Something possessive and protective that I was pretty sure could suck the life out of me.

Then I sagged when I saw Bailey coming up around the side of the house, gliding across the lawn, which was hugged by the sprawling rose gardens and the massive house.

She was grinning.

Grinning her sweet little grin, carrying that damned Beast that I half wanted to rip out of her arms and shred, or maybe press my face to it, breathe it in like it might be able to bring us back to that day so I could be that guy I'd wanted to be.

Those thoughts drained just as fast when I realized she was holding a small package with it.

"We got a present!" she sang. "Is for Mommy!"

"Bailey." Faith flew around me, her steps as urgent as her voice. "You aren't supposed to go out front by yourself."

"I didn't. I stay right here on the grass." Her brown eyes were wide and emphatic.

Faith sank to her knees in front of her and pulled the box from her hands. "Then where did you get this?" Faith turned it over in her hands, frowning.

There were no markings on the box, but it was taped up.

Bailey looked at her like she was crazy, and she pointed to the edge of the rose garden. "Froms my friend. He was right there."

"Where did he go?" Faith rushed, terror sliding from her mouth.

Bailey's eyes went wide. "I's don't know."

Faith gasped. Distraught, she shot up and started to run around the side of the house.

Like she was going to chase down whoever had left this herself. "Faith!" I shouted.

She cried out a sound of rebellion against it, a beaten-down desperation taking her whole, fury and terror escaping from her lungs.

I ran behind her, and she pushed herself harder.

I caught her, close to tackling her to the ground when I wrapped my arms around her from behind, the two of us on the ground panting as Felix blew by at a flat-out run, shouting as he did, "I've got this. Fucker isn't getting away this time."

Mack was right behind him, his hulking frame slower than Felix's long legs.

With my arms around Faith, I tried to see through the hot hatred, torn between holding her, staying there in that spot to protect her and Bailey, and joining Felix and Mack.

But I couldn't seem to pry myself away from her. Couldn't stop from experiencing the agony she was feeling.

Holding her as she began to weep.

Frantic, she started to tear into the seal, and I was hit with a bolt of that protectiveness, alarm riding in on the breeze, this feeling raising and suffocating.

Faith pulled out one of the blocks that I instantly knew had come from Bailey's room.

She started shaking. Shaking so hard her shoulders were jutting up and down as she unfolded a note that was tucked in with the block.

I kept a single arm around her tremoring body as I pried the note from her hands.

I squinted at it beneath the rays of light.

*The next time I come looking for it, it'd better be there. I know you have it. Stop protecting Joseph. You have nothing left to lose. Well, I guess you do.*

Printed on the back of the sheet in black and white was a fuzzy picture of Bailey playing on the grass.

Fury hit my veins. So violent I couldn't see. I drew Faith tighter, at the same time reaching out to grab Bailey to drag her into my arms.

Wrapping both of them up.

Holding them tight.

Refusing to let anything happen to either of them.

Sobs erupted from Faith, her words whimpered, "I don't understand. I don't understand. What do they want?"

I could feel Bailey's confusion in the way her little body swam with the unknown, her little heart so innocent and sweet as she wrapped her arms around her mother's neck. "Is okay, Mommy. Is just a present."

Felix and Mack came back around from the front, both panting and trying to catch their breath.

"Fuck," Mack hissed. "Not a fucking trace."

He took the note I had crumpled in my fist. At the same time, his cell rang. He answered it.

"Yeah."

"What?"

"No."

He paced off, and I could feel his own hostility coming off him. Lashes and whips.

"Fuck," he hissed. "Okay. Give me thirty. Have a situation here, too."

I wouldn't have heard what he'd said had I not been listening so intently, my ear craned to his conversation while I hugged Faith and Bailey to me as tightly as I could.

Courtney scooted around to the front of them, glancing at me, a plea in her expression. She gently edged into the hug, whispering, "It's okay, it's okay."

Faith gulped over a cry and let her friend wrap her up.

I stood.

Anger streaking across my flesh as I turned and stalked for Mack.

His lips were pinched, a heavy paw roughing over his face, his voice coming as a quieted growl the second I was in earshot.

"An alarm was going off in an office building downtown. Turns out, it was one leased by one of the companies owned by Joseph's umbrella. Someone is digging . . . finding out his holdings. Place was tossed."

"Shit," I hissed. I could feel it. That ugliness lying siege. Sinking into every cell in my body. The willingness to do absolutely anything to protect the people who meant the most to me.

Mack squeezed the outside of my shoulder. "We're getting close, man. We'll find whoever this bastard is. Find out what happened to Joseph. End this."

I let my eyes travel back to Faith. Broken on her knees, her daughter in her arms where she wept.

Something swelled in me. That feeling I shouldn't allow myself to feel. I shoved it down and turned back to Mack. "Do it fast."

Because I was aching to do a little of that *ending* myself.

"Is she asleep?"

Warily, Faith nodded as she took another step out the door, sadness pouring from her as she looked to where I was sitting on the double swing that was strung up in the corner of the porch.

I was antsy.

Itchy.

Aching to take matters into my own hands even though Mack made me promise to keep my cool.

Reminded me I couldn't afford to get myself into any more trouble.

That I couldn't compromise the investigation by running off to fight a battle I wasn't qualified to fight.

But that's what I wanted to do.

I wanted to fight.

I wanted to crush and destroy and eradicate.

Which was why I'd forced myself out back. Trying to breathe in the cool while a fire torched my nerves.

Mack had stationed a cruiser out front, which was about the only solace I found in all of this.

I looked up at Faith who was just standing there.

She was in the shadows of the night, the moon a sliver that shed the barest light on the yard, Faith protected by the walls of the old house.

Still, I swore they howled and yelped. Cries of the ghosts that were held within.

That chocolate hair was a river around her shoulders, a white V-neck tee and fitted, holey jeans hugging her body in all the right ways and making my heart do crazy things.

Thumping and thudding and thrashing.

Fuck.

I was going to lose it.

Wanting to protect her.

Wanting to wipe that expression from her face.

Wanting to *love* her.

That was the crux of it all.

I wanted to *keep* her.

Which was so goddamned stupid. But loving her had always made me do stupid things.

She clutched that same monitor in her hands and edged farther onto the porch.

Coming my way.

Every step torture.

Lighting on my flesh.

Teasing my restraints.

She eased down beside me, tucking her legs up to her chest. She set her cheek on her knees and looked over at me.

"I don't understand what's happening, Jace. What someone wants from me when I don't have the first clue what they want or what they're looking for."

A stake of guilt cut right through the center of my chest. Did she really not know about the shit Joseph was into?

"What Joseph was into." Her words were soggy, coming from her like she'd tapped right into my thoughts. "He . . . he was working so hard, saying he was doing everything he could to get the money together to fix up the house."

Anger surged.

Joseph had always been a liar. Saving face. Manipulating every situation to look like the good guy when he was setting things up to land in his favor.

"He didn't say anything to you? In the days or months before he died, that seemed out of place?"

Faith blinked. From the corner of her eye, a tear streaked free.

And there I was, wanting to reach out, gather it up, kiss it away.

"He . . . he never said a whole lot about work. He just said it was busy." She blinked again. "Honestly, the last couple of years, he hadn't been around all that much. Working long hours. Traveling."

She shook her head, her face pinching like she'd just caught on to something. I waited, watching her profile as her mind worked.

"God, I was a fool, wasn't I? Blind?" she said in that sweet, sad way. "I mean, there were these times when I got this feelin' . . ."

She touched her chest right over her heart. "This intuition that something wasn't right. I ignored it, Jace. I ignored it because I didn't want to believe my husband could be involved in anything illegal."

*She will hate me.*

*She will hate me.*

When she found out, she was going to hate me. I deserved it, and at the same damned time, I wanted to reject it.

Lay every ounce of blame on Joseph, the piece of shit.

But even if it was his fault, it didn't mean I wasn't responsible.

She blinked into the distance. "And now . . . someone somehow thinks that I was involved?"

Her face pinched in rejection of the idea. "That's what this is, isn't it? They think I have knowledge of something? Possession of something that Joseph never should have had? Tell me he wasn't corrupt, Jace. Tell me I'm being crazy."

She looked at me with that pleading expression.

A million lies danced on the tip of my tongue, desperate to do anything to take the blame away from her.

"The shipping yards . . ." I hedged, shifting to lean my forearms on the top of my thighs, my feet slowly rocking us where they were planted on the porch.

I glanced over at her. "They invite trouble. There is so much crime down there, shit being moved around that shouldn't be."

I tried to deliver it gently. As soft as the girl. Didn't want to taint her with any of the nastiness that thrived and lived in that area. The guns and the drugs and all the shit that came through. All masked by what looked like legitimate businesses.

Laundered and shaken and put right back onto the streets.

Guessed I should have thought of that before I got everyone mixed up in that world in the first place.

Even with those words, she squeezed her eyes shut. "Joseph wouldn't . . ." she started to say before she trailed off, gasping over a cry in her throat.

Then she opened to me. "I feel like an idiot, Jace. Like a complete idiot, doing nothing but living with the wool pulled over my eyes."

I shook my head at her, hand trembling, wanting to reach out and hold her. "No, Faith. You just always saw the good in people. Believed in them when they didn't deserve it."

Her teeth clamped down on her bottom lip. Pain streaking across her face as her eyes flicked all over mine. "Sometimes those are the people who need the belief the most."

Energy crackled.

Warmth and grace and *Beauty*.

I wanted to breathe it in. Taste it. Live in it.

I inhaled, leaning her direction. "Faith—"

Like she felt the magnitude of what was coming, she hopped to her feet, cutting me off, fumbling over the words, "I . . . I . . . I need to go check on Bailey."

Dropping her head, she scrambled for the backdoor, taking all that intensity with her.

I pushed out a frustrated sigh.

Fuck.

Finally, I climbed to my feet and headed inside, going for the front window and pulling open the drape. A cruiser sat in the shadows under the trees.

I blew out a little relief. The little that I had. The fact that Mack wasn't taking any chances any more than I was willing to do.

Needing to give it up, to clear my mind, I headed upstairs to my room. Only I stumbled when Faith was slipping back out of Bailey's room and into the darkened hall.

Just looking at her had energy replacing the air around me. Sizzling and shivering through the atmosphere. Could feel it radiating from her skin. From her heart and that sweet mind.

My mouth went dry, and she whispered, "Jace."

And I was there, in front of her, drawn in a way I shouldn't have been. In a way I couldn't stop. I wanted to press her to the wall. Kiss her. Touch her. Carry her into my room and get lost in her.

It felt like I was right there. In that moment when I'd had to say goodbye.

If I could go back, could I do everything differently?

Or had we been destined for destruction?

Me thinking I could have something good when I'd been nothing but trash?

She blinked up at me with those chocolate eyes. So warm. Glinting with something different. Like there was a chance she was feeling some of the need twisted through my guts.

I inched closer, and she fumbled back, hitting the wall outside Bailey's door. I hovered there, our noses an inch away, our breaths mingling.

I could count every beat of her heart as it thundered into the enclosed space. Could feel her torment. Could feel all the same questions swirling through me.

I planted both my hands over her head. "Faith," I murmured.

She panted. Gasped. Then twisted out from under me, backing away with her hands pressed over her heart. "I can't do this, Jace."

I stared at her silhouette, her eyes alive in the shadows.

"I missed you," I told her, admitting a little of what I'd been needing to tell her all along.

She took another step back, her hand on the knob of her door. "And you destroyed me, and I'm not sure I can risk that happening again."

I stood there wanting to tear something apart as she stepped inside and her door clicked softly shut behind her.

The beast raging.

Wanting to punish something for taking her away.

Or maybe he was just plotting exactly how he was going to get her back.

# twenty-two

## Jace
### Eighteen Years Old

*J*ace hustled down the trail toward the trailer. He'd just gotten

off work, and he was anxious to grab a shower, knowing he'd be sneaking back out to meet with Faith.

He slowed when he saw that same shiny car parked out front. Anger wound up in his chest, and he gritted his teeth as he spat a curse at the ground.

Was it wrong that his mama absolutely disgusted him? That his guts got all tied up every time he thought of her and what she represented? The things she'd allowed to happen in their *home*.

Jace's eyes traveled the rusted trailer, the cardboard wedged in the windows that were busted out, and the trash strewn about the yard.

*Home.*

Yeah right.

With a harsh shake of his head, Jace bounded up the steps and blew through the door. He stumbled again when he caught sight of what was going down inside.

That slimy bastard his mom had been hooking up with was on the shabby couch, leaning over all the salacious crap left on the coffee table.

Both Ian and Joseph were sitting on the floor at his feet, listening to whatever bullshit he was filling their heads with.

If they listened that hard at school, the two of them would have straight A's.

The prick looked up when Jace stepped inside. He cracked a grin.

Unease rumbled through Jace's spirit. "What's going on here?"

The asshole sat back on the couch, leveling Jace a stare. "Just having a little conversation with your brothers."

Anger pulsed.

The cocksucker didn't even know Joseph wasn't their brother. And there he was, sitting on that couch like he owned the shithole.

With the way he was dressed, Jace was pretty sure he thought he owned the world.

"I don't think either of them need to hear a thing you have to say." The words left Jace's mouth like gravel. Hard and pitted. Full of hate.

"I think they are very interested in everything I have to say." He cast his wicked eyes over them. "Aren't you?"

Ian looked to the ground and Joseph fucking nodded.

What the hell?

"Well, it doesn't matter if they want to hear what you have to say or not. I'm telling you they don't." Jace pushed open the door. "I think it's time you leave."

The guy had the audacity to laugh, pushing to his feet, his head angled as he crossed the space, coming toward Jace. "Aren't you the big man?"

He tipped his head farther, like he was assessing Jace, adding up his worth. "Maybe you should be the one I'm talking to. I like someone who's loyal. A fighter."

Fear and fury vibrated all the way to Jace's bones.

"Stay away from them." Jace's teeth ground together so hard he could hear his jaw clicking in his ears.

This guy would probably destroy him in a fight, but Jace didn't care. He'd gladly go down in a blaze if it protected Ian and Joseph from the seedy shit he was so clearly wrapped up in.

The guy grinned. "I'll see you around." He reached up and straightened Jace's collar, pulling hard as he brought them nose to nose. "Jace."

He released Jace and ambled out like nothing had been said. Jace slammed the door shut, glaring at Ian and Joseph, who were still sitting on the ground. "What the fuck do you two think you're doing?"

Ian blinked, hugging his knees to his chest. "He just wanted to talk to us."

"About what?" The words were an accusation.

Joseph pushed to his feet, lifted his chin. "About a business opportunity."

Rage blistered across Jace's skin, this horror that took him hostage as he thought of Ian and Joseph getting caught up in that world.

Jace flew across the room, getting in Joseph's face. "Stay away from that guy. Do you hear me? He is nothing but trouble."

"We were only listening to what he had to say," Ian said quietly.

Jace's attention darted toward him, his words hard. "Well, don't. They're lies. There's nothing that he can say to you that will amount to anything but you becoming exactly what the world thinks you are."

"Maybe you're just jealous he asked us instead of you." Defiance radiated from Joseph, and Jace swung his gaze back on his cousin.

"I'm warning you, Joseph. Stay away from that guy."

A snarl curled Joseph's face, taunting Jace with his own words. "Whatever it takes to survive, remember? We look out for ourselves. Do whatever we have to do to make it."

Jace looked between the two of them. "Not when it comes to us. We look out for each other. Take care of each other. And I'm telling you that you aren't sniffing up anything but a dead end with that guy."

Most likely a body bag.

Joseph shook his head. "I think the problem is that you're so wrapped up in that stupid girl, trying to impress her, that you've forgotten who you are."

Ian nodded, his anger over the time Jace had been spending with Faith flooding out of him in a streak of jealousy.

But Joseph's jealousy was different.

Jace knew it. Felt it in his gut.

Before he even realized what he was doing, Jace pushed Joseph against the wall. His back slammed against the paneling and the trailer shook on its rickety foundation. "Leave Faith out of this."

Hating the instant reaction, the instant aggression, Jace took a step back, trying to get himself together. His voice trembled when he pointed at Joseph, praying he'd get it, that he'd understand. "I'm warning you. Stay away from him. I'm telling you for your own good."

He looked at Ian. "Both of you. You hear me?"

Ian nodded.

"Whatever you say, Boss Man," Joseph said, nothing but venom on his tongue.

Jace stumbled, his hand still on the doorknob as he peered into the darkened trailer. A moan echoed back from somewhere within.

Dread curled through his insides, and he held his breath as he fumbled to flick on the light switch.

Hazy light filtered into the space, and the dread he was feeling turned to horror when he saw his brother in a ball on the floor in the corner.

He rushed that way and dropped to his knees. His hands were shaking like crazy when he gently rolled his brother over.

A shocked gasp rocked from Jace's lungs.

Blood covered Ian's face. It dripped from his nose, and his upper lip was busted open. One of his eyes was swollen closed, purple and black bruises already beginning to rise to the surface.

"Ian," he wheezed. "What happened?"

"I . . . Steven. You told me to stay away from him, so . . . so I tried to keep him out of the house when he showed up here. I tried, Jace. I promise, I tried to make you proud."

Jace's jaw clenched.

Fury blistered. Scoring into his consciousness. Penetrating to the ugly, dark spot in his soul.

That piece of shit did this?

"It's okay," he attempted to murmur, to comfort his brother, his words raking from his raw throat. "It's okay."

Ian nodded and then winced in pain as he moved.

"It's okay," Jace whispered again, helping his brother to stand. Knowing it wasn't even close to the truth.

The pompous fucker straightened his suit jacket as he stepped out of his car and onto the sidewalk. Jace didn't hesitate. He rushed up behind him and shoved him as hard as he could.

His back bowed as he stumbled forward a step before Steven whirled around. He cracked a grin when he saw Jace. But Jace wasn't smiling back. He was throwing a fist. As hard as he could.

It cracked against the guy's face. His head rocked back, and Jace didn't slow, didn't wait, he dove for him, tackling him to the ground.

A frenzy lit inside Jace. All the anger and hostility he possessed rising to the surface.

Freed.

"You hurt my brother. You piece of shit, you hurt my brother."

Jace threw punch after punch. They landed on the guy's chin. His jaw. His nose. Bones crunching and flesh splitting.

It only fueled the fire.

The hot hatred that burned inside Jace.

He wanted to end him.

Erase the threat.

All of it.

The drugs he was feeding his mama, the hook he had in Joseph.

Most of all, he wanted to get retribution for Ian. His brother who was so brave and so damned stupid.

"You disgusting piece of shit. I'll kill you. I'll kill you."

Jace didn't even know what he was saying, his rage so intense, red was the only thing he could see.

He could barely feel the blow that jolted through him when a fist landed on his cheek.

Blinding.

Feet pounded around him, and voices shouted.

He didn't slow. He pounded and pounded and pounded.

Hands were suddenly on him, dragging him back, pinning him facedown on the ground. Cuffs were slapped around his wrists.

Jace lifted his head.

Blood dripped to the sidewalk from his mouth, and he could barely make out the figure who was pushing up to sitting, wiping the red from his face, grinning at Jace like he was the one who'd won.

"I'll kill you," Jace shouted.

He was jerked up, his feet coming out from under him, two officers dragging him away.

"I'll kill you."

The cell door buzzed, and Jace warily fumbled out, his head hung low as he was released.

Questions swirled around him, the worry of his fate and wondering how his mom had scraped together the money to bail him out.

He'd never hated his world more than right then. Who he was and where he came from. He'd never regret what he did—sticking up for his brother. Protecting him. But he would always regret what lived inside him.

Regret the fact that he was supposed to meet Faith last night and he hadn't shown. He could only imagine what she'd thought when she'd been out in front of that house in the middle of the night and he wasn't there.

Fear trembled through his spirit. Because he'd never been so sure than right then that he would never be good enough for her.

He stepped out into the sunlight, blinking against the bright day, only for his guts to twist when he saw the asshole leaning against the side of the building.

He pushed from the wall and grinned at Jace like they were the best of friends. "Ah. Jace Jacobs, the little destroyer. What you did last night wasn't very smart, but I can't say I'm not glad you did it. You owe me. Now get in my car."

Jace's guts curled in the tightest knot, his spirit pulsing with dread.

## Faith

"*I* think it'd be best if I just stayed home." I wasn't in love with the way my voice cracked with a shot of uncertainty.

But that was the way Jace Jacobs had always made me feel.

Uncertain and confused and itchy and wanting things I shouldn't want.

"I have to go, Faith. And that means you're coming with me."

He was leaned against the kitchen counter, hands gripping the white stone, so casual and powerful in his stance that I didn't know how to process what it was I felt when I saw him standing there.

A week had passed since we'd received the last threat. It was like having to start all over again.

Each time one came, I felt as if I were back at square one. Preparing for a new fight, and still, trying my best to go on livin'.

Moments forgetting all about it as I went about my days, only for the next minute to have the reality of my situation slam me from out of nowhere.

The dread and the fear and the anxiety.

Though standing there right then?

I was experiencing an entirely different sort of anxiety.

I had no idea how to step out with him. Not with the way he made me feel. Not with the confusion that lined my insides and tugged at my spirit.

I'd known he'd been about a second from kissin' me last weekend outside of Bailey's door. The scariest part was how badly I'd wanted him to. How I'd been silently begging him to erase the space. To hold me. To whisper that it was goin' to be all right.

Maybe I was a fool for feeling like it was actually going to be okay when he was there.

"It feels too strange to go out. Not with everything going on."

"And it's not okay for you to hide away in this house, either. Plus, I won't be able to enjoy myself if you aren't there, and half the force is going to be there. It's the best way for me to look out for you."

A sigh bled free, and I hugged my arms tighter over my chest. "You can't be watchin' out for me all the time."

He pushed from the counter. "You sure about that?"

"Jace," I said, trying to make sense of this man. Or really, I was just trying not to get lost in him as I blinked up at his striking face—defined jaw, plush lips, and intense eyes.

"Faith," he taunted right back. He let a smirk glide onto his mouth. "What would Mack think if you didn't show for his thirtieth birthday?"

My eyes narrowed. "Are you trying to play me, Jace Jacobs?"

He edged forward, his voice dropping into a caress. "Oh, I can think of all kinds of games we could play."

More seduction.

"Jace," I whispered, feeling hot and sweaty and off-kilter.

He'd been doing that more and more lately.

Tripping me up.

Stealing my air and ripping the ground out from under my feet.

"I told you that you can't go sayin' things like that to me."

In frustration, he roughed a hand through his hair before he angled close, his head cocked so he was breathing against my cheek as he murmured, "Maybe I'm getting tired of not saying what we're clearly both thinking. Not saying it doesn't mean it's not right there, playing out in both of our minds."

Desire flashed across my skin, seeping into my pores, igniting something in me that I wasn't sure I could ignore much longer.

He straightened and touched the spot he'd just set fire to with his words. "Now, go get ready. You're coming."

# twenty-four

## Jace

*I* stepped out of my bedroom into the quiet dusky hall, coming up short when I found Faith coming out of hers.

She was in this slinky royal-blue dress, which barely hit the middle of those lush thighs, and high heels, which made her appear even taller than she was.

The breath punched from my lungs.

This girl was so fucking gorgeous I was beginning to suffocate beneath the weight of it. Beneath the want and the need and the love for her that refused to die.

Uneasily, her hand fluttered up to her slender neck. She fiddled with the teardrop diamond earring that dangled from her ear. "I hate dressin' up. I feel ridiculous."

I gazed at her. Knot in my throat. Dick so deprived and balls so blue that I could feel every inch of my body hardening just from looking at her.

Fuck.

This was getting messy.

But I couldn't *not* say something when she stood there shifting self-consciously, couldn't *not* reach out and let my thumb trace the little divot on her chin.

"You don't look ridiculous. Not even close."

Twilight flooded the hall, like it was taking up space, forcing us closer, and she sucked in a choppy breath against the feel of my thumb on her skin, those lips parting a fraction.

Shit, I wanted to dip my thumb inside that sweet mouth of hers.

Maybe lean in for a taste.

Just one little taste to quench the thirst that left me parched and needy every damned day, growing stronger with each one that passed.

"I ready!"

I jumped back when the door beside us banged open.

Bailey was grinning from her doorway.

Fucking cutest kid on earth. So full of life and belief. So full of *faith*.

She hauled a tiny pink suitcase behind her, two dolls and that Beast tucked under one arm as if she were heading on some week-long vacation rather than spending the night at her grandparents' house.

We'd decided that was the safest place for her to stay. Funny how that might be the place I dreaded stepping foot onto the most.

"Are you sure you want to go?" Faith asked her.

"I's a *big* girl, Mommy."

Faith sighed a restless sigh, her worry bounding through the hall.

"Okay, let's go then," she relented.

We headed out to my car.

With no sign of anything else, Mack had finally lifted the twenty-four-hour watch, a cruiser rolling by at random times of the day and night, Mack telling us to call him directly if anything seemed out of place.

Swore, it was a bitch that we could find absolutely nothing solid—no evidence, no names to actually point us in the right direction of the culprit—and still feeling like someone was constantly watching.

Thank God the construction crew Felix had hooked me up with had shown on Monday. That put at least five men at the house at all times, which eased some of the pressure because there was safety in the sheer numbers.

It was probably the only reason I felt comfortable taking Faith out tonight. A party with a bunch of cops and detectives was the safest place to be.

This afternoon, I'd put Bailey's car seat in my car, and Faith buckled Bailey into it while I put the suitcase on the floorboards in front of her. We climbed into the front, and I started down the drive.

Those branches stretched over us, blips of the setting sun breaking through as we bounced over the holes and bumps carved out in the dirt road, covering us in glittering golds and hues of orange and pink.

Silence filled the cab as we traveled.

Faith was jittery and anxious, continually fidgeting and shifting in her seat next to me.

She wasn't alone.

Because every fraction of a mile that passed had my own anxiety increasing.

Growing and clawing and reminding me of what I'd fought so hard to escape.

The eyes of this town that had watched me. Looked at me like I was trash. Like I was a thief.

Faith's father hadn't been any different from every other asshole in this town who'd cast their stones, cast their judgment, without giving us a chance to prove otherwise.

It wasn't like I'd given him a reason to trust me. Treat me differently.

But fuck.

I could almost taste how much I'd wanted it. How fucking badly I'd wanted to be different.

How I'd wanted her father to look at me and see past the grungy clothes and the rumors that flew and see a guy who just loved his daughter.

A guy who'd do absolutely anything for her.

She and I both knew how well that'd gone.

"Are you sure you want to do this?" she asked as I took the last turn into her parents' neighborhood.

I chuckled out a rough sound. "Since when do you know me to give up when I want something?"

She cut me a glance. A hard, bitter, pointed one.

*The day you walked away.*

She might as well have screamed it at me.

Gulping around her silent accusation, I shook my head. "We're going. Mack is turning thirty. We can't miss rubbing that in." My brow lifted as I shot her a grin, doing my best to lighten the mood.

God knew, she deserved a night to just have fun.

She barked out a sudden laugh. "You're right. We definitely can't miss that."

"And when's the last time you went somewhere and just had fun?"

"Fun hasn't exactly been on the agenda lately," she said, raising those brows.

God, she looked fucking fantastic sitting there in the front seat of my car. All legs and sweetness and sexiness.

"Then I guess we'd better jot it down. Tonight Faith Linbrock is slotted for some fun."

So what if I used her maiden name? Couldn't bear the thought of her branded with Joseph's.

"Is that so?" It was almost playfulness in her tone when she said it. Like she felt comfortable enough with me to maybe entertain it. I was determined to give it to her. Even if it was just for a little while.

"Yeah, that's so," I tossed back out.

"Fun and birthday cake! I's want a big piece," Bailey shouted from the backseat.

I swore, the kid pulled an affectionate chuckle right out from the center of me. "Have you seen Mack? I think he might eat it all."

"Mack *wooks wike* a dragon *swayer*." Bailey's voice got quiet in wistful awe, and I glanced in the rearview mirror at the way her dark, dark eyes went wide in some kind of fantastical excitement.

The kid.

"I don't know about that. I bet he keeps dragons as pets," I told her.

Hell, the guy was a dragon.

"You better not *let* him get my unicorns."

Faith was worrying at that bottom lip when she turned her attention toward her daughter, letting that warm gaze slide to me, trying to keep from laughing at the cuteness of it all.

"I'll be sure to tell him."

"And cake!"

"Whatever you want, sweet one."

Faith released a strained sigh as I pulled to a stop in front of the house she grew up in.

Both of us feeling the pressure.

It was crazy that it felt like Faith and Bailey had become the center of my life, and I'd yet to have to face her parents.

The times they'd come to the house, I'd made myself scarce.

Just like Faith had called me that first day.

A trespasser.

There when I didn't belong.

A fucking coward who didn't want to face them. To see the hate and questions in their eyes.

The house looked exactly the same as it had then.

I was pretty sure I was feeling about the same as I had then, too. I tugged at my collar, which suddenly felt too tight.

I might as well have been wearing my jeans that had been three inches too short rather than this suit that had been tailored to the last centimeter.

Might as well have been anxiously walking Faith to the door for the first time rather than pulling to the curb in a hundred-thousand-dollar car.

Guessed it didn't matter how much fucking money I made. It never erased who I was at my core. The surface shined but the heart remained the same.

Because there was Faith's father, standing on the porch in the same spot he'd been that day. That day, there had just been the flickers of fatherly concern in his eyes, suspicion of any boy who would walk his daughter home.

Tonight? There was outright hate. Rage bristled across his skin as he came out to guard over his family.

The guy had always been a couple of inches shorter than me, though then, I'd been nothing but a scrawny kid who was just getting ready to grow into his skin, even though there had been no denying I could scrap it out in a fight.

No one knew how much strength there really was in self-preservation until they were fighting for their life.

Her father's eyes narrowed as he looked me over where I filled up the seat behind the wheel.

I refused to allow myself to go back to those days when I wanted to cower and shrink under scrutiny, a feeling that had grown and mutated to become this underlying rage.

Yeah, I'd grown into all that strength and hostility. Had learned how to harness that intimidation and make it work for me.

Turned it into an empire that had earned me millions.

But none of that could change what I'd done, and if Faith's father wanted to throw a couple punches, I'd stand there and take them.

God knew, I deserved them.

Faith reached out and grabbed me by the forearm. "Don't you dare get into it with my daddy. The last thing Bailey or I need is to see the two of you fightin'. You hear me?"

I blew out a sigh, scraped my fingers across my lips, and did my best to get it together. To remember my purpose. Why I was here. What I was protecting.

"No fightin'. You hear me?" Bailey parroted.

God, these two women. Bossy and right.

"You really think I'm going to get into a fight with your dad?" I said, brows lifted to my hairline, like I was completely offended by the idea.

Faith shot me a look that called bullshit and reached out to open her door. "I mean it."

At the backdoor, she ducked in and unbuckled Bailey, who

scrambled out, shouting, "Hi, Grampa."

Faith started up the walk behind her, and I reluctantly unlatched my door and stepped out into the approaching night.

The man seemed to have to tear his hatred from me, every inch of him softening as he turned his attention to the little girl who beat a path for him.

She clamored up the two short steps, tripping a little but still smiling when he swept her into his arms.

"Hey, Daddy," Faith called.

"How's my girl?" he asked, his eyes soft as he glanced to her before they bored into me from over her shoulder.

"Good!" Bailey shouted, thinking he was talking to her.

He patted her little leg. "Well, things are about to get better since you get to spend the whole night here with me and Grandma."

He took that opportune time to send me a warning glare.

Just fucking great.

With just that glance, the guy made me feel like a worthless seventeen-year-old kid.

I ducked into the backseat and grabbed Bailey's suitcase, keeping my head held high as I rounded the front of my car.

The screen door unlatched and Faith's mother stepped out. She'd aged too, graciously, her cheeks softened and a few new lines creased her face, but the kindness she'd always shown was still there.

Just like her daughter.

Like it was fundamental to them.

Part of their makeup.

"My . . . look who is here. Jace Jacobs."

"Good evening, ma'am."

I mentally cringed. Yup, there she was, making me feel like that seventeen-year-old kid, too.

Not the powerful mogul who commanded every meeting. Took what I wanted. Made it mine.

"I knew you were gonna do big things with yourself. Look at you, so handsome."

Redness hit my cheeks.

What the hell?

It seemed this whole line of women knew how to hit me at the knees.

I set Bailey's suitcase down on the top of the porch. "There you go, sweet one."

"Thank you, Jace," she said in her little drawl.

"You're welcome, Button," I said, that nickname coming too easily. Sliding right off my tongue with affection.

Damn it.

I was getting in too deep. Getting too close. I had to be careful, or I was going to fuck this all up.

I was pretty sure Faith's mom swooned right there, while her father slit my throat with a metaphorical knife.

Breaking the tension, Faith strode up the two steps, dropping a kiss to her father's cheek and peppering a bunch of them on Bailey's. "Be a good girl for Mommy, okay?"

"Okay, Mommy. You be a good girl, too."

I would have laughed if her father weren't clearly stabbing me over and over in his mind.

Faith's mother took her by both of the cheeks, searching her face. A real mother. The way a mother should be. The way Faith in turn had become for her own daughter.

Sometimes it chafed, seeing it displayed so profoundly. So real.

"You go and have some fun and don't worry about a thing. You deserve a night out, you hear me?"

Faith reached up and grasped her mom by both wrists, giving her a squeeze, something transpiring between the two of them. "Okay, Mama."

Her mom smiled a wistful smile. "All right, then. Go on."

Faith turned and passed by me on the walk. Pinned to the spot, I watched her go, feeling her unease, how hard it was for her to leave her daughter.

We both knew Bailey would be fine with her parents and that a cruiser was set to come by this address several times during the night, but the worry was still there.

Sometimes, knowing something and trusting in it was the hardest thing to do.

I blew out a strained breath, again wishing I could change it. Take it on for her. Let her know it would all be okay.

I watched her climb into my car, that feeling I kept trying to fight stirring inside me.

The fact that this woman was supposed to be mine.

I wanted to go after her. Comfort her. Make her promises I didn't deserve to make, but I knew I owed her father a word or two.

I tried to work myself up to it, figuring out what to offer him, what I could say that would make any of this better, but he beat me to the punch. "You've got a lot of fuckin' nerve."

I swung my attention over my shoulder to where he stood glowering at me from the porch.

Bailey and her grandmother had already disappeared inside.

Anger surged through my veins.

He had no idea why I was there. What I was willing to give.

I beat it back.

He deserved his indignation. I'd let him have it.

"Excuse me?" I said, feigning like I hadn't heard correctly, gearing myself up for him to lay into me.

I could feel Faith watching us from my car that idled at the curb.

"You know, I was right inside the day it happened," he said, his teeth clenching as he gritted the words.

I frowned at him, not exactly sure what he was getting at.

"I heard the sirens. They just kept coming and coming. It seemed like it was going on for hours."

Disquiet pulsed. Stretching tight against my chest as I slowly came to the awareness.

"I knew it." His face contorted. "I just had this feeling that whatever it was, the sirens whizzing by, the helicopter flying in overhead, that everything was getting ready to change for us, and not in a good way."

Grief and guilt.

It reached out and grabbed me by the throat.

Squeezing hard.

"I wasn't even surprised when Mack showed up at my door,

asking me to come with him to give Faith the news."

Agony clawed at my spirit. This mix of hatred and sorrow.

His eyes squeezed closed, and his hands fisted at his sides. Preparing to fight against going back to that day. Or maybe he was just holding himself back from coming at me.

Taking a swing.

*Blame it on me. It was my fault, anyway.*

"Faith . . . she crumbled in my arms that night, Jace. Weeping. Screaming her denial."

*I could have stopped it. I could have stopped it.*

Anguish pushed at the night, and I swore I could physically feel Faith's in that moment. Could feel her from behind where I thought maybe she was chained inside my car, unable to bear witness to what her father was telling me.

Like she couldn't experience it all over again.

His eyes latched on to mine. A dark threat, the brown color lighter than Faith's but just as genuine and real, holding nothing back.

"And I have to wonder . . . wonder if her grief that night came even close to being as bad as it was when you left her."

The man had to have sucker punched me in the gut. Or maybe got me with a swift kick of a steel-toed boot.

Because a pained wheeze gusted from my lungs, the impact of it close to buckling me in two.

Denial pulsed from the darkest place inside me.

She'd chosen Joseph. I had to remember that.

But her father kept right on, driving knives into my consciousness, the pain so intense I was sure I was seconds from blacking out.

"You don't know what you did, Jace Jacobs. The pain you caused. And now you're back, and you think I'm gonna stand here and watch you hurt my daughter all over again? You might have rolled up here in a fancy car and wearing a fancy suit, but that doesn't change who you are."

I whirled all the way around to face him, anger coming off me in menacing waves. "Are you joking right now? Have you forgotten why I left? You were there that night, remember?"

"Yeah, I do remember." There was a threat behind it. "It was the choices you made that got you there."

A disgusted snort blew through my nose. "You don't know the first thing about me. You never have. You saw what you wanted to see, just like the rest of the town. If you knew me at all, you'd know the last thing I want is to cause Faith any more pain."

I was there to stop more of it.

Do my best to fix what had gone wrong.

His gaze narrowed. "Is that so? Then what exactly are you doing here?"

My attention swung to the car.

Faith was angled to the side, watching us, like she was trapped inside.

My eyes flew back to her father, hard and emphatic.

"I'm here to fix what Joseph wrecked."

Uncertainty blanketed his face. "What are you saying?"

My head shook. "Don't act like you didn't know Joseph was rotted to the core. Or did he have you blinded, too?"

Her father fidgeted.

"And you thought he was what was best for her, didn't you?" I continued, unable to stop the accusations from dripping from my tongue.

"You were the one loaded down with all that shit."

*You have no idea the circumstances. What I was protecting,* I wanted to scream. I didn't. I knew it wouldn't matter, anyway. It wouldn't change who he thought I was.

Disgusted, I started walking backward as I faced him, my head held high.

Right where it should have been back then.

"Think you should know, I'm not the same scared, pathetic kid I was back then. I cower to no one, least of all you. I'm not going anywhere."

Not until I was sure their world was a safe place. Until I could give back a little of what I'd stolen.

The asshole almost grinned. "We'll see."

# twenty-five

## Faith

*J*ace hustled around the front of his car after he passed off the key to the valet.

I shivered watching him, the way his lithe body moved beneath his fitted dark-gray suit, his face striking in the spray of headlights that lit him up like he was supposed to be the jaw-dropping finale of some Fourth of July fireworks display.

At least that was the way he left me.

Feeling awed and stunned and a little stupefied.

Foolish girl.

But it didn't matter how much I chastised myself or tried to scold my thoughts into submission.

It didn't matter how many times I tried to tell myself it was too soon.

That I wasn't ready.

That I was never going to be ready for someone like Jace Jacobs.

The reaction was the same when he got to my side, opened the door, and reached in to help me out.

I let him wrap my hand in his.

Heat flashed up my arm at the contact, and my breath left me on a stuttered rasp, every inch of me shaken by the force of the energy that roared. So loudly I could hear the howl of it in my ears.

He helped me onto unsteady feet, and still I wobbled forward.

"You okay?" he asked, his own voice seeming a little strained, which I was betting had a whole lot to do with whatever my daddy had told him back at the house.

I'd warned my father not to say a word. Told him I was grown, and I could make my own decisions and that I got to make my own mistakes, too.

The fact he obviously hadn't listened had made me angry, but I'd decided to hold back, figuring it was better to let them get out whatever the two of them needed to say to the other, anyway.

Jace had my hand clasped in his, held between us and up close to his chest, watching me with concern where he stood a few inches from me. That space between us felt just as heavy as the night.

I swallowed hard. "I'm fine."

"Are you sure about that?" A tease glinted in those copper eyes.

Getting away from the house had seemed to lighten Jace. Something easy gliding into his demeanor the farther we'd gotten away from Broadshire Rim. Maybe, to him, it'd felt as if we'd been leaving the threat behind.

To me, it was as if I were getting the chance to put some distance between all the grief and hurt.

I huffed out the semblance of a laugh. "Um . . . no, Jace, I am definitely not sure that I'm fine. But I'm tryin' to be."

Warily, I looked around us. Strangers whizzed by, this area so far away from the outskirts where I lived that there wasn't a soul that I knew. No one to look at me with pity or disdain or questions.

Oh, but inside, there would be plenty.

He squeezed my hand. "Fun."

My head shook, and I could feel the smile trying to climb to my mouth. "Fun. Tons of it."

The words were nothing but a mockery of the way I really felt.

"I'm serious. Tonight, you're having fun. Letting go for a little while. First on the list is getting you inside to get you a drink."

"I think I need about ten of them."

His laughter boomed, bouncing against my thrumming chest, and I decided right then, that I was.

I was going to let go for a little while.

Rest in his security.

Even if it would be short-lived.

"Don't tell me I'm going to have to carry you out of here over my shoulder before the night is over," he teased.

Swept up in the lightness, I knocked into him as he led me through the door. "It wouldn't be the first time, would it."

I peeked over at him. Wondering if he remembered all the things we'd shared. How we'd once been. The way he'd made me feel.

And I was wondering how it was possible he still made me feel all of it.

I beat back the guilt that rippled inside me. What threatened to rise up and take me under.

*Not tonight.*

Tonight, I was just gonna breathe. Let him hold some of the burden that constantly weighed down on my shoulders.

He leaned in, his mouth suddenly at my ear. "Do you remember that night?"

A flush raced my skin, hot and heated and so very wrong, but I was whispering back anyway, "I remember everything. Do you?"

Oh, I was a fool, inviting him into those memories.

Memories that spun and danced and enticed.

He set his hand on the small of my back, and a tremor rolled up my spine and spread out, his words sending goose bumps racing across my skin.

"Do you think I could ever forget a single moment with you? Not ever. Not for a second. You were the only good thing I ever had."

My heart tumbled right in the center of my chest.

For a beat, his eyes flashed beneath the glittering lights so severely I was pretty sure he could see all the thoughts inside my head.

Loving him.

Needing him.

Adoring him.

Then he straightened, situated the button on his suit, and guided me inside.

We stepped deeper into the trendy bar. Inside, the walls were dark, the wood aged, and the brick roughened. Lights dull and hazy.

The bottom floor was a big, open space, and a long bar stretched the length of the back wall.

The three levels upstairs boasted smaller spaces, specialty bars and secluded rooms filled with leather furniture, coves for conversations, and private rooms for intimate parties.

Nooks everywhere, making a person believe they could get lost and forget the rest of the world existed outside of the secreted walls.

I couldn't help but think how nice that might be.

Jace scanned the massive room, looking for the group within the people moving on the dance floor and packed close to the stage, a band called Carolina George clearly drawing a huge crowd.

Or maybe it was just the atmosphere.

Darkness cut by the flashing lights.

The air heated, dripping with sex.

Almost suffocating.

Or maybe it was just that the only thing I could feel was this man. Every step he took reverberated against the floorboards.

Splintering out, becoming mine.

The energy overwhelming.

Too much.

Making me feel flushed and overheated and a little dizzy.

Jace squeezed my hand a little tighter.

Giving me calm.

Strength.

"Ah, there he is. The party can begin," Ian called when he

caught sight of us making our way through the packed crowd, a glassfull of something dark like a beacon lifted in the air. "Or are you actually here to tell us to watch out for ourselves?"

There was a gleam in Ian's eye. A tease and something true.

Jace laughed, not removing his arm from around my waist when he reached out to shake his brother's hand. "What are you talking about? Parties are nothing but a bore without me."

"Sure, sure. This from the asshole who was always telling us what to do." Ian was all smiles as he looked at Mack for backup, pointed at Jace as if he were the brunt of the joke. Proof that he had been a downer when he'd always been the one protecting them.

My chest stretched tight when I was struck with that truth. He had. He'd worried so much about them all. And then he'd just . . . walked away. I still couldn't make sense of it.

"Ah, I guess he can be fun once in a while," Mack said with a wink. He stood from the round table where he was sitting to shake Jace's hand.

Then he turned to me, edging Jace out, and hugging me tight. "So glad you're here tonight."

He really was a good guy. Worked hard at his job. But I knew what happened to Joseph had struck close to home for him. That the case haunted him in a way that I was sure kept him up at night.

"It's your birthday. I wouldn't have missed it," I said.

He edged back, looking me in the eye. "You're a good girl, Faith."

"Ha, that's just what she wants you to think."

My attention jerked to the side to Courtney, who'd broken through the crowd, Felix wrapped all around her from behind, his face pressed into her hair.

"Just because I'm standing next to you, it doesn't mean I'm reflecting who you are," I shot back.

Her mouth dropped open. "That hurt, Faith. Hurt bad."

But she was grinning the way she always did, and she stepped up to hug me. Then she grabbed me by the outside of both shoulders, looking me up and down.

"I told you to wear something sexy, I didn't tell you to come in here and completely show me up. You make every single person in this room look bad."

My chest heated, the warmth crawling my neck to land on my cheeks. "Courtney. You're ridiculous. Have you looked in the mirror today?"

"Have you?"

My head minutely shook.

She swung hers in Jace's direction. "Of course, it doesn't help that you're with him."

That blush became a full flush.

Clearly, she'd been pre-gaming, a buzz making her words come fast and unfiltered. But that didn't mean she wasn't completely right.

The man was something to look at. So dark and powerful and massive where he stood two feet off, watching me say hello to everyone.

The man delicious.

Decadent and dangerous in a way that was making my belly twist and my mouth water.

There I went, mind tumbling down that treacherous path. A path that led right to the man I'd promised I'd never allow to hurt me again.

I had to rip my attention away from Jace when Mack started introducing a bunch of his friends from the station and some of his other friends. Everyone had taken up residency at a few of the round tables along the wall. Close to the stage, but far enough back that everyone could still relax.

I smiled, recognizing a few of them, wondering how many others had heard what I'd been through. If any of them were speculating. Judging me for being there.

But I couldn't contemplate that.

Not when Jace was suddenly back at my side, his arm firmly planted around my waist, his voice nothing but a growl in my ear. "Stay close."

To him?

It'd always been impossible to be anywhere else.

# twenty-six

## Jace

*A* couple of hours had passed since we'd first arrived. The club had gotten busier, packed wall to wall, droves of people crowding into the enormous space.

Carolina George had just finished playing an incredible set.

The country band was well-known in the area, traveling from Southern city to Southern city to play in dive bars and huge venues alike, their following growing greater.

People flocked all the way from neighboring states to get a chance to listen to the angelic voice of Emily, their lead singer, whose talent was out of this world.

When they had ended their set for the night, a DJ had taken over. Dance music pumped from the speakers, a low resonating bass, the vibe shifting into something seductive and dark.

I'd been surprised when Courtney had managed to lure Faith onto the throbbing dance floor.

But there she was, out there in a circle with Courtney and some of their other friends.

Having fun.

Just like I'd promised her.

I leaned against the wall, watching her. Satisfaction buzzed through my being, another part of me itching because she was more than an arm's length away.

But, God, I loved seeing her this way. Removed from the sorrow and the grief and the trauma. Removed from the need to constantly watch over her shoulder.

I was doing my best to focus on that and not on the way that she was moving.

This sexy, slow rhythm as she danced. Hips jerking and swaying. The movement of her body casting some sort of spell.

I wondered if the girl had any idea how captivating she was. How every asshole in the place was watching her, wondering if he had any chance of taking her home.

Like I was any better.

The only thing I could think about right then was edging up behind her and claiming her as my own.

Wrapping my arms around that slender waist from behind, tucking her ass close, my nose at her neck as we moved.

A hand clapped down on my shoulder. I jumped about ten feet in the air.

Ian smirked, voice wry. "Jumpy."

My eyes narrowed. "Not like we haven't been dealing with some scary shit."

That was right when Mack broke away from the group of detectives he was chatting with, their laughter loud, their mood rowdy.

Grinning wide, the guy sauntered our way, nothing but muscles and tattoos.

All night, he'd been throwing back shots like they were water.

Celebrating hard.

The same way he did everything.

Ian lifted his glass as he approached. "To Mack, the biggest, burliest, oldest motherfucker I know. Happy birthday, man."

"Eat rocks, asshole. You mean the baddest motherfucker you know." Mack lifted his thick arms out to the sides, his beer sloshing over the rim.

"Ah, pretty sure he meant oldest, my friend," I said, unable to stop the grin from riding my mouth. "But since it's your birthday, I'll let you go on believing that," I continued with the raise of my glass. "You know, since you're going senile and all."

"You just wish you could be me with all my wisdom." His blue eyes gleamed, a chuckle on his lips. "And I thought we'd already established not to go knocking the years, considering you're right behind me."

He was right. The years went by faster than we expected. On instinct, my gaze moved back to where Faith was dancing with her friends.

Courtney grabbed Faith's hand, moving with her, the two of them free and completely letting go.

Swore I got lost in it, in the years separating us. Through all the experiences we'd each had. I had to wonder if even a single one of them mattered to me without her.

I was jarred out of the trance by Ian's hard chuckle. "You going soft on me now, brother?"

My attention whipped back to him. "Never."

"You sure about that?"

He took a pull of his whiskey, his attention trained on Faith, who tilted her head toward the ceiling and . . .

Laughed.

She fucking laughed.

My heart twisted in my chest, beating wild at the sight.

Ian pointed at her with the hand he had clutched around his glass. "She's always made you that way."

"And what way is that?"

"A believer."

"And why do you make it sound like that's a bad thing?"

"It is if it makes you do stupid things."

Everything clenched. She had. That belief making me both strong and weak. But Ian was wrong to think any of the choices I'd made had been Faith's fault. The choices I'd made were on me. Were on Joseph.

Mack sobered. "How's she holding up?"

"She's the strongest person I know."

A sigh pilfered from his mouth. "I hate this, man. Having no leads. These assholes keep getting in and out without leaving a trace. Right under our fucking noses."

Mack gave a harsh shake of his head. "The call we got on that office downtown last weekend yielded nothing. The only thing I could take from it was they were looking for something specific and came up empty-handed, and that did not make them happy. Entire place was trashed. But that's where the clues ended. This is no hack job. Whoever is behind this knows what they're doing."

Unease rustled through my consciousness. "But we already knew that, didn't we, that these assholes know what they're doing? Joseph couldn't have been involved in this for as long as he had without his dumb ass getting caught."

"We assumed it, yeah, but how the fuck can I prove it when every name we have runs dry? It's driving me crazy."

Pointedly, he swung his gaze to me. "You tell her yet?"

Dread clotted the blood sloshing through my veins. Cold ice sliding down my spine, freezing everything, because I knew what confessing everything would do. "Just can't stand for her to go through any more," I told him.

And I knew this was going to gut her.

"You can't protect her from everything."

"Can't I?" I tossed back out, my eyes narrowed as I watched her, those legs so damned long and that body so damned tempting.

I wanted to cross the room and take her in my arms.

Pull her against my chest.

Put my hands and my mouth all over her body.

Let every asshole in the room who was salivating over her know she was mine.

Seemed it was me who she needed protection from. Knowing I was going to shatter that all over again was torture.

And still, I couldn't slough the determination I could feel like a steel lining beneath my skin.

Mack released a low rumble of amusement. "For someone who was just coming here for a short time to make sure she was safe, make a little amends for the guilt you've been wearing, you sure seem to have your foot firmly planted in the door."

*Soft*, Ian mouthed again.

I shot him a glare. "Such an asshole."

He quirked a brow. "You say that as if it might offend me."

He said it like a joke, but there was no missing the truth behind it.

A low chuckle rumbled from him, and he leaned back against the wall where I was standing.

"Seriously, Jace . . . you're slipping. I can feel it," Mack cut in, drawing attention back to the situation.

"Nothing's changed. I'm here for one reason, and one reason only," I gritted, refusing the hope that threatened to climb into my spirit. The love that wanted to grow. God knew, that love was dangerous for us both.

I needed to remain focused.

Focused when I could feel myself losing sight.

Falling deeper and deeper. Buried in the bliss of being with the two of them, refusing the torment of knowing I could never keep them.

Ian's laughter was dry. "One reason? You think I can't see all kinds of *reasons* playing out in your eyes? Pretty sure most of those *reasons* include the two of you naked."

"Watch it, little brother." There was a chuckle in my threat.

He laughed. "Wasn't it you who always said no bullshit between us? Not about to start now."

"Told you already, I'm here for one reason. That's to be here, protect them, until this bullshit is behind them. I owe them that."

Ian scoffed. "You don't *owe* anyone anything, Jace. No matter how much you try to convince yourself this was your fault, it wasn't. Joseph did this. Not you."

"I owe them everything." Didn't mean for the bolt of fury to line the words.

A smirk grew on his face. "Nah, man, this isn't a question of owing. It's a question of owning. Because that girl *owns* you. You need to be careful with that. When people like us love someone, we lose, remember? And I'm pretty sure what you experienced the first time around was a shut out."

Those were the words I'd drilled into Ian's head over and over as a kid.

*"No one gives a shit about us. No one cares about us or loves us. All of that is bullshit. It's just us—me, you, and Joseph against the world. Don't ever forget that, Ian. Never. We fight for what we want, for what we need to survive, any way we have to. As soon as we let our guard down, love someone? That's when people like us lose. Do you understand what I'm telling you?"*

"Maybe I was wrong," I told him.

Ian blinked at me like he didn't recognize me. "I don't get it, why you feel obligated. Why you're willing to sacrifice everything for that girl. But what I do know is you never forgot her. You changed after you lost her, and the only thing I want is for you to get some of that joy back."

His brow pinched in emphasis. "But if you go after it? After her? Make sure you're doing it for the right reason. Not because you fucking feel guilty or you're trying to make amends for what Joseph did. You always taught me to look out for myself and no one else. But that girl right there? She's the only one who ever made you think changing that belief might be worth it."

I watched Faith across the space. Her grace filling the air. So pure and goddamn sweet. I swallowed the lump in my throat and chased it with a gulp of scotch. "Not a question of *might.*"

Ian cracked a grin. "Then I'd say it's time to go after what you want. It's what we do. We fight for what we want. You walked away once. Don't make the mistake of doing it again."

Shock moved through me. "I thought you didn't like her?"

Ian gave a somber shake of his head. "I didn't not like her, Jace. I was terrified of her. Of what she might mean to you. That I might lose you because of it. It made me make my own stupid choices. I'll regret that for the rest of my life. I'm not any good, Jace. You and I both know it. But the last thing I want to do is stand in the way of your happiness for any longer."

"You're wrong, Ian. You are good."

His head shook and he choked out a laugh, clearly diverting the direction our conversation had gone. He pointed at Faith. "So, what are you waiting for, brother?"

Mack huffed. "That's a bad fucking idea, Ian, and you know

it." He shifted his attention to me. "Your judgment is clouded. You're going to fuck everything up. All the progress we've made."

Wasn't sure I'd call it *progress* when they had nothing. Knew it wasn't Mack's fault, but I was close to going out of my mind.

"You've got to nail this fucker, Mack," I suddenly said, words gravel. I drained my drink. "Or I will."

"Don't be stupid, Jace. You're only here as a lookout. Nothing else. You got me?"

I cut him a glare. The only thing I *got* was I'd do anything for Faith. Anything for Bailey.

Mack exhaled, a strained push of his lungs. "Fuck, man. You're getting in too deep. It's written all over you. It was clear that day when you dragged all our asses out there to work on her house. Not that I minded, but all of us know why you're doing it. I never should have said a thing."

If I was too deep, then I'd gladly drown.

"What do you say we drop this for now, yeah?" Ian said, taking a swill and looking around the room. "This is supposed to be a party. Don't you think Joseph has ruined enough?"

"Fine by me . . . so long as your brother here remembers his place." Mack's eyes glinted with the warning.

Ian slung his arm around my shoulders. "Oh, Jace here totally knows his place . . . or at least where he wants to put it."

It was pure innuendo. The prick actually sent me a wink.

He was lucky I loved him so much or I'd take him out back and teach him a lesson the way I used to.

Ian locked his elbow around my neck, giving it a tug. "Come on, let's celebrate. Mack only turns thirty once, and the night is wasting away. I'm done spending it in the corner."

Ian turned to face me as he started to back into the crowd. "I'm ready to find me a little fun."

I grunted.

Knew exactly what his form of fun was. I'd wasted away in the same shit for the last ten years.

He shrugged. "Suit yourself. I'll just go dance with your girl. She is the hottest thing out there tonight."

That grunt turned into a growl.

A grin filled up the punk's face. "That's what I thought."

He disappeared into the fray, and Mack cinched a hand down on my shoulder. "Not trying to be a dick, man. I just need your head clear."

I nodded, and he edged back, shaking his head like he didn't believe a thing I said, which was about right because I didn't believe it either.

I headed to the bar and ordered a water, hoping it'd give me a little time to cool down.

Time to sink back down to reality.

To focus on my mission and not the chaos that whirled through me. A tornado ripping everything apart.

Then I fucking panicked when I turned around and a shadow was moving in front of Faith.

Her friends were having way too much fun to even notice this huge asshole was backing her away from them, deeper into the throbbing mass, crowding over her as he encroached.

Rage beat a path through my veins, possession a life-beat inside me, drumming like a snare.

I pushed through the crush on the dance floor, not giving a fuck about the glares and grumbles I was getting.

I promised her I wouldn't let anything happen to her.

It sure as fuck wasn't going to happen here.

My jaw clenched as I finally made it to where he was leaning down, the fucker whispering something in her ear.

There was no missing the anxiety that rippled from her in a wave. Her uneasiness mine. I swallowed it, let it feed the frenzy that lashed inside me.

A gasp of relief wrenched free when I slid my arm around her waist. I wasn't sure if it was hers or mine.

"Hey, baby," I murmured loud enough for the asshole to hear. I jutted my chin out at him, uttered a cold, "What's up? I'm Jace . . . and you are?"

That's right.

*Leaving.*

A shot of air burst from his nose, like he didn't want to give up his play, the piece of shit leering at her in a way that had me close to coming unchained.

Chinks coming loose.

Rational mind completely lost.

"Back the fuck up," I gritted.

His dark gaze moved to me, anger in his stance. "What the fuck did you say to me?"

The guy was instantly in my face, reeking of booze, too much confidence for his own good.

He leered at Faith. "Seems to me she can make the decision for herself."

This from the dickhead who didn't even notice her cowering. Didn't notice her shake when he tried to move around me and get another step closer.

Panic surged through my body.

Hot and intense.

I flew in front of him and pushed him back. "Stay the fuck away from her."

He swung an arm, and I ducked back, barely missing his meaty fist. "Come on, asshole," he taunted. "You want a fight?"

I guessed I did.

Because rage spiraled through me.

A blackout.

Everything boiling.

Rising to the surface.

Everything too much.

I threw a fist. It cracked against his nose.

A few people scattered back, and I was going to go for him, ready to take the asshole down, beat all my aggression out on him, when someone was there, hauling me back.

Mack.

"He's not worth it, man. Not worth it. You're going to land your ass in jail if you throw another punch."

I looked up, catching Felix and some of the other guys watching, ready to jump in.

I blew out some of the frustration, shoulders sagging as I released some of the hostility.

The asshole I'd hit wiped the blood dripping from his nose

with the back of his hand, clearly wanting to come back for some more, giving it up when he saw everyone surrounding me.

He shrugged it off, spat, "Pussy."

Like I wasn't the one who'd just busted his nose.

I had half a mind to go after him.

Teach him a little respect.

The other half of me wasn't letting Faith get farther than a foot away from me again.

The second he disappeared, Mack released me. "Cool it," he warned low.

His badge had never been so distinct between us.

I was having a hard time acknowledging it.

He stood there for a few seconds, guarding me like I was the one who was looking for trouble, before he cut me a glance and sauntered away, shooting me another look of warning over his shoulder as he went.

Faith pressed against my side, relief sagging her shoulders as she leaned her sweet body into mine.

Fuck.

I wanted to hold on forever.

Never let go.

"Are you okay? What did that asshole say to you?" I whispered at her ear, though my voice was elevated so she could hear me over the music.

She shook herself off. "I'm fine . . . it's fine. He just . . . asked me to dance. It was nothing. I freaked out for no reason at all. You didn't need to go punchin' him."

I turned her toward me. "Yeah, I did. Things aren't going to end well for anyone who gets near you."

"I think you might be taking it a step too far."

"I'm not taking it far enough."

That asshole was still out there. Unknown. Lurking.

I fisted my hand that still stung from the crack. Hell, that asshole could have just as easily been him as anyone else.

"I don't want you gettin' into trouble because of me. Gettin' hurt because of me."

"You don't get it yet, Faith, that I'll do anything to protect you."

She looked at me like she still didn't get it.

I leaned in closer to her. "Get used to it."

A shiver rushed through her, and her eyes darkened, her voice going deep. "Well, I guess I do have to thank you for savin' me. You seem to be doing a lot of that lately."

Fuck.

She was killing me.

Looking this way. So fucking sexy. So fucking good.

We got stuck there. Both of us entranced by the other.

In sudden discomfort, she took a fumbled step back to put some space between us. "I need to use the restroom."

"I'm coming with you."

She shook her head. "That's not necessary."

I erased the space between us, murmuring at her ear. "Yes, Faith, it is."

I followed her to the restroom door, and I hesitated. She looked back at me, something close to a smile on her face. "I'm fine. I'll be right inside."

Unease rustled through my senses. "Scream if you need me."

Soft laughter filtered from between her lips, but her eyes . . . they were serious. So soft. Her voice softer. "Beast."

Everything clutched as I watched her push the door the rest of the way open and walk inside, giving me a full view of the back of her dress, those heels driving me right out of my mind.

I stood at the door, my chest heaving, ragged pants leaving my lungs as I contemplated barging in there anyway.

Drag her out. Pull her into one of those dark alcoves. Kiss her senseless.

*Senseless.*

Just like she was making me.

I stumbled back when the door flew open.

Courtney was there, smirking up at me. "Jace Jacobs. Dance with me."

The vicious look on her face had my dick shriveling up.

Still, I quirked a brow, kept my tone as light as possible. "Right here?"

"Right here."

"You want to dance with me that bad?" It was a rigid tease.

She rolled her eyes. "Oh, give it up, playboy. You're hardly my type."

"Is that so?" I stepped forward, my hold light when I wrapped an arm around her waist.

"Um . . . yeah, so very so."

She barely rested her hands on my upper forearms as I pulled her two steps from the door and into the very back of the hall.

"You're really breaking me up here. Way to ruin a guy's ego."

"Oh, I'm sure you have plenty of that to last."

"Wow, you really are my biggest fan, aren't you?"

She eyed me, the playfulness diminishing, a flare of protectiveness coloring her expression. "You do realize that, if you hurt her, I will kill you."

I laughed.

I'd always liked this girl.

"I don't doubt that for a second."

"Good . . . because I'm not joking. Faith's been through enough."

My voice softened. "You think I don't know that?"

"Do you?" It was both a challenge and true question. Like she was standing there, wondering if I actually got it.

"I do."

The problem was, I was going to hurt Faith. In the end, I was going to hurt her all over again.

Not because I wanted to.

But because what was done was done, and I couldn't take it back, no matter how much I wished I could.

A puff of relief left her, like she'd heard my sincerity. "Good. It'd be a shame to have to maim you. You're way too pretty for that."

She wouldn't have to worry about that. I'd be destroyed at the end of this, anyway.

My voice turned serious. "I'm here to help her. Protect her. That's it."

Disbelief had her eyebrows rising to her hairline. "That's it?

Because that sure isn't how you've been looking at her."

"And how have I been looking at her?"

A huff of sarcasm left her tongue. "Oh, come on, Jace. You think I didn't witness that pissin' contest out on the dance floor? Throwing a punch over someone just lookin' at her? You might as well have whipped it out and taken her right there on the floor. Or maybe the bar would have done just fine for what you had in mind."

Lust curled, and my teeth clenched. Didn't she get I was trying to keep control and losing it? I sure didn't need those kinds of visions planted in my mind.

She grinned and then patted my chest. "Mm-hmm . . . that, right there? That's exactly how you've been looking at her. You act on it? Then you'd better plan to stay. Because Faith is the exact same girl you left that day. Kind and pure and gentle, and she doesn't need any of your games. You say you're here to protect her? Then protect her heart, Jace, because that's what is really at risk."

I flinched. That's where she had it all wrong. "The threat is serious."

Her brow pinched. "You think I don't know that? But at the end of the day, Faith's heart is what's on the line. What's always been. Neither you nor Joseph fully appreciated that."

"I never wanted to hurt her."

Courtney stepped back, expression knowing. "Then prove it."

She turned around like she hadn't said anything, leaving me there staring at her as she melted back into the crowd.

Heat raced my arm when a hand squeezed my forearm. I whipped my attention that way. "Faith."

"Tell me she wasn't botherin' you. I swear . . . she puts her nose in all the places it doesn't belong."

I grinned at her, shaking off the unease. "I think I can handle it."

"Well, I'm glad you can, because I sure can't." She was grinning, too.

"She is *your* best friend."

A giggle slipped from her mouth. Fuck. I loved the sound of

that. It seemed impossible that she could, that there would be any joy left. It only proved the type of person Faith really was.

"She's a handful. But she'd do anything for me."

"I'm glad you have her."

"So am I. Not sure I would have made it without her."

My voice softened. "Faith—"

She held up her hand, stepped closer, hitched my goddamned breath when she slid her hand up my chest and set it over the thunder of my heart.

"Shh . . . tonight's the best night I've had in as long as I remember. Let's not ruin it."

Like a fool, I took a step toward her, nearly erasing all the space between us.

I dipped down, whispering at the shell of her ear, "Told you that you were going to have all kinds of fun."

*Fun*, she mouthed back with a subtle swish of her hips.

Good God.

Ruined.

Completely ruined.

Blood pumping hard, rushing straight to my dick. Straining and begging.

My hand moved to her hip, the other moving high up on her slender waist.

It was instant.

The way tension climbed to the air.

"Jace," she whispered, staring up at me in that way I recognized from so long ago. In the way that'd made me feel as if I were different.

Better.

A believer, just like Ian had said.

"Faith," I murmured back, unable to stop myself from pulling her closer.

Which was so goddamned reckless.

She'd had more than a few drinks.

Clearly, her inhibitions were down, the armor she wore loosed, her body lax.

I should get her home, tuck her in bed, leave her there to sleep it off.

But I'd promised her a good time, and I didn't want my dwindling resolve to ruin that. I had to steel myself.

Get control so I could . . .

She leaned into me.

Sparks. That energy that was always alive a strike in the bare space between us.

My guts twisted into a thousand knots, and I swore I could feel the resolve I was just trying to fortify splinter under the pressure.

Chocolate eyes stared up at me. The strain stripped away and something else in its place.

Something so mesmerizing and enthralling.

*Magic.*

The girl had always invoked the impossible, but there was nothing dark about it.

Bright, bright light.

Goodness and grace.

I felt drunk on it. Drunk on this girl who clutched my upper arms.

Heat binding. Wrapping and enveloping.

I pulled her flush, her sweet body tucked against mine where we stood tucked alone at the end of the hall.

A whimper left her full lips, and those chocolate eyes flared.

Shit. Shit. Shit.

This was so bad.

I was in deep. Deeper and deeper.

Losing myself.

But the problem was, I'd been lost for years.

And with her in my arms? The only thing I could think was that I'd been found.

Rescued.

Which was so goddamned stupid.

Clearing my throat, I inched back, hating that I had to put a damper on the night.

But my need had risen to dangerous levels.

"Come on, I should get you home."

Faith all but stumbled forward at the loss of contact. Dropping her gaze, she shifted in discomfort and tucked an errant strand of hair behind her ear. "Yeah. That's probably a good idea."

I set my hand on the small of her back. Bad idea, too. Seemed there was nothing I could do that didn't spark the need that strained and pulled inside me.

We wound back down the hall and into the crowd, and from the corner of my eye, I glimpsed Ian with some chick pinned against the wall.

His attention flicked my way for a beat, his expression devoid of anything but a desperate hunger.

Like he'd consume everything and anything in his path.

Burn it all away for the sake of a second's pleasure.

I hated it for him.

Wanted more for him.

Wanted more for me.

Wanted her.

Fuck.

I wanted her.

Wanted her so desperately, I could feel that tacked on restraint coming unglued. Pulling up at the edges. All the reasons I couldn't do this failing to matter any longer.

I rushed her out of the bar, through the throng of people crushed in the space. Didn't even take the time to say our goodbyes.

I had to get out of there before I lost my mind.

I gave the valet my slip then wanted to lash out like some kind of deranged lunatic when the kid eyed my girl like he was imagining licking her up and down.

My car pulled to the curb, and I quickly helped Faith inside, trying not to watch the way those long legs slipped into the darkness of the car.

Trying to ignore the way I was dying to run my hand up the silky flesh, beneath the hem of that skirt to find what I knew would be burning underneath.

Sweat beaded on my brow, muscles clenched in restraint.

I ran around the front, tipped the kid—who I still really wanted to deck—and hopped inside.

I really was losing it.

I hit the road and cranked up the air, needing to cut the heat out of the space.

But it only radiated and grew and compounded.

I took the city streets.

Lights blinked down over us, flashes of darkness, streaks of hazy light.

I took the corners harder than I probably needed to, trying to beat my frustration out on the road.

But nothing worked.

Faith's breaths filled the car, and I couldn't help from peeking over that way.

She was in the seat, shifting uncomfortably, squeezing her thighs together like she didn't know what to do with herself any more than I did.

She pushed her back against the door. Searching for a way to put space between us.

It was almost sadness that filled her tone, all wrapped up in a needy vibration. "Why have you always made me feel this way?"

"Shit," I cursed at no one but myself.

I blinked hard, should have kept my mouth shut but couldn't stop the confession from bleeding from my tongue. "And you somehow think you don't affect me? That I'm not dying right now?"

She squeezed her eyes closed, her hands pressed to her heart, words coming free that I was pretty sure she was going to regret tomorrow. "You killed me, Jace. Shattered me. I didn't think I'd survive when you left. It hurt so bad. It all hurt so bad."

She slurred a bit, the alcohol dulling her defenses.

The only buzz I had was her.

She vibrated my bones.

Shivered through my senses.

Once I got out of the city, I took a left down the main road of our small town. We raced through the quiet hum.

"It killed me, too," I finally admitted.

She choked over a sob. "Why? Then why did you leave me if you didn't want to go?"

Pain compressed my entire being. "I had to. I'm sorry, but I had to. You deserved so much better than me."

Tears lined her face as she stared over at me. "You were the only one of us who believed that."

"Faith," I murmured, rubbing the back of my hand over my lips. A reminder to keep them shut. That there were things that would hurt her so much worse than my walking away had.

I made the last right onto the bumpy dirt road that followed along the stream at the back of town and then a left onto the tree-lined path.

Moonlight streaked through, shining down to illuminate the girl who continued to watch me from the seat.

Silver streaks on her cheeks.

Hate and love in her eyes.

I came to a stop, feeling so fucking wrecked, wondering how we'd gone from *fun* to our hearts bleeding all over my leather seats in a second flat.

But that was what I got for dipping my toes into dangerous waters.

I'd waded in until I was swallowed.

And I just kept going deeper.

Deeper and deeper and deeper.

Got the unsettled feeling I'd never again be able to break the surface.

Hopping out of my car, I scanned the area, making sure it was clear before I rounded the front. Opening her door, I took her hand and helped her down.

She sagged into me.

Vanilla and rose.

Delicate purple petals.

I wanted to bathe in them, too.

Our feet crunched on the pebbles, her heels sinking in, her weight against my side.

She leaned away a bit when we got to the porch steps.

This part of the porch was complete thanks to the crew that had worked through the week, this gorgeous place sitting in the darkness, a shadow of what we'd wanted.

Of all I'd lost.

I was the fool who tortured myself with the barest taste of it. Taunting myself with what it might have been like.

*She is worth it. She is worth it. She has always been worth it.*

I fumbled through the locks while Faith waited two steps behind me. Her breaths heaved. Held in the humid night air.

A gust of relief hit me when I finally had the door open. Needing reprieve. To get away.

Because I could feel myself tipping.

Sliding.

Stumbling at the edge.

I started to walk inside but froze in my tracks when I heard the ragged word that came from behind.

"Jace."

Prickles lifted at my nape, and I knew I should ignore it. Ignore her and her plea, go up to my room, and lock the door.

But she'd always made me weak.

Slowly, I turned around. Faith was right there, staring at me.

So goddamned gorgeous she was the only thing I could see.

Inciting the energy that whipped and churned.

It lashed at my skin. Lashed at my spirit.

It pressed and pulsed. The connection we'd always shared pulled taut. Her fingertips stroked the glowing flesh of her exposed chest, right between her breasts.

That was it.

I snapped.

Erased the space and had her spun around and pinned to the exterior wall in a second flat.

It was as if my whole damn soul moaned in relief.

My hands burrowed in the twist of her hair, and my mouth took over for my brain.

It wasn't gentle. This brutal kiss was a demand.

My tongue plundering. Ransacking. Searching for what had been mine.

Right in the exact same spot where we'd always found ourselves all those years ago.

Delicate hands clutched at me, nails digging into my skin.

Hate. Hurt. Love. Desperation.

They swelled and crashed, her emotions overpowering. Filling me. Invading me.

"Beauty," I muttered at her mouth, pressing against her body, needing more.

Needing everything.

I rocked against her.

Heat blazed.

She whimpered. "Jace. Jace. Why?"

I could feel it shattering. The flimsy understanding we'd made. It'd been nothing but a fool's game from the start.

My hands slid over her body.

Cupping her curves.

Memorizing.

Remembering.

I cinched down on her narrow waist and pressed my aching cock to her belly. Dying to be inside her. To take her and love her and promise I'd never let her go.

Fuck. What was I doing?

I searched for strength. To remember why I was here. What I was going to *ruin* if I gave in.

I forced myself away, my breaths ragged where I panted them into the inch of space between us.

Hers were choppy, hiccupped cries that filled the night.

I stumbled back a step, and she stared at me in shock.

That was right before she clapped her hand over her mouth and released a horrified sob.

"Faith." I reached for her.

Squeezing her eyes closed, she backed away. "Please, don't touch me."

I roughed a frustrated hand through my hair.

*I knew better. I knew better.*

"I'm so damned sorry."

She shook her head, cutting me off before she turned and fled up the stairs.

# twenty-seven

## Jace
## Eighteen Years Old

*S*weat dripped like a leaky faucet down Jace's back, his shirt drenched from the adrenaline that pumped overtime, shame oozing from his pores.

Steven yanked on the straps of Jace's backpack, jerking Jace forward, their noses close to touching.

The stench of greed and corruption filled Jace's nostrils.

"See, that wasn't so hard, was it?" Steven said, his voice hard, words a threat. "You pick it up here. You take it across town and let me know when it's delivered. Nothin' to it."

Disgust twisted up Jace's face, the weight of what Steven had just placed in his backpack feeling like a million pounds.

Or maybe the fucking world.

"Hard? We all know you take the easy way out. You don't give a shit about anything but money and the fastest way to get it."

Jace should have kept his mouth shut. But he couldn't stop it. Couldn't stop the spill of hatred from his tongue.

Steven cracked a menacing grin. "Didn't your mama ever tell you to work smarter, not harder. Although, I have to admit, I don't mind working her over nice and hard."

Nausea swirled in Jace's stomach, and he knew the piece of shit was baiting him. "You think I give a shit about her?"

A cool, wicked arrogance seeped from Steven. "No. I don't. We all know what's important to you. Who is. You wouldn't want your poor little brother to have to pay for your mistakes now, would you?"

Jace gulped around the bile that climbed this throat. He had to physically will himself not to throw up on Steven's shiny fucking shoes. Showing weakness was not going to win him any points.

And Steven had already found his.

*Ian and Joseph. Ian and Joseph.*

Steven grinned as if he'd watched their faces play out like a plea in his eyes. He clapped Jace on the shoulder. "That's what I thought. Now go make that delivery, like a good little boy."

# twenty-eight

## Faith

My hands were tremblin' out of control as I fumbled with the coffee pot. I was both exhausted and wired, my chest achy with this heavy feelin' I couldn't shake no matter how hard I tried.

I hadn't slept for a second last night. Tossin' and turnin'. Listening for any sounds coming from Jace's room.

Last night, when I heard him finally come upstairs after about two hours had passed, part of me had willed him to come to me. To knock at my door. To come inside.

To hold me and make every question and hurt go away.

The other part was nothing but terrified that he would.

Guilt had consumed my senses. Saturating every cell. Makin' me feel like a horrible, horrible person for letting that kiss happen.

Begged for it, really.

Desperate for the man to make me feel the way he once had.

Nerves had gripped me when his footsteps had thudded up the stairs.

They'd grown wild when I'd heard the squeak of them outside

my bedroom door.

I had felt the blister of his torment radiating through the walls, rushing across the floor, slamming into me.

I had no idea how long he'd been out there before I'd heard him retreat, his footsteps quieted but heavy as he'd closed himself inside his room.

Now, the shaking in my hands took to my entire being when I heard him rambling around upstairs, the groan of the stairs, the worry in his approach.

His presence pummeled me from behind.

Potent and powerful and raw.

Energy crawled the walls and scraped across my flesh.

He stopped just inside the doorway, his heavy breaths taking to the air, filling the space with everything that was him.

The man bigger than the sun.

Hesitation brimmed, uneasiness a force that ricocheted between us.

"Faith," he finally grated. I could hear it. The plea in the word that begged me to turn around. To look at him.

A shiver raced my spine, and I pressed my palms flat to the counter, gathering myself the best I could before I slowly spun around to face him.

The breath left me on a rasp.

The man stood there wearing nothing but a pair of thin sleep pants, his chest bare and his shoulders wide, his chiseled abdomen rippling with all the strength his spirit possessed.

But it was what had still been obscured last weekend when I'd seen him without his shirt that punched me in the gut.

A tattoo peeked out from the band of his pajama bottoms.

The word had been missin' when he'd gone away. When he left me all those years ago.

*Faith.*

It was written in a bed of roses, all black and shadows and curly letters.

He cringed when he realized what I'd noticed. He roughed one of those big hands anxiously through his hair, his voice gruff when it hit the atmosphere. "I told you, Faith."

Terrified, I drew my gaze up his body, afraid of what I was gonna find there. Desperate to see it at the exact same time.

His jaw clenched, the confession jagged. *"It killed me to walk away from you."*

"You took my heart when you left," I whispered.

He took a slow step forward, his confession cracking in the air. "And I left mine with you."

Oh God. This was torture, but I should have known it was comin'. That we couldn't ignore this forever.

Courtney was right.

We'd left so much unfinished between us, everything I'd held for him tucked way down deep in that spot that would always belong to him.

Ignoring its existence when it'd been there all along.

The acknowledgement of it only made the guilt come crashing over me. Welling up from my spirit and spilling over. I clutched my hands over my drumming heart. "Joseph was there for me."

Why'd it come out sounding like a defense?

And why'd it hurt so bad to see the hurt and guilt strike on Jace's face when I said it?

"I loved him, Jace. I really did."

Slowly, he nodded, though somehow it looked as if he might be sick right there on my floor.

Or maybe he was restraining himself from flying around and putting his fist through the wall with the way his muscles jumped and ticked as he curled his hands.

"I know," he said, voice hoarse.

"But it was different." I wanted to reel it back in, stop the flow of words that just kept coming. I didn't know how to stop them. If I was wrong for speaking them or right for admitting the truth.

He took another step farther into the kitchen.

The ground shook beneath my feet.

Fear and questions started to ramble from my mouth. "I . . . I just don't know how to move on from there. From promising all of my life to him."

Would I be a fool for moving on in Jace's direction? More than that, would it be a betrayal to Joseph?

An echo of Joseph's voice stroked through my mind. He'd come home in the middle of the night a few years ago, and his voice had been slurred and his breath pungent with alcohol.

*"I want to erase him from you. Make you forget he ever existed. Tell me you don't still love him."*

I wondered if he'd heard my answer in my silence.

If he'd hate me for bringing Jace into our home. Into our lives.

But I didn't have to step that direction because Jace was already moving my way. Making the decision for me. Predatory in his stance, possession in each measured stride.

Trembles raced through my body when he reached out and let his fingertips flutter down the side of my cheek. His touch soft and those coppery eyes fierce. "I only want to take care of you. Let me."

There was so much to his demand. So much more than protecting us. So much more than fixing this house.

"I don't know if I'm ready for this, Jace. If I'm ever gonna be."

The problem was that my heart was already racing for him. Screaming out from the confines of my chest that I'd always belonged to the man in front of me.

"I'll take whatever you can give." Stark vulnerability oozed out from between his ferocity, the man a live wire waiting to go off.

He was right there, towering over me, filling my head with the scent of cloves and expensive leather.

Fillin' my belly with lust.

"I'm terrified of you hurtin' me all over again," I whispered. "I can't take any more."

Flinching, his eyes dropped closed. "I don't want to hurt you, Faith. Never. I never wanted to. I'd give anything to stop that from happening again."

With the grief that struck through his expression, I wondered if it was inevitable, him leaving me again.

His throat worked hard, his fingers trembling on my face.

His tongue darted out to wet his lips.

The man wavered.

Gathering what to say.

"If you knew every terrible thing I've done in my life, Faith, every mistake I've ever made, could you forgive me?"

Confusion crashed through my heart and mind, his question nothing but misery on my soul.

What was he asking me? To forgive him for walking away that day? My spirit clutched with the pain of it, the devastation I'd felt when he'd left.

But it felt like something more than that, and I couldn't help but wonder what he'd done to achieve what he had. The place where he drove a luxury car and wore ridiculously expensive suits.

Had he hurt people along the way?

A shudder rocked through me, and I wanted to reach inside of him, search deep for the boy I'd once known.

That angel-boy in pauper's clothes.

My gaze swept him, head to toe.

The man so beautiful. So potent and raw and bristling with a goodness that I wondered if he could even see.

No.

I didn't believe it.

He wouldn't hurt someone to win.

And Jace . . . he'd become so much more than I'd ever imagined.

More than the things he'd had to do to survive growing up, the lying and the stealing to put food in Ian and Joseph's mouths.

"I told you I saw great things in you. Look who you've become. I told you, you would. If you wanted it badly enough. Is that what it took? You walking away from me to realize who you could be?"

It was amazing how deep love could go. How big it could be. Because I realized right then, if that was what it had taken, I would have given him up.

Freely so *he* could be free.

If he'd just have told me. Warned me. Would it have hurt any less?

His body jerked, and his head swung to the side as his face pinched. As if he didn't want me to see everything written in his expression.

A harsh breath left his nose and he turned back to me. "I told you, it killed me, Faith."

"Then why?" I begged.

Did I really want the answer? Could I stand him tellin' me that I wasn't worth it?

His hands clutched down on the counter on either side of me, every part of him strained. His eyes pierced me to the spot. "I went to prison, Faith. That was why."

A gasp raked from my lungs and horror ripped through my consciousness. "What?"

Anguish blistered through my soul at the thought. For the boy I'd loved with all of me being shackled, shoved into a cell.

"Because . . . because we were here?" I fumbled to get out.

That night whipped through my mind.

*My stupidity. Jace wanting to give me everything. Me cracking open the window, gliding it up, giggling as we snuck inside.*

*The bedroom upstairs.*

*Our bodies twisted. Sweat on our skin.*

*The police waiting for us outside when we'd snuck back out.*

When Jace had shown at our spot the next day, I'd thought it was all right. That it was all gonna be okay. That we weren't in trouble, after all.

We were just stupid kids.

Chasing a dream.

Then he'd shattered my heart.

"How is it possible I didn't know?" I begged.

There was a part of me that was wishing he would tell me that he couldn't have stayed. That he'd left because he needed to find himself the same way I'd always believed.

Not that he'd been stolen away.

"It was the one thing I asked of Ian and Joseph. To spare you knowing." His teeth ground hard. "I didn't want to make you wait through that."

Instead, they'd let me believe he'd left me behind.

Anger swelled. At Joseph. At Ian. At Jace for putting them up to it. At myself for being too ignorant and naïve to understand there were true consequences to our actions.

"I would have waited," I whispered, hurt spreading fast.

His expression shifted.

So soft.

So soft.

The boy I'd loved.

His thumb brushed across my chin.

Back and forth.

Back and forth.

"I know you would have. And that was exactly the moment I finally accepted that you were so much better than that. That you deserved more than that life, more than what I could give you."

Something brittle filled his voice when he edged back to look at me. "I'd warned you, Faith. Warned you that I'd do anything to protect my family. To see them survive."

A frown stitched up my forehead, confusion winding through my spirit. "What does that mean?"

He blinked as if he were blinking away what he was going to say. "It doesn't matter. The only thing that matters is that I was protecting them. Protecting you. And that's what I'm going to do now. Whatever it takes."

"I—"

My response was cut off when I saw the emotion streak through his expression. The pain. The devotion. The love.

It sucked the oxygen from the room, replacing it with him.

Too big.

Too much.

I struggled through the tightness in my chest.

"I don't want to live in the past. Not anymore." His voice was sharp. Jagged and harsh.

My words were a wisp. "And I'm not sure how to move on from it."

"Kiss me and see." It was a growl, his mouth an inch from mine.

He was all around. His presence thick. Consuming in a way that only this boy could be. Trembling and shaking through me.

Like the first time I'd seen him.

Something that vibrated through the air that I could taste.

An omen.

A premonition.

My world about to change. For the better or worse, I couldn't be sure.

All I knew was this man stripped me bare. Peeling back the hurt to expose all the love that'd been left there.

My lips parted, and I inhaled, and God, I was such a fool.

Because I rocked, indecision cracking underneath his stare.

"Kiss me," he demanded again.

There was no resisting his command. My toes lifted as if he were controlling the action. Body and soul arching for him.

I set my mouth on his, our lips barely touching. The two of us just breathed in the splendor. The need and the fear.

I'd never loved anyone the way I'd loved him.

He was a fire that consumed. A strike in the night.

So wrong.

So right.

I tumbled through it, the emotion that knocked me from my feet.

Jace was right there to catch me. He grabbed me by the sides and hoisted me onto the counter. Then the man took over the fragile, tentative kiss.

With both hands cupping my face, he explored me tenderly. Passionately.

His lips soft and smooth, plush where they caught mine in soft, dizzying pulls. He nipped and pressed and sucked.

Tingles spread. Gliding across my skin.

He tucked me closer and wrapped my legs around his waist.

Heat flashed.

Fire.

Desire.

Everything I'd been missin' for so long.

Oh God, what was I doing? But there was no stopping it. The need that blistered through my flesh. The desperation to get closer. To get lost in this man.

I started rubbing shamelessly against him, the only thing separating us our pajamas.

Part of me wished they weren't there to keep us apart.

I needed him.

Oh, I needed him.

The love and the pleasure and the release.

Jace pulled me from the counter and started carrying me across the floor, murmuring between his frantic kiss, "I'm going to take care of you, Faith. I'm going to take care of you."

"Jace . . . I'm—"

*Scared.*

*Terrified.*

*Desperate.*

I couldn't make any of those words come from my mouth.

"I know, Faith. I know. *Slow.* Just . . . let me take care of you. Let me make you feel good."

A gasp jetted from my lungs when he sat me on the edge of the big, round dining table, the air rushing between us as he tore himself away. His stare potent as he looked down at me.

My palms were planted on the table, and my feet were barely hooked on the edge.

He set those big hands on my knees and began to slowly slide them up the insides of my legs.

Chills flashed.

My insides ached. A tingly madness that surged and danced.

"Beauty," he whispered.

Tenderly.

I almost shattered right there.

"Jace," I begged, my back arching. Reaching for him. Trying to breach the distance that had separated us for all the years.

But how could we cross it with everything littered in the middle?

And my mind screamed out that my heart and body might be moving too fast. But I didn't want to stop. Didn't want him to stop. That vacant space called out to be filled.

"Please," I whimpered.

Jace's teeth clamped down on his bottom lip. Oh God, he looked like a plunderer when his eyes raked over me that way. As if he were measuring all the ways he was gonna eat me alive.

Ransack and devour.

My belly trembled.

How was it possible I wanted him to?

I wondered if he could scent the desire on me when his nose dropped to the flesh of my inner thigh and he inhaled, gliding up as he fisted the edges of my sleep shorts in his hands.

Quivers racked through my body as he slowly peeled them down. Cool air blasted across my skin, all mixed up with the heat of his breath.

My legs lifted as he dragged them completely free, and a sharp hiss fell from between his lips.

"You are so fucking gorgeous."

His hands were back on my knees. Spreading me. I didn't think I'd ever been so exposed.

"You always made me feel that way . . . like I was beautiful."

Copper eyes glinted in the rays of the sun when they flashed to my face. "You were the only good thing I had in my life, Faith. You were the one who made me see it when the only thing I could see was the dark. My light in the dark. You made me believe in it. Beauty."

His confession pulled and pressed and weaved.

Healing a few more of those cracks in my broken heart.

"My beast. The most beautiful boy I've ever seen."

I let it slip out. My own confession that staked through my spirit. Letting go of a little of the reservations. Walls slipping. Letting him see. It didn't matter that it came with a streak of guilt painted like a scarlet *A* slashed across my chest.

*I never forgot you.*

*You always held a secret place inside me.*

*I've always, always loved you.*

I ached to say all those things aloud. But I couldn't make them form on my tongue.

Instead, I stared, my gaze tracing over the magnitude of him. His wide, wide shoulders and the strength in his ripped, carved abdomen.

Lust twisted low in my belly, a pool of desire that welled, overflowed as it slipped like liquid fire across my skin.

The boy I'd once known was all man.

A picture of sheer masculinity.

His fingertips brushed through my center. An illicit gasp wrenched from my throat and struck in the air as he touched me.

"So wet. So sweet," he murmured.

Those big fingers parted me and slowly slipped into the heated well of my body.

My walls clenched around the intrusion.

*It's been so long. So long.*

I wanted to feel all of him. Wanted him to take me and love me and promise me it would all be okay.

The realization of it brought a tremble of fear shaking through my body. The questions of how I'd allowed things to get this far between us when I had no idea what direction we were going.

The only thing I could feel was my heart tipping that way. Asking him to hold it. Carefully.

I swore, Jace felt it, sensed it, those eyes so soft as he reached up and cupped my face with his free hand as he explored me gingerly with the other.

Soft pants rose from my mouth.

Everything at odds.

My need and my regret and my guilt.

They were a blaze in the room.

Amplified in the energy that thrashed and whipped in that living space between us.

"I've got you, Faith. Relax, baby. Let me take care of you. I won't hurt you. Just . . . please let me. Don't want to go on a second more without touching you."

There was no longer any resisting.

Nothing I could do but give. On a needy sigh, my back hit the hard table.

The man lowered his big body into a chair.

Trembles rolled.

Was this really happening?

He tucked me closer to him, his hands up high on my thighs as he dragged me right up to the very edge.

That was where he had me. On the edge and tumbling over.

Falling faster and faster. Where I'd no longer be able to claw my way back up to safety.

He slipped his hands under my thighs, wrapping all the way around until he was holding me by the tops, wedging those big shoulders between them.

"Shit, Faith. Do you have any idea how many nights I spent dreaming of this? Thinking about you? Wishing I was the one who was with you?"

Oh, God, he needed to stop saying those things. But he was dipping down, running those soft, soft lips up the inside of my leg, his voice a rough murmur at my overheated skin. "You marked me, baby."

A shiver rushed, and part of me wanted to beg him to stop, because I didn't think I could handle this. The onslaught of emotion coming up from the depths, breaking free of the dam that'd held it back.

But it was too late. Because he continued, his lips and tongue roaming higher.

Higher and higher.

Dizziness slammed me.

An assault of need.

My hips jerked from the table in their own plea.

A dark chuckle rumbled from his massive chest. "Tell me you want me, Faith. Tell me you want this."

"Yes . . . please . . . make me feel good. I need you, Jace."

For a beat, he looked at me.

His gorgeous face could have been smug with what he did to me.

But no.

There he was, his expression written in stark adoration.

Maybe that was what scared me the most. But I didn't have time to contemplate it before he dipped down and gave one long lick through my slit.

I jumped.

Body and soul.

"Oh, God."

My fingers searched for something to hold on to, scratching at the wood as he started to explore me with all the devastation of that mouth.

His lips sucking. Soft, delirium-inducing pulls at my clit.

Desire lit. A throb through my body.

Arrows in the air.

Staking me.

His hot tongue licked and lapped, delving deep into my folds before he was back to laving at that sweet, sweet spot, setting my flesh ablaze.

"Oh, Jace . . . Jace." His name was all a whimper. A plea.

Mumbles fell from his mouth. Promises as much as a demand. "I've got you. Let me take care of you. I told you I was going to take care of you."

He pulled back for the barest flash when he said it, copper eyes somehow aglow, glimmers of gold in the sun.

So beautiful I forgot to breathe, rasping sounds barely making it into my lungs when he drove three big fingers into me while he pinned me with his stare.

Possessively.

Pumping slow and sure while I writhed and continued to cry out his name.

"That's it. Do you feel that, Faith? Do you feel what I do to you? What I was always supposed to do to you?"

Then he ducked back down and flattened his tongue against my clit.

Rolling and pressing.

His fingers drove deeper.

Deeper and deeper while I went higher and higher.

Climbing right into the darkness where the boy had always lived.

My beast.

I rode on it. Holding on. Falling into this man. Where my body splintered and shook.

Broke apart.

I was lost to the most mind-blowing kind of pleasure. The kind of pleasure that streaked and surged and consumed.

Filling every hollow.

Every inch.

Erasing every question. Where he became the answer.

Until he possessed everything.

My fingers drove into his hair, pulling him closer while he continued his assault, tongue lapping and suckling, keeping me held high, a hostage to everything he was.

Finally, he slowed. My breaths catching as he did. He nuzzled the inside of my thigh with his face, and his hands cinched down tight, holding me as I came down.

"There's nothing more beautiful in this world than watching you come," he murmured. "I could look at a million other women. A thousand sunsets. Every exotic beach. And you would still be the most beautiful thing I've ever seen."

And I didn't know how to process what it was that I was feeling.

Swept up.

Caught up.

Trapped.

Freed.

I didn't know.

All I knew was I was slipping from the table, sliding over him as I went, dropping to my knees.

A sharp wheeze pulled from his heaving chest. "Faith . . . I—"

"Shut up, Jace Jacobs. Don't say a word. Don't make me think about what I'm feelin'. Just *let* me touch you. Give me this."

I needed this. Maybe proof that I wasn't the only one who was subject to it.

The energy that swelled.

Obliterating.

Annihilating.

My mouth was pressing all over his chest, wanting to devour him the way he'd just devoured me.

I kissed down, across the flat planes of his abdomen, and licked over the spot where he'd written me on his body.

It was like tastin' what we'd lost. The sweetest flavor of what might have been.

His muscles jumped and twitched when I did, and before I lost my nerve, I let my fingers find the waistband of his pajamas.

He was already straining outside of the confines of it.

As if the man couldn't be contained.

The fat head of him swollen and glistening with his own need.

I ripped the fabric down, and Jace hissed as he was freed.

Instantly, his fingers plunged into my hair. "Shit . . . Faith . . . what are you trying to do to me?"

I pulled back so I could look at his face. "What you've always, always done to me."

He angled up, kicking his pants the rest of the way free. That was right as a rasp of a sound was leaving me at the sight of him.

The man so hard and big as he strained from the chair.

"What is it I've always done to you?" It was a grated challenge from his mouth.

Maybe he wanted a confession.

Proof.

My hand was shaking like crazy when I wrapped it around the velvet flesh. Then I added the other. I gave a firm squeeze, and my tongue darted out to wet my parched lips. "Make me want things that I shouldn't have. More of you."

*Always, always, more of you.*

Copper eyes glinted.

Fire.

Flames lapping at my soul.

"Who says you shouldn't have them?"

I almost laughed. It would have been maniacal, frenzied, a mirror to the way this boy made me feel. The way he'd always made me let go. Forget every worry and reservation.

I stroked the long, hard length of him.

A shiver rippled across his golden flesh.

Oh goodness, was the man beautiful like this.

Bare and ready for me.

And I knew I had to be delirious.

Because I was taking him in my mouth. My lips stretched around the hard mass of him.

So big.

Too much.

*Everything. Everything.*

I wanted to possess him the way he possessed me, and he growled out a sound that shot straight to my core when I licked at the underside of him.

"Fuck . . . Faith . . . you feel so good. So damned good. No one . . . no one has ever made me feel like this. No one. Not ever."

I couldn't stop them, the tears that sprang to my eyes as I began to suck him. As I opened myself up to him. Taking him deeper and deeper.

I'd wanted to possess him.

But it was Jace Jacobs who was possessin' me. Filling my mouth with the measured surges of his cock.

Filling my mind.

Filling my heart.

My knees dug into the floor, and he twisted his hands tighter into my hair, the man rocking harder, deeper, taking more.

Taking all of me.

And I wanted to give it.

But I was so scared. So scared of fully lettin' go.

Only, sometimes, we didn't even realize we'd tripped before we were in a free fall.

Unstoppable.

The ground gone.

Ripped right out from under our feet.

I was just terrified of where we would land.

"Fuck . . . Faith . . . baby. That mouth. You have the sweetest mouth. Take it, Faith. Take me."

He started cursing, barely sitting in the chair, wedging deeper and deeper into my mouth, hitting my throat, desperate for more.

*More.*

*More.*

*More.*

I let go of the chains that were holding me back, and my hands moved to either side of him on the chair. Holding on to it before I floated away.

He was holding on to it, too, the other hand on the table as he jutted and rocked, as if it was the only thing that was keeping us grounded.

Then those hands were back in my hair, tugging hard as he pressed himself as far as he could into me, my jaw sore and burning from the force of him.

And still, I relished every second.

His cock jerking.

His pleasure given to me.

He roared. A prayer he offered to me. His come in my mouth and my name on his tongue.

For a second, I owned it.

Relished it.

This boy I hadn't been able to keep.

Panic climbed into my chest.

I couldn't lose him again.

I couldn't.

I'd never, ever survive.

I realized my eyes were pinned shut when he eased out of me, and I only squeezed them tighter when I felt his hands on my face, tipping it up so he could take me in.

"Faith, sweetheart." His voice had gone soft, and his thumbs were brushing my cheeks, gathering the moisture I hadn't realized soaked my skin in hot, terrified streaks.

"Don't cry. Fuck. Please, don't cry."

Oh, I was a mess. Such a mess. But I didn't want to hide from it anymore.

So, I let him wrap me in his arms.

Let him hold me while I wept.

The problem was, I didn't even know what I was weeping for.

The future or the past.

Or maybe it was for what had come in between.

Because I felt another piece of its hold break away.

Like all of those memories had gone into a free fall with the rest.

Jace sighed into my hair. "I've got you."

The scariest part of that was I'd never felt so whole.

# twenty-nine

## Faith
## Seventeen Years Old

*F*aith gulped around her nerves, around her fear and trepidation and what threatened to be a broken heart as she stood at the end of the lane.

"Stop being a coward," she scolded herself under her breath, forcing her feet to keep moving down the road that was little more than a path carved out by tires with a bunch of weeds growing up the middle.

Her heart beat harder and harder with each step she took, her mind racing with the different scenarios of what might have happened two nights ago.

Of where he might have been.

She hadn't heard from him in all that time.

Faith faltered when she came around a leafy bend, trees growing wild all around her, and saw the trailer sitting in the middle of it, rundown while the foliage seemed to try to swallow it whole.

Her heart climbed her throat, throbbing and pulsing as she tried to shove her reaction down.

Jace was always so worried what she'd think about where he lived, but what he didn't get was it could never make her think less of him.

It only made her want more for him.

Made her hate it all the more that he had to live this way.

She was trying to instill the courage inside herself to knock on the door when it banged open.

A surprised gush of air left her, only for a slight smile to find her face when Joseph came out. "Joseph," she said as a soft hello.

"Faith . . . hi." He was all timid smiles and slightly curly, dark brown hair.

Cute in an almost studious, boy-next-door way.

"What are you doing here?" he chanced, shoving his hands in his pockets and rocking back on his heels.

She raked her teeth over her bottom lip, trying to stave off the nerves. "I'm lookin' for Jace. Have you seen him around? He was supposed to meet me a couple nights ago, and he didn't show, and I haven't heard from him since. I'm worried about him."

A glower streaked through Joseph's expression, and his lips pursed in concern. "You shouldn't worry about a guy like that."

Taken aback, Faith frowned. "What does that mean?"

Joseph took the three steps down to the ground, and he came her direction, his voice lowered like a warning. "It means he's not a good guy, Faith. It means you deserve someone better than that."

She rubbed her palms up her arms, chills lighting on her skin even though it was blistering hot outside.

"How can you say that?" she whispered. Her question wasn't out of anger. It was bred from an insecurity she didn't want to feel.

The barest hint of some of those worries had needled their way into her consciousness.

The what-ifs.

What if he didn't really love her the way he'd said?

What if he'd found someone he liked better?

What if her dreams of staying in this town weren't big enough for him?

"It means he got arrested for assault."

Air shot from her lungs, and she stumbled back as if she'd been kicked. "What?" she wheezed.

Joseph started to say something else, but both of them froze when there was a clatter from the trailer.

Jace was suddenly standing in the doorway, staring at them both, his entire body vibrating with that same hostility that had both terrified her and captivated her the first time she'd seen him.

Faith's heart started to beat wild, that attraction and disorder racing through her veins. Overcome by that sensation she'd only ever felt with this boy.

Copper eyes flashing their turmoil, she was sure she was bein' held hostage by their intensity. Almost scary in their severity.

But it was the cut on his cheek that had her stomach twisting in tight compassion, with all the love she felt for him.

Instantly, she was moving his direction. She had an overwhelming urge to reach out and heal anything that might hurt him.

"Jace," she whispered into the heated day, squinting up at where he stood at the top of the steps.

Jace swallowed hard. Shame etched all over him like a stain. "What are you doing here?"

"I came to check on you. Obviously, you needed it. What happened?"

"Yeah, Jace, what happened?" This from Joseph, who was standing behind her.

Jace suddenly flew off the steps. She spun around to see Jace had pinned Joseph's back to a tree. "I'm warning you, Joseph. I told you to leave Faith out of this."

Joseph thrashed, and Faith rushed up behind Jace, touching his back. "Jace, what are you doing?"

Jace released Joseph, and Joseph shrugged away, shaking himself off. "Told you," Joseph told her as if he were offering a warning.

She didn't respond, just stared dumbfounded at Joseph's back as he retreated toward the trailer. He sent her a single glance over his shoulder before he slammed the door shut.

She whirled back around. "What is happening?" she pleaded.

Jace's shoulders slumped. Defeat in his stance. "Exactly what I warned you was going to happen. I'm not good enough for you, Faith. I told you I was going to mess this up."

She blinked at him, not believing a word he said, and she reached out a trembling hand to gentle her fingers across the cut on his cheek.

Her head angled to the side as she searched his face. "Don't tell me you're not good enough for me. Just tell me what happened."

Turning away from her, Jace blew out a strained breath and walked to the edge of the lot where he stood in the high weeds.

She stood behind him, and he dropped his head, his shoulders sagged as he muttered toward the ground, "This guy . . . he's been hooking up with my mom. Feeding her drugs. Basically, the same bullshit we've had to deal with all our lives. I came home the other night, and he'd beaten Ian up. I was done with it, Faith. Done."

His entire body quaked. "I went after him. Forced my mom into telling me where I could find him, and I waited for him until he showed."

He looked back at her, his expression twisted in remorse. "I couldn't see anything but gettin' revenge. Couldn't stop myself from going after it. Seeking it out. I warned you—"

"That you would do anything to protect your brother and your cousin," she cut in. "You're right, Jace, you did. And there is no shame in that . . . there is absolutely no shame in protecting your family."

His lips pursed in disgust. "I got arrested, Faith. I wanted to end this cycle. That's all I ever wanted, and now the only thing I've done is—"

His admission cut off, so much pain and regret oozing from the words that Faith couldn't do anything but jump in to try to ease it.

"It will all work out. There's nothing you could have done that would make things worse when the only thing you're tryin' to do is make things better. You'll see."

He shook his head. "It doesn't work that way."

"Why not?"

He suddenly spun around and wrapped her in the strength of his arms, stealing the little breath she had, hitching it right in her throat where her heart was drumming mad.

He buried his face in her hair. "I wish it was, Faith. I wish it was all that simple. That I could just believe and it would all come to pass. That I could get out of this mess. It's all I want, but every time I turn around, I'm getting deeper into it."

She hugged him tighter, her nose in his neck, breathing him in. "It will. It will all work out."

"What do you see in me?" he murmured.

Her hands fisted in his threadbare shirt. "Everything."

She squeezed him tighter. "I see everything, Jace. My future. My hope. All my firsts. I want all of them with you. To experience everything with you. For you to find a future with me, too."

She could feel the restraint billow through his body. Fighting her when she would always fight for him. "Faith . . ."

"I'm yours, Jace." She pulled back and looked at his face. "And the next time we're alone, I'm going to prove it."

# thirty

## Faith

"**Y**ou were right . . . oh, God, you were right," I rushed with a

strained whisper into the phone. I was pacing my room, clutching my towel to my chest as I tried to decide what in the world I was supposed to do.

Once I'd finally stopped crying, I'd needed to separate myself from him.

Gain some clarity.

He'd carried me all the way to my bedroom door where he'd kissed me gently.

Tenderly.

Giving me the encouragement I hadn't known how much I needed.

Then he'd nudged me toward my room, told me to get myself a shower and that he'd see me in a little bit.

The only thing the water had been good for was washing away the tears staining my cheeks. Definitely not for washing away the cloud of confusion and guilt lining my insides.

By the time I'd stepped out, I was nothin' but a ball of anxiety. Wondering how I was going to move on from there.

So, I'd called the one person I could always rely on to tell me straight.

"And what exactly am I right about?" Courtney asked, totally droll. But I heard it, the all-knowing in her voice.

The brat already knew exactly what I was talkin' about.

She was gonna force me to admit it out loud.

"He kissed me." I tried not to sound completely freaked out, but I was failing. My voice dropped even lower when I whispered, "Put his mouth on me."

Silence.

It echoed back.

Before Courtney laughed. "Tell me you aren't complaining about that man puttin' his mouth on you. I'd bet my favorite Louboutin's he knows how to work magic with that mouth."

"Court." It was a low chiding.

"Faith," she shot back, sarcasm in her voice.

I could almost see her shaking her head. "Oh, come on, Faith. Tell me you aren't surprised. There was no mistakin' the fact that man wanted to eat you up last night. Hell, I'm shocked he didn't devour you right there on that dance floor. He's lucky one of Mack's cop friends didn't arrest him for indecency with the way he was lookin' at you."

I pressed my palm against my forehead, paced some more.

What had I done? The guilt twisted up like an impossible knot in my belly, and the overwhelming shiver of need racing through my veins made me feel as if I was gonna come right out of my skin.

This feeling that Jace Jacobs was a necessity.

It sure didn't help that the shower was running in the room next door and images were filling my head.

Jace naked.

Rivulets of water running over that body. His length bobbing up to his belly button. Swollen for me.

Oh, my.

That was definitely not helping things at all.

"Why are you bein' so nonchalant about this?" I hissed.

As if it weren't earth shattering.

Life altering.

"Because that first day when he showed back up, and he was standing there watching you on the sidewalk as if he was prepared to jump in front of you and take a bullet for you? It was written all over his pretty face. Even if he didn't know it himself, he was there to take you back. Honestly, I'm kind of stunned it took him this long."

I wondered if I had known it then, too. If I had known the second I saw him back in this town that he was there to stir things up. Toss me into turmoil. Or maybe he'd been sent to save me from the pits of despair.

"Tell me what to do."

I'd given up knowing anything myself.

Courtney chuckled something salacious. "Are you sure you want to be askin' me what to do? Because I have all kinds of good tips I could give you."

"Oh, I'm sure you could. And the last thing I need around here is to get any more out of control."

"Maybe losin' a little control is exactly what you need."

"Well, I definitely did that up good."

I guessed she could hear the admission in my voice, because her tone dropped. "Tell me what you did."

"I put my mouth on him, too."

With the way the words dropped low, I might as well have been sharing secrets with her back in her bedroom when we were teenagers, looking at those magazines.

But this wasn't embarrassment over experiencing something for the first time.

This was rooted deep.

The overwhelming tumult that I was heading down a path that I couldn't return from.

Taking a sharp turn that would lead to a head-on collision.

Pure destruction.

"You little slut," she teased. Of course, she did. She couldn't be serious for five seconds.

"Courtney," I hissed.

"What? I just like to be in good company."

"Why in the world am I tellin' you any of this?"

"Um . . . hello. This is your best friend you're talking to. The keeper of all your secrets. It's your duty."

I sucked in a breath, my voice going emphatic as I pressed my phone a little harder to my ear. "I'm serious, Court. Help me. I feel like my life is slipping right out of control. That I'm losing my grip."

While another part felt as if it was coming together.

Mending to where it belonged.

My gaze moved to my bed and the wedding picture sitting on my nightstand.

*Joseph.*

He'd said in that letter to look at our wedding picture. He'd said that moment was the most honest of his life.

Grief swelled as I thought of the man who'd shared that place with me for so many years. How could I forsake that?

Her tone shifted. "You want to know what to do, Faith? You do what feels right. You do whatever it is you can't stop thinking about, what you can't stop wantin', and you do your best not to allow the fear and the guilt and the loss to rule you while you do it. Because you know better than anyone that none of us know what direction our lives are gonna go. When the world is gonna rip the rug out from under us. Who's gonna hurt us and who's gonna love us."

She paused for a second before encouragement flooded the line. "We can only do our best . . . treat the people around us with as much love as we want in return. Then we sit back, enjoy the ride, and pray for the best. And don't worry . . . he hurts you, I've got my huntin' knife."

A burst of laughter left me at the last.

"Should I be concerned you might be secretly hoping he is up to no good just so you can deliver on that offer?"

Her chuckle was dark. "Nah, there are plenty of assholes out there to keep me entertained."

This was why I'd called Courtney. She always made me feel

better.

I blew out a sigh, hesitated, before I admitted, "Part of it makes me feel like I'm cheatin' on Joseph."

The part of me that still loved him, the one that stood at the altar and promised I'd love him forever—that girl felt as if loving Jace was nothing but a sin.

That was the same girl who'd settled on believing Jace had been a sin all along.

He'd left me. Hurt me. When he turned his back on me, I'd convinced myself that he had left all of me behind. That his excuses were nothing but lame and stupid. An easy reason to get away.

I'd thought maybe my dreams hadn't been big enough for him, after all.

Especially after I had found out how successful he'd become. The company he'd built from the ground up, buying up businesses and land, investing and turning all of it into big, big things. So much bigger than my simple dreams could ever compare to.

Now everything felt like this huge, complicated, convoluted mess.

I was getting an unsettled feeling that there was so much I didn't know.

It was so hard to reconcile the two—that I had spent ten years believing he had left me willingly and the fact that Jace had gone to prison and still managed to make something of himself.

I looked at the worn floor, contemplating, then asked, "Did you know Jace went to prison when he left here?"

Did that mean he'd really left or was the reality of it that he'd been taken away? Because of my own stupidity? Wanting to play house so desperately that I'd put us both in danger?

Blame raced through my veins.

God. What had I done? And what had he suffered for me?

Shock rippled through the line. "What?"

I rubbed at my forehead. "That's what he said."

"Why?"

"I guess because we broke in here that night?" I whispered, almost a question. "I . . . I thought we were free and clear, but I think Jace took the fall for me."

"Shit . . . are you kiddin' me?"

"No."

She laughed.

"Why in the world are you laughin'?"

"Because I'm getting the feeling that man is so much more than either of us ever gave him credit for."

## Jace

*G*od damn it.

What had I done?

Fucked it up in a way there was no chance I could reconcile, that was what.

But there'd been no stopping it. No stopping how I felt or what I wanted.

No stopping what I was going to take.

Keep.

Devotion pumped through my blood, right along with the sinking reality that there was so much I couldn't change. So much that she still didn't know that would ruin her if I stayed.

I'd barely been able to admit to her that I'd gone to prison, the reason I'd been sent there frozen on my tongue while she'd stood there in all her belief and innocence somehow thinking that it might have been her fault.

As if slipping inside this place would land me in prison for three years.

I was only supposed to be here to fix what I could. What would she think if she knew?

She would hate me, which was why I'd been pleading with her for forgiveness even though the girl didn't have the first clue what I was asking her to forgive me for.

Would she?

Could she look past the greatest treason?

Fuck.

I didn't know.

All I knew was there was no chance I could pack it up and walk away when all was said and done.

I toweled off.

The smell of her was still on my skin despite the shower I'd just taken.

Liked she'd been etched there.

Written on me.

Dropping the towel to the floor, I looked in the mirror where I wore her name on my hip like a scar.

A brand.

A reminder of who I was. Why I was. The sacrifice I'd made.

Bottom line? All of it had been my fault. Right from the very start. It hadn't mattered that Joseph was responsible. The one who'd committed the act. I was the one who'd led him there.

Fed him all the bullshit that had made him into the man he'd become.

Then I'd turned my back when he'd needed me most.

I scrubbed both my palms over my face, cursing at myself to get it together.

I was stronger than this.

But that was the thing about *Faith*.

Having it made me weak.

And she was making me weaker. Making me believe all the bullshit she'd made me believe back when we'd been kids.

Look where that had gotten me.

Exhaling heavily, I forced myself into my clothes—jeans and a tee. The bedroom door creaked as I stepped out into the hall, my ear inclined toward her room.

Silence echoed back.

Realizing she was no longer on the second floor, I bounded downstairs, heading for the kitchen, when I caught the sight framed in the big window that overlooked the side of the house from the living room.

My chest tightened.

Faith was out there. In the rose garden. Her fingers brushing over the petals and her face lifted to the sky.

Like she was seeking any wisdom that might fall from above.

I stood there watching her.

The girl my dream.

Something that had become an impossibility when it was getting harder and harder to stop from wanting her to be my everything.

Considering I was the source of her torment, I should give her space.

Time.

Guess I'd never exactly been known for what I *should* do, because I was slipping out the front door, quietly crossing the porch, and moving that way.

I knew she felt me.

Could feel her energy rippling back.

Warmth and light and grace.

They hit me like stones.

I was a bastard.

Such a bastard because I couldn't stop myself. Couldn't stop myself from edging up behind that sweet, sweet body, from setting my hands on her slender waist, from pulling her back against me.

Against my aching body and my hammering heart and my dick that was already hard for her again.

One taste, and I needed more.

I nuzzled my nose in the flesh of her neck, my face lost in the soft fall of chocolate waves.

Vanilla and roses.

She released a sigh, and she sank back into me. Her hands came to settle over the top of mine where I held her tight across her belly.

My voice turned rough. "This . . . this is the picture I held of you for all these years. You standing right here, in these roses, whispering that you loved me. It was what got me through the days. Remembering the things you'd told me. Who I could be. Who you saw when you looked at me. I wanted to be that guy, Faith. God, I wanted to be him. I wanted to follow that light in the darkened sky."

"You could have been." There was pain in her voice.

"Will you let me be him now?" I murmured into her hair. A plea. Begging with this girl for that forgiveness.

"This is all happenin' so fast." Fear cracked through her murmured words.

"I'll give you all the time you need."

She snuggled a little deeper into my arms, hugging me tighter to herself. Relishing in the connection. "Why do you make that sound like you're stayin'?"

"Because that's what I intend. If you let me."

"God, Jace, you're ruining me."

I let my hands sweep down her thighs. "I'll ruin you in the best of ways."

Deeper and deeper.

Couldn't stop.

Didn't want to.

I needed her to know how much I wanted her.

I half expected her to go rigid and push me away, especially when I'd just promised her *time*. But I figured with what had just gone down in her kitchen, I would take the chance.

God knew that was what Faith and I needed.

A chance.

Even if it was going to be a fighting one.

She released a little laugh, her amusement gliding into the humid, summer morning. "You're awfully sure of yourself, aren't you, tough guy?"

A chuckle rippled from me, and I could feel it slide right through her, a tremble under my hands.

My lips moved against the delicate shell of her ear. "Oh, good girl, you have no idea what I'm dying to do to you. What I've been dreaming of. I've had plenty of years to think it through."

Couldn't help but put it out into the atmosphere.

My intentions.

Dragging her back to where we'd once been and all the places I wanted to go.

*I'm going to take you. Fuck you and love you and make you scream. Drive you mad until you realize that you're mine. That you've always been. That we were always supposed to be.*

Those were the words I held back. With the rumble that thundered at my insides, I knew it was the truth.

A motherfucking promise.

I was going to make sure it was the truth.

The problem was, I had no idea how to broach the issue of Joseph.

How we were going to deal with that ghost.

With that loss.

Some piece inside me wanting to shatter with the idea of her still loving him.

God, I wanted to claw my eyes out, thinking of the two of them together. And somehow . . . somehow I still couldn't even picture it.

Something shy worked its way into her posture, but when she peeked back up at me, her full lips were quirking up at the sides. "You did a pretty good job of it back in the kitchen."

I brushed my fingers through her hair. "I was just getting started."

That feeling filled up the air. Like it was breathed from the sky.

Pouring down from the place she'd just been looking.

"Is that what this is? A start?"

"Seems to me, we're only picking up where we left off."

For a beat, her spine stiffened, and I knew where her thoughts had gone. Those years coming between us, getting closer and closer until we'd have to face the consequences of them.

"Come on . . . let's go get that little girl of yours," I said.

I had to get out of there or I'd be taking her places I knew she wasn't ready for.

The way she'd fallen apart in my arms this morning was proof of that.

I wasn't sure I'd ever felt guiltier than in that moment when the girl had fucked me with that sweet, sweet mouth and then had broken up after.

Torn. Tormented. Confused.

And I kept pushing her.

Problem was, I didn't know how to stop.

Not when this girl had always been mine.

I wasn't going to settle until she knew it.

Blowing out a breath, disappointment or relief, I wasn't sure, she swiveled out of my arms. I caught only the tips of her fingers.

This soft kind of wariness had filled her features when she looked up at me. "She likes you."

Emotion gripped me everywhere.

*Magic.*

The way I felt about that little girl had to be proof of its existence.

"I like her, too." I barely forced it out.

Because I couldn't quite put my finger on the way I felt about her.

Honestly, the thought of that innocent face kind of made me want to do some of that weeping, too.

"She's my world, Jace." There was some kind of warning in it.

I touched her face. "Which is exactly what she should be."

A smile ticked up at the corners of her perfect, plush lips.

Joy.

I saw it.

Right there, waiting to reclaim its spot. To become the brightest part of her.

I stepped back so I could fully take it in. See the wholeness of it. Let it tease me with a little of my own.

"You ready?"

Faith hesitated for the beat of a second before she stretched out her hand to take mine. "Yeah, I'm ready.

Five minutes later, we had made it into town, and I took the last turn into her parents' neighborhood.

Big trees hugged each side, and well-kept, modest houses were tucked in their protection. Lawns fronted the houses, and the walkways were edged in bright, blossoming flowers.

Faith swung her gaze at me, a smile riding her face.

The tension and the strain from earlier had evaporated.

Damn.

She was radiant.

Fucking brilliant.

Blinding.

"I seriously thought you and my daddy were gonna have it out right there on the stoop last night."

A grin perked up on my lips. Keeping it light when there hadn't been anything funny about it. "Uh, yeah, I was waiting on him to come at me, too. He's not exactly my biggest fan."

She laughed quietly. "Ah . . . my daddy's a big ol' teddy bear. He only wants what's best for Bailey and me."

"He always has wanted what was best for you," I told her, remembering the things he'd said to me.

How they'd affected me.

How I'd wanted to prove him wrong when the only thing I'd done was prove him right.

"My daddy's not about words, Jace. The only thing he cares about is, if we say them, we'd better mean them."

My nod was slow, and there was not a damned thing I could do but reach over the console and take her hand.

Squeeze it.

Savor the fire.

"And if I showed up there right now and told him I was staying, what would he think?"

"He'd probably think you were feeding him a line." She squeezed my hand back, her quiet voice filling with that hope. "And both of us would silently be rooting for you to prove him wrong."

I smiled at her as I pulled to the curb. That feeling took hold of me again. Something perfect. A feeling I wanted to keep forever.

Faith had already hopped out of the passenger side by the time I made it around, and I stepped up to her side, planting my hand on the small of her back as we took the walkway and then edged up the steps.

A shiver caressed that soft, soft flesh.

I wanted to trace it. Capture it. Explore every inch.

The front door swung open, and there was Bailey, all wild curls, bright eyes, and dimpled chin. "Mommy and Jacie!"

My chest tightened again.

Laughing, Faith shifted her attention my way. "Well, it seems someone earned himself a nickname."

The kid was so damned adorable, winding her way right the hell in.

My brow quirked up. "Jacie, huh?"

Emphatic, Bailey nodded and started to sing, "Jacie, Jacie, Jacie."

All right then.

A soft rumble of laughter pilfered free. "You can call me whatever you want, Unicorn Girl."

Bailey beamed. "Unicorn Girl! I a unicorn girl."

God. That hooked me, too.

Faith's mother was suddenly there and pushing open the screen. "Well, are you two gonna stand out there all day or are you gonna come in? Might as well be a fire out there for how hot it is."

Faith stepped inside, quick to pull Bailey from her feet and hike her onto her hip. At the same time, she dipped in to peck a kiss to her mother's cheek. "Hey, Mama. How was my girl last night? Did she sleep okay?"

"She slept just fine. You worry too much."

"It's a mama's right to worry, isn't that what you always told me growing up?" There was a tease to Faith's tone.

Her mother laughed. It was a free sound that bounced through the entry. I had to wonder what it might have been like as a kid to come home every day to something that sounded like that.

"Don't go using my words against me, girl."

"It's the only defense I have." Faith winked, and her mom just grinned.

God.

I roughed an uncomfortable hand through my hair and

dropped my eyes to the ground.

Suddenly, I felt like I was overstepping.

Out of bounds.

Getting into things I knew better than to get involved in.

This wasn't why I was here.

The problem was, I was starting to forget the reason. Hell, I was pretty sure the second I'd touched her last night, every single one of those reasons had flown out the window.

When I looked back up, Faith had disappeared down the hall in the direction of her old room, Bailey rambling about needing to get her Beast.

My heart stuttered when I found her mother standing there staring at me.

"Well, Jace Jacobs."

Unease bounded through my nerves.

She'd always been too warm. Too nice. It made me feel like I'd let her down, too.

"Now, don't go lookin' at me like that."

Confusion had my brow twisting, and I was barely able to get the question out. "How's that, ma'am?"

Yup. There I was. A stammering, seventeen-year-old kid.

She eyed me seriously. "Like you don't belong here."

She reached out, and a shiver raced down my spine when she pinched my chin between her thumb and forefinger, forcing me to look at her. "You look up with your head held high. Strong like you are."

My throat locked up.

"You think I didn't always know it?" she asked, her voice soft and somehow hard as she craned her head to the side. "The man you are inside? The rest of the world might have been blind to it. The rest of the world might have wanted to beat it down and hold it back. But I saw it right there, burnin' from your bones."

"I've done some things I'm not exactly proud of." Couldn't keep the admission from sliding free.

She gave a slight nod. "Haven't we all. And it's a real man who admits when he makes a mistake. Does his best to make it right. Is that what you're here to do? Make it right? Only a real man would come in the middle of a mess as monumental as this one. I see you, stepping in and putting yourself in danger for the sake of them both. That . . . that is what counts. There is no better judge of character than the sacrifice a man is willing to make."

There was a gleam in her eyes.

God damn it. If I wasn't already crumbling at Faith's feet, her mother sure has hell would have had me a puddle on the floor.

"I'll do everything I can to make sure they are safe. To make this right." At least I could give her that truth.

"Good." She straightened herself out. "Because you damned near broke my heart as much as you broke hers when you walked away."

Surprise sent my head rocking back, and she turned and started for the kitchen, muttering the whole way, "You were the one, you know? You were always the one. Almost went and found you myself and dragged you home where you belonged."

I didn't even know if she meant for me to hear it.

Faith and Bailey were suddenly at the end of the hall, Bailey dragging her suitcase behind her, that ratted Beast hooked in her elbow. "I's ready!"

"Not yet, you're not." It was a shout from the kitchen. "You didn't really think I was gonna let you show up here and not feed you, did you? Late lunch is on the table. It's family time. Don't care how busy y'all are. Time to put some food in those bellies."

Faith jerked her face to me, worry written all over her expression.

I angled my head, smiled, and then followed her into the kitchen.

It was the same way as I had that day so long ago. Though, this time, I did it the way Margot told me to do.

With my head held high.

Because her mother was right. It was time I made amends. Did things right.

I scooped Bailey into my arms. Her head was lolling to the side, half asleep at the table where we'd sat for the last three hours while Margot had filled her head with stories of Faith growing up.

Lightness filled me in a way it hadn't in so damned long. A comfort like none other. Imagining Faith that way. A little girl like Bailey. Picturing her through the years that had passed, as she'd grown and learned and loved.

Shined.

Filling the world with all her light.

It almost made it feel like the menace lurking in the shadows wasn't real. Like she could shine a little more and every single shadow would be exposed as nothing more than a vapor.

That's what I wanted. For all this shit to disappear so we could move on. Figure out who we were and if we could make it without anything else interfering.

Her dad had been pretty much quiet, grunting a few things here and there, watching me like he was ready to haul ass over the table and come at me if I said the slightest thing wrong.

Or maybe he was just silently trusting me to do what I'd set out to do. My care for his daughter as great as his, but entirely different.

Bailey was close to falling asleep as I carried her out the front door and buckled her into her car seat in the back of my car. My actions gentle, still wary of getting too close but getting sucked in without my permission, anyway.

Faith was whispering something to her mother on the stoop.

With the way her mother kept grinning over her shoulder at me, I was pretty certain of the topic.

Faith finally climbed into the passenger seat beside me. I pulled away from the curb, the engine a quiet hum against the late afternoon where the sun began to sag toward the horizon.

It tossed the town in gorgeous colors. Pinks and blues and reds.

Like the girl next to me.

So bright and beautiful it made it hard to see.

I came to a stop at the stop sign at the end of the road and looked both ways, getting caught up with the way Faith was looking at me when I turned that direction.

"Thank you," she whispered.

"For what?"

"For making me forget for a little while. For making me feel like my life is normal. That I'm surrounded by the people who care about me and won't stop working until this mess is set straight."

Reaching out, I trailed my fingertips down the sharp angle of her jaw. "That's exactly what you are—surrounded by the people who care about you."

Her smile was so soft, so full of trust that I couldn't stop the way my heart gave an extra beat.

Commitment.

Devotion.

Turning right, I accelerated down the road. My hand was on hers, caressing slowly, softly, letting her know I was there.

I wasn't going anywhere.

I came to a stop at the stoplight that led out of town toward the plantation, unable to stop myself from looking her way, my grin so fucking wide I probably looked like a blundering fool.

But the one she returned me?

It wound through my spirit like a storm. Desolating in its severity. Binding and perfecting. Never the same where I was left in its wake.

Because it was the smile I'd been waiting for.

Real. Genuine. Filled with *faith*.

This girl.

I was still smiling at her when everything crumbled around us.

My body lurched forward, and a deafening crash rang through my ears.

Confusion and chaos.

*What the fuck?*

Time set to slow as I watched Faith's eyes widen with fear. Shocked as the car jolted forward.

Then she screamed. Screamed in the middle of the crushing sound that resonated through the air. Her hands flew out like she could defend herself from the collision.

My fucking heart nearly ripped from my chest.

Overwhelming terror gripped me as I was struck with the grating sound of twisting metal and the squeal of tires and the realization that there was nothing I could do.

Nothing to stop my car from spinning, from being tossed out into the middle of the intersection like it weighed nothing at all.

It rocked one direction and then the other before finally coming to a standstill.

Jagged breaths jerked in and out of my lungs and dizziness swept my senses, ears ringing with a high-pitched drone. Confusion clouded my mind, but I shook it off, focused on the reason I was there. "Faith, baby, are you okay?"

Her mouth trembled open as she whimpered the one thing that mattered to her most. "Bailey."

*Bailey. Bailey. Bailey.*

Instantly, my attention darted to the rearview mirror, eyes desperate as I searched for where she was buckled into her seat. Cries jetted from her mouth, these shattered, wails of fear, and her little hands were reaching out for someone to help her.

*Bailey.*

Fumbling, I released my buckle so I could climb out and get to her.

That was when in my periphery, through the shattered side window, I caught the movement.

The car that had hit us was backing up.

Motherfucker was going to run.

Anger blistered through me when I thought of it. Someone just up and leaving without checking to make sure everyone was okay. Bastards who didn't give a fuck about anything but themselves.

Then that anger shifted, spiraled into a vortex of horror when I realized they weren't running.

They were gunning it back in our direction.

Tires squealing as they rammed on the gas.

"Faith!" I yelled in terror, wanting to get to her, climb over her, protect her.

But there was not a thing I could do but grab for the steering wheel like it was a life preserver, fingers slipping when the piece of shit slammed us hard from the side.

Under the force, my head snapped to the side.

Glass shattered as it cracked against the driver's side window.

An explosion of sound.

An explosion of pain.

Sight dimming.

Agony splintering through my being.

Sight going red.

*Bailey. Faith.*

Hate and fear and possession. My car rocked to a shuddering stop.

Faith was staring at me.

Wide-eyed and in shock.

And I wanted to go to her. Wrap her up.

But that fucking car was shifting gears again.

I wasn't going to let this happen. I wasn't.

I flung open the door and staggered onto the street.

My feet nearly gave out from under me as my consciousness blinked. Squeezing my eyes closed, I fought it, the fade that wanted to suck me into black.

Barely able to see, I rummaged under my seat, adrenaline lighting in my veins as my fingers came into contact with the metal where it was strapped to the underside.

The shock in Faith's eyes shifted to straight fear when she realized what I was holding. "Jace . . . what are you . . ."

But her words trailed off with the squeal of the tires the lit on the road, the smashed to shit black town car skidding backward in reverse.

With my gun drawn, I stalked around the front of my car.

Squinting, I tried to see through the thick, sticky wetness that blanketed my face.

Sun glinted from above, and the only thing I could make out through the car's windows were the two massive, silhouetted figures in the front seats.

I lifted my gun higher, striding that direction.

Numb except for the fact I'd fight to the death for these girls.

My finger on the trigger, I started shouting, deranged anger bleeding from my mouth, "Come on, motherfucker. Come at me.

You want to hurt an innocent woman? A little girl, you sick fucks? Come at me."

Their engine revved, and I kept marching that direction.

Two seconds of a silent war.

Me facing down the front of that battle-ram car. Trembling finger on the trigger.

Then the car suddenly whipped around and peeled out, flying down the street. The only trail of it the taillights that bloomed in the distance before it screeched as it careened around a corner, disappearing from sight.

A scream echoed from behind me. Faith's torment coming from the front seat of my car where she stumbled out onto the road.

"Oh my God, are you okay?" There was another voice coming from the outskirts of my consciousness, a woman running to help me from across the intersection.

I dropped my gun to my side. The shock sliding through me and draining like a pool of tar onto the ground when I turned back around to see the wreckage.

"Oh, God," the woman whispered, rearing back.

No doubt, she was terrified when she saw my state, the blood that streaked from the wound on my head.

Or maybe she just saw the violence shining in my eyes.

I didn't care. Didn't give a fuck what I looked like.

"Call 9-1-1," I told the woman as I sidestepped her, going right for Faith, who was shaking, barely able to stand as she struggled with the bashed-in door to get to Bailey in the backseat.

By the time I got there, she'd managed to wrench it open, her screams hitting the stifled air. "Bailey . . . oh God, Bailey, my baby, my baby. No. No."

Bailey's cries echoed from the backseat.

I looped an arm around Faith's waist, glancing again over my shoulder, making sure the fuckers were gone.

This time, I sure as hell wasn't going to be unprepared if they rounded for another attack. I'd already let emotions cloud my mind.

There was nothing. Just the hiss and whirr of the engine, the woman in the intersection on her cell, begging for the ambulance and police to hurry.

And Faith . . .

Faith who wailed against me, this frantic terror bleeding from her lips. "Bailey. Oh, God, Bailey. How could they do this? How could they?"

"Shh," I whispered, desperate to give her solace. Refuge while every cell in my body screamed for retribution.

To silence the threat.

"I've got you, Faith. I've got you."

*I've got you.*

She writhed and cried out, "Why's this happening to us? Why? Oh, God . . . someone help us. Please."

Torment rang from her mouth.

Filled the air.

Tortured my heart.

"Shh . . ."

I struggled to get myself together. Focus on that second. What was happening and what needed to be done. I tightened my hold on Faith while I edged her to the side so I could look at her kid.

*Her kid.*

Her sweet, sweet kid.

And I realized right then that there were no longer any reservations. There was no longer trying to stop myself from falling completely for this child.

Because I felt the snap.

Every hard, bitter idea I'd had of Joseph's child cracking beneath the crater of devotion that sank into my spirit.

*Bailey.*

Faith crumbled a bit, letting me hold her, and I angled her to the side as I stuffed the gun under the front passenger seat. I kept her close while I set my knee on the floor in the back so I could get a better look at Bailey.

Fear and fury ripped a hole through the center of me.

Blood dripped down her chin and soaked her shirt.

Oh God.

But her eyes, they were open wide, her chocolate gaze filled with all her trust.

"Jacie . . . I's need you. My *mouf* hurts." She said it in that little drawl of hers, her voice scared but strong.

Relief hit me, harder than that fucking car, and I tried to keep my cool. To keep it together and not break down in a fucking heap of tears that would be nothing but relief.

I needed to be strong. For them.

Possession spun a web around me.

My heart and my soul.

It took every ounce of control I had not to pull her from her car seat, every warning I'd ever been given about never moving someone in a crash up against the all-consuming need to wrap the little girl up.

Hold her.

"You've got me, Unicorn Girl. You've got me."

And I wasn't about to let her go.

I eased back out and pulled Faith closer, praying my voice would break through her fear. "She's okay, baby. She's okay. You're okay. I've got you. I've got you. I won't let anything happen to you."

It was the brutal fucking truth.

I could hear the sirens strike up from the fire station just two streets over, the whir of them coming closer and closer.

I just stood there, a rock between my girls while we waited, an arm around Faith's waist and my hand holding Bailey's tiny one.

A cruiser flew up the street and skidded to a stop at the intersection. The officer stepped out, eyes quick to assess the situation.

Two seconds later, an ambulance came to a stop beside him. Paramedics piled out, their heavy footsteps pounding on the pavement.

Was it fucked up I didn't want to let go when they approached? That I wanted to stand in front of them?

A shield.

A guard.

But I relented, feeling as if a physical piece of me was being pried away. Four paramedics enclosed the space.

I didn't go far. Hovering right there, my feet pacing, my body unable to sit still as my insides began to boil.

As anger grew.

As retaliation became a living, thriving being that beat through my blood.

It only amplified when I thought of the possibility that Bailey had been hurt worse than she appeared, when she cried out when they cut her free from the seat, when Faith quietly wept at her side.

My spirit trembled and hate screamed.

A paramedic touched my arm, jerking me out of my frantic thoughts. "Sir . . . we need to take a look at that cut on your head."

"I'm fine," I growled at him.

The guy had the nerve to grin. "Don't look so fine to me. You're gonna need a couple of stitches, and we need to check for a concussion."

Shit.

The last thing I wanted was to worry about myself.

But I let him sit me on the curb, his gloved fingers poking and prodding, a light shined into my eyes.

During the exam, there was no missing the eyes of the officer penetrating me. Clearly, he had been calculating the disaster.

Coming to realization that nothing was right.

This wasn't an accident.

It was an attack.

His shadow fell over me as the paramedic dabbed a cotton ball on my cut.

I winced. Took that sting and buried it with the bitterness that was building into something that should be impossible.

So intense that I could taste the bitterness of it on my tongue.

My stomach nothing but fists and knots of aggression as violence replaced the blood in my veins.

I knew these people were disgusting.

Out for themselves.

Money the almighty end.

Nothing else mattering but lining their pockets and protecting themselves from the consequences of their corruption.

I'd just not expected the depravity. The type of wickedness

they could sink to.

The officer stepped forward, and I looked up at him. "I need you to call Mack Chambers. Get someone here to get what evidence they can. This was intentional."

Premeditated.

A warning I wasn't going to leave unanswered.

"I can't believe this fucking bullshit. Right in our town? In broad fucking daylight? No different from with Joseph. Like they can't be fucking touched."

Mack ranted outside of the emergency room door where I silently raged.

I'd just had a line of stitches placed in my head, but it was my guts that were raw and bleeding.

Faith was with Bailey, who was having additional scans done to make sure she didn't have any hidden injuries, covering all the bases.

As far as they could tell, her only injury was a cut to her lip, which accounted for the blood on her shirt.

Faith had been unharmed other than the damage that was steadily being done to her psyche. These bastards wearing her down. Carving her out. Looking for something that wasn't even there.

Her parents had rushed over as soon as they'd heard, terrified, her father's jaw clenched shut. I wasn't sure what to expect when he'd approached me, my insides lined with steel as I'd prepared for his anger.

But he'd reached out, squeezed my shoulder, unable to say anything, only giving me that silent show of gratitude before he'd turned and disappeared into Bailey's room.

If only I could have done more. Ended it this afternoon. Helplessness spun through the space, and I tried to blink away the blinding torment and vengeance possessing me.

Mack had shown up looking every bit the deviant I felt. His anger as deep as mine. The venomous tattoos that screamed death and destruction on his arms coming alive beneath the bristle of his straining muscles.

All my screaming was on the inside. Spirit exploding with fury. Soul shaking with the wrath it pumped into my veins.

I gritted my teeth, doing my best not to lose it right there in the quiet hall. "They fucking rammed us twice, man. It was no accident. Wasn't even close to being a simple hit and run. It was them. I know it."

"No shit." He gripped the longer pieces of his blond hair between both hands. If he tugged any harder, he would have yanked it free.

He dropped his attention to the white-and-gray speckled linoleum floor, like he was reading some hidden message written in the design. "It has to be . . . some kind of fucked-up warning. Otherwise, they would have stayed and finished it."

*Finished it.*

His words cut through me.

Daggers and knives.

My back hit the wall, and my head rocked back hard in my frustration. A fresh round of pain splintered through my head when it knocked against the plaster.

I welcomed it.

Let it stoke the fire.

"They could have been hurt. Killed." Grit and hate. They seethed from my tongue.

Mack swung his attention back up to me. "You sure you didn't get a good look at them? Anything that I can go on?"

I gave a harsh shake of my head. "Could barely make out two guys. Nothing of their faces. Didn't get the license, either, but the front of the car was smashed to shit. Not sure how they even drove away."

Frustrated, he pushed out a sigh, warily looking up at me in his own sort of desperation. "They found it abandoned about a mile outside of town. Wiped clean. It had been reported stolen this morning from Raleigh. Wouldn't have mattered if you caught the

MORE OF *You*

license, anyway."

"Shit," I cursed at the floor.

His voice was a harsh murmur, "These guys aren't fucking immortal. They can't just disappear. There has to be something. Something I'm missing."

Didn't help that the only name I had been able to give Mack had come up as a dead end.

Steven in the ground a few months before Joseph had been killed. Not that I was mourning that piece of shit.

The monster who'd started the entire chain of events.

Forcing me into running that poison for him.

Nothing but a slave.

Shackled.

Every bit as real as the bars I'd found myself behind.

Mack angled his head so he could meet my eye. "I'm going to find these assholes, Jace. I will. I promise you."

I lifted my chin. "I sure has hell hope so, Mack . . . because you aren't going to like it if I find them first."

I wound around him, and he snatched me by the wrist. "Jace, didn't confide all of this to you to get you hurt."

Yanking my arm out of his hold, I backed away. "You should know me better than to think I wouldn't gladly die for them."

Spinning on my heel, I started down the hall, faltering to a stop when Mack's grated words hit me from behind. "They killed Joseph, man. Put a gun to his head and pulled the trigger."

His voice was jagged. Cracked and bleeding. His own regret filling the narrow hall. A plea for me to think twice. "I couldn't stand it if I let that happen to you."

I swung back around, my brow twisting so tight I could barely see.

Couldn't see through the hate.

The devotion.

The protectiveness that wound inside me.

"You, Mack? You didn't let that happen. I did. Don't think for a second I'm going to stand aside and let it happen to Faith and Bailey."

My heart thrashed in my chest. Like it had teeth and claws.

Looking for a way out to avenge.

His attention dropped to his boots. "No, I don't. It's just . . ." He lifted his gaze. "You have to tell her everything. What he did. What he had himself into."

"I know." I took another step back, drawn to the door Bailey was behind. I gulped for the nonexistent air. "I will . . . I promise."

The selfish part of me wasn't ready for this. Because I could feel it coming—everything I'd been a fool to think I might be able to keep slipping through my fingers.

My hands fisted.

Tightly.

Because I refused to let go.

## Jace
### Eighteen Years Old

*J*ace did his best to ignore the way Joseph and Ian had stopped talking the second he'd come out into the living room.

He was already on edge.

Watching over his goddamn shoulder.

Fighting the misery of what he'd become.

The last thing he wanted was for either of them to know what he'd succumbed to, and he sure as hell didn't want them to know he'd done it for them.

Most of all, he hoped to God they wouldn't do something stupid.

Go behind his back and get deeper into that sort of sordid trouble.

Steven, that cock-sucking lowlife, had been lurking. Spending more and more time at the trailer.

Jace doubted it had much to do with the *allure* of his trashed-out mother.

He always worried that they'd slip into the lifestyle they'd been bred into. He knew it was so much easier than fighting it every step of the way. He could only pray that they got that fighting was worth it.

He dropped his backpack to the ground at the door, glaring at it like it held some of the culpability. Doing this?

Yielding?

It was his own form of fighting.

"Where you been, Jace?" Joseph called, something sour in his tone.

God, Joseph was pissing him off more and more.

Ian laughed. "He was probably off getting himself a fine piece of ass. Pretty obvious, isn't it?"

Jace tried to control his temper.

Hating the way it constantly flared.

The way he was constantly on edge.

He looked at them where they sat on the couch watching a movie. "I was out."

He sure as hell wasn't gonna let on where he'd been.

"To see Faith?" Ian goaded, grinning wide. "You lucky bastard."

Jace shook his head. "She's not a joke."

"But she *is* hot."

Joseph glared daggers at Ian and then turned them on Jace. Angry in a way Jace hadn't ever seen him before. He had no idea what his problem was lately.

Joseph climbed to his feet and headed for the door. Jace swiveled around as Joseph jerked it open. "Where are you going?"

"Out." Joseph tossed out the same excuse Jace had just given them. Jace knew that was exactly what it was. A cover for something.

Worry sloshed with the anger, like two rivers coming together and forming white-water rapids.

"Where?" he demanded, taking a step in Joseph's direction.

An incredulous smirk twisted Joseph's mouth into something defiant. "You don't have a say in what I do, Jace."

Panic surged, and Jace had him against the wall again. "Stay away from Steven. I already warned you."

Joseph pushed Jace back.

As hard as he could.

Jace barely stumbled, glaring Joseph down, ready to fight the insolence out of him if that's what it took.

"You want to fight, Jace? Bring it on. I'm finished listening to you . . . spouting all your holier-than-thou bullshit while you're off having all the fun."

Scornful laughter rocked from Jace. "All the fun? That's what you think? That I'm off, *having fun?*"

The time of his fucking life.

Yeah, right.

Joseph didn't have the first clue what Jace had done for him. What he was still doing for him. The sacrifices he'd made.

Jace pointed behind him. "Now get your ass back on that couch. I need to take a shower and meet Faith. When I get back, I expect you to be sitting right there."

Bitterness bled from the snort Joseph emitted. "That's what I thought."

Forty-five minutes later, Jace rushed back out to the small living room.

He was running late.

Quickly, he shoved the blanket he'd washed and folded into his backpack, looking back at Ian and Joseph who were again sitting on the couch behind him.

"I'll be back in a few hours." He stood, slinging the backpack onto his shoulder, and pointed between the two of them. "Don't either of you go anywhere."

Ian mock-saluted him. "Aye-aye, Captain."

Joseph just rolled his eyes, and Jace slipped out into the night.

Tonight, the moon was high and full. Washing the leaves and the ground in a milky spray, a breeze blowing through from the ocean filling his nostrils with the scent of the sea and the summer.

Jace raced up the bumpy trail, running through the night toward the one place he wanted to be. He didn't slow until he was at the base of the porch, staring up at the girl who stood at the door.

271

His own definition of a dream.

A fantasy.

Wearing this flowy dress, her hair a chocolate river, rolling over her shoulders, her skin glowing in the traces of moonlight.

She curtsied as if she had stepped out of the eighteen fifties. "Why, sir, welcome to the BBB."

Jace felt the smile twitching all over his mouth, and he did his best to play along. "It's a pleasure to be here, ma'am. It's been a long trek, and I'm eager for a comfortable place to rest."

"Oh, I plan on making you comfortable, all right," she drawled, sweet seduction on her tongue.

Unable to stay still for a second longer, Jace started up the porch steps, his breaths coming shorter and shorter with each one he took, until he had the girl backed against the wall in their spot.

She grinned up at him. Jace's heart clanged in the confines of his chest.

She threaded her fingers through his. "Let's go inside," she whispered like a secret.

Confusion pulled a frown to Jace's forehead. "You mean . . . inside, inside?"

She only grinned wider. "Come on, Jace. Dream with me. Follow me."

She was giggling as she moved around the house to one of the smaller side windows, glancing back at him as she pushed it up.

He choked out a laugh. "Did you know that was unlocked this whole time?"

"Yep," she said. "I've gone in before. This time, I want you to come with me."

He roughed a hand through his hair and looked around the property. "I'm not sure that's a good idea."

Faith slipped through the window, her hand outstretched through the frame. "Follow me, Jace. Let's dance with the ghosts. Introduce ourselves. Let them know we'll be stayin'."

He couldn't help but smile. "You're insane, Faith Linbrock."

"Insane for you." She edged back, her gaze sweeping the room where she stood. "This is our place, Jace. Our castle. Let's claim it."

How was he gonna resist that? He didn't want to.

He slipped through the window and into the shadowy, hazy light, watching the way the tender smile ridged her lips.

She backed farther into the darkened silhouettes that danced and played on the walls.

"Can you imagine what it will be like? Living here? People coming in and out the way they used to do? Can you imagine all the people who've been inside these walls before us? All their experiences? Their loves and their losses?"

"Would you really want to know all those things?" he asked, following her through the rooms on the first floor, watching her wistful expression as she explored.

She looked back at him. "You can't know the full goodness of someone without being able to see the bad. Otherwise that vision is distorted. Then we'd never understand what they might have endured. Their hardships and their blessings."

He stepped forward and ran his fingers through her hair. "You have an astonishing soul, Faith."

The most beautiful soul.

He was terrified he was going to tarnish it.

The things he'd been forced into the last few weeks made him sick.

Physically ill.

But Steven had warned him that, if he didn't do as he was told, he'd make what he'd done to Ian look like a walk in the park.

And Joseph would be next.

What else was he supposed to do?

God, Jace had never wanted to be different more than he did right then. Had never wished he'd come from a different world than the one he had more than when he was standing in front of Faith.

She suddenly pulled away, giggling as she raced for the main big room, looking over her shoulder as she went. "I dare you to come find me, Beast."

Jace froze right there, wrapped in the sound of her laughter ricocheting from the walls as she disappeared at the end of the hall, his heart thundering harder with the echo of her footsteps as she moved upstairs.

Or maybe it was just the howl of the ghosts.

And right then, he couldn't remember his ghosts. Who he was and what was holding him back. None of the reasons he could never be good enough for this girl.

The only thing he could process was that she was his and he was hers.

He believed.

Believed in the way he loved her. In the things he would sacrifice for her happiness and her joy. The way he would always take care of her.

Right then, that was the only thing that mattered.

That and the fact she was somewhere upstairs waiting for him.

His stomach tight and his pulse a thunder in the darkness, he edged up the sweeping staircase he'd only ever seen through the window.

Inside, it appeared even more massive than the mere picture he'd gotten, the entire place worn from disuse and age, and still screaming with all the possibilities Faith had in it.

He got to the landing and looked down two long halls. Instantly, he went left, drawn that direction as if he could feel her life force bleeding through the walls.

Her energy alive.

That feeling he had been terrified to feel taking over every part of him.

His heart and his mind and his body.

He stopped at the first door on the left. It was open a crack, and he nudged it farther, the old hinges creaking as it slowly swept open.

That feeling radiated back.

Real and alive.

Intoxicating.

He stepped inside.

Faith's back was to him, and she stood looking out the window. She peeked back at him. "I was gonna hide, but I got distracted."

He inched up behind her. Her fingertips traced the window. "Look at that. I bet this is the best view in the house. I call this as our room."

The only thing visible from the window was the garden of roses, the expanse of them seeming to go on forever before they disappeared in the distance toward the trailer where he lived.

"So much beauty in the middle of something so ugly," he said, words a soft gruff from his chest.

She slowly turned around to face him.

"That's funny, because I only see the beauty."

He ran his knuckles down the side of her face. "That's because that's what you are."

"Let's make more of it," she whispered, a tremble in her needy voice.

And he wondered if she was as nervous as he was. If she understood he was holding something so precious in his hands.

That she was offering it to him.

Trusting him with it.

She was holding his hand when she knelt, and he sank to his knees in front of her.

He let the backpack slide off his shoulder, and he opened it so he could pull out the blanket he'd washed and packed for them. He spread it out on the floor and helped her lay down on it.

Moonlight poured across her face, and he wondered if he'd ever witness anything so perfect again.

"I love you," he said, carefully climbing over her.

"I love you more than anything," she murmured back, letting those fingers trace his face, nothing but fire to his body.

He slipped the little straps of her dress from her shoulders, kissed her softly.

Carefully.

As carefully as he loved her.

They slowly undressed each other. Like both of them were memorizing every second.

He watched her through the shadows as her eyes went wide and her lips parted. As she whimpered his name and he groaned hers.

He loved her in the shadows.

With the howl of the ghosts whipping around them. With the

promise of what this place might be one day.

After, he held her tenderly, Faith snuggled up in the crook of his arm, her head on his shoulder as she played her fingers across his bare stomach. "Are you goin' to marry me, Jace?"

"The second you'll let me."

He could feel the force of her smile against the thrumming beat of his heart.

"How many babies are we goin' to have?" she all but whispered, her mind racing into the future. He wanted to be right there, catch up, pray he could maybe be the father he'd never had.

"How many do you want?"

"Two," she immediately said. "A boy and girl. Bailey and Benton."

Jace laughed lightly, leaning up to kiss the top of her head. "You just want to add them to all those B's."

She was grinning wide when she looked up at him. "Oh, come on, Jace, this has to happen," she teased so quietly, with so much love, parroting his words from the beginning of the summer.

Somehow that seemed so long ago.

"It does have to happen," he whispered.

Like his own prayer.

He had to find a way to make this happen. Find a way to get himself out of the scary shit he'd somehow fallen into.

They stayed like that for the longest time, Jace just holding her and not wanting to let go before he finally sighed. "We should get you home."

"I want to stay right here. Forever."

"Me, too. Someday. Someday," he promised.

They dressed and he stuffed the blanket back into his pack, held tight to her hand as he led her down the stairs and back to the window where they'd slipped inside.

He stepped out first, reaching back into help Faith through, when a streak of light hit him on the side of the face.

The blinding glare of a flashlight. "Freeze, right there."

Jace froze, every inch of him going cold.

Jace sat at the cold metal chair at the cold metal table, cold cuffs around his wrists. He pressed his palms to his face, shook his head again. "I told you, it's not mine."

The sheriff frowned in disbelief. "Really? It was in the bottom of your bag."

Jace pressed his eyes tighter, trying to believe. To believe that he could somehow get out of this. "It's not mine," he begged.

He'd already gotten rid of everything Steven had forced on him earlier that day.

Three goddamned stops where his heart had been in his throat, dread coating his skin in a slick of sweat as he'd slinked into three rotten apartments.

"Then who's is it?"

Ian's or Joseph's. Ian's or Joseph's.

It'd had to be.

Somehow . . . somehow one of them had gotten wrapped up in this mess, too.

Besides, Steven had been giving him large, wrapped bundles. What they'd found in his backpack were little packets of coke already ready to sell on the street.

"I don't know," he said.

The sheriff laughed. As cold as the rest of the room. "Seems to me that you've got a problem. You had enough coke in there that we have you on intent to distribute. Not to mention the breaking and entering with that girl."

That girl.

That girl.

She was the only thing he cared about right then. Her and his brother and Joseph.

Oh, God.

What was he going to do?

The problem was that Jace knew there was no getting himself out of this.

Not without getting his brother or cousin in trouble.

That, or he could give Steven's name, which would more than likely do nothing but get Jace killed.

Either him or Ian and Joseph.

That was not a result he could contemplate.

And there was no chance he could talk his way out of the breaking and entering.

There was no way he was letting Faith take the fall for that, and he knew she was in the next room over, trying to do exactly that.

Convince them that it was her fault.

Her idea.

Jace swallowed hard, searched inside himself for courage, for the determination to do whatever it took to protect his brother and his cousin.

To protect Faith.

He lifted his head and looked the officer head on. "I'll plead whatever you want. I just need two things from you."

"I need to talk to you."

Joseph immediately shot to his feet when Jace banged into the trailer.

Jace had sent Ian to run an errand for their mother, telling him he needed him to do him the favor. Really, he'd just wanted Ian out of the house so he could talk with Joseph in private.

Guilt was written across Joseph like it was written in a book, all mixed up with the hostility that continued to bleed from him.

Jace wanted to take it out on him. Demand a confession. Make Joseph give him confirmation that either he or Ian had been the ones who'd stuffed those drugs in Jace's backpack, surely finding the quickest place to hide it when Jace had come out of his room.

He'd bet a million bucks Steven had shown up and coerced one of them into it, just the same as he'd done to Jace. The threat too great to resist.

How could Jace blame either Ian or Joseph for the same thing that he'd cowarded to? It wasn't as if it was a negligible risk.

No question, Steven would stand on his word.

None of these guys were to be toyed with.

So instead of railing on Joseph, Jace swallowed down all his anger that he felt toward the world, and he made a plea. "I know things have been weird between us lately, and I know you're younger than Ian, but I need you to step up. Take care of him the way I've been taking care of you."

Jace sucked in the heated air. Feeling as if he were being consumed.

Incinerated.

Then he begged, "I don't know what either of you have gotten into, but I need you to promise me, Joseph, promise me, whatever it is, it ends now. Or you're going to end up just like me. Maybe worse."

Joseph stared at him. Appearing dumbfounded. Maybe shocked. "You want me to take care of your brother?"

Grief clawed at his throat. "And Faith. Watch out for Faith. You and Ian have to promise not to tell her that I'm getting sent away. She'll be devastated. Riddled with guilt. Let her think I left her. That's all I'm asking of you. Here's the key to the little safe I have under my bed. It's all the money I've saved working at the store. Can I trust you to do this?"

Joseph took the key and rolled it around his fingers. "Of course, you can trust me."

Rays of blinding light streaked through the moss-covered branches that stretched across the old dirt road like a living canopy.

It was a road they'd walked together what seemed a thousand times.

Their secret spot.

Their *sacred* spot.

He stared at her from where he stood five feet away.

His hands stuffed in the pockets of his ripped jeans, rocking with the guilt and the grief, trying to keep from rushing her. Holding her.

"I don't care what anyone thinks."

The pleas poured from her mouth, every single one like a knife driven right into his heart.

"I don't know what kind of trouble we're in. The only thing that matters to me is that you're standing right here, in front of me."

Sadness rippled through her features. The only thing he wanted was to reach out. Take it away. Promise her that it would all be okay.

But it wouldn't be.

He had to embrace his circumstances.

He was going to prison.

He had to cut himself off from her. He couldn't ask her to wait. He knew she would.

By doing it this way, he was giving her a choice.

Like a caged bird, he was letting her go.

He'd find out if she really belonged to him if she still loved him when he returned.

Only he'd be the one in the cell.

It was the only way he'd ever really know if she was his or if it was all a fantasy. A dream he could never live.

"It doesn't matter, Faith? How can you say that?" His voice was bitter and hard, every bit of disgust cast at himself.

She took a pleading step forward. "It doesn't. The only thing that matters is you and me."

He took a weary step back, trying to put distance between them. To ignore the energy that blasted and raged. His voice twisted in emphatic sincerity. Praying she'd get it. Finally understand. "You matter, Faith. Who you are and who you're going to be. And I won't stand in the way of that any longer."

He nearly buckled and told her the truth when he saw the tears gather in her eyes. "No," she whispered.

He shook his head. "I'm sorry. The last thing I ever wanted to do was hurt you, but that seems to be the only thing I can do. What happened last night is proof of that. It ends right now."

Jace forced himself to turn around, to move, to leave.

He felt her panic slamming him from behind. "Jace . . . please, don't do this. Don't leave me."

Fingertips brushed down his back. Fire crackled from the connection. The way it'd always been. Since the second he'd seen her.

He tried to ignore it, to run, but he whirled around and grabbed her face in both of his hands. His eyes traced every line.

Every inch.

Memorizing.

But it wasn't enough. And he was nothing but a thief. Needing one more taste.

He dipped down and captured her mouth.

Fighting his own tears.

Wishing he could tell her how much he loved her.

Cherished her.

That last night had meant more to him than any other moment in his entire life.

Feeling like he might collapse, he dropped his forehead against hers, his eyes tightly closed as he breathed her in.

Vanilla and roses.

As if she'd been dancing in a bed of them.

That was the way he would remember her.

Blowing her belief on the wilting petals. Breathing new life into them. Praying it would be enough to sustain him.

Then he gripped her by the shoulders, physically having to pry himself away.

Then he turned, and he left her standing there.

In their spot.

Hoping he wasn't a fool to believe when he returned she might still belong to him.

# thirty-three

## Faith

*T*hrough the shadowy darkness of the old house, Jace carried

Bailey up the sweeping stairs. I'd almost wanted to argue with him. Tell him I was capable. That I wanted to do it. *Needed* to do it.

But it was the look on his face when he'd pulled her from the backseat of the rental car that had silenced every question begging to be released from my tongue.

That hatred that had blazed in the depths of those coppery eyes as he'd searched the property as if he were prepared to run into the whipping shadows with a sword drawn.

A warrior who was preparing for war.

A fight to the death.

It was as if a switch had been flipped, and that menacing, terrifying boy who'd do anything to protect his family had been zapped back to life.

Born in that accident.

Or maybe he'd just been there all along, waiting to be released. The presence of it crawled the walls and buzzed in the atmosphere.

Crackling.

Snapping where it struck.

I could feel it, flames against my skin.

Inciting a terror inside me unlike anything I'd ever known. Not of him, but of what was to come.

I could feel it. The threat of it rising in the air. Clouds that rained disaster.

I struggled to breathe against it. Everything up to this point had felt as if whoever this was wanted to scare me. To warn me into handing over whatever it was they wanted.

Didn't they know I would if I could?

But now . . .

A shudder tumbled down my spine, the trauma of the accident so fresh it was the only thing I could see when I closed my eyes.

This had to end.

Jace stepped over the gate at the end of the hall, and I followed him into Bailey's room where he carefully laid her onto her tiny bed.

His hands were shaking when he pulled back the covers, his jaw clenched when he tugged off her shoes.

But what destroyed me was when he knelt beside her, when he kissed her forehead and brushed her hair back from her face and looked down on her sleeping form as if she had become the focus of his world.

As he tucked the Beast doll into her arms as if it were a promise to watch over her all night long.

Terror shivered through my being.

The what-ifs.

What if they'd hit a little harder or a little differently?

What if they'd backed up and slammed us again?

What if they returned?

But my tiny girl? She was safe.

Safe because of Jace, the man so stupidly brave when he'd faced down that car as if he were invincible.

Dragging his attention from Bailey, he turned the force of that gaze toward where I stood uneasily in the middle of the room.

Right then, he was wearing the same expression he'd worn this afternoon.

Devotion and love and hate. A glow in his eyes.

It pinned me to the spot.

Energy blasted.

Rushing and racing and spiraling.

His mouth trembled as promises fell from his lips. "I will kill them, Faith. I will hunt them down and destroy them before I let them hurt you or Bailey."

A tremble ridged my spine, and I found myself voicing the question I didn't even want to entertain. "What is it they really want from us? I don't have anything anyone could possibly want."

Why did I get the devastating impression that he knew? My mind filled with the vision of him in that intersection, going for that car with a gun drawn.

Stricken, he blinked at me, and the accusation flew from my mouth—gratefulness or confusion or blame—I didn't know. Whatever it was, it left me on a whimpered cry. "You had a gun."

His head jerked to the side before he slowly pushed to his feet.

The man towering.

A blistering shadow in the darkened depths of Bailey's small room.

He stalked my way. Slowly, though his strides were purposed.

A shiver rushed across my skin, and my back banged softly into the wall. His voice was rough, caressing across my face like a sharp promise. "Yes, I had a gun. I told you that I was here to protect you. I won't leave you defenseless."

My eyes slammed closed for a second, trying to find my senses.

I could feel the questions twisted across my face in deep lines when I opened my eyes again and stared up at the man who looked so dangerous and forbidding standing there.

"Tell me what's happening, Jace. What did Mack tell you? Do you know who hurt Joseph? What do they possibly think I could have?" My voice cracked on the last.

A consuming kind of grief was sucking the life from my spirit. Stealing away the flickers of joy I'd felt the last couple of weeks. That shimmer of hope that had risen from the depths of me.

As if maybe we could escape all the grief and sorrow. Never forget but find joy in the shadows.

The questions were coming too fast for me to entertain that any longer, though.

"What did he do?" I finally whispered the culmination of it all.

As soft as he tried to make them be, his words scraped across my soul.

A lash.

A blow.

"Joseph was never honest with you, Faith."

Tears streaked free, and my mind was tumbling back to those days when Jace had been taken from me. When Joseph had warned the exact same thing about Jace.

What was I supposed to believe?

Jace's mouth pinched. As if he were holding something in. Holding something back.

My eyes slammed closed, the accusation a low, pained cry. "What aren't you tellin' me?"

God, I was a fool.

Falling so fast and so hard.

But that was the way this boy had always had me. Hooked in his grips with nothin' but a glance of those knowing, fierce eyes.

It seemed impossible with the savage state that he was in, but I was sure it was hurt that blanketed Jace's being when he jerked back. As he blinked at me as if he were trying to see through his own questions.

His own torment and grief and guilt.

*What was happening?*

*What did he know?*

Jace paced, roughing a hand through his hair, his voice quieted as he hissed the words. "If I knew who was responsible, I would erase them, Faith. If I knew exactly who Joseph was involved with, I would have had Mack beating down their door the second this happened. But I don't."

He hit his fingertips against his chest, pain wheezing from him on his sharp breaths.

"The only thing I know is Joseph was *never* good enough. *Never* deserved you. And I *never* should have given him the chance to let him steal you from me."

Steal me away?

I stood there shocked when he blew out of Bailey's door as if it'd all become too much of a burden for him to bear any longer.

Footsteps pounded down the hall, and I craned my ear, listening for him to take the stairs and disappear out the front door the way I'd been terrified that he would do all along.

Forever.

But then I felt it. Jace came to a sudden stop.

As if he hadn't expected to do it, either.

His hesitation bled through the old walls before I heard the creak of the hinges of the neglected door.

The room I'd scarcely been able to bring myself to enter for all these years except to clean it every now and again, hit by a landslide of memories every single time I went in there.

There was nothing I could do to stop myself from moving that direction.

Drawn to the magnet.

Drawn to the light.

I was a shaking mess when I came to the door that was left open an inch.

When I nudged the crack wider, I found Jace standing in the middle of the room with his back to me, staring out at the garden of roses that filled the window as if the gorgeous scene had been framed.

All that hostility and rage brimming from his muscles.

My beast.

His shoulders tensed when he felt me inch in from behind him, and his hands fisted at his sides.

Shock reared me back a step when he suddenly whirled around.

It was almost fear that skated through me with the look on his face.

He pointed toward the wall. "When I came here, I thought I'd hate her."

Hurt blistered beneath the surface of my skin, unable to fathom that he'd even let a thought so cruel slip from between his lips.

He took a looming step forward. "I wanted to. I wanted to hate her so badly because she wasn't mine."

If it weren't for the deep sincerity breaking in his voice, I would have walked out. Turned my back on him. Instead, I was blinking at him, trying to process what he was saying. What was hidden in the deep emotion that burdened his words.

His eyes pinched closed, and when he opened them, they were blazing.

A thunderbolt.

Striking through me the way he always had.

"You want to know why I came here, Faith? You really want to know?"

My head started bouncing all over, as if I were begging for the answer but couldn't control the quakes that rocked the floor.

His fist came down hard on his chest. "Because I never stopped loving you. Not for a second. Not for a day. Because you've consumed every one of my goddamned thoughts since the second I left."

His body angled toward me. "Because I'm. In. Love. With. You."

He punctuated every single one of those last words with the desperation that rolled from his tongue.

"Because I always have been, and I'm always going to be."

His tone softened in some sort of grief. "And I fucking love her, too."

Oh.

I almost folded in two, slammed with the magnitude of it.

Because I'd finally caught up to what he was sayin'. I finally understood the way he'd been looking at her.

Desperation lit, caught up in the dense, dense air.

The strike of a match.

Tossed right into the rippling energy.

Gasoline.

My throat grew dry in the same second my heart boiled over, and there was no containing what I'd tried to keep buried deep inside me.

"And I never, ever stopped loving you. I might have hated you in the middle of it, but I never stopped, Jace. How could I? Not when you were the boy who made me realize what it was like to really love. The one who'd taken a fantasy idea in my mind and made it a reality. You touched me in a way no one else ever could. I think I've loved you since the day I met you."

The admission fractured out of me. Just like the last pieces of those memories that I'd been so desperately trying to cling to since Joseph was ripped out of my life.

Guilt churned at admitting it aloud, as if it might be a dirty secret I'd kept for all these years.

But it wasn't close to being as great as the love that poured free with the confession.

Because Jace Jacobs?

He could never be erased from me.

## Jace

The room echoed with our proclamations.

As if the words were etching themselves onto the walls. A knife dug deep into the wood.

A statement made.

Permanent.

No going back.

It was the room where I'd first taken her. Loved her. Where she'd taught me that life might hold more meaning than simple survival.

More than just a struggle.

More than just brutality.

With her?

It'd been *more*.

It'd been everything.

I'd lost it. Let it slip through my fingers like a fool.

I stalked toward her, no longer able to tolerate the space between us. Every echo of my footsteps vibrated through the floorboards.

Because it was fucking alive.

The air and the energy and the feeling.

The *connection*.

The truest thing I'd ever had.

Faith was trembling when I dove my fingers into those long locks of chocolate hair and captured her mouth.

Possessively.

Desperately.

With all the fear I'd felt this afternoon.

With all the devotion I felt in that moment.

All my defenses down.

My lips pressed and pulled and sucked, and she whimpered into the assault, "Jace."

I pressed her against the wall, my forehead rocking on hers, the words a breath of a whisper against her lips, "I mean it, Faith. I fucking love you. I love her. This . . . this was what I was always meant to do. Protect you and love you. I'm supposed to be here with you."

Her fingers gripped my shoulders, pulling me closer than I already was. Like she couldn't get close enough. "Then why's it feel like I'm the one who has finally made it home?"

Her fingertips fluttered up over my face.

Across my lips.

My nose.

My brow.

Not quite touching when she flitted them over the row of stitches that had been made at my temple. Like she'd give anything to heal them.

What she didn't know was that, just by standing there, she already was.

Until that moment, I wondered if I'd ever really known what devotion meant. As a kid, I had been too scared and broken and insecure to realize what she'd really needed was me.

"Because that's what this place was always supposed to be. *Ours.*"

Didn't care if it was some kind of blasphemy. A straight shot of betrayal sent Joseph's way.

Fuck him.

After today? After seeing what he'd gotten them into? I couldn't find it in myself to give half a shit about what he might want.

He'd stolen what was mine.

And I was taking it back.

My hands found the angled curve of her face, lifting it to me, and I stared down at her through the flood of moonlight that poured into the room.

Or maybe it was just the girl who was lighting it up.

"Do you remember?" I asked her. "The night you gave yourself to me? What I told you?"

"That you'd love me forever." Her hands wrapped around my wrists. Her voice dropped.

Low with seduction.

Still, the girl was so damned sweet that it still managed to come out sounding shy. "I remember everything. The way you touched me. The way you loved me. But I'd already belonged to you, Jace. Just like I do now."

I pressed her up harder against the wall, her back hitting it with a soft thud, an echo that wound with the promise that fell from my mouth. "I lost you once. I won't let it happen again. I won't let you go."

"I don't want you to. Don't ever let me go. I need you, Jace. I need you to stay."

My hands slid down the perfect curves of her body, landing on her waist and cinching tight. "Tell me again," I demanded.

She lifted her chin toward my face, her voice so devastatingly soft, and still, the loudest thing I'd ever heard. "I'm in love with you. I love you so much it hurts."

I was going to erase the sting.

Eradicate the hurt.

Touch her and please her until there was nothing but pleasure.

Protect her in a way that she would always know she was safe.

Softly, I brushed my fingers through her hair. "And you're the only one who's ever taken my pain away."

"I guess maybe we've always just been better together," she whispered in that soft accent that she wore so well. Goodness on her tongue and trust in her eyes.

"Together," was my only answer, and then I was sweeping her off her feet and pulling her into my arms, cradling her like a treasure against my chest.

I carried her through the dancing shadows of the room to the massive four-poster bed.

The carved wood was dark and gleaming, lush in the light of the moon, the plush, satiny, cream-colored bedding screaming luxury in what had once been the master suite.

Luxury was fucking right.

There was no greater extravagance or indulgence than being inside Faith. No greater riches than holding this girl in my hands.

And I was about to get greedy.

Those slender arms clung to my neck as I leaned down and peeled the covers back.

I laid her in the middle.

Chocolate hair spilled out all around her, and that tight body arched.

I hadn't even touched her, and she was already quivering with need.

Her breaths panted into the dense, dense air, stirring up the memories that were ready to stand and fight for a future.

I'd let her go, thinking it was what was the best for her. It had been the most foolish thing I had ever done.

No more.

I stepped back and stared down at her where she was laid out like a vision on that bed.

A fucking fantasy.

The girl I'd been dreaming of for all these years. A tease in my mind and a scar on my body.

My body that raced, muscles clenched tight, my dick begging at the seam of my jeans.

*Mine.*

Her hand fluttered up.

A whisper.

A plea.

"I don't wanna be alone. Not anymore, Jace. Take it from me . . . that place that's been achin' for you for all these years. It's always belonged to you, anyway."

Lust roared through my veins. Pumped steadily with the devotion.

I set a knee on the bed and climbed up over her, hands planted on either side of her head.

I dipped down.

Kissed her.

Slow and tender and profound.

Gentle sweeps of my tongue and soft bites of my teeth.

Fuck. She tasted so good. Felt so right.

A glimmer of a warning glowed deep inside my soul.

*She doesn't know.*

*She doesn't know.*

I shoved it down where it belonged. Refusing it. Because it didn't matter anymore.

My purpose had shifted.

My *reason* was her.

I set my palm on the side of her neck. Her pulse a needy drum, drum, drum.

Hard and fast and desperate.

It was enough to set me off. Make me dizzy. This girl filling my lungs.

Vanilla and roses.

My palm slipped down, gliding over the frantic beat of her heart, her body trembling under my touch. My fingers fumbled with the first button it met on her blouse, then the next, and the next, until the material was splayed open.

Her chest heaved, her tits covered in pink lace, her belly soft and flat and trembling. "No woman could ever compare to you. You are the sexiest, sweetest, most tempting thing I've ever seen."

"Jace," she whimpered.

"It's the truth. You are my perfection. Everything I've ever wanted. Everything I've ever needed. Everything I've been *missing*. *My Beauty*."

The last word came out on a harsh gush of air.

Need a fucking pounding force inside me.

Demanding that I take her.

I nipped at the shell of her ear, sucked at the pulse point that throbbed below it, tongue stroking out as I made my way down her throat, tasting the whimpered sounds that escaped her.

"I missed you. More than you could know." Her fingers were in my shoulders when she said it, ripping at the material of my tee. "I need to see you, Jace. *Feel* you."

Who was I to deny her that?

I shot up to sit on my knees, straddling her waist on both sides, and slowly peeled my shirt over my head, ignoring the sting of the fabric raking over the stitches when I did.

She was worth it.

So damned worth it.

Especially when she looked at me like that. Her lips parting on a sexy sigh as her eyes rushed over me.

Lashes of fire.

Heat and love and greed.

She reached her shaking hand out to trace across my chest. "And it's you, Jace. You who's the most magnificent thing I've ever seen. The most gorgeous boy who stumbled into my life. You stole my breath the first time you came through that office door."

Her fingertips brushed down. Stroked across my abdomen.

Every damned muscle tightened, rippled with unbearable need, this feeling that I might lose all control.

"Little did I know you'd soon be the keeper of it. The keeper of my breath. The keeper of my heart."

She reached out and grabbed me by the shoulders to hoist herself up, angled so the words came as sweet caresses across my face. "The keeper of my soul."

I pushed her back down onto the bed, my hand splayed across her chest. "And I'm not going to give it back."

There was a warning in there, but the girl took it as a tease, her teeth worrying on that bottom lip as redness splashed across her silky flesh. "You'd better not."

I dipped down quickly and raked my teeth across the defined

curve of her collarbone.

She jumped.

Gasped.

Whispered, "More."

*More.*

I jerked back both sides of her blouse, winding them off her shoulders, lifting her upper body from the bed so I could drag it the rest of the way from her arms.

It bound her all up, and I attacked her neck as I did, kissing that soft column as if it sustained my life.

Her head rocked back to grant me better access.

"Jace." It almost sounded like confusion. "Every touch. Every time. How do you do this to me?"

Her scent flooded me.

Filling my head.

My heart.

My soul.

And I was going to worship her forever.

Intensity whipped the air, that energy alive in the room that was ours.

Ours.

Hunger raced through my veins and poured onto my flesh.

Severe and strong.

Uncontainable.

Brighter than anything I'd ever felt.

Blinding.

I tore her shirt the rest of the way free, loving the tiny shock of surprise that jetted from her lips when I reached out and tugged down the cups of lace to expose the tight buds of her rosy nipples.

Her tits were full and pouring out over the top.

"Motherfuck . . . you are sublime."

I ran the knuckle of my index finger over one.

She arched, mumbled, "Yes."

I let my thumb take its place, rolling and teasing as I angled down to lap at the other with my tongue as I pushed her back to the bed.

Sucking and loving and *living.*

That was what it felt like when I was touching her.

Coming alive.

I reached behind her back and freed the clasp of her bra, and I relieved her of those bindings, too.

Free.

I wanted her free.

To live in me the way I wanted to live in her.

Without the chains of the past to hold us back. To beat us down.

And her hands were suddenly everywhere. Nails in my shoulders, scraping down my back, their own plea that meshed with the cries that fell from her mouth.

*More.*

I ripped myself back and went to work on the button of her jeans, moving away from her only long enough to slide them from her legs.

Good God.

She stole my breath.

Hitched and hooked it, my heart caught up in the middle of it, hammering wild.

Long, long legs that went on forever, pale flesh and slender curves and fucking perfect body.

Her cunt was bare, wet and glistening for me.

I tugged her jeans from her ankles, and my fingers were right there, dragging through her pussy.

I sank my fingers into all that attraction and desire.

Enraptured.

Fucking lost in the *magic* of this.

I leaned forward, still touching her as my tongue darted out to wet my dry lips. "Look what I do to you, baby. Look at the way I make you feel."

I burrowed my fingers deeper, in all that tight, slick heat, relished in her shudder that raced up my arm.

"You," she whimpered, her hips coming from the bed.

"You," I murmured back, kissing her softly, trying to find some semblance of control when this girl had stripped it all away.

Every vulnerability exposed.

The girl always making me so damned weak.

But this time . . . this time I felt the strength in it. The purpose. The reason.

This girl could bring me to her feet, but I'd always stand for her.

Devotion and loyalty hummed through my being. All mixed up with the frenzied heat, and I was back on my knees, ripping at the button of my jeans and shoving them from my body.

My cock jutted free, bouncing at my stomach, as devoted as the rest of me.

"No one. No one, Faith. Only you." The promises tumbled out, leaving me like I was drugged.

Dizzy on this girl.

It'd always been her. It always would be.

I felt half crazed when I wedged my hips between her trembling thighs.

So warm.

So right.

Short breaths ripped from my lungs, mingled with her own, everything becoming one.

Bated. Held and caught up in this moment.

I pushed up onto my hands and stared down at the girl, my heart a thunder where it beat at my chest.

"You," I told her again.

Heat blazed from her body, and I watched the bob of her delicate throat when she swallowed and watched me with all that trust that I didn't deserve, but I'd do everything in my power to earn.

"You," she rasped.

Energy billowed and bloomed. A fire that raged in the remaining space between us.

I had to remind myself to go slow when every part of my body wanted to fuck her wild.

Claim her.

Mark her.

I swallowed hard, dipped down and kissed her, and Faith dropped her legs open wide.

An offering.

Emotion tightened my chest, and I edged back an inch, letting my cock barely slide through the arousal between her lips.

A lick of need.

A lash of desperation.

Lust prowled my spine. The base instinct to take what was mine.

"I can't wait to feel you again. I need it. I need to feel your body on mine," she whimpered.

It felt like what was meant to be was finally catching up, matching time. Everything shifting back into its rightful alignment.

For a beat, our eyes tangled, and her nails burrowed deeper into my shoulders. "Take me. Make me remember every reason I've always been yours."

I gripped her behind her neck, the other at the top of her thigh, holding on to that soft, delicate skin as I pushed her wider.

I pressed just the head of my dick into her. Nudging into her folds.

A grunt fell like a stone from my mouth. Didn't matter that I was barely an inch inside.

The impact of her hit me like a landslide.

Too much.

Too perfect.

Too right.

Faith struggled to draw air into her lungs, her body bowing up as she struggled to accept me as I slowly spread her.

Finally, I couldn't take it anymore. No restraint. No self-control.

I slammed home.

I'd never, ever felt it more than then.

*Home.*

Her mouth dropped open at the side of my neck, her nose at my flesh, breathing me in.

My entire body shook, curling around her.

I pulled out before I rocked back in.

Hard.

Hip to hip.

Taking all of her.

"So good," ripped from my throat. "Nothing has ever felt so good."

Pants lifted into the air, her sweet lips parted.

"Are you okay?" I murmured, terrified I'd pushed her too far and too fast. Unable to stand the thought of it at the same damned time. The fucking desolation of her thinking about him.

"Nothing has ever felt so right."

Relief left me on a gush of air, and I began to move in her. Slow and hard.

Half-delirious, half-sure I'd never seen anything so clearly.

Every thrust was a promise.

Every fuck of my body a claim.

Soft cries of pleasure struck the air, and I held her, took her deep and hard while I kissed her gently.

My treasure.

My prize.

While I adored and cherished and murmured that I was never going to let her go.

I could feel it, her pleasure building, the way her body began to simmer under mine.

Heat and friction and need.

Her head rocked back, and I sucked at her chin before I kissed down the column of her throat.

Energy lapped. A slow build at first, a steady increase that lit in a frenzy.

Those eyes met mine, so intense.

And the feeling that I'd been fighting since I returned gripped me whole.

She opened herself wider and lifted to meet every hard thrust.

Our bodies a wave.

Rolling.

Floating.

Building.

"Jace," she whimpered, begging my name.

Pushing up onto a hand, I wedged the other between us, finding her clit, loving the sounds she made as I did.

Sounds of desire.

Of pleasure.

All of it for me.

I could feel her winding up.

Her body stretched thin.

She gripped my ass.

Urging me deeper as she rubbed her body against me.

Harder, faster, more.

Our skin was slicked in sweat, heat rising.

Short wheezes ripped from her delicate throat. Chants of my name.

And there was no question.

This girl. She'd always fucking been mine.

And she was going off.

Bliss a crack in the room.

Thunder.

Pleasure bound and pummeled the walls.

She took me with her. The most powerful emotion raced down to gather at the base of my spine.

Physical and emotional and alive.

All her.

I felt it splinter out.

Detonating.

Energy bursting when I came, body pouring into hers. My cock jerked and spasmed within the tight clutch of her walls.

Her body so sweet.

So perfect.

Owning all of me.

Her teeth were in my shoulder, and her hands were in my hair.

Like she couldn't get close enough to me. Like she wanted to sink inside. Share every part. Invade every recess.

She was already there.

I held her through it, the two of us riding wave after wave. I swallowed her whimpers while she swallowed my praise.

"I love you. Fuck, I love you. So much. There's nothing better than this. Nothing."

Shivers rolled.

Hers and mine.

Finally, I slumped down onto her in sated-out bliss. My heart still beating madly, and my spirit thrashing in the confines of my chest.

I rolled to the side, taking her with me. I brushed back the hair that was matted to the side of her face.

There was so much intensity ricocheting in the room that I was almost nervous as I tipped her face up to look at me.

It'd fucking gut me if I'd taken her to a place she wasn't ready to go.

But then the girl . . . she smiled.

Smiled that smile.

The one I'd told her I was there to see.

One that was genuine and filled with joy.

*Joy.*

I couldn't help it. Couldn't stop it. I wanted its existence more than anything I'd ever known.

I'd settled for a life of greed. Money and mindless sex and labels that meant absolutely nothing.

And there I was, holding the meaning of my life in my hands.

I brushed the pad of my thumb across her swollen lips. "Beauty."

My light in the darkness. If she couldn't chase it away, she'd promised she would at least be there to help me see through it.

She tapped her fingers across my heart.

"Beast." She chewed at her bottom lip. "I'd always been afraid of you disappearing. Of you burnin' out before I got the chance to keep you."

"I never wanted to leave you."

Our hushed voices were contained in the space between us, trapped by the four walls.

As if we could admit anything, and the wood and plaster and ghosts would hold all our secrets.

I stared at the lines and curves of her gorgeous face in the shadows, and I finally found the courage to ask her the one question I'd been both desperate and terrified to ask her all along. "You named her Bailey."

Sadness streaked across her features.

I wanted to reach out, wipe it away, but I needed to know. It'd been gnawing at me like a bitch since the first time I'd heard her utter the name.

Her fingers were back on my face, eyes so intense as she searched for understanding. "I told you, sometimes dreams don't die. Sometimes they don't burn out even when the light is taken away."

"I'd wanted it, Faith. To share that with you. I did."

*Bailey and Benton.*
*Bailey and Benton.*
*Bailey and Benton.*

Old hopes spun around us, sucking me back to that time, like the girl was casting her hopes amongst the rose bushes.

"I'll love her the same," I murmured. Hard and soft. Lined with truth.

"How does you saying that break and heal my heart all at the same time?" she asked, a wisp of grief working its way into her words.

My grief.

Hers.

Ours.

"I promise, Faith. I will. I'll love her like she was mine."

"Is it wrong I wanted her to be? That the second I saw her, that name came out of my mouth before I could stop it? One look at her, and I was in love, Jace. The level of it was something I'd only felt one other time, and it was dropping free like a claim."

Regret prowled beneath my flesh.

"If I could have stayed, I would have. I had to leave. I had to."

"Because we broke into this house?" She searched for the answer in my eyes, her own horror there, like she could have been the one responsible. "That's the reason you went to prison? Because we broke in here that night?"

"Partly," I told her, unable to stomach the idea of actually telling her why. What I'd done. The effects that had spiraled through the years.

"Why didn't you come back for me?" she whispered.

There was no missing the hurt that slashed across her face. So goddamned real I could feel it spear through the center of me.

"I tried. Sometimes we're too late. Sometimes no matter what we intend, we fall short."

"Oh, God, Jace." Regret swam with the love in her eyes.

I tried to give her the only encouragement I could find. "But we can't regret our lives or our pasts or the decisions we've made. We can only learn from them and live in the day. For *right now*. For *forever*."

"Just . . . promise me one thing."

I took her hand that rested on my chest, brought it to my mouth, and brushed kisses across her knuckles. "What's that?"

"Don't walk away from me *for* me without telling me why you're doin' it. Don't make that wrong decision for me. Not again. Don't ever hide what's happening in your life to protect me. You should have let me make that decision."

"I won't," I promised her.

Silence climbed back into the room. Like the questions crawled in from under the crack in the door.

Penetrating and invading.

"I need you to tell me everything you know about Joseph," she finally said, her plea small and insecure.

If Joseph weren't already dead, I might jump from that bed, hunt him down, and kill him myself for that sound alone.

For the terror that trembled through her body.

I knew there'd come a time when we had to lay it all out. Mack's warning from earlier rambled through my mind and clawed at my consciousness.

*"You have to tell her everything."*

I knew I did.

But how was I supposed to put her through that?

I wanted to protect her.

Wrap her up and hold her and promise her that everything would be okay.

Reaching out, I yanked her closer. "Come here."

I rolled onto my back so I could envelop her in my arms.

She rested her cheek on my chest, angled so she could still look up at me.

"It's going to be okay, Faith. I promise you."

Mindlessly, she ran her fingertips over my stomach, her thoughts going far. "You know that's what Joseph told me, too? When I asked him what was happening, that's what he told me."

A bolt of agony slanted through my spirit. I shifted so I could look at her better. "Is that all he said?"

Her head began to slowly shake, taken back to that time. I wanted to grab her and pull her out of it, tell her to stay with me, right here, in this moment, but I needed to know.

I kept my mouth shut and let her continue. "One night, he got up from the dinner table with the excuse that he needed to go back into the office. It was the same excuse he'd been making more and more. I'd finally called out after him—to his back as he was walkin' out the door—and asked him to just tell me. Whatever it was, to just tell me."

Insecurity bunched up in her shoulders. "I guess I'd figured he was cheatin' on me. Maybe it makes me pathetic, but I wouldn't have been surprised in the least since sex between us always seemed kind of . . . unfulfilling. Our relationship was . . . different, Jace. When we first got together . . ."

She trailed off, searching for what to say, her eyes blinking up at me for understanding. "He was there for me when you walked away. You have to know I had no idea where you'd gone or why. Had no idea you'd been sent to prison. I thought you left me. Joseph kept me company, being a friend and telling me one day I wouldn't miss you so much."

Sadness blanketed her spirit. "About nine months after you left, he kissed me. Right out by the roses. I started to cry because it felt so wrong. So off. I told him I was always goin' to love you, that time wasn't going to change that, and he told me that was okay. That he'd love me enough for the both of us."

She winced. "In time, I did love him. Different from how I loved you. It was a comfortable kind of love."

I wanted to claw my eyes out at the vision. Joseph with her. Touching her. I'd bet my ass for Joseph it hadn't been *unfulfilling* at all. The fucker had no idea how to treat her right, and she'd taken that inadequacy on herself.

Or maybe . . . maybe she really just hadn't ever felt a spark.

Regret filled her sweet gaze. Like any of this could ever possibly be her fault. "But things had started to change. He'd been acting different for about six months before he was killed."

Her eyes narrowed, like she was trying to look into the past and figure out what she'd missed. "He was acting anxious. He had always been a little jittery. Watching over his shoulder. But something had changed. Something that kept him up at night. I tried to ignore it. To chalk it up to the fact that we all have different moods, and that we're all going to go through different phases in our lives. I'd thought it would pass."

She met my gaze. "That night? After I'd finally confronted him and told him to tell me what was wrong. He came back just before dawn. He'd been drinking . . . obviously upset. He'd said he wanted to erase you from my memory. He promised he was going to take care of us, that he was going to fix everything. Crying when he said everything was goin' to be all right."

Guilt blazed in her eyes when she looked up at me. "I ignored it, Jace. I ignored it and shoved it away as some drunken nonsense he'd been spoutin'. Ignored it because he'd said he wanted to erase you from me, and that was the last thing I wanted him to do. I ignored it harder when I got the call that he'd been killed."

Her fingernails clawed into my skin. "I should have known. I should have said something."

She choked over a cry. "How could he do somethin' that would put Bailey in danger? I don't understand, Jace. I don't understand."

I hugged her closer, desperately trying to release the confession, but the words were hanging on as tight as a man about to go overboard.

Nothing but death and darkness waiting below.

*She'd hate me when she knew.*

I toyed with a lock of her hair. Trying to find the nerve. My words were measured as I prepared to lay it all out. "How much did you know about what Joseph did for work?"

I always wondered how the slimy asshole had convinced her he was legit.

She blinked at me, stuttered a bit, "He . . . he'd started working down at the shippin' yards right after you left. He got promoted quickly."

I cringed and then gently prodded. "Do you remember how quickly?"

How he went from a minimum-wage job in the warehouse to claiming to own the cargo front in a handful of years?

But it was Joseph who had been owned.

Her brow squeezed. Like she was fighting the truth of everything that was written in front of her. "He said . . . he said he was working hard to give me the life that I deserved. So that, one day, we could buy this house and I'd be able to live out my own dream."

Hate fisted my guts. So fucking tight.

*She didn't know. She didn't know.*

She blinked at me. "Did . . . did you know he was involved in something he shouldn't have been? Did Mack? Oh God," she whimpered, the pain I'd wanted to shield her from slid out. "How didn't I know? How didn't I know he was involved in somethin' he shouldn't have been?"

Horror filled her words. Grief clouding over her like an eclipse.

The love she had for him showing through. The care. Her own regret.

"It wasn't your fault, Faith. There was nothing that you could have done that would have stopped what was coming."

That was on me.

"What was comin', Jace?" she pleaded. "Did you talk to him after you left? Did . . . did he tell you somethin'?"

My tongue soured with the confession that gathered there. Everything I knew. Unsure if either of us was prepared to take the blow.

I sucked in a deep breath, the words dying on my tongue when the little voice echoed through the wall. "Mommy?"

Chocolate eyes went wide, her guilt stripped away. In its place was a flustered panic. "Oh, goodness. Bailey."

I brushed my thumb over her cheek. "Hey . . . it's okay. I told you, I'm in this with you. For you. For her."

Faith eased a little, and I sent her a soft smile before I rolled out of the bed and pulled on my jeans, quick to head out of the bedroom like it'd granted me a stay of execution.

A moment's reprieve.

Reprieve that came in the form of the tiny thing that stood in the hall outside her door, rubbing one of those tiny fists in her eye as she clung to the Beast.

"Jacie," she whispered in some kind of relief when she saw me there. "I's had a bad dream."

Like she found comfort in my presence. That just for the fact I was standing there, she was protected and safe.

A belt of emotion tightened around my chest.

Never had I known it stronger than right then.

I'd never allow anything to happen to her.

Not to Faith.

Not to us.

Joseph had left enough wreckage behind.

I was going to pick up the pieces.

# *thirty-five*

## Jace
## Twenty-One Years Old

*J*ace didn't think he'd ever been so happy to see his brother. Ian
leaned against his car in the parking lot, looking like freedom and
the road to Jace's second chance.

He was going to take it.

Run with it.

Run home and to the one thing he never should have left
behind.

It'd taken locks and bars and cells to finally figure out who he
was and what she'd seen in him, and he was determined to become
that man.

The lock buzzed, and the heavy metal gate slid open.

One second later, Jace was free.

Released two years earlier than his five-year sentence. Let's just
say, he'd been on his best behavior.

A little harder than he'd once been. Three years behind bars
would do that to a man.

He'd thought he'd seen it all—the worst in people—but he hadn't had the first clue.

He'd learned a lot of tough lessons, but he'd finally embraced a bunch of good shit, too.

His only worry was the letters. The letters he'd written over the years that had never been answered. He guessed some things had to be confessed face-to-face.

He walked toward his brother, determined to never repeat what had gone down. He was reclaiming his life. Taking back what was his.

Ian straightened when he approached, and they measured each other for a second before Jace threw his arms around his brother and hugged him tight.

Ian hugged him just as fiercely. "Fuck, man, I missed you like crazy. Don't ever leave me like that again."

Jace squeezed him like his next breath depended on it. "I don't plan on it."

Ian nodded, pushing away, shaking himself off. He rounded to the other side of the car and hopped into the driver's seat. Jace slipped into the passenger's.

Ian turned over the ignition. "Where are we headed?"

"I need to get to Faith. Explain all this bullshit."

They were more than a hundred miles from Broadshire Rim. Jace had been carted off to some dump penitentiary that was hidden in the mountains on the west side of the state.

Something passed through Ian's expression. Worry and sorrow and pity.

Jace's hands fisted on his thighs, and he stared across at his brother, who tried to busy himself by fiddling with something on the dash.

Dread spiraled through his system, and he heaved a breath, forced out the words. "Just tell me, Ian."

Ian stilled his fiddling and inhaled deeply before he slowly looked back at Jace. "She's married, man."

"What?" Disbelief fisted his spirit, drenching his heart and mind.

No.

It wasn't possible.

Not after he'd sent all those letters promising he'd be back.

Denial pulsed through his being. Ian had to be wrong. He'd made a mistake. That was it. A mistake.

"I'm sorry, Jace. I couldn't tell you while you were in there. I just . . . couldn't."

Grief constricted Jace's throat, so tight he was sure he was being strangled. Right as a fist punched into his chest and ripped out his heart.

"To who?" he barely managed.

Ian hesitated, wavered as he rocked in the seat, holding on to the steering wheel as if it might make delivering the blow easier. "To Joseph."

Agony sliced him in two. It was a misery unlike anything he'd ever known.

Amplified by the blinding fury that beat within his broken heart.

Betrayal.

He couldn't stop it. The way his mouth worked and moisture filled his eyes.

No.

Fuck no.

He couldn't believe this shit.

Ian jerked his head away, shaking it, filled with turmoil. Then he cursed and jerked his gaze back to Jace, so much brutal sincerity in his voice that it rocked the car.

"I didn't do it, Jace. Those drugs? I didn't have anything to do with them. I promise you. I know you were trying to take the fall for me, but it wasn't necessary. I know you didn't believe me when I told you I wasn't involved. But it's the truth. I wouldn't have done anything that piece of shit said. I didn't fucking care if he'd killed me. Not after what he did to me, and sure as hell not after what he did to you."

"I know." I could barely manage to form the words.

His head dropped again. "Joseph was always jealous of you. Of everything you had. Of everything you stood for. He knew he could never compare to you."

Ian looked back at Jace. "He's been working for Steven since the day you got hauled away."

Turmoil blistered through Jace's body. So hot, he was sure he was being incinerated from the inside out.

Joseph had been responsible?

"Take me there," he demanded. "I need to see it for myself."

Ian's eyes went wide. "Why would you want to go and do that?"

"I have to, Ian. I have to."

Maybe Jace needed the confirmation. Or maybe he just needed the proof that dreams really didn't last. That dreaming them was nothing but a waste of time.

Because three hours later, he and Ian were parked in a lot on the other side of the small apartment complex.

Jace was gutted all over again when Faith stepped out of the apartment door.

Joseph right behind her.

Heartache howled through his insides, seeping all the way to his bones, saturating to the marrow.

He fisted his hands on his thighs and squeezed his eyes closed against the sight. "Get me out of here. Take me to the old house where she and I used to meet."

Ian looked at Jace like he'd lost his mind.

Jace guessed he had.

# thirty-six

## Faith

$\mathcal{S}$haking through the last button on my blouse, I took another glance around the room.

The bedroom that I'd always thought of as mine and Jace's—locked away and hidden like a treasure that was right there.

Out of sight but not forgotten.

It'd felt as if he were inviting me to step back into that time. Back to when we'd lost each other. It eased so much and somehow only bred more questions.

Heaving out a breath, I slipped out the door, not sure how I was supposed to explain any of this to my innocent daughter.

How could I when I wasn't sure myself?

When it still felt like there was a fog of confusion holding me hostage. This afternoon had been one of the most terrifying experiences of my entire life.

*Joseph.*

The loss of him still cut and marred. Especially with the way he'd been so violently taken.

He'd been there for me when I'd felt so utterly alone and abandoned. My friend who'd slowly grown to be something more.

My supporter.

My lover.

But reluctantly, I could almost admit that something had always been off.

*Joseph, what did you do? You were always so sweet and devoted. Why didn't you trust me enough to tell me you needed help?*

I would have been there for him.

Helped him the way he'd always helped me. Regardless of the fact that we'd been little more than friends, living our lives the best way that we could, I'd been devoted to him.

Loyal to him.

Had he really not been loyal to me? Fed me lies by omission?

Or had they really been bold-faced lies? Every time he walked out the door, had it been under false pretenses?

*No.*

I couldn't fathom it.

Maybe he'd gotten caught up in something he didn't fully understand.

Had been as confused then as I was as I tried to ponder it all out.

I slipped out the door and took one step in the direction of my daughter's room, only to stumble to a stop.

A bittersweet breath pulled deep into the well of my lungs.

Surety fell over me like I'd just been wrapped in the warmest blanket after I'd been left for dead out in the middle of a freezing snowstorm.

Comfort and security.

It was written right there.

In the way Jace knelt on one knee in front of her, his fingers gentle as he swept the unruly mass of her waves from her face.

In the tenderness of his voice as he murmured, "It's okay, I've got you. I'm right here. You don't have to be afraid."

He pulled her into his arms, hugging her close to his chest. She wrapped her little arms around his neck. "Don'ts never leave me, Jacie."

My heart twisted and pulsed. Just seeing it made it hard to breathe.

So much of this felt wrong. Seeing my daughter in Jace's arms.

Because I felt like some kind of terrible person when my first thought was it was meant to be that way all along.

"I won't, sweetheart. How could I ever leave my Unicorn Girl?"

"You *sway aww* the dragons?"

He squeezed her tight. "Always."

My spirit soared. So high. So high.

I felt as if my feet might not be touching the ground as I followed them into her room where he was tucking her back in.

Her sweet eyes found me from the doorway. She sent me a smile that shattered me a little.

The amount of love that continually burst from the middle of me when I looked at her still sometimes shocked me.

And to think I could very well have lost her today. How terrified I'd been when that car had hit us earlier.

I felt like I was being sucked from one direction to the other. Waves coming at me from every side.

Mercy and grief.

Mercy and grief.

Pulling and pushing. Both fighting for dominance.

Filling me with life and threatening to drown me in the midst of it.

She looked back up at Jace, who was still kneeling at the side of her bed. "Mommy and Bailey and Jacie."

She said it with a wide, wide grin, though there was no missing the question behind it.

Jace turned that penetrating gaze on me. Copper eyes flashed. Filled with too much.

The most wistful kind of smile pulled up at the corner of my mouth.

Jace turned back to her and answered for all of us. "Yeah. Mommy and Bailey and Jacie."

He tucked her under her covers, kissing her forehead, and I edged across the room so I could tell her good night again.

I peppered my love to her temple. To her nose. To her chin. "Good night, my sweet girl."

"Night, Mommy."

"We're right here if you need us."

"Oh-kay," she said, sleepiness falling back over her.

Reluctantly, I moved back toward the hall. If I could stay right there, in the safe confines of that room, just the three of us?

Forever?

I would.

Jace seemed to be feeling the same way because a distinct wariness had taken him over when he pushed to his feet.

As if the stress of the day and the last few weeks had finally caught up to him.

As if, when he'd been sitting there at her side, he'd been struck with the same what-might-have-beens from this afternoon that had struck me.

The torment of something happening to my baby girl more than anything I could bear.

Was it wrong it felt like a gift that he might feel some of that, too? That he promised to love her as if she were his own? That I trusted him to love her and keep her?

Keep me?

How was it possible? After all these years?

How was it possible that the thought of losing him again felt like the cruelest sort of devastation?

Was I nothin' but a fool for allowing myself to take that chance?

But not taking it was an impossibility.

My love for him was so intense, so big and overwhelming, that it felt like a swelling mass growing inside me.

Stunning and extreme.

Another of those waves coming fast.

It'd always been that way with him. My love had always been almost more than I could bear.

Seeing that wound on his head only brought it out into the open.

Because I could have lost him just as swiftly as I could have lost my daughter.

It shivered through me, locking my throat in the tightest ball as I stared up at the man who edged across the space.

Towering.

His presence so vast.

"Jace—" I started to mumble, to take us back to the moment back in that room where I needed to face what was really happening in my life.

Begging with him to answer that question.

*What do you know? What happened to my husband?*

Jace pinned me to the wall. "Shh . . . just . . . give us one day, Faith. One day to live. To be. Just . . . please . . . give me one day with the two of you."

I choked over the despair that radiated from him.

A new kind of trepidation taking over.

Again, I could taste something vibrating in the air.

An omen.

A premonition.

He set one of those big palms on my face.

A plea on his.

"Please."

# thirty-seven

## Jace

*H*eaven.

I woke wrapped in it. Floating on some kind of goddamned cloud. Comfort and grace.

Could only pray that it might be strong enough to hold us up, and it all wouldn't come crashing down when I gave her everything.

When I shattered her heart all over again.

I was terrified of where those pieces might land.

I released a heavy exhale into those soft locks of chocolate hair.

Strands fluttered through the early morning light that streaked in through the window, her body so warm and right where it was tucked in the well of mine.

Hadn't let her go for a second last night.

Coming to her again and again.

Addicted to the feeling of that *connection*. Needing her skin against mine. A promise that she was fine, knowing all of this was coming to a head, her safety right there in the palm of my hand.

Possession swelled. I would never let what happened yesterday happen again. We had to find these assholes.

I felt her stir, could feel the beat of confusion that rippled down her spine when she remembered she was lying in bed with me. I felt the force of her smile as she shifted closer.

Wrapped in the well of my arms.

I loved that it was her first response.

What came naturally.

One of those smiles.

Gently, I rolled her onto her back, the girl so fucking stunning with sleep still heavy in her eyes and the sting of my kisses still plumping her lips.

Couldn't help but reach out and touch. Relishing in that instant burn that raced through my being.

"Morning," I rumbled.

Shyness peeked up at the corners of her mouth, redness on her cheeks, those eyes tracing my face the same way mine had been tracing hers. "Best morning ever."

She reached out, touch tentative as she traced her fingers across my lips. "It's the first morning in my life that I've ever gotten to wake up lyin' next to you."

A growl tore out of my chest.

I couldn't help it. The way her saying it made me feel. Like a goddammed king.

Grin riding onto my face, I scrambled to crawl over her, attacking her with a bunch of kisses all over her face.

Only thing I wanted to do was shower her with my love. With some reprieve. With some of the belief she'd always rained on me.

Faith squealed in surprise. Laughter climbed into the air and bounced off the walls.

Free.

Exactly the way I was determined to make her.

"Jace, what do you think you're doin'?" she wheezed. Frantic giggles started to roll from her when I started tickling her sides.

I couldn't resist.

Couldn't resist from provoking that sound.

*Joy.*

"What do you think I'm doing?" I teased her, tickling her harder and smacking a bunch of kisses to her chin and chest as I did.

She flailed and swatted at me, trying to catch her breath.

"I think you've gone and lost your mind, that's what I think you're doing."

Pressing my mouth up under her jaw, I slowed my assault. "No, Faith. I've gone and lost my heart."

On an exhale, her fingers stroked into my hair. Softly. Coaxing me to look at her. "Funny . . . 'cause you found mine."

I slowed, staring down at her, brushing my knuckles down her cheek. "Lost mine a long time ago. Been searching ever since."

She tucked her bottom lip between her teeth. Awe swept through her expression. "I'm so glad you came back to find it."

I leaned forward and pressed my lips to hers. "Me, too. Me, too."

I pulled away before I let myself get distracted. Body hard, nudging at me to go that direction. "Come on before I keep you in this bed all day."

"Sounds like a fine idea to me."

I gripped her hand and gave a little tug. "As much as I like the sound of that, I'm pretty sure that girl of ours is going to be pounding on your door in a minute or two."

Yup. There I went. Making those claims.

*Ours.*

Surprise streaked through her eyes before the emotion shifted. Sheer adoration took its place.

God, I wanted to be worthy of that. Of the way she was looking at me like I was good and right. Like I was everything.

Nerves spun, and I shoved them down.

I'd face all that tomorrow. Today . . . today was about us. And I was finished wasting time.

"This way," she whispered with her little, awed voice, her tiny hand wound up in mine.

She tugged at me, quietly padding forward as she led me through the thicket of spindly trees that edged the back of the property.

As if it were a secret. As if we were stepping into a different world.

A magical one.

Lush green grew up on all sides, the narrow trail hugged by shrubs and bushes and a variety of trees as we got closer and closer to the brook that trickled over the smoothed rocks beyond.

The sound of it filled my ears. The memories fierce where they beat through my mind.

That peace was compounded by the energy blasting into my back. A steady, burning pulse.

Thrum. Thrum. Thrum.

Every one of Faith's footsteps behind us was like fuel that reminded me of my purpose.

"You hear that?" Bailey rushed low, looking at me from over her shoulder.

Swore to God, the child hitched my breath.

Stole the air right out of my lungs.

Dimples and chubby cheeks and chocolate eyes.

Filled with wonder.

*Faith.*

"What is it?" I murmured back, just as quietly as we cut deeper into the copse of limbs and trunks and thick leaves.

Sunlight speared through the dense canopy above, sending glittering rays through the crannies and cracks, as if straining to find their way to the damp ground floor.

Lighting in the heavy humidity clinging to the air.

A kaleidoscope of iridescent colors scattered across the ground to merge with the scent of mud and grass and summer that wisped and churned in the slight breeze that blew through.

"A dragon," she whispered, faking the shudder that ran through her body. "Is a bad one."

The lightest laughter billowed from behind.

Joy. Comfort. Light.

"A dragon?" I whispered back, catching on to the child's game. "I hope your unicorns are around."

"Don't you see them? They ev'where."

A bird rustled through the branches above. My eyes grew wide. "Is that one?"

"Yes. Did you see it? It got pink wings, Jacie. She *fwies* so high." Excitement billowed through her voice.

"I saw it," I told her. "We better hurry and help her."

I swung Bailey into my arms, wondering if it wasn't because I couldn't stand the thought of not holding her any longer.

She squealed when I hugged her to me and then she quieted like she'd just realized she'd slipped out of character.

"Be super quiet." Those brown eyes were wide with her play. Lost in her little world. "We got to *sway* the dragon."

Faith's energy flowed. Quiet as our play and as fierce as Bailey's belief.

I would.

I would slay all of them.

Faith wandered the edge of the rose garden.

Silently.

Lost in thought.

Wearing this yellow sundress that made her shine. The girl was like a torch that burned in the pitch of night.

I'd been on a blanket in the grass with Bailey under that big shade tree that grew up at the edge of the magnificent house.

We'd played by the stream for more than an hour before Bailey had decided she was hungry. But it had to be a picnic, she'd insisted, the little girl seeming unwilling to let go of the day we'd spent out under the sun.

Faith didn't seem to mind all that much, either.

It felt like we'd stepped into a reprieve. A time-out. A moment given to make sense of the direction we were stampeding toward.

Like all of us could feel it.

The rumble coming from underneath. Coming closer. Growing stronger.

Bailey was humming under her breath, a few words coming out here and there as she played with her dolls and books, caught up in her own little make-believe world with the Beast propped up in the middle of it.

I brushed my fingers through her hair, and she turned to grin up at me before she slipped right back into that sweet imagination that ruled her mind.

Part of me was wondering if that was what I was doing.

If I was lost in my own imaginary world. Pretending I could stay here. Be a part of something beautiful.

I'd rarely had anything beautiful in my life.

Every second that I had? It'd been wrapped up in one single woman. The woman who lightly brushed her fingertips across the satiny petals, her face cast up to the sky as she swayed.

Sunlight pouring down.

I got the distinct feeling she was gathering it. The girl taking on that energy.

A reflection that glowed.

*Beauty.*

Drawn, I pushed to my feet and edged that way, couldn't stay away a second longer.

She felt me approaching

She always had.

A tremor of awareness slipped down her spine, need a force that blistered across her damp, soft skin.

I pressed my nose to it, to the light sweat that had gathered on her nape.

I inhaled.

Tucked her down.

Everything I was determined to keep.

"You are a vision," I whispered at her flesh.

Chills skated. I kissed across them. Gathering them on my tongue.

"Jace," she whispered, barely turning to look at me from over her delicate shoulder that carried so much weight.

That's what she was.

Delicate and strong.

Fragile and compelling.

Her attention traveled to where her daughter played quietly on the quilt she had set out for her.

I followed her eyes, my heart doing that crazy thing again, my words rough where they hooked in the air. "She is the most incredible thing."

Impossible in her perfection.

"I'm doin' my best . . . to give her the life she deserves."

I felt the intensity of Faith's stare where it landed on the side of my face. I looked back at her. "She's incredible because of you. Because she is filled with you. With your belief and your love and your strength."

Her throat bobbed when she swallowed, her voice pensive. "She's not going to remember him. Soon, she'll forget. He'll be nothing but a vague memory in a picture book."

Part of that felt like a slap to the face. The other totally got it. Her worry. Her devotion to her daughter bigger than either of us.

Needing the connection, I reached out and trailed my fingers down her bare arm. "I'm so sorry. That you both lost him."

I didn't know how to relate to that.

The idea of Joseph being here.

Not when these two were the only things I wanted.

I also didn't want to be the dick who discounted what he'd been.

Her face pinched, and her tone turned wistful, as light as the gentle breeze that whispered through the blooms of purple roses.

"After it happened, I'd felt this consuming need to keep his memory alive. To constantly talk about him to her and show her pictures."

Pain etched her gorgeous face when she let her attention travel back to me. "And I can feel all that slippin' away, Jace. His memory. Who he was. And now, I'm left wondering if I even knew him at all."

I cupped her cheeks in my hands. "Everyone has their secrets. We all have good in us, and we all have evil in us. We are all going to make the world better in some small way, and we're all going to do some damage. You're the one who taught me that. That we're not all good, and we're not all bad. That we each deal with the circumstances we're placed in differently. It makes us who we are. Joseph included."

Why was I talking that bastard up?

But it was true.

He'd been who he was because of his circumstances. Because he'd done it the best way that he knew how.

I was the one who'd taught him that we had to do anything we had to in order to survive.

And he'd been her husband.

Bailey's *father*.

I couldn't erase that truth. Couldn't blot out the importance of it. No matter how badly I wanted to.

Problem with Joseph? I was pretty sure the bad had spoiled the good. That every part of him was rotted.

Moisture filled that knowing gaze, and she tucked one side of her bottom lip between her teeth. Her head swung to the side to look at the hedge of roses.

I reached out for one, for the tiny bud of pink that was all curled up, waiting to blossom, to grow into something beautiful.

My fingertip trailed down the stem, and I let it catch on a thorn, let it prick my flesh.

"Remember how this garden had been left for dead? Dried up and wilting?"

I swore that both of us could still hear it, her encouragement that had flooded my ears at that time. The girl filling me with her belief.

I tried to give the same to her, my words nothing more than a breathy whisper. "You are going to come out stronger on the other side. Because I *know* how great you are. Look at all the amazing things you've achieved, and there are so many more waiting for you in the future. I know it, Faith. You just have to believe it's going to get better."

"I always believed in us," she murmured.

I palmed the side of her head, dipped in to kiss her softly.

Slowly.

With the promise that I would make this right.

Whatever it took.

I suddenly felt the tiny presence at my side. Faith and I peeled our mouths apart, though we were still clinging to the other.

There stood Bailey at our feet, grinning up at us. "Bailey and Mommy and Jacie forever. Like magic."

She threw her hands in the air. Casting a spell into the garden surrounding us. The little girl an enchantment all on her own.

I dipped down and swooped her up. Relished the weight of her in my arms. So tiny and perfect and real.

No thorns to be found.

"Like magic," I rumbled at her head.

She wrapped those little arms around my neck. Squeezed tight. "I *wuv* you, Jacie."

My heart stuttered in my chest. Then took off racing like a wild beat inside me.

I'd done a lot of fucked-up shit in my life. Deserved the pain I'd received. Had done absolutely nothing to deserve the love these two were showering on me.

Worst part was knowing I'd done nothing but stolen it.

And I couldn't shake the uneasy feeling that I was no fucking better than Joseph.

# thirty-eight

## Jace
## Twenty-Six Years Old

*J*ace tried not to crawl right over the massive desk to the piece of shit who sat on the other side from him.

Sniveling the way he always had. Just like when they were kids, Jace could smell the pathetic, self-pity oozing from his pores. "Jace, I'm telling you, man, I need your help. Just this once."

Just this once?

Yeah, right.

Jace was still shocked every time Joseph came crawling to him. Like he should owe him any sort of loyalty when he'd offered none to him.

When he'd stolen everything.

Framed him and then went in for the kill.

The first time Joseph had come to him for help Jace had nearly lost his mind.

Went over the edge.

Did something that he couldn't take back and destroyed his

own future because he'd thirsted so viciously to destroy Joseph's.

And like a pathetic loser, Jace had given in.

Helped the bastard out. Maybe it had been because in the end, Jace knew it'd be helping Faith.

Faith who remained his weakness. It didn't matter how many years passed, he couldn't shuck the memory of her from his skin.

Couldn't erase the marks she'd etched into his spirit.

Joseph had always been a master manipulator, anyway. His looks alone gave him the appearance of an innocent, good kid, but he'd never been anything but a slimy cocksucker, always looking out for himself.

Maybe Jace had taught him that way. Raised him to be a fighter. A survivor.

But he'd always thought his loyalty to the kid would earn him some in return.

Maybe it was Jace who'd been the fool for sacrificing anything for him—for lying and cheating and stealing for his cousin and thinking it would count for something.

He hated the man in front of him.

This fiery loathing that boiled inside him.

He managed to pretend it wasn't seething inside him as he sat back in his massive executive chair, rocked back as if he didn't have a care in the world.

"And what's your excuse this time?" Jace asked, so dry they could have been standing in Death Valley.

"I'm breaking out on my own. It's time that I lived my life right. The way you taught me to do." Joseph was all eager lies.

Jace almost laughed.

He almost fucking laughed aloud at the line Joseph was feeding him when he knew firsthand that Joseph had gambled every last dollar away.

Jace's friend Mack kept him appraised of all the bullshit that went down back in Broadshire Rim. The sordid, sleazy mess Joseph had himself entangled in.

Like Jace should care.

But he did.

He could never rid himself of that vacant spot that throbbed inside him. Could never scrape the itch from his skin. Could never rid himself of the thoughts of her.

His worry over the life she might be living and the cutting jealousy that he wasn't the one living it with her.

Jace had built an empire. Worked and strived and fought until he'd come out on top.

He'd taken his brother with him, put him through college and law school, kept him close and protected until Ian could stand on his own without the threat of that seedy world pulling him back down.

And still, this useless excuse for a man had everything Jace wanted.

Nothing but a common criminal.

A puppet and pawn.

Working for Steven.

The same way as he'd been all along.

"I have nothing to offer you," Jace told him, cool and calm while that fire raced his veins.

Joseph snorted. "Is that right?"

"That's right."

"But you have the one thing she wants, don't you?" There was spite in Joseph's tone.

Jace rocked forward, his movements crawling with menace as he breathed, "And you have a wife and a kid on the way that you're putting in danger."

"You don't give a shit about my kid," Joseph spat.

"Do you?" Jace accused.

Joseph blinked. The first real emotion Jace had seen from him since he'd come through the door. "Of course, I do."

Jace should shove him out the door. Toss him out on his ass. Because he shouldn't care, either.

He hated the idea that Joseph had touched her. That they were going to have a child. A family.

Hated that Joseph fucking knew that Jace would do about anything to ensure Faith's happiness.

That there were some dreams he'd never stand in the way of.

"Then I'll make you a deal." His voice was hoarse. Ragged.

"The deed for their safety. You truly walk away from all that bullshit, from Steven and the rest of his crew, and you don't look back. I'll even throw some money on top of it."

Jace pointed over Joseph's shoulder. "And then you don't ever step through that door again. Do you understand me?"

Face pinched, Joseph nodded.

Jace squeezed his eyes closed for a beat.

Against the agony.

The grief.

The crushing of a dream.

But he was granting one in the same token.

Sacrifice.

He'd always been willing to make it for the ones he loved most.

And he'd never, ever stop loving her.

## thirty-nine

### Jace

"We finally got something." Mack's voice was thin and hard on the other end of the line.

The last of the day had sunk on the other side of the window, the late dusk filling the room.

Bailey had been tucked into bed a half hour ago, the monitor positioned on the nightstand next to me.

Faith had slipped away to grab a shower and wash the day from her skin.

I'd been contemplating joining her when my phone rang.

I immediately started to pace.

God, we needed news.

I just prayed it was the good kind.

Any lead to grab on to that might finally point us in the right direction.

"What did you get?"

Strain pulsed through Mack's sigh. "I shouldn't be telling you this."

I roughed a hand over my head. "Yeah, well you probably shouldn't have told me a lot of things, but it's too late now, don't you think?"

I could almost see his reluctant nod. "Do you remember Doug . . . one of the officers on the case? You met him at my birthday party?"

"Yeah, of course. He's driven by the house quite a few times to check on things, too."

"He and Felix have been digging through the few bits of evidence we've been able to uncover. They found an address in some of the files found at Joseph's office. It's a warehouse. Main name on the trust was Joseph's—but when Doug and Felix searched deeper, they found Steven tied to it."

Mack inhaled deeply. "We'd thought we'd rooted out all of Steven's holdings, but clearly, it went further than we'd imagined. Did a drive by myself, and there's definitely activity at the address. This is a building that belonged to both Steven and Joseph—both of them are dead—and there are still people moving shit in and out of there? Shouldn't be a soul around."

I could hear the implication in Mack's words. Adding the facts up and coming to a quick sum.

"Shit." I roughed the back of my hand over my mouth.

"Yup. This has to be the break we needed. I can feel it. We're right there. Gut tells me we're going to find what we've been missing behind those doors. We're finally going to be able to put these bastards to bed."

"What's the plan?" I asked, tone harsher than I intended.

Mack hesitated.

"Don't try to freeze me out now."

Tension rippled between them, and then Mack cursed under his breath. "With two murder victims tied to the same building, we easily got a warrant. Going in at midnight."

"I'm coming."

"No, you're not."

"Yeah, I am. You can't expect me to sit here when we're this close to nailing the bastard."

"And the last thing I need is you getting in the way. You already know my ass is on the line for telling you any of this. You show up, it's gonna look bad."

My heart stuttered when I heard the shower turn off, and I lowered my voice. "I won't even get out of my car. I just need to be there to watch you haul the monster out in cuffs who tried to hurt Faith and Bailey."

The guy who killed Joseph.

I shouldn't care.

I shouldn't care.

But I did.

Still hadn't forgiven myself for my part in it all. This might finally be the retribution my soul needed to put all this in the past.

Agony splintered through me. My guilt and remorse. Everything I should have done differently. All the things I'd go back and change.

I couldn't, but at least I could help bring justice.

For Bailey.

For Faith.

And fuck . . . maybe for Joseph, too.

"This shit is real, Jace. Dangerous. We have no idea what we're going to come up against in there."

"Not up for discussion, Mack. I'm sorry, but I have to do this. You know I do. I think that's why you called me in the first place."

I heard muttering on the other end of the line, Mack talking to someone else before he came back on.

"All right, Jace. Felix volunteered to go out and keep a lookout at the plantation while we do this. But you stay in the car. Do you understand me?"

"I will. I promise"

"Be here by eleven. You can ride with me. Felix will head over by then."

Silence filled the space between us before he finally said, "It's time."

"It's time," I returned.

That was the hardest part.

The fact that it was time.

The fact that I couldn't keep it from Faith any longer.

She stepped out the door, hair soaking wet and body wrapped in a towel, that energy surging when she looked at me from across the room.

Beauty.

Grace and light and everything I'd ever wanted.

I just prayed after everything, she would still want me.

## Faith

*I* stepped out of the shower and started to towel off. A muted

voice echoed through my bathroom door.

One I would recognize forever.

The one my spirit had quietly called to for all these years.

There was something about the tone of it, though, that sent dread skating across my dampened skin and had me quietly edging toward the door and pressing my ear to the thin wood.

Maybe it was wrong, eavesdropping this way. The way my heart fumbled around in my chest as if it were struggling against the chains of fear that wanted to wrap it up.

But the man *was* in my room, and there was nothing I could do but listen.

Nerves trembling through me, I angled my head and bit down on my lip as I listened to one side of the conversation.

"I won't even get out of my car. I just need to be there to watch you haul the monster out in cuffs who tried to hurt Faith and Bailey."

"Not up for discussion, Mack. I'm sorry . . . but I have to do this. You know I do. I think that's why you called me in the first place."

"It's time."

Something rustled, and I heard Jace curse under his breath, as if he were upset over whatever Mack had told him, while a torrent of fear billowed through me, taking to my veins.

Because I could feel it.

Coming closer.

Gaining speed.

Everything I didn't want to know.

Everything I wanted to pretend wasn't real.

And maybe that made me the biggest fool in the world.

Pretending something wasn't real didn't keep it from happening.

But I didn't think I could take any more. Couldn't take any more before my spirit cracked.

The fragile seams Jace had made as he'd stitched me back together felt as if they were being pulled and stretched. So close to rending under the pressure.

With my heart beating somewhere in my throat, I quietly turned the old knob on the door and stepped into the shadowy darkness of my bedroom.

Night pressed at the window, the fade of the moon slicing through the leaves that billowed and waved at the glass.

It sent the room into a slow dance of shadows.

Hypnotizing.

Jace stood at the end of the bed.

His own shadowy figure. Dark and somehow the brightest thing I'd ever seen.

That fierce, protective fury coming off him in waves.

My beast.

And there I was, making a thousand wishes.

That all of this would actually be okay, just like he'd promised.

That he wouldn't allow anything to happen to us.

That he would love us and protect us.

As if he felt every single one of my questions, he took a step my direction.

His presence thrashed.

A life force that cracked.

A boom against the walls.

I could almost feel it shake the foundation of the old house. The impact of him looking at me that way.

He slowly edged forward, so much power in each step that I found myself taking one back with each that he took. No longer sure that I could stand under the magnitude of it.

Mystery written in his face and questions written on my heart.

I wanted him to erase them. Write over them in his own words.

*Love me. Love me.*

The only cover I had was the towel that was wrapped around me, and I clutched it tighter. Throat dry and stomach heavy.

Trembling with fear, that feeling at odds with the desire I felt for this man.

His face so beautiful.

His body so gorgeous.

Unlike anything I'd ever seen.

Shirt gone, it exposed those shoulders that were so wide. The expanse of skin on his muscled chest so smooth.

Carved and chiseled, his abdomen was the thing fantasies were made of.

This . . . this was what I'd imagined when I'd pressed my eyes closed and dreamed for so many years.

But there he was, real and whole and massive in the middle of my room where he stood like a darkened storm.

The only thing the man wore were those same sleep pants he'd been wearing yesterday morning, teasing me with this perfect picture of him.

Powerful and imposing.

Heat blistered through the compressed, thickened air, chills lighting on my skin beneath the burn of those copper eyes.

"Who was that?" I rushed out, knowing the answer but not sure I really wanted him to give it to me.

Not sure I was ready.

I didn't know if Jace was either as he stalked closer to me.

I was sure I looked a mess. A drenched rat that shivered and shook. No place to hide.

The problem was, the only thing I wanted was for this man to find me. To find me and keep me and make it all go away.

The way he had today.

The way he'd ripped every worry away. Brought his quiet peace to my spirit and our home.

I wondered if he knew it.

That in all his torment, I'd never felt safer than with him at my side.

Maybe he did.

Because a flash of something struck through his expression.

Bold.

Brutal.

Savage.

Perfect possession.

His fingers dove right into my soaking hair. A growl rumbled in his chest as he tugged me against his hard body.

"Mack. He found something. We're close. So close. This is going to end, Faith. You won't have to be afraid anymore."

My knees rocked and my spirit churned.

"Tell me you trust me," he demanded. "That you understand that every single thing I've ever done, I've done for you."

"I trust you." I said it.

I gave him the very thing I'd promised myself I'd never be fool enough to give him again.

Because you couldn't cut yourself open wider than offering someone your trust.

It was giving them your heart.

Your dreams and your vulnerabilities.

It was placing all your *faith* into their hands.

And Jace Jacobs held every piece of me.

"I'm going to prove to you that you can, Faith. You're not going to want to, but I need you to hold this truth . . . you can trust me."

Confusion spun, and my lips parted, rimmed with the question.

But Jace . . . Jace took it as an invitation.

Those hands tightened in my hair, and he yanked me closer to him.

Flames flashed. My wet skin against his heated flesh. His mouth came down on mine.

Hard.

Possession in his kiss.

A command. Demanding that I give him everything.

I opened to him, and his tongue swept inside. It reignited that ever-raging fire inside me.

Every insecurity burned.

Ashes.

Because I was his.

Our tongues tangled, and his hands roamed, gliding out of my hair and down onto my neck.

Could he feel my pulse pound?

My heart and my love?

Because I could feel the power of it surging out of me. Reaching for him.

"God, Faith, you are ruining me. Ruining every single thing I'd forced myself into believing."

"You ruined me a long time ago," I whispered between his demanding kisses.

He walked me back across the floor, and my bottom hit the edge of the massive dresser that took up almost the entire back wall in the room.

The dark hard wood was carved and detailed, and the massive ornate mirror affixed to the top was hazed-over with age.

He pressed me to it, his cock hard against my belly, pleading for me through the thin pants that he wore.

Need tumbled through me.

Desire dense.

And I remembered . . . remembered what it'd been like to want a man so desperately.

To hunger for his touch.

Body begging for the kind of pleasure that only he could give.

A whimper rocked free and became one with our kiss.

"Nothing has ever felt as good as you touching me."

Oh, it was the truth. Because those flames were lapping, growing so hot in my belly, that space between my thighs glowing bright.

Aching for him to fill me.

The need of it almost felt like too much.

As if I might burst if he didn't take me.

He ripped only his mouth away, his hands back to my face, those eyes penetrating where they stared down at me through the murky darkness.

"I've had to fight for everything I've ever wanted for my whole life, Faith. I've had to lie and steal and cheat. None of that even compares to what I'm prepared to do for you. Loving you makes me feel like I'm no longer just surviving. Loving you is living. I love you. So much. So goddamned much."

And I swam in them.

The confessions of his heart.

Waded through the emotion that filled the room.

Dense and deep and dark.

But somehow, I didn't think I'd ever felt so light. The man bearing the weight. Holding me up when I'd forgotten how to fly.

"I love you, Jace. I've never loved a man the way I loved you. The way I *love* you."

And there I was, confessing my own.

Offering him the secrets of my heart.

Devotion pumped through the room. Fierce pulses of energy. Stretching out. Growing taut. The band connecting us alive.

So alive.

That was what I felt.

Alive.

As if I could finally breathe.

And then Jace was stealing it. Pressing himself back against me and kissing me like a madman.

His touch was rough and demanding and somehow gentle at the same time.

A promise that he would never hurt me.

He tugged at the towel I still had clutched to my chest and yanked it away, leaving me standing there bare.

Vulnerable.

My trust in his hands.

Those eyes flashed.

Copper and gold.

Dark with desire.

A tremble ripped through his massive body.

And maybe some of his trust belonged to me, too. Because this boy had been broken.

Beaten down.

I was still awed and amazed that he'd clawed out of that desolate world and made a new place for himself.

Yet somehow, I wasn't surprised in the least.

"You are everything I believed you were. Everything I saw, I see it right now, staring back at me."

A rumble blistered through the air.

A shot of devotion.

A bolt of intensity.

"And you are the same girl I saw that first day. Peering at me like she knew she'd just stumbled into a place she shouldn't be and wanted to go there anyway."

"That girl always saw something great. Something amazin' getting ready to be exposed. And you did. You amazed me. You still do."

Shame blanketed his face.

A flash before it was gone, and then he was grabbing me at the waist and spinning me around.

My hands flew out and grabbed onto the edge of the dresser to keep myself steady.

From behind, Jace gripped me by the waist, his fingers sinking into my skin.

"Look at you." The words were gruff. The lowest demand.

And I realized what he was doing, turning me toward the mirror, our expressions captured in the dingy glow.

Our reflections were like charcoal drawings in the muted light.

Both beautiful and ominous.

A hand slid down my bare back, chasing the chill that crashed along my spine. My bottom jutted out, begging for his touch.

He was all too eager to comply, and his big palm ran over my cheek, making me shudder when he gave a squeeze.

"You are what is amazing. That you look at me the way you do."

My gaze caught his in the mirror. "I never could stop looking at you."

He angled himself over me, and my chest sank down onto the top of the dresser as he pressed his chest against my back. The hot length of him pushed at my bottom, and his lips traveled across my shoulder.

Oh God.

This man was gonna wreck me.

Because I could feel my knees trembling. Could feel myself slipping more and more when it should have been impossible.

That was the thing about Jace Jacobs.

He'd always been *more*.

More of everything.

"And even when you weren't there, when I closed my eyes, I still saw you. I wanted to watch you. See you. Understand who you were," I admitted through a rasp of words.

His heart thundered at my back, a manic boom that beat into my blood. "You saw me clearer than anyone. Knew me better than anyone."

"And that boy who was gettin' ready to become a man was stunning. I knew it. Knew it, Jace."

A hand spread around to my belly, tucking me closer, the other winding around to hold me by the front of the throat.

His mouth was at my ear. "No. It's you who's stunning. This body and that face and your glorious heart. You gave me more than you'll ever know."

My fingers clung to the edge of the slick wood, so close to coming apart right there. "I never gave you anything."

The only thing I had was a young girl's love and all my naivety. I was still reeling with the grief of knowing that had been what had sent him away.

He held me tight, our skin slick, so close to being one. "You gave me everything. The courage to see myself as someone else than the rest of the world. You are the reason I fought. You are the reason I worked my way out of that life. It didn't matter that I didn't have you. I still did it for you."

Love bloomed in my chest. Like the awakening of petals. A rose coming to life.

Dizziness swept through my head, the man stealing reason and thought.

"Jace . . ."

How was it possible he could make me feel this way?

He grunted, still holding me by the front of my throat as he inched back and fumbled to push the pajamas from his hips, his words low, hard where he released them at my neck. "I'll give anything for you . . . anything for you and that little girl sleeping across the hall."

"I trust you."

*I trust you.*

The hand on my throat slipped around to the top of my back, and he pressed me tighter against the dresser. Cool wood hit my bare breasts, and one of his knees nudged my legs apart.

Exposing me.

He ran his fingers between my thighs.

A gasp pulled free, and my body arched with a pulse of pleasure.

A needy sound came from the base of my throat, and I was pushing back, begging for more.

No shyness found.

Only me and this boy.

This boy who'd been mine and who'd become this intense, fierce, dominating man.

And his fingers were pressing deeper. Pulsing and receding into the walls of my body. Winding me up so fast I couldn't make sense of it, the feeling that gathered like a ball of fire at my core.

My knees came close to buckling. The man so staggering he knocked me from my feet.

"Jace," I begged. I wasn't sure how much more I could take, and somehow, I knew, he was just getting started.

And he was suddenly kneeling behind me, gripping me by both

sides of my bottom, spreading me. His tongue swept through my folds, kissing and lapping and fucking and . . .

"Jace . . . oh . . . that feels so good. What are you doing to me?"

He bit down on one side of my bottom. Not enough to cause a whole lot of pain but enough to shoot a spear of need through me, my body burning up, lit from the inside and those flames spreading fast.

I'd never felt anything like it. Not in all my life.

He ran his nose up my cleft. "You have no idea what I plan to do to you, do you, good girl?"

His old nickname that'd been nothing less than a warning pulled from the smirk I could feel imprinted on my flesh, his mouth quirking up as he kissed up my back.

Shivers rolled.

He was everywhere.

I met the arrogance in his eye.

"Show me."

He stepped back, showing me that body, fisting that hard, massive length in his fist.

My mouth watered.

And then he was right there, pushing the fat head of himself into my lips, and a strangled breath was leaving my lungs.

Because he was so big. Consuming. Overwhelming as he gripped me by the hips and slammed into me.

A yelp ripped free.

Echoed around my room.

I was overcome by the perfect burn.

By the way he felt, taking all of me.

Possessing.

Every inch.

A grunted curse fell from his mouth. "The question is, what are you doing to me? What are you doing to me, Faith?"

He cinched tighter on my waist, yanking me back to meet every solid, hard thrust as he began to pound into me.

"What is it you're doing to me? You're making me crazy. Making me do crazy things. God. Fuck. You feel so good. I don't ever want it to stop."

His hand was in my hair, fisting and guiding me until my neck arched and he dropped his lips close to my ear, his chest pressed to my back. "Look at you."

I couldn't resist taking in the reflection staring back at me, my eyes so big, dark and somehow bright. Lips parted in need beneath his masculine sexuality.

I looked different.

Bolder and harder and needier at the same time. The little pleas that whimpered from my mouth were nothing less than a demand, "All I see is you. Touching me. Taking me. I'm yours, Jace. Yours."

Jace started running those big thumbs up and down the crease of my bottom, a tease of illicit desire. My stomach filled with this ball of need so intense I could barely see.

So intense it glowed.

I could feel it all around us.

Brighter and brighter.

His body pounded into mine while he touched me in a place I'd never been touched before.

A gush of a plea whispered from my mouth, and I was pressing back, begging for more, the front of my body writhing against the wood.

"You're so sexy. So damned sexy, Faith. Underneath all that sweetness, you are the fucking most devastating thing I've ever seen. Did you think of me? Did you picture me? Owning you this way?"

Oh, God, and I couldn't take it, his words and his assault, and that feeling that was gathering tighter. Getting closer and closer.

"Please," I whimpered, needing him to put me out of my misery.

"What do you need?"

"You. I need you, Jace."

Instantly, my body was jerked up, my back to the strength of his straining chest, his fucks so deep as he held me up with one arm across my chest, the other winding around and touching me.

Jace watched me through the mirror. Him stroking my clit, my body stretched out across him, his hand cupping one breast, thumb flicking at that sensitive spot, too.

He was everywhere.

Driving me wild.

His expression devout.

His thrusts relentless.

Hard.

Fast.

Deep.

Taking all of me.

Giving me everything. The way he promised me he would.

Pleasure glowed, a shimmer in the periphery. He touched and flicked at that ball of need, every stroke sending me higher.

Spinning and tightening and twisting until there was no other place I could go.

Pleasure cracked wide open, brilliant in the night. The orgasm ripping through me was bigger than anything I'd ever felt.

Infiltrating, invading, stealing every part of me.

And I could feel it.

Jace weaving his way in. Deeper and stronger. Those fragile seams of healing he'd made growing thicker. Binding the pieces back together.

I was just praying Jace would sew himself right there in the middle.

*Stay. Stay. Stay.*

Jace increased his pace as I was crying out his name, and he was holding me tight, angling his body as he rocked into me again and again.

So big.

Pushing deeper.

Owning me.

His breaths came short, jagged and hard, and then he was trying to stifle the shout of my name as he clenched down on me so tightly I could feel every twitch and ripple of his body.

The pulse of him as he shook and poured into me.

And we were there together. Floating through that dark, dark night. Me and this beautiful boy.

My beast with the brightest heart.

So bright I wanted to reach out and hold on to him forever.

"Oh, shit . . . fuck . . . Faith. Perfect. Perfect," he rambled at my skin.

He was gasping for breath where his mouth was pressed into my neck, my head canted to the side. Then he settled me onto my feet, steadying me when I nearly slumped to the floor.

Limbs spent.

Energy gone.

And he held me up, turning me around, and picking me up. There was no better place than the safety of Jace's arms.

He carried me to the bed and sat me on the edge of it. Carefully, he wrapped the towel around me, every touch tender as he kept looking up at me as if he'd just broken me, glancing at me often as he pulled back on his pants.

Finally, he came to kneel in front of me.

My heart gave a nervous kick. "What's wrong?"

His lips pursed. "I'm sorry for that. I needed to touch you one more time before this night ends."

"Loving me like that does not require an apology. You don't have to apologize to me for needing me."

He brushed back the hair matted at the side of my head. "Yes, Faith, I do. I have so much to apologize for."

I searched his face, trying to make sense of the sudden shift in his mood.

Not sudden, I realized. The man had been spun up since he'd received that phone call.

On edge.

Desperate.

It was the shift in me that I couldn't keep up with.

The sheer bliss that had beat through every cell in my body—that heat and devotion that rushed from him with the stark intensity of what we'd just shared—and the sinking fear I could feel settling into its place.

"Is this about what Mack told you on the phone? About the lead they got?"

He gave a tight nod, and he reached out a trembling hand and toyed with the end of my hair. "They found something . . . an office downtown that Joseph owned. One that was pretty much hidden."

He paused before he said, "It was tied to a well-known drug trafficker . . . a man who was found dead about six months before Joseph was killed. That building . . . it should be shut down. Vacant. And there's evidence of illegal activity. People moving stuff in and out."

I didn't know if the news delivered relief or another punch to the gut.

"What kind of illegal activity?" I chanced, my eyes dropping toward the ground, not wanting to know.

"Drugs. Smuggling. It was coming in on the ships and being packed for the streets. Gambling on top of it."

My spirit moaned.

Oh God.

How could he? How could he?

Why would he do something so horrible?

"Does Mack know how long he was doin' it?"

A stir of dread and unease whipped through the room, and Jace paused before he took me by the chin, forcing me to look at him. "He'd been involved for a long, long time."

I didn't want to hold his eyes, but there was something in them that I couldn't look away from.

Guilt.

Remorse.

"How long?"

"Faith," he murmured, so carefully, with so much regret, that I felt it like a strike.

"No, Jace. Don't do that. Tell me how long."

"Since right after I left. Probably longer. I've known since I got out of prison, Faith."

A frenzy screamed through my chest. Betrayal and hate and remnants of that love.

Confusion, too.

So much confusion.

"When I got arrested," he hedged.

I blinked at him, the knot in my throat so big I felt as if I were being strangled.

"There was cocaine in my bag, Faith."

Pain blossomed across my body. I might as well have been being beaten.

Blow after blow.

"No." My head shook.

"It wasn't mine. I thought it was Ian's. So, I took the fall for it. I was scared that, if I denied it, Ian would end up in jail or dead, and I would rather die than see that happen to him."

Jace scraped a palm over his face, a rigid guilt bunching up his shoulders as he looked at the floor for a beat. "I have to tell you something, Faith."

Dread flooded my senses. "What?"

"I . . . that guy . . . Steven? Do you remember me telling you about him? The guy I got arrested for assaulting?"

My nod was shaky. "Yes. He's the one you were protectin' Ian from. How could I forget that?"

Jace's expression twisted in shame. "He forced me into moving stuff for him. That night, the coke that was in my bag? It wasn't mine. But I *had* been doing deliveries for him. Picking up packages at the dock, running them across town to different stash houses. I got the feeling he really didn't need me to do it for him. He was only using it as a way to get me under his thumb. As a way to control me. I should have known right away that his intentions were to get all three of us—Ian and Joseph and myself—into that world."

Jace reached out and grabbed me, his hold pleading.

"I didn't want to, Faith. I swear to you, I didn't want to. But he told me if I didn't, what he'd done to Ian the first time would pale in comparison to what he would do. He wanted to make me obligated to him. He knew once I was, Ian and Joseph would follow."

Disbelief whooshed through my consciousness, my heart sluggish as I tried to catch up with the information Jace was giving me.

Could I ever blame him?

Jace had told me he would do anything to protect Ian and Joseph. It wasn't until then that I finally understood the lengths he'd actually go to in order to do it.

Anger lifted in him again, a blaze across his skin.

"I'd thought I was taking the fall for Ian . . . protecting him . . . so I'd confessed that it was mine."

"Jace." His name was a whisper. Torture and devotion. How was it fair that he'd gone through all of this and I'd not even known? "I thought it was because we broke into this house?"

Maybe I really was naïve. Nothing but the same stupid little girl who'd convinced Jace to sneak into this house.

Jace shook his head. "If that was all it'd been, I'd have gotten away with a slap to the wrist."

He swallowed hard. "The day I got taken away, I made them promise me . . . made them promise me that neither of them would go anywhere near Steven again. I didn't know he'd already sunk his claws into Joseph before I left, didn't know that Joseph was the one who put the drugs in my bag. I found out the day I was released from jail. I still don't know why he did it. He never would confess that he was the one who actually did."

Shock jarred me back. "What do you mean never confessed it? You talked to him?"

Nervously, Jace yanked at the front of his hair. "Yes, Faith, I talked to him."

Agony sliced through the center of me.

As if it were hacking through the two men I had loved.

Because I hadn't known Jace had even talked to Joseph in all those years.

Joseph had told me Jace was dead to him.

Dead to us.

It'd hurt, but I'd had to accept that Jace had left me behind. Left us behind.

I'd accepted it and lived my life the best way I knew how under those circumstances.

The fact it was so different sent ripples of anguish splintering through me like shockwaves.

"He came to me through the years for money when he'd get himself into trouble."

I blinked at Jace. "What do you mean, he came to you? You

*saw* him?"

I clutched the towel around me, scrambling back a little. I couldn't stop the horror in the words. The accusation in them.

But Jace hadn't mentioned that he'd ever seen Joseph. Not once in all this time he'd been here.

In all we'd shared.

And Joseph sure had never said he'd seen Jace in all the years that we'd been married.

Hurt bottled in my chest, and unrest whipped through the atmosphere. These fierce lashes of anxiety and worry that clawed through my bones. As if I was about to get sucked away into a vortex.

A hurricane I couldn't escape. One that would destroy everything.

"He . . . you talked to h-h-im?" I asked again through a stuttered whisper, still unable to process how that was even a possibility.

Pain streaked through Jace's face.

Torture.

"Yes. Through the years, yes, Faith. I talked to him. And I knew he'd gotten himself in deep. That he was living the way he shouldn't. He'd come to me when he needed something. When he'd gotten himself into trouble and didn't know how to get himself out of it."

Sorrow rushed.

How could Joseph have hidden this from me?

How could I not have seen it?

Anger rose inside me, this slow beat through my blood that increased with each thrum.

Something horrifying flashed through Jace's being.

The way his big body shuddered in the moonlight, his voice going so low.

"I warned him, Faith. I warned him that I was done. That I wouldn't get involved anymore."

My throat went dry, and I swore that I could feel my heart shriveling right in the center of me. "What do you mean?"

"He came to me . . . and . . . fuck."

Guilt twisted his face in a grimace of his own torment.

"I sent him away, Faith. He came to me. Begged me to help him. Told me they were going to kill him, and I sent him away."

All the air was gone.

The empty space it'd left swelled with the most gutting kind of pain.

"No," I whimpered. "You wouldn't do somethin' so horrible. I don't believe you."

Jace's voice turned rough with the admission. "I sent him away. I told him I didn't give a shit what he'd gotten himself into. That it was his fault, and I was no longer responsible. I'd warned him that I was done. I warned him."

The last cracked on his own grief.

Grief that was overwhelming.

Slamming between the two of us.

The awareness of what could have been stopped.

Jace brushed his fingers over my face. My face that was pinched with the horror of it all.

With Joseph's choices.

With Jace's.

With what he'd ignored.

What could have been stopped.

"I'm so fucking sorry."

I winced against the feeling of his hand on my face.

Was that another betrayal, too?

Another lie?

"You . . . you knew they were gonna kill him, and you turned your back on him? You let him die?"

It was all a spill of horror. Pain and guilt and remorse as tears broke free and streaked down my cheeks.

"You came here . . . knowing all of this? What Joseph was into? And you didn't tell me any of it? Why didn't you tell me, the first day you showed up here, what you knew? Why didn't you tell me?"

The last left me on a screech of confusion. With too many emotions binding up my insides. The reality of everything feeling as if it was goin' to finally bury me.

Jace was tied to Joseph in a way I'd never known. Had had an inside into everything Joseph had been involved in, even a say in it. All the while, both of them had left me a fool floundering in the dark.

Shame.

Jace had always worn some of it.

But I wasn't sure I'd seen him wear as much of it as he was right then.

But this was the quiet kind.

Because it was real.

Maybe for the first time, he had something to feel shameful for.

I clutched the towel to my chest. "How could you have kept that from me?"

A sob wrenched free.

One for Joseph.

One for me.

One for Jace.

How could we ever get past all these things?

"I loved you. Trusted you. I don't understand how you could just lie to me this way."

He sat back on his heels. "I told you a long time ago I'd never be good enough for you. Do you finally believe it?"

That was the problem. I didn't want to believe it. But the truth glared back at me.

Both men who I'd loved, trusted, had lied to me.

Kept me in the dark.

Made me a fool and put my family in danger.

I stared at the man I could feel crushing my heart with each second that passed.

"It was never a question of you being good enough for me, Jace. It was a question of what you did with your life. The choices you made. And you made the choice to lie to me."

Those fingers fluttered across my face. So soft and full of sorrow.

His and mine.

I didn't think either of us knew what to do with that.

"I knew you would hate me before I left here. But coming

here? Protecting you and Bailey. I won't regret that. Not for a second." Jace's expression crumpled. Just as quickly, determination raced in. "I have to go. End this. For the two of you. Felix is going to be parked outside as the lookout. I know you hate me. I accept that."

His voice twisted in deep emphasis. "I just want you to know that my love for you? It was always the truth. I could never tell a lie that great."

Then he pushed to standing, turned his back, and strode out the door.

Grief crashed into me.

Stunning and extreme.

Annihilating.

My body swayed, and I slipped from the bed and onto my knees.

Sobs ripped out of me.

Loud and pummeling.

Blows against the walls that echoed and shook.

I wanted to scream out for him. Beg him to stay.

A new kind of fear rumbled through my spirit as I heard him grab a few things from the room next door, his hesitating footsteps out in the hall before he hustled down the stairs.

The front door slammed closed with the type of finality I didn't ever want to consider.

## Jace

*P*ain lanced through me.

Cut after cut.

Excruciating.

I stumbled out into the darkened hall of the old house. I swore that I could hear ghosts screaming from where they were chained to the walls. Metal clanging and scraping. Shrill howls as spirits begged.

An echo of Faith and me.

A wail from Joseph.

A tangle of thieves and liars and cheats.

What had I done?

But I knew she'd hate me when she found out. I'd known it.

It didn't make it hurt any less.

It did nothing to lessen the agony that sheared through me.

Violent and piercing.

Ravaging every part of me.

I stumbled down the hall, hand darting out to keep me

standing. To keep myself from dropping to my knees and crawling back to her.

But I'd hurt her.

Hurt her in the worst way that I could.

I knew it. I knew it.

And it just made me that much more of a bastard that I hated him too.

That I hated Joseph for putting her through what he had.

For being such a selfish prick that he hadn't cared that he'd put Bailey and Faith in danger.

I hated the look of grief on her face when I told her that I had sat back and done nothing. That I could have stepped in and prevented what had happened.

Refusal tried to grab on to my heart and mind. This fucked-up piece that wanted to refuse it. To lay all the blame on Joseph.

I'd told him.

Warned him and pleaded with him to stop. Gave him every chance. Played his fucked-up games for years before it'd all become too much.

Before I couldn't take any more and the only thing stopping me from coming back here and taking Faith and that little girl from him was cutting myself fully out of his life.

Maybe that was what I should have done right from the beginning.

Come back and taken them.

I staggered into the darkness of the room where I'd been staying, quick to throw my things into my suitcase.

It wasn't like I had all that much there, anyway. The only things that mattered in those walls was Faith and Bailey.

Faith and Bailey.

My spirit roared. Roared and thrashed and demanded that I go back into her room. Take her back.

Make her mine the way she was always supposed to be.

Instead, I slung the strap of my overnight bag over my shoulder, grabbed my suitcase, and forced myself out into the hall.

Heart slamming against my ribs, I tried to go directly for the stairs, but I was trapped. Drawn to the door of that little girl who'd made me believe.

*Magic.*

I could feel it radiating from the room.

Unicorns and sunshine and fucking rainbows.

I wanted to get lost in it.

In the fantasy.

But that had never been my world, and every single time I'd attempted it, teased myself with the idea that I could have something *more*, it'd only brought on a greater loss.

Guessed I was just a sucker asking for the pain.

I set my palm to Bailey's door, imagining that I could feel it, her life-beat thrumming from the other side where she was lost to sleep.

Eyes pinched closed, I left the rest of what I had right there.

My love and my adoration.

Because I'd never love anything as purely as I loved her.

Struggling for a strangled breath, I dropped my head, sucked down the pain, and forced myself downstairs.

I knew the only thing I had left to give was helping Mack wipe out any threat.

I tried to quietly latch the door shut, but a gust of wind slammed it, as if that storm was beating from the inside.

Quick to shut me out.

I forced myself across the fucking porch that gleamed white.

*Safe.*

That was all I'd ever wanted them to be.

After tossing my suitcase and bag into the backseat of the rental car, I climbed into the front seat.

My phone rang.

The only relief I got was the number that was flashing on the screen. "Felix."

"Yo, man, you on your way out?"

"Yeah."

"Good. I'm on my way. I think it's important you're there. You've been right in the middle of this mess from the get go."

I hesitated, not knowing exactly what to say, but not knowing how to just let go of the two who were inside.

It was like I could feel the agony bleeding through those old walls, the ghosts stretching out with the spindly, bony fingers, trying to grab onto me.

Refusing to let me go.

I just didn't know if I could stand to ever have Faith look at me the way she had when I'd finally confessed my involvement. "Just . . . watch over them, okay? Don't let anything happen to them. They don't deserve any of this."

Felix blew out a sigh. "Of course."

"Thank you."

Felix dithered for a second before he finally said, "No problem, man."

Grateful, I hung up and gunned the engine as I headed toward Mack's.

Remembering my mission.

Why I'd come here in the beginning.

I was doing this for them. Because I owed them their safety. The ability to move on.

And that was exactly what I was going to give them.

# forty-two

## Jace
## Twenty-Nine Years Old

"What the fuck are you doing here?" Jace's hands fisted on top of his desk as he shot to standing from his plush leather chair.

Unable to believe what he was seeing.

*Who* he was seeing.

Shock blistered through his senses, his eyes narrowed as he stared at the man who'd just walked through his office door.

Hot hatred spiked at the center of him.

He'd have thought that, after all this time, it would have abated. Dimmed to a slight disdain.

But it was this ugly mass at the center of him that had only rotted and festered and grown.

Like a cancer that fed off the whole parts of him until there was nothing left but decay.

Joseph took a step forward.

Anxious and antsy.

Itchy.

A bead of sweat gathered at his temple and slipped down the side of his face.

"Jace," he said, his name both contempt and an appeal from his tongue.

"What do you want, *cousin*?" It was nothing but a sneer. "I thought I told you I didn't ever want to see you again?"

There was a threat behind it.

Because Jace was done. He had no sympathy left. Nothing left to give.

Joseph had already stolen it all.

Glancing away, Joseph roughed a hand over his face. "I need your help."

Unbelievable.

"I told you the last time that it was the *last time*. You were supposed to get your shit straight and never show your face here again. That was the deal, remember?"

It was the damn deal, yet there he stood, sniffing up the money tree like the sleazy, cheating bastard he was.

So goddamned squeaky clean on the outside while the inside was foul and dirty.

"Things changed, Jace."

"How's that?"

He didn't answer, just shifted uneasily on his feet.

"You gamble it away?" Jace demanded. He could feel another piece of himself breaking free and slipping down into that vortex.

Deeper and darker and bleaker.

Joseph swallowed thickly. No words were needed for the admission.

Motherfucker.

*How could he do this to them?*

Jace wanted to end him.

Or maybe run to Faith and tell her everything.

Convince her to walk away from her husband. Wrap her up and drag her to safety.

Seeing the fury in Jace's expression, Joseph chuckled through scornful laughter, like he had the right to be angry with Jace.

"Let's not pretend like what you did was for me when we both know you did it for her. It's your fault I'm in this mess."

"My fault? You're the one who came here begging for help. You're the one who was all over that deal the second I offered it."

"Because it's the only thing she ever wanted." Bitterness filled Joseph's gaze when he looked over at him. "But you already knew that, right? Which was why you gave it to me."

Jace's hands tightened almost painfully as he pressed them to the wood and tried to remain rooted when the only thing he wanted to do was fly over his desk and throw a fist or two.

Mouth watering with how sweet that kind of vengeance might taste.

Joseph laughed as his eyes moved over Jace's face. Like he was amassing the proof and quickly coming to a guilty verdict. "You still love her, don't you?"

Jace's teeth ground, restraint crumbling. "I'm warning you, Joseph—"

His scoff was straight disrespect, his own hatred bleeding through. "How does it feel to want what's mine?"

Jace was around the desk and across the floor before either of them could make sense of it. Joseph's back was slammed against the wall, Jace's forearm pinning him at the throat.

The piece of shit squirmed, trying to break free.

He'd once been as close as a brother.

Once.

"And why's that, Joseph? Why do you have what I want?" Jace spat in his face.

*You thief. You fucking thief.*

He grunted his response, the answer always clear.

But Jace had walked away like a fool.

That day he'd gone back to Broadshire Rim, he should have flown out of Ian's car like he'd wanted to do and told Faith everything.

Made her see.

Instead of going after the one thing that would ever truly make him happy, he'd turned his back and embarked on a mission to prove every motherfucker out there wrong.

He never should have had his brother dump him in an

unfamiliar city where he'd thought his only option was completely starting over.

If he could do it all over, he would.

But he couldn't.

And he could no longer be any part of that world without losing his mind.

He had to move on.

Forget it all.

"Get the fuck out and don't ever come back," Jace gritted close to his face, pushing him harder against the wall. "Do you understand me? I don't care what you got yourself into. I don't care what you owe. I don't care what you have coming to you. Do you get what I'm saying to you?"

Jace took a quick step back, and Joseph slumped forward, panting for a strained breath. That single bead of sweat had bloomed to a fucking sheet of perspiration soaking his shirt.

It took a second flat for his entire demeanor to shift. He stumbled a step forward, that look he'd mastered when he wanted something twisted through his expression, written in manipulation.

Desperate.

Needy.

Fake.

"Please, Jace, I didn't intend to come in here and act like an asshole. I just . . . I need your help. Please. They're gonna kill me, man. Please."

Jace cracked a grin. "They're gonna kill you, huh? I hope so."

It was his own taunt.

His own disrespect.

Besides, Jace knew better than to believe a single word Joseph spouted. He stepped back and pointed at the door. "Get out before I kill you first."

Three Weeks Later

Jace picked up his cell where he sat at his desk. Atlanta was spread out below him where he took in the view from his high-rise apartment.

He felt a single thud in his chest when he glanced at the screen. "Mack," he answered.

On the other end of the line, Mack pushed out a shaky sigh. "Jace, I have bad news."

Jace's heart froze in the middle of his chest.

"We found Joseph in his car in front of the grocery store. A bullet through his head." A bottled sob scraped up Mack's throat. "They killed him."

# forty-three

## Faith

*T*ears kept streaking down my face where I was on my knees on the floor. The room spinning as I tried to make sense of the news I'd received.

I didn't want to accept it.

The betrayals that had been meted at the hands of Joseph and Jace. I didn't know which hurt worse.

My phone vibrated on my nightstand. A string of blips calling out.

With my insides twisted in pain, I forced myself onto my feet and stumbled that way, barely able to see through the bleariness of my eyes.

Through the loss that thrummed and churned and seethed.

Oh God. How was I ever gonna get through this?

How had I been so blind not to realize Jace knew more than he was telling me? How could he come into our home and keep this kind of secret?

There was no reconciling the two. No way to patch it or glue it or fix it.

Joseph was dead. Failing himself. Failing me.

And Jace was caught somewhere in the middle of it.

My soul cried out.

Horrified to realize I really hadn't known Joseph at all.

That he'd been into all the things he'd promised me he never would.

Promising me that he was different.

That he would give me the kind of life that I deserved.

Maybe it was all my fault, anyway.

My fault for letting myself love him but knowing I could never love him all the way.

Maybe I was the one who was truly selfish, taking somethin' for myself and knowing I couldn't give all of myself in return.

Maybe I was the one who'd betrayed and shamed and gone the wrong way.

A wave of grief and guilt slammed me.

My knees knocked, and a raw sob clawed out of my throat.

Everything hurt.

Excruciating.

Blinding.

I tried to pick up the phone, and it clattered back down when it slipped from my trembling hands, and I sucked in a breath as I forced myself to focus, to pick it up.

To remember the only thing that really mattered was the little girl sleeping across the hall.

Her safety and her future.

I thumbed across the screen.

**Jace: Felix is on his way over to stay with you until this is ended.**

**Jace: The last thing I will do is leave you unprotected.**

**Jace: Even though you hate me, I won't leave either of you unsafe.**

**Jace: I'm so sorry, Faith. So sorry. The one thing I ask is that you never forget that I truly loved you.**

I felt the force of his devotion through the words. His love and his regret. It nearly dropped me to my knees again.

My attention moved from the words on the screen to the picture I still had at my bedside.

Joseph and me on our wedding day.

My insides curled with grief.

*How could you?*

I wanted to scream and shout at him so loudly he would hear my words from beyond the grave.

*How could you?*

Immediately, the words of that letter I'd found filled my mind.

*Faith,*

*The first time I saw you, I wanted you. I guessed I'd always chased after the things that weren't mine. I'm so sorry for that. But I don't regret it.*

*Do you remember the day we got married? Look at that picture, Faith. Look at me. It was the most honest day of my life. But even that honesty was tainted because you never really belonged to me.*

*I could never regret you. The only thing I wish is that I'd done it all differently.*

*Look at that picture, Faith. What you see there, it's the truth.*

*Joseph*

Tears blurred my eyes as I stared at the image. Both of us so young. What I felt for him so different from what I'd ever imagined for my wedding day.

But I'd been happy. Happy in a resigned, compromised way. Resolved to love him the best that I could.

Suddenly, I was struck with an urge. A frenzied desperation as I lifted the frame and threw it against the wall.

Glass shattered, the frame bent, and the picture shifted from its position.

I gasped when I saw something peeking out from underneath.

I dropped to my knees and grabbed the metal, shaking the glass loose, the knot in my chest expanding in this blossoming pain when the small folded piece of paper slipped out.

Blinking through the bleariness, I carefully grabbed it and unfolded the letter.

My heart twisted in two.

**He was always your beast. I never should have tried to compete with that.**

Instantly, I was taken back to the day we'd argued, when he'd screamed at me to throw the Beast away, that he didn't want any memories of Jace in our home.

I hadn't had the heart to get rid of it and had hidden it in the back of the closet.

I'd almost regretted not throwing it away the day Bailey had found it and started carrying it around as if it was her best friend, the quiet yielding hurt that had blanketed Joseph's eyes when he'd come home and found his daughter carrying on about how much she loved it.

*The Beast.*

*The Beast.*

Choking over the sobs in my throat, I climbed to my feet, raced to my dresser, and pulled on a tee and sweats.

Without slowing, I rushed to my daughter's room and I gently pulled the tattered stuffed animal out from under her arm, careful not to wake her as I knelt beside her bed and frantically searched.

Hands pressing hard over the face and the arms.

I froze for a beat when I patted down the blue jacket and felt the crinkle in the sewn-down pocket.

Shooting to my feet, I hurried back out and into my room, fumbling for the scissors. Frantic, hiccupped sounds jetted from my mouth as I cut it open and found another note.

This was a series of six numbers.

And I remembered the key.

The key in the drawer with the letter.

A trail that Joseph had left me because he'd known.

Oh God, he'd known he was leaving this world.

Memories flashed.

Joseph and I on the top floor as we made plans to clear a few things out. He'd brought attention to the old safe up there, winked at me when he'd said, "This baby holds all my secrets."

I'd thought he was joking.

Teasing me.

Breaths heaved in and out of my aching lungs, and my heart stampeded, so out of control as I rushed to the drawer and grabbed the key and fumbled upstairs to the third floor.

Darkness spread out over the rambling, open space. Antique furniture was everywhere, some covered in sheets and drapes, other pieces covered in dust.

I scrambled for the old safe where it was hidden inside an armoire, hardly able to get my hands to cooperate as I shoved the ancient key into the lock, my spirit screaming as the old door creaked open.

Inside was a small, newer safe. The kind that had digital numbers to enter the code.

My entire body rattled as I pulled it out and tried to squint at the numbers on the sheet.

Then I froze when I heard the creak from behind me.

I wasn't quite sure what it was. What made the fine hairs at my nape stand at attention.

The ugly presence that billowed through the space.

Fear banged through me, so intense it whipped against my skin like physical blows.

A warning.

*Intuition.*

Terrified, I turned my head to look over my shoulder.

Felix stood at the top of the stairs.

"Felix?" I asked, almost like a question. "Hey . . . hi . . . I'm so glad you're here."

But I wasn't glad he was there. Wasn't relieved to see him. Because I couldn't escape the feeling that something was off.

His normal fun-going casualness wiped away in his slow approach.

He was wearing his uniform . . . but somehow . . . somehow looking at him right then, it fit all wrong.

His eyes looked . . . different.

Harder and meaner.

As if a mask had been ripped from his face to reveal what was really hidden underneath.

My blood ran cold.

"Looks like you knew where it was all along. I was beginning to think you really were ignorant."

He cracked a twisted grin when he looked between me and the safe sitting on the floor in front of me.

Awareness hit me, sending a bolt of terror ripping through my consciousness, and my eyes started to dart all over the place, trying to find a way out.

A way to get to my daughter and get us free.

A way to scream loud enough that Jace might hear.

I did.

Oh, I screamed.

It didn't matter.

There was no one there to hear it. No one there to save me. So, I did the only thing I could do.

I pushed to my feet and I ran.

He caught me from behind, and a big hand clamped over my mouth.

The stench of wickedness filled my nostrils when Felix leaned over and breathed against the side of my face, his words a threat at my ear. "Joseph owes me, Faith. Looks like you're the only one left to pay."

## Jace

Heart beating out of control, I clutched the dashboard like I might be chained to it as I watched Mack and his team bust into the warehouse from where Mack's car was parked across the lot.

Wearing SWAT gear, their weapons intimidating as they filed in through the door once they were given the clear.

My blood was in a frenzy, and I had to physically force myself not to jump out.

I was trying to remain respectful.

Because Mack was a damn good cop. He knew what he was doing.

But fuck.

It was brutal sitting there, wanting to be the one who stopped this monster, and having to sit there like a pathetic kid who didn't know how to wipe his own ass.

Flashes of light lit up the windows as flashlights drove out the darkness, my body so hitched on what was happening inside I thought I could feel every pound of their boots, the way they moved in and out of rooms, climbing to the top floor.

Every second that passed, my pulse raced harder, my chest squeezing as I angled closer and closer to the windshield, trying to get a better view.

There was nothing I could do when I saw Mack reemerge through the door where they'd entered.

I flew out and ran across the pavement.

His expression was frustrated.

Grave and confused.

"What happened?" I shouted.

He scrubbed a palm over his face. "Nothing fucking happened. That's the problem. There isn't a trace of anything in there. No files. No computers. No contraband. It's wiped clean. Like not a soul has been in there in months."

"What? How? I thought Felix and Doug found something?"

"Thought so, too."

A bluster of helplessness moved through me, all mixed up with the torment that had been written on Faith's face when I'd told her. The combination of the two nearly dropped me to my knees.

Mack squeezed my shoulder. "We are going to find them."

Unsettled, I shook my head. "None of this sits right with me. You guys found the address a few hours ago, how did they have time to up and disappear like they'd never been here in the first place?"

He squeezed my shoulder again. "They could have caught wind of the raid and got the hell out of there. It wouldn't be the first time it has happened."

I wanted to take him at his word. But there was something about it that didn't sit well.

Hell, nothing had been sitting well since the second all of this shit had gone down.

But I couldn't stop the commotion inside me. This throbbing mayhem that warned nothing was right.

"Listen, I'm going to go back to the office. Read through the report again. See if there's anything that we missed. I'll drop you at your car, then you need to go and get some sleep."

I huffed out a sound. That was funny because I had nowhere to go.

"Seriously, man, I know you are going crazy right now, and believe me, I want to nail these fuckers as badly as you do. But sometimes it takes time."

Problem was, I was worried we were running out of time. The loss swirling around me, so dark and bleak. What had gone down in that intersection two days ago was proof of that.

"Fine," I told him.

Reluctantly, I climbed back into Mack's car, part of me wanting to go into that building and do a little hunting for myself. Sure we had to be missing something.

What I really wanted to do was to go back to Faith's place.

But I wasn't welcome any longer.

I called Felix instead, needing to check in. The reassurance that everything was all right.

It went straight to voice mail.

"Shit," I muttered under my breath.

"What?" Mack asked as he took the last turn into the station.

"Felix isn't answering."

Mack's brow lifted. "That's because he's working. Doing his job rather than gabbing with you on the phone."

He tried to make it come out light, but I wasn't feeling so light.

Everything felt heavy, unable to escape that feeling that had my guts twisted and tied.

I knew its source.

The fact Faith would never forgive me. My mind haunted by the horror and hate that moved through her expression when I'd admitted what I'd known and, like a fool, had never disclosed.

Had never helped when I'd had the chance. Laughed in Joseph's face instead, my last words to him nothing but spite.

I hit the road, not even knowing where the fuck I was going to go but knowing I couldn't go too far until this was solved.

Then I would go.

Leave and never return.

I forced myself into the rental car, my sight bleary as I hit the road. I headed in the direction of Ian's condo back in Charleston, figuring I'd crash there.

Streetlamps blazed and glimmered from above, and I blinked hard, trying to erase Bailey's little face that started to take hold of my mind.

Flash after flash.

*Jace, you sway aww the dragons?*

I could hear her little drawl pleading with me so clearly that it was like she was right there, whispering in my ear.

My heart hammered in my chest. This bam, bam, bam I could feel all the way to my soul.

I squeezed my eyes closed against the assault and tried to convince myself they were fine.

Safe.

Tried to remind myself of what I'd done. How deeply I'd fucked up.

It didn't matter.

Bailey's little voice was there.

*Mommy and Bailey and Jacie.*

Wrapping and winding and prodding.

I didn't know how to go on. How I was going to survive from here. Because nothing had ever hurt more than this.

Losing both of them.

Who knew the love of your life could grow into something bigger? That it could magnify and compound and become this vast, stunning need that glowed at the center of you.

What made it worse was this sticky feeling that skated my skin, crawled over me like a disease, drenching me in sweat.

I tried to force myself to drive to Ian's place.

Instead, I was flipping my car around and heading back toward that tiny town. Pushing harder on the accelerator.

Drawn.

Drawn back to where I shouldn't go.

I sped through the city and hit the road that led back to Broadshire Rim.

My mind was already back there at that massive house.

Our sanctuary.

The place where our dreams had been made and crushed in

what had felt like the same moment.

All those memories collided, pushing and pulling and screaming out for reclamation.

*Hurry.*

That word sounded through my mind like the clanging of a gong.

I gunned the accelerator, sweat dripping from my temples.

What the fuck was happening to me?

Maybe this was what it was like to have my sanity slip right through my hands, dripping through my fingers like the finest sand, spilling all over the ground.

A frenzy around me.

Spurring me on.

Driving me faster.

Harder.

I skidded around the last turn and barreled down the dirt road that ran the back edge of the town. I forced myself to slow as I drew closer to the old house.

I wasn't welcome.

It didn't stop the devotion that burst in my blood. This feeling that wouldn't let me go.

Moonlight clung just over the line of towering trees that hugged the narrow lane, stretched thin and tossing the night into a thousand pulsing shadows.

It didn't matter that everything was still.

Silent.

I could feel the energy.

Throbbing.

Thick and foreboding.

Screaming through the bottled hush that held fast to the air.

Cutting my lights, I slowly started to ease the car down the drive. I came to a stop halfway down the lane.

Swallowing hard, I reached into the glove box and pulled out my gun, ensured it was loaded before I stepped out into the humid night and tucked it into my jeans at the small of my back.

The soles of my shoes crunched beneath me as I hastened through the night. The barest shot of relief hit me when I saw

Felix's cruiser parked at the circular drive in front of the porch.

I should turn around.

Go.

But that feeling wouldn't release me.

All around, bugs trilled and branches rustled.

The quietest howl that screamed.

Unsettled.

Distressed.

I swallowed around the lump that grew heavy at the base of my throat and eased around Felix's car.

I peered up at the house.

All the windows were blacked out. The thickest kind of night echoed back.

There was something about it that felt off.

Wrong.

Like the peace of the place had been stripped from the walls.

Anxiety pulsed. Mixed with the driving, pulsing urge to race across the porch and bust down the door.

The door.

It struck me right then, and my gaze flew that way when I realized what it was that had made everything feel off.

It was darkened, obscured by the sway of the shadows that moved across the covered porch. But when I looked closely, I could see that it was sitting open a crack.

Terror cinched down across my chest.

A vise.

Constricting.

Without another thought, I was moving, trying to keep my footsteps as quiet as possible as I crept up the porch steps and across the planks.

I craned my ear, listening.

Silence echoed back.

A dark kind of silence. Something grim and wicked and evil riding on the dense, dense night. Like I could taste it, pull it into the well of my lungs.

Violence skated my skin and twisted through my insides.

I'd told Faith I would do whatever it took to keep her and

Bailey safe.

I'd meant it.

I'd never meant it more than right then when I realized I could scent it.

Malice.

Rage seeped from my flesh and dripped from my pores. I'd take out anything, anyone, who would hurt them.

I eased open the door another inch, cringing as it creaked on its hinges. I bit down on my lip like it might keep the sound contained.

The only thing there was the stilled vacancy of the room.

I stepped inside, eyes rushing around to take in the stillness.

Where the fuck was Felix?

Terror rode my spine.

What if I was too late? What if Felix hadn't been enough to protect them?

Heart slamming against my ribs, I inched deeper into the darkened house, the old antiques big and imposing, as imposing as the silence that reverberated back.

Quieting my feet, I eased up the sweeping staircase, moving as fast as I could without making a sound.

I went straight for Bailey's door.

Somehow, I already knew it'd be sitting wide open, her bed empty, covers a mess where they'd been dragged to the floor.

Sweat drenched my forehead and dripped down my back.

No.

*No. No. No.*

Blinking through the staggering pain, I pushed right back out, and did the same to Faith's room, eyes sweeping the place, knowing it would be the same.

Emptiness bled through the door. Pooled on the floor. The picture frame that had remained on her nightstand had been shattered on the floor.

I started to rush out, to run for the door, to grab for my phone as I did.

Then I heard it.

A rustle from upstairs.

A small bang.

A barely heard moan.

But it hit my spirit so loudly I could have sworn Faith was screaming it in my ear.

*I need you, Jace. I need you in a way I've never needed anyone.*

Little fingers digging into my neck.

*You sway aww the dragons?*

Pulse crashing through my veins, I eased up the narrow staircase that led to the third floor, not knowing what to expect but preparing for the worst. I paused only long enough to send Mack a text.

**Me: Get to Faith's now. Bring backup.**

I inched the rest of the way up the steps, cringing every time the old wood groaned, praying I could make it up without being noticed.

If the girls and Felix weren't alone up there, it would be me against who knew how many. The last thing I wanted for them to know was that I was coming.

The banging grew louder the higher I got, and I eased up into the open space of the rambling third-floor above.

Dust and boxes and old furniture sat everywhere. It'd been cluttered the last time I'd been up here, but since then, it'd been torn apart.

Ransacked.

The barest light glowed from a corner at the very back, and my heart clanged, the desperate clawing of the beast when I found Faith huddled on a worn couch on the other side of the expansive room, rocking Bailey in her arms.

Her expression was terror-stricken, her energy bowed and twisted and tied. Stuck on this moment.

Life in the hands of the bastard who raged in front of her, gun clenched in his hand.

Felix.

What the fuck was happening?

Confusion spun while horror climbed into my spirit.

*Felix.*

My mind flashed with all the threats. The fact someone had been able to get in and out without being noticed. Almost like they belonged.

*Felix.*

He'd been right there under our noses this whole time.

Watching her.

Waiting.

Motherfucker.

How could I have let this happen?

That lead had been nothing but bait to lure me away. And I'd left Faith right in the palm of his hand.

Rage blistered and blew. I didn't know how he couldn't feel the storm whip through the room, the lashes that struck in the stagnant air.

Thunder.

Swore, I felt a bolt of lightning strike through the center of me.

A stake to my body.

"Where the fuck is it, you stupid bitch?" Felix ranted, angling down toward her where she did her best to hide in plain sight, her hand over the back of Bailey's head like she could protect her from the words he spat.

"I told you . . . I . . . I don't know what you're talkin' about. I don't know anything about Joseph's business."

Roaring, Felix whirled to the side and kicked a huge cardboard box. Glass shattered when it crashed onto the ground, contents spilling out.

Bailey screamed, and her mother held her tighter.

While I almost came right out of my skin.

No one would hurt them.

No one.

Not ever.

I'd die before I let that happen.

Felix was back in Faith's face. "Give up the bullshit innocent act. I know you know. I gave you plenty of chances to come clean. Warning after warning. I didn't want it to come to this, but I'm out of time. Just the same as you. Now tell me where that piece of shit hid it before I beat it out of you."

Anger surged. So intense I almost went running across the room.

But I held back, eyes scanning, trying to figure out the best way to lure the asshole away.

Faith whimpered. "I told you, I don't know anythin'. I swear. I'd tell you if I did. Please . . . let us go. I won't say anythin'."

Malicious laughter rolled from him. "You're just as greedy as that little fucker was, aren't you? This big ol' house, all for yourself. Isn't that right?"

"No," she wheezed. "Please . . . I beg you . . . you can have anything. Just let my baby go."

He reached out and touched Bailey's hair, his voice turning menacingly soft. "She's always been the answer, hasn't she, Faith? Do I need to take it out on her to get the answer out of you?"

A sob wrenched from Faith's throat, and there was nothing I could do.

My body vibrated with the need to destroy. To take out any threat.

Gun aimed at his back, I stepped out of the shadows. "I'd think twice about that."

## Faith

$O$h, God, Jace was here.

He was here.

Maybe he'd heard me screaming, after all.

Because there he was, coming around an armoire that sat to the side of the stairs, gun in his hand and vengeance in his eyes.

Felix whirled around, his own gun lifting. "I was wondering when you'd show your dumb ass back here. Was hoping we'd be long gone by then. I guess plans have to change sometimes, don't they?"

I still couldn't process that it was Felix. That the man had somehow inserted himself in our lives and I hadn't suspected anything was wrong.

Courtney hadn't known.

Oh goodness, Courtney.

My best friend.

I had no idea if she was fine. If she was home sleeping and had no clue or if this vile man had hurt her, too.

Jace laughed. Laughed a sound unlike any I'd ever heard him

make before.

Cruel and every bit as savage as the man who'd held my daughter and me hostage for the last two hours. "Yeah, you're right. Sometimes plans change. Because the last thing I expected to have to do tonight is take you out. Yet, here I am."

Felix's nostrils flared, and he took a step in Jace's direction. It was as if they both were magnets. Drawn to the flames that were gonna burn all of us alive.

Because I could feel it.

Something cruel and depraved pulsing through the air. Sucking out the oxygen. Leaving the gut feeling that none of us were gonna walk away from this unscathed.

I wanted to beg Jace to go. The only thing I wanted was for him to take Bailey with him.

Protect her and provide for her.

Because Joseph's debt had come due, and I wasn't going to let Bailey be the cost.

I'd pay it. I'd pay it if it meant my baby would be okay.

"Jace," I whispered.

For the barest moment, those copper eyes flashed to me.

But in that glance, I heard a million pleas.

*Don't move.*

*Don't say anything.*

*Let me pay.*

*Let me pay.*

*It is my fault.*

*I owe you this.*

And I wanted to take back every single thing I'd accused him of earlier.

Tell him I understood.

That whatever Joseph had done, he'd done himself. He'd brought all this on us. Put us in danger.

Felix erased another inch of space between them. And I saw it, Jace easing back, almost imperceptibly, but I knew.

I knew he was luring the man away.

Protecting us the way he'd always promised he would.

"Joseph has something that is mine," Felix said. "I'm not

leaving here without it. I want that log."

A log.

That was what he'd been looking for all this time? Breaking into my house and terrorizing us for some stupid log I hadn't even known existed?

Felix had been enraged when he hadn't found it in the safe. He'd been sure I'd been hiding it all along . . . that I'd already removed it and had hidden it somewhere else in the house.

He'd been ranting, spouting a bunch of names that I wanted to purge from my mind.

Names of people I had thought had been Joseph's friends who were nothing but a disgusting family tree of organized crime.

Felix thought I was still trying to protect Joseph.

Never.

Hate glinted in Jace's eyes. "Putting a bullet through his head wasn't enough?"

"He was responsible for my uncle being killed. He stole from our family. He knew the rules. He broke them. His grace period had run out."

"Then what do Faith and Bailey have to do with it?"

Felix shrugged. "Collateral damage, I suppose. I was sure she knew where it was, that she was protecting that traitor, but I'm beginning to think she was telling the truth. It's too late now, though, isn't it?"

He said all of this as if none of our lives mattered.

All of us expendable. Greed the greatest game.

Sickness clawed at my insides, and sitting there, I wanted to weep.

Weep at the cruelness of it all.

"She doesn't know anything. Just . . . put down the gun, let them go, and you and I will find that log."

"Right . . . I'm just going to let them walk out of here. She knows everything, and even if she doesn't, I can't take that chance."

"You don't let them go, and you're going to be the one who isn't walking out of here."

Felix sneered, a hateful twist of his lips. "Awful sure of

yourself, don't you think? Should have taken you out the second you rolled up here like a knight in shining armor sent to save the day. There's no saving, Jace."

Jace?

Jace just cracked a smile that was all taunt.

He was windin' Felix up.

Stoking his anger.

Aiming it at himself.

"You're right. It's over. Over for you."

Needles and knives. I could feel Jace driving them into Felix's flesh. The way rage rippled through Felix, his pinpoint focus narrowing in on Jace.

But Jace's . . . Jace's might have been more intense. His drive greater than anything I'd ever witnessed or seen.

Fear tumbled through the center of me.

A different kind.

It was the terror of losing him all over again.

It rang with finality.

I could see it written all over him.

What he was willing to give. What he was gettin' ready to do.

"That's where you're wrong. Steven is dead. I find that log? End this threat to our family? I take his place. Taking out that traitor Joseph was only a bonus. Now . . . back the fuck up. Me and your girlfriend here are going to find that log. She cooperates, and maybe, I'll let the little girl go."

Oh God, that was the only thing I wanted. For Bailey to be safe.

Desperately, I looked around as if it might conjure that log he was so desperate for.

Maybe . . . maybe I could use it to get us free. The only thing inside the smaller safe had been a stack of letters.

Felix had scattered them onto the floor like garbage, shooting into a rage before I'd even been able to figure out what they were.

He'd dragged me downstairs to get Bailey before he'd dragged us right back up here and had begun to tear apart the third floor.

Screaming at me to tell him where *it* was.

*A log.*

That's what this had been all about?

As if I'd protect that over my daughter.

"You aren't going anywhere," Jace said, "and sure as hell not with Faith or Bailey. You want to walk out of here? Let Mack continue to hunt you down? Be my guest. But you aren't hurting either of them."

I could see it in the firm clench of Jace's jaw. In the way his finger flexed on the trigger of his gun.

The two of them had started to dance around the other, moving slowly as they began to circle like hawks.

Predators after their own prey.

Both of them beasts. Coming from the same ugly world.

But that was where the similarities ended, their hearts so strikingly different.

I felt the burn of Jace's.

The bolt of light.

The streak of love.

And I knew . . . I knew I couldn't just sit there. He was getting ready to go down in a blaze. I had to do somethin'.

If Felix had been responsible for Joseph's death, no doubt Felix wasn't going to think twice about killin' any of us. I shook when I realize it'd probably been his intention all along.

Get the log, and then he was goin' to get rid of us the same way as he'd gotten rid of Joseph.

I couldn't allow that to happen.

With none of their attention on me, I quietly eased off the couch and onto my knees.

In the lapping shadows, I ran the palm of my hand over Bailey's mouth, my eyes begging her, silently praying she'd understand I was asking her not to make a sound.

Silently telling her how much I loved her.

That she was my world.

I hid her in a crevice between the couch and a massive dresser, and I pressed the softest kiss to the top of her head. A promise that I would always love her. No matter what happened.

My little thing hugged my neck, sending her own silent plea.

But somehow her heart was beating steady. Filled up with that understanding that was too great for someone her age. The child always too keen.

Pressing my lips to her chubby cheek, I breathed her in, held her little spirit tight to my heart.

Then I gathered the little courage I had and crawled back out, peering around the couch only far enough to see the two men still circling each other.

"You should know better than to think any of this works like that. Joseph killed my uncle, and he was holding that log over our heads like it was going to save him. Nothing would have. Just like there isn't anything that is going to save you or her."

Felix was in the middle of the room. Seething. The stench of hate coming off him was so great, I knew there was no chance any of us were making it out of there if someone didn't stop him.

The vile man stood like a fortress between Jace and Bailey and me.

The only thing coming between us.

I had to do something.

Anything.

Anything to distract Felix so Jace could have a shot at saving us.

I wrapped my hand around the base of a tall glass lamp that had been shoved to the floor.

Everything shook, as devotion and fear warred.

The latter was so strong it turned my stomach and soured on my tongue.

But I needed to be brave. Brave the way Jace had always been. Willing to sacrifice myself for the ones I loved.

It was the rawest, barest form of it.

Giving it all.

Slowly pushing to standing, I emerged out of the shadows with the lamp held high. I ran for Felix, praying I could make a difference.

Stop this madness, once and for all.

Those copper eyes flashed with terror.

With the most startling kind of fear when Jace realized what I was doing.

I swung.

"No!" Jace screamed, and he was racing my way, flying across the floor.

Gunshots rang out. The piercing sound ricocheted against the walls.

Deafening.

Agony.

I swore I felt the sting of it just as I felt the impact of the lamp across the top of Felix's back.

Jace was there, ramming into Felix and pushing me out of the way at the same time.

Flying back, I landed hard before scrambling back and out of the way.

Eyes wide as I watched the scene unfold in slow motion.

Felix staggered. Shock written on his face as he clutched his chest.

His big body fumbled back, and he slammed into the big window that was covered by a black drape.

It shattered and the fabric ripped free from the rod. The milky night poured in as I watched the massive figure tumble backward through the frame.

A shriek pulled from my lungs at the finality of it all. Relief and horror and shock.

That Felix could do this.

That Joseph could put us in this position.

And Jace, he was looking at me, relief and the truest kind of love pouring from the glinting gold in his eyes.

It was as deep as the blood that saturated the front of his shirt.

Dread spiraled through the center of me.

"Oh God, Jace," I whimpered, and I tried to climb back to my feet so I could get to him. So I could stop this from happening.

*No.*

This couldn't happen.

Pain flashed across his face, and he crumpled to the ground.

Panic surged, as thick as it sloshed through my blood.

Desperate, I crawled across the floor, frantic to get to him, another sob breaking free.

"Jace."

I fumbled for him in the darkness, and my fingers ran over his face.

His beautiful, unforgettable face.

No, no, no.

Shivers ripped through my body, and I wanted to crawl over him, protect him the way he'd protected me.

"Jace," I whimpered, hovering over him, hands shaking as I set them on his cheeks. "Jace."

He reached up, his hand on my face.

His voice was raspy, gurgling in his throat. "Anything, Faith. I told you, I'd give anything for you."

With the softest smile on his face, his hand dropped away and his body went slack.

And I screamed.

I screamed as I clung to him.

Begging him not to leave me.

Big hands were on my back, dragging me away while I fought to remain at his side.

To stay.

"Faith . . . you've got to let go, honey. You've got to let go." Mack's voice was in my ear.

Asking me to do the one thing I didn't want to do.

# forty-six

## Faith

*I* could feel the tentative footsteps edge up behind me. The heavy breaths released into the dark, subdued air. The grief that saturated everything.

"He always loved you."

Tears streaking free, I shifted to look over my shoulder at Ian.

Another bolt of sorrow crashed over me. The man resembled his brother so much that my heart panged at the sight of him.

Ian eased up to my side, strain so heavy in his shoulders I could feel it radiating from him.

Wave after wave.

"You were his entire world," I whispered.

Ian grunted. "No, Faith, that position belonged to you. He would do anything for me, but when it came to you? He gave up everything. For a long time, I hated you for that. Terrified you were better than me, that he would like you better, and he'd forget all about me. Selfish, right?"

"You were only a kid," I whispered. "I guess I'd felt the same way—had thought that he'd forgotten all about me when he walked away. I still don't understand why he wouldn't have just told me when he was gettin' sent away. I would have understood. Would have supported him."

Ian huffed out a tortured sigh. "Because Jace never saw himself the way the rest of us did. He never thought he was good enough for you."

"He was *more* than enough for me." I glanced over at Ian. "He was everything."

I watched the grief streak across his face. "He's the last thing I have, Faith. The only thing. I don't think he ever really knew it. Understood it. He was everything to me, too. I wouldn't be here without him."

And I knew in my heart that Bailey and I wouldn't be either.

That yesterday would have been our end if Jace hadn't come to me.

"He gave it all for us," Ian murmured, his voice catching in the quiet, the intensive care near deserted, just the quiet shuffle of nurses' feet as they moved from one place to the next.

I turned back to the window that overlooked the darkened room, the barest glow inside where Jace was covered in tubes and wires, the man left to the hands of the machines.

I pressed my palm to the window. "And the only thing I want is to give it back."

Ian pushed out a soft sound, the hard, hard man turning to look at me. "Do you know what he loved most about you?"

My eyes squeezed closed for a beat, and my knees shook, barely able to stand beneath the devastation that thrummed in my chest.

I couldn't form the words, couldn't make a sound except for the sorrow that wobbled at the base of my throat.

His words filled the air, "He loved your belief. That you looked at the world differently than anyone else. That you looked at *him* differently. It scared him, but it was what he loved most. There's a reason you're here. I think there always has been."

He angled his head, getting close to my face. "You saved him . . . saved us from the life we were set on. From living the kind of life we were destined for. You were the reason. You were his courage. You were his belief. Don't give up on that *faith* now.

Because that? I think that is what would kill him."

Then Ian, the guy who wore the biggest chip on his shoulder and an easy smile that was nothing but a wicked grin, turned and walked out.

I turned back to the glass separating Jace and me.

Pressing my palm harder to the cool surface.

Praying . . .

Praying . . .

*Come back to me.*

I sat at his bedside.

A day.

Then two.

Then three.

Unable to sleep. Only able to pray.

Exhaustion weighed down my shoulders, and grief weighed down my spirit.

But he was no longer on life support. His heart beating on its own. The man slipping in and out of a disoriented consciousness every so often.

That was the only thing that mattered. The only thing I clung to as I listened to the steady *beep, beep, beep* of the machine that tracked his heart.

I laid my head on the side of his bed, my hand wrapped in his, my eyes drifting closed as I poured all my belief into him.

I guessed I'd drifted because I startled when I felt the hand squeezin' mine. I jerked my head up to see that copper gaze staring back at me.

Soft and hard and everything between.

My beast.

"Jace," I whispered. His name my confession.

I shot up and rushed out into the hall. "He's awake," I shouted at the nurse.

She came right in, and I anxiously stood back while she checked his vitals and helped him take a drink of water.

Some of that anxiety drifted away when she said that everything looked good and the doctor would be in soon to check him out.

The second she stepped outside the door, I rushed for him, my hands moving across his face, and I started to ramble, the emotion and fears finally cresting in a tsunami that poured from my mouth.

"Jace . . . you're going to be okay. You're here. I'll . . . I'm going to take care of you. I'm so sorry . . . God, I'm so sorry. You're goin' to be okay."

Nervously, I tried to adjust his sheets. To make sure he was comfortable. Desperate for something to do with my hands.

"Faith—" My name cracked on his tongue, but the words kept coming from me in a nervous rush.

"We'll put the renovations on hold, and I'll take care of you. The way you have always taken care of me. It'll be okay, I promise—"

He grabbed me by the wrist. "Faith, stop."

I blinked at him, fighting the tears.

But they were there.

"Please, stop," he begged, grief and torment etched onto his face.

A choked sound left me, everything catching up. Everything we'd been through becoming a chasm that echoed between us.

"I don't think that's a good idea," he murmured.

"What do you mean?"

"When I'm released from here, I'm going to go home with Ian."

My head shook. "No."

Moisture filled his eyes, and he searched my face, so tenderly that I wanted to drop to my knees.

"I failed on the one thing I promised you. That I would never let anything happen to you or Bailey again. I walked out and left you in that bastard's hands. I can't do one thing right."

"No . . . you saved us. You saved us."

His head shook, and he turned his attention to the far wall. His jaw worked, and I saw him gathering the words before he looked back at me.

"No. You almost died because of me. Because I was too much of a coward to admit to you what I knew and who I was. I put you and Bailey in danger, again and again."

I squeezed his hand as tightly as I could. "No."

He smiled softly at me. Affection and the most intense kind of remorse. "It's the truth, Faith. You know it as well as I do. I saw it written on your face when I admitted it to you. You know I'm responsible for Joseph. For stealing your husband. For stealing your daughter's father. For failing you time and time again. I can't bear the thought of you thinking it every time you look at me."

"Jace, please," I rushed, flying to my feet and gripping his shoulders.

He winced.

Pain bleeding through even though they were pumpin' only God knew what through that bag that dripped into him.

I could imagine all the pain he was feeling came from his spirit. The guilt that moved through his face. The same shame he'd been watching me with for all those weeks, the shame I hadn't been able to understand.

"I'm so sorry," he murmured, winding his hand out of my hold and setting it on my face. "So sorry. But I can't stay here. Not after everything."

"Jace," I pleaded, and he was giving me that smile again.

"I came here for one thing, Faith, and that was to make sure you and that little girl were okay. To protect you. Now there's nothing keeping me here."

His thick throat bobbed when he swallowed, and his eyes dropped closed before they were open again.

Blazing as they pierced me.

Slamming me with all that intensity.

"Go. Live your life. Take that house and make it something special the way you always wanted. No one is left to stand in your way."

Tears streaked down my face. "Jace, don't say that. Please, don't say that."

His smile softened farther as he reached out, a tube secured to his wrist, his fingers gentling through my hair. "There's too much history between us. Too much hurt. Too many lies. Go, good girl. Live a good life. I refuse to taint it any more."

"Jace . . . please . . ."

It was a sob that broke.

A cracking in my spirit.

The last thing holding me together.

*Please.*

Those fingers brushed down my face. "I need to go. Figure out who I am after all of this. I am responsible for the death of my cousin. Because I was angry at him, I turned my back on my family. I'm not sure how I'll ever forgive myself for that, but I do know that I can't do it here."

Weeping, I buried my face in his hospital bed, wanting to cling to every inch of him.

Knowing he was broken.

Because of Joseph.

Because of me.

Because of us.

Maybe I'd been right that night when he'd admitted it all. There would be no way for us to piece *us* back together. No glue strong enough to hold all the frayed threads that knitted our lives.

Unable to take it a second longer, I stood and leaned over the bed, never opening my eyes as I pressed a kiss to his mouth.

Because I wondered if he was right.

If Joseph's ghost wouldn't haunt us forever. Destroy us bit by bit.

I ripped myself away, the most striking kind of grief stabbing me as I forced myself out of his hospital room.

Because I realized right then. My heart had never truly been torn between two men.

And I was leaving all of it right there at Jace's feet.

## Jace

"What the fuck are you doing?" Mack raged behind me,

asshole taking up all of the confined space in the hospital room. Didn't help that my brother was leaning against the wall with his arms crossed over his chest.

Both of them sucking the life out of the room.

Oh wait, that was just my insides shriveling up.

Turning to stone.

Been heading there all along. Wasn't sure why I was idiot enough to think I might change it.

I threw a hard glare at Mack. "What does it look like I'm doing? I'm packing all my *nice* things."

Sarcasm dripped from my tongue as I shoved all the bullshit the nurses and the discharging doctor had given me into a plastic bag.

Bandages and scripts and care instructions and a fucking pink water pitcher that I was sure was gonna go great with the décor at Ian's condo.

I'd be staying at his place for at least a week while I finished recovering and then I'd be dragging my sorry ass back to Atlanta where I belonged.

"I know what you're doing, asshole. I just want to know why you're doing it."

My head shook as I continued to shove the shit inside the bag with a little more aggression than necessary. "You know why."

"Uh, think you might need to clarify that, because neither of us knows what the fuck you're thinking." This from Ian, who was watching me the same way as I'd watched him his whole life.

My head shook. "Just leave it."

"Not leaving anything," Mack gritted.

Anger surged. This violent twist that churned through the middle of me.

All of it directed at myself.

I whirled around, faster than my wounded body was ready for.

But I welcomed the stab of pain.

Deserved it.

"You want to know why I'm leaving?" My head craned to the side as I stared Mack down. "I'm leaving because I can't fucking stand the thought of her looking at me and knowing what I did."

Mack shook his head. "She loves you."

My voice lowered. "It doesn't matter how much she loves me, she won't ever be able to look at me the same, and I can't stand that. Knowing I can't be everything because I took part of her away."

"That's bullshit, man. You saved her."

My chest squeezed, and I trained my attention on the floor. "Yeah. And that's what I came to do. And I promised both you and myself I'd be out of here the second she was safe. We all knew I wouldn't be able to stay, and I was a fool to think I might be able to."

# forty-eight

## Faith

*I* shifted in the chair where I sat across from Mack at his desk.

It was the same spot where I'd sat when I'd made my first statement about Joseph. When he'd asked me for any details of what I might have known and I'd felt like a complete fool because I hadn't known anything.

Where I'd wept and had thought I'd never been so unsure of anything in all my life.

It was the same spot I'd sat when I'd come to him after someone had been in my house. After the true threat had been revealed. When I'd been given what had turned out to be a warning.

Felix believing I had actually known the location of the log Joseph had hidden and thinking he could scare the information out of me.

Now, I sat there while Mack gave me all the details I wasn't sure I wanted to know. I listened numbly as he told me that Joseph had been involved in illegal activity for as long as I'd known him.

Quickly rising through the ranks, working for Steven Ricci and his crooked family, the man Jace had tried to protect both his cousin and brother from.

Drugs.

Smuggling.

Money laundering.

Gambling.

With each bit of information he gave, a new piece of me was peeled back and pared down.

My love and respect for Joseph stripped away.

Piece after agonizing piece.

Mack looked away, seeming to waver, before he looked at me pointedly, dealing yet another blow. "I told you he'd been laundering money through the shipping company for the Ricci Family, but he was also siphoning off some of that money that belonged to their supplier for himself. Joseph made it look like Steven was the one pocketing the money. A few months before Joseph was killed, Steven was found floating in a lake somewhere in Massachusetts. Steven's family, Felix included, blamed Steven's death on Joseph, which I have to assume is the case."

Only Felix wasn't actually his name.

Caleb Ricci had been his name, his family's ties so powerful they were able to get him onto the force with falsified information. Getting him on the inside and close to me.

Hooking up with Courtney had only gotten him closer.

Doug had also been one of the Ricci family's men. He and Felix had been sent to *fix* the problem that had been Joseph. Mack assumed it had been Doug who'd been slipping in and out of my house.

Pain sliced through me.

A sharp blade that cut and mangled.

How could Joseph have been involved in these things?

How hadn't I demanded more answers rather than playing the fool?

I choked over a pained sound. Horrified that I'd been so blind. Horrified for Courtney, who was still dealing with the guilt of bringing Felix into our lives, as if she ever could have known what the man's intentions had been.

Mack swiped his wrist across his mouth, his own regret and guilt showing. "Felix killed Joseph because of his betrayal to Steven. But he still needed the log that Joseph had been using as a shield. I think Joseph thought if he held it over their heads, made them believe he was going to turn it over to the detectives, it would keep him safe."

He gave a harsh shake of his head. "But I guess he knew that wasn't going to work, that it was already too late, because he had a note for me hidden in those letters you found. It was information on where to find the log. He had it stashed in a locker at the gym. It contained a slew of names and information to put these guys away for the rest of their lives."

A pang shot through my spirit.

*What a waste*, was all I could think. What a waste of a life. Living that way for no reason. He could have been such a good man.

Hurt and confusion and pity rocked through me in a bolt of feeling I wasn't expecting.

*What a waste.*

Mack pulled open a drawer, blowing out a breath as he pulled out whatever was inside. Slowly, he slid the stack over to me.

They were the letters that had been in the safe, the ones Felix had scattered before I had the chance to figure out what they were.

"These are for you, Faith. I think you should go home and read them through. In private. It's important."

Tears streaked down my face.

Hot.

Hurt.

My insides such a mess I didn't know up from down.

The loss of Jace had become this festering mess inside me.

Each day, it only grew, amplified, became more painful.

I wasn't sure I could take any more piled on top of that.

The truth was, I was angry.

Angry at Joseph for doing all of this.

Angry at myself for falling for it, for ever saying yes to Joseph in the first place.

"I don't want those," I told Mack, squeezing my eyes closed

and turning my head away.

He pushed them farther my direction. "Yes, Faith, I promise, you do."

Fifteen minutes later, I pulled up in front of Courtney's little house, that stack of letters bound by a rubber band, screaming from the seat as if they had their own voice.

As if they possessed their own energy.

I still hadn't gathered the courage to turn them over to see what they were because my gut told me they were going to destroy me a little bit more.

And I was desperately sure I couldn't take any more breakin'.

That the only thing left holding me together was Button.

Button.

She came running out the screen door, taking the one step down and beelining down the red-bricked walk.

Holding that Beast.

My insides clutched in a tortuous curl.

God, I didn't know how to stand. But I did. I unlatched the door and slid from the car in time to catch her as she jumped into my arms.

Just holding her was a balm moving through me.

She'd been acting as if nothing had happened. As if we hadn't been held hostage by a madman. As if she hadn't seen Jace get shot.

Instead, she'd been living in her little fantasy world where she rode on unicorns and the world was always right.

I knew someday, those fears were bound to come out.

"Hi, Mommy."

I kissed the top of her head. "Hey, Bailey Button. How's my favorite girl?"

"I good."

She nuzzled her face in my throat, and I wondered if that trauma was right there, lurking under the surface.

The only thing I wanted was to be strong enough to make it right.

To provide her with the kind of life I'd always wanted.

We'd been granted a second chance.

Freedom.

Life when we'd been so close to losing it.

I was trying so hard to cling to that and not the loss that banged around inside me.

That vacancy so vast.

Jace's presence missing.

Courtney had followed Bailey out, and she wandered down the walkway, her arms crossed over her chest as if she were trying to protect herself. Nursing her own broken heart.

"Hey," she said.

I rocked Bailey a little, looking over at my best friend and just wishin' all of this could be wiped away.

Magic.

"Thank you so much for watchin' her."

Nodding, she swallowed thickly. "It's the least I could do."

My head shook. "Please, don't do that."

"Do what?"

"Feel as if any of this is in any way your fault. You didn't know."

A tear slipped out of the corner of her eye, and I knew her well enough to know she was going for sarcasm, trying to make things light the way she always did, but the words cracked. "If I didn't have such terrible taste in men, none of this would have happened."

"You didn't know," I told her again.

Her mouth trembled. "I should have."

"I didn't know, either. I guess sometimes we miss the most important things."

Neither of us knew what Joseph and Felix had been involved in.

The truth was, we'd been blinded. Trusted too easily. Saw the best in people, when really, there was little of it to be found.

"Are you okay?" she asked.

I winced, hugged Bailey closer. "No, I'm not. But one day I'm goin' to be. You will be, too."

"I know."

I gave her a smile. "I love you, Courtney. You know that,

right?"

"And you know I love you."

My nod was somber and true. "I know."

If I didn't stop this train, I was going to break down right there, so I cleared my throat and shifted my daughter. "I'm going to get home, get her some lunch, and then put her down for a nap."

"Okay, I'll call you tomorrow."

"All right. If you get lonely, you know where to find us."

Her smile was weak. "Oh, I'm sure I'll find some trouble I can get into."

Only Courtney could make me grin. "I'm sure you will."

I buckled Bailey in, drove us home to that massive house, wondering what I was goin' to do now.

Sell it, I guessed. Turned out, the ghosts living there were really too much. Too scary and dark.

God, I hated the idea of someone else living there, but I didn't think I could handle all of it on my own.

We went inside and into the kitchen. I made us lunch, which we barely touched, and then told Bailey about fifteen stories where I knelt at the side of her bed before she finally fell asleep.

Her fears were right there, even though she wouldn't admit them.

When her breaths had finally evened out, I tucked her under her covers, kissed her temple, breathed her in.

Lavender and baby powder and hope.

I was struggling so hard to find any of it in the middle of this.

Warily, I pushed to my feet and trudged out the door and into my bedroom, moving to the massive dresser where I'd set the stack of letters and had wondered if I'd ever have the courage to actually open them.

I stared at them as if they might catch fire.

But I knew I needed to put all of this in the past. To finally, finally move on.

Because I couldn't be stuck this way. I had to be strong for my daughter.

To do that, I had to read what he'd written.

Hand shaking, I reached out and took the stack of envelopes

that were wrapped in a single piece of paper that had a single word written on it in Joseph's distinct handwriting: "Faith."

I carried them to my bed, where I sat on the edge. My heart hammered, banged at my ribs.

Anxiety pulsed as I eased off the rubber band and the piece of paper came loose.

On a gasp, tears streaked free. So fast and so intense I couldn't see. Couldn't see anything but the first envelope that sat on top.

It was addressed to me.

But it was where it had come from and the date that crushed me like a speeding car that had come from out of nowhere.

It was from a correctional facility and was postmarked a year after I'd thought Jace had simply walked out of my life and hadn't looked back.

Hands shaking uncontrollably, I flipped it over and opened the lip that had already been ripped open. Mack or Joseph, I wasn't sure. But none of that mattered.

Not anymore.

I swiped the tears away from my eyes, racing to read the words on the page.

*Faith,*

*I should have sent this a long time ago. Hell, I shouldn't have walked away that day without you knowing the reason I had to leave. But I'd thought it was for the best. That I was letting you go so you could live the kind of life that you deserved.*

*Sitting in here for the last year has made me realize that I should have known better.*

*I know you and I belong together. I know I can be the man you believed I was going to be. I will. It might be harder than ever, but I will.*

*I'll explain why I'm here to you when I get home. I just need you to know that's where I'll be going—home to you. And when I get there, I'm going to give you everything. Never give up on that dream.*

*All my love,*

*Jace*

I pressed a hand to my trembling mouth, trying to hold back the sob, but it was no use. It ripped out of me.

Jace had intended to come back for me.

*I didn't know.*

*I didn't know.*

Hit by a frenzy, I ripped into the next letter and the next. Reading the words of his love.

His confusion that I hadn't responded.

His growing fear, and his mounting worry that I'd begun to think of him the same way as the rest of the world.

As trash and not worthy of me.

Heartbreak crested in waves. One after another. A rising tide that was going to sweep me away.

Joseph had kept these from me. Hidden the truth. Took the chance away from us.

Lied to me.

Not the way Jace had done. Jace had done it to protect me because he loved me.

Joseph had done it to benefit himself.

Hatred ran through my veins. The kind of hatred I'd never felt before. A gutting sorrow that pummeled and pounded, tearing until there would be nothing left.

I felt ravaged, devastated as I devoured every word, faster and faster, pouring over the letters that had come for *years*.

It shouldn't have been possible for me to crack any further, but this one—this one destroyed me.

*Faith,*

*I'm being released in one week. I haven't heard from you in three long years. Beauty robbed from my life and a darkness taking its place. I ache—every day I ache because*

*I haven't heard from you.*

*But I can't forget your words. The hope you instilled in me. You told me I could be anything if I believed in it enough.*

*I believe in us. In our dreams. I want to live them with you. My only hope is that when I see you, face-to-face, you'll remember exactly who I am. That boy who fell in love with a girl who became his world. The only thing I want is to give the world to you.*

*I'll be waiting at our roses. Let's dream again.*

### Jace

I buckled in two at the words, bent over on the bed as I wept.

I imagined him there, in that garden, waiting for me. How long had he stayed? Waiting and wondering and worrying?

I hadn't come.

Because I was already married to Joseph.

Oh, the hate and horror that burned through my spirit. The ugliest feeling I'd ever endured.

*How could he?*

*How could he?*

I could hardly bear the thought of continuing, but there were two more letters at the bottom.

These were different. They weren't from the correctional facility. Neither had a stamp or a postmark.

The one on top was printed with my name across the front in Joseph's same handwriting.

Part of me wanted to rip it to shreds. End it. His voice and his malice and his greed.

Rocked with the greatest sort of sorrow, so deep I could feel it vibrating through my marrow, I forced myself to continue. The tears were so heavy, I could barely see through them as I unfolded the small stack of papers and began to read . . .

### Faith,

*I know by the time you find this . . . by the time you read this . . . I'll be gone. Wish I would have had the guts to tell you the things in this letter earlier, but I've always been a coward. Always have been a liar. Always have been nothing but a goddamned thief.*

*I know you hate me. I deserve it. I deserve everything that is coming to me, and I can feel it coming fast.*

*I need you to know that I'm sorry. I don't expect you to forgive me, but I do need you to know that I am sorry.*

*I'm a prideful man, but all that has caught up to me. I have nothing left to hide. Nowhere left to run.*

*I wish I could go back and do it all over again.*

*The first time I saw you, I wanted you. I wanted you so badly that I did whatever it took to have you.*

*But I should have known you would never truly belong to me. How could you when you'd always belonged to him? But I thought that, if we just had the chance . . . one chance, you'd see we were meant to be together. I was a fool. A callous, clueless, selfish fool.*

*I tried not to be. Tried a million times to man up and leave. Let you go back to the one you cried for at night. I knew. Fuck, of course, I knew. But I stayed, and I stole, and I cheated, thinking someday, someday you would love me the same.*

*I was never worthy of that love. Not for one day. I'm sorry for the pain I caused, but I can't say I regret it, living one day with you. I never said I wasn't a selfish bastard.*

*I stole you away from the one man you truly loved. The one man who truly loved you.*

*Because he did, Faith. He was willing to do anything for your happiness, while I continued to steal it away. While I continued to watch him suffer.*

*Jace sacrificed for us all. All the years growing up—he went hungry so we could eat. He took punches so we could sleep. He took the fall when he wasn't to blame.*

*He went to jail because I wanted you, and then he continued to sacrifice, thinking it was making you happy,* and still, he looked out for me until the day I finally drove him away.

I can make no amends, but I'm leaving you with this—he loved you. He gave up everything so you could live your dream. I know better now. Know I was wrong. I'm not ignorant enough to think I won't rot for eternity for what I've done. But I won't leave this world without you knowing.

When I was younger, I was convinced that I could be the one to give you that dream. What I didn't know then, what took me years to admit, was that your dream was only half of one. He was the other half, he always had been.

I wish I could tell him how sorry I am to his face. I should have held him on a pedestal for all he did, and instead, I knocked him to his knees.

The only thing I can do now is give him back what belonged to him all along.

I loved you, Faith, but it wasn't the right kind. Now go, live in his love. Don't be afraid. Wherever he is, find him. Fight for him. I'll no longer stand in the way. Love him freely, Faith, without regret. Without question. Let him love you back. Don't let him walk away thinking he is less than he is.

### Joseph

Shattered, gutting cries tore from my mouth, my chest heaving as I read his words.

The page underneath slipped free, and with shaking hands, I picked it up, confused by the document.

It was a deed.

One that had been transferred. It originated in Jace Jacob's name.

I gasped when I realized it'd been signed over to Joseph.

This house.

Oh, God, he'd given us this house.

*Our dream.*

*Our dream.*

A staggering surge of emotion flooded me.

Love.
So much love, I couldn't see.
I climbed to my feet, and I knew one thing.
I'd let him walk away once. I wasn't about to do it again.

# forty-nine

## Jace

"Are you sure you have to go?"

Ian rocked on his soles on the edge of the curb where we stood at the front of his building, my new car parked at the valet.

I tossed my suitcase and laptop case into the trunk, my shoulder still aching like a bitch but not coming even close to the ache in my heart.

"You know I do. I can't stay here with her that close. It just hurts too fucking bad."

Didn't have anything left to hide.

No reasons to give other than the one that was the truth.

It just fucking hurt.

"You haven't even talked to her, Jace."

My head shook as I pushed the button to close the hatch. "Don't start on me, Ian. You know why I can't do this. You know why I can't stay."

"You're a fool."

"Yeah."

I'd been a fool for thinking I could find a life here with Faith.

I'd put her in danger again and again.

Lied to her.

Hurt her.

I'd never forget the expression on her face when she realized just how far those lies went.

I refused to hurt her any longer. Refused to drag her back into my life that had always been filled with turmoil. A disaster from the start.

She was free.

Finally free.

That was the only thing that mattered.

Ian pursed his lips, his hands stuffed in his dress pants, his sleeves rolled up and showing off the scars that lined his arms, covered in all those tats that screamed his pain.

Dude was a storybook not a soul could read.

Except for maybe me. Because I knew all those stories. I'd done my best so that they might be written differently, but I'd failed there, too.

God, if I could write all of them differently, I would.

He looked up, carefully eyeing me. "What if I said I wanted you to stay?"

"Then I'd tell you to come visit me. Atlanta is a big place. Plenty of room for all of us."

"That's not home," he told me, voice hard.

"And this is?" It came out a little more bitter than I meant for it to.

He huffed out a frustrated sound. "I think you know the answer to that."

I blew a strained sigh through my nose. "You didn't see her face, man. I saw it, all the way to her soul, and she won't be able to look at me the same. I don't want to live with that. I don't. She and I both deserve better than living with his ghost."

I moved toward him, hesitating for a second before I hugged him tight, not caring that my shoulder screamed. "I'm not even sure who I am after all of this. After everything I've done."

Ian squeezed me back. "You're my brother. The best guy I

know. You are more than you'll ever see."

I squeezed my eyes, fighting the emotion, fucking hating to say goodbye but knowing I couldn't stay. "I love you, brother. Take care of yourself. Settle the fuck down and stop being stupid. Don't make me come back here and kick your ass."

I attempted to tack some playfulness on the end.

I pulled back, but Ian wasn't smiling. "I'm not the one who's being stupid."

I gave a tight nod, knowing what he meant. "I'll talk to you soon."

He sighed. Shook his head. "Drive safe."

"I will."

Without another word, I hopped into the driver's seat. When I pulled out onto the street, my guts were in knots and my heart was bleeding all over the fucking seat.

Dripping out with each mile that passed.

My cell rang, the number lighting up on the dash.

My first instinct was to reject it. Put it all in the past. Leave it the way I had to do.

But the rumble in my spirit had me pushing the accept button on the steering wheel.

"Courtney." Her name was grit.

"Jace . . . you need to go out to the plantation."

Concern lit, but I bit it back. "I'm already on my way out of town."

"Then turn around," she snapped.

"I'm not playing games, Courtney. I'm leaving."

"Neither am I, and you need to turn your ass around. Faith *needs* you."

"Is she hurt?" I was unable to stop the panic, the throb inside me that drew me right back to the girl. That place that would always belong to her.

Courtney's voice quieted. "Yes, Jace, she is hurtin' like crazy, and I'd venture to say you are, too."

"Don't do this to me," I almost begged.

"I already warned you I'd kick your ass if you hurt her, Jace Jacobs."

"I didn't want to hurt her."

"Then don't."

A sigh pilfered from between my pursed lips.

"Don't make me hunt you down and maim that pretty face. Don't want to do it, but I will."

"Courtney."

"Jace," she returned just as hard.

Silence wavered between us. "Just . . . go out there before you leave. That's all I'm asking of you. After everything, please do this one thing."

"Fine."

This was such a bad idea. Such a terrible idea because walking away again was going to be the most excruciating thing I had ever had to do.

Leaving for good.

I ended the call and made a quick U-turn. My sluggish heart instantly racing.

I made it back through Charleston and hit the quiet streets of Broadshire Rim.

I swore that I could look at the sidewalks and see all those ghosts.

Speeding through it, I felt unprepared for the million memories that slammed me as I made the last turn onto the dirt road that ran along the backside of town.

The car jostled down the bumpy dirt road, and I remembered the stake to my heart the first time I'd seen her.

Standing there in that corner of the office like she was trapped by a wild animal.

The feeling she'd invoked.

The care she'd given.

Meeting her on this road what felt like a million times. Falling fast. Loving her hard and so stupidly.

But not as stupidly as when I'd come back here, when I'd tripped into all that grace and found comfort in the one who I never could keep.

I'd known it.

And I'd tried to keep her anyway.

But I'd always been that kind of fool.

My heart hammered like a bitch as I got closer to the plantation, grief climbing my throat when I thought of seeing them again, as I worried what might be wrong.

I slowed when I noticed something in the distance, right at the end of the turn to the plantation.

I squinted into the bright sunlight, my pulse kicking, blood pounding through my veins.

Faith and Bailey were standing at the end of the drive.

A big wooden sign had been erected, painted white, an outline I couldn't make out etched over the top.

Terror hit me hard when I realized it had to be a *for sale* sign.

Everything churned when I came to a stop and killed the engine.

Just staring out the windshield at Faith who was staring back.

Energy thrashed.

A shockwave through the humid air.

Drawn, I clicked open the door and warily stepped out, that feeling rising higher.

Her grace so full.

Her spirit so warm.

I wanted to rest in it forever.

My heart tumbled in my chest when I glanced down at Bailey who swayed at her mother's side, hearts and rainbows printed all over her shirt and magic in her brown, brown eyes.

My Unicorn Girl.

My throat grew thick, so thick I could barely speak, but I finally forced out the choppy words. "Courtney said you needed help."

Faith nodded, blinked, and let her gaze sweep to the sign. "I'm going to need some help paintin' this."

I shook my head. "I won't help you give up your dream, Faith. I won't. Please, don't do it."

But Faith . . . Faith smiled. She smiled that smile that annihilated me.

Joy and life and light.

My goddamned knees went weak.

"I'm not givin' up my dream, Jace. I'm asking you to live it with me."

She took a tentative step forward.

Stealing air.

With that one footstep, I was hit with a crush of need.

"I know what you did," she whispered, her voice so soft it was a song.

"What do you mean?"

She gestured toward the house that was hidden in the protection of the row of spindly trees. "You gave me this. My dream. Even when you thought you couldn't be a part of it."

She wasn't supposed to know. Not ever. My head shook, trying to stop her from coming closer, but she didn't stop.

She just took another step while she stared up at me with those chocolate eyes.

Bailey trotted along with her, holding onto her thigh, the little thing an extension of her mom.

"You bought this house, didn't you? For me?"

God damn it.

My hand went to my chest. Like I could physically rip the pain from where it lived.

Reluctantly, I nodded. "It was always supposed to be yours."

Her lips pursed, so soft, so goddamned soft that I wanted to dip down and taste them one more time.

Her words cut off that thought. "No, Jace, it was always supposed to be ours."

My chest tightened, and she edged an inch closer. "I knew the second you barged into my life that I was never goin' to be the same. I wasn't. You changed me. Changed me in the best of ways."

Grief climbed my throat. "I failed you, Faith."

She reached out and set her hand on my cheek. "You saved me. You saved me and my daughter."

"I lied to you."

Emotion twisted across her face, and her head canted to the side. "Because you loved me."

"I hurt you."

She brushed those fingertips across my bottom lip, and I nearly came undone. "Because you had to."

"I . . ." I struggled for the words, the sound of them gruff when they finally broke free, my heart cracking right there in the open. "I can't stand the thought of you looking at me and seeing what you lost instead. What I stole from you."

Moisture gathered in her eyes, and I thought she'd step away, but she moved closer, so close I could feel the warmth coming from her sweet, sweet skin.

Roses.

Like she'd just run through the gardens.

All I wanted was to bury my face in her neck, to breathe her in.

"When I close my eyes, I see you. When I think of you, I see us together. When I look at you, I see where I belong. I *see* you."

My teeth gritted. "I betrayed Joseph, Faith. My own blood."

Her head shook. "You saved him, again and again. I know what he did, Jace. It was Joseph who betrayed us. I will forgive him . . . someday . . . I will."

She searched my face, those eyes caressing every inch. "You asked me in my kitchen if I knew all the horrible things you'd done in your life, if I could forgive you, and I promise you, there is nothing to forgive. The more I know about you, the more I love you. You are the best man to ever walk into my life."

She searched my face. "Do you remember you once told me I taught you how to believe? That I had given you the hope that you were worth so much more than the world gave you credit for? That I helped you accept you were destined for great things?"

She ran her fingers down my chest. "It was you who brought all of that back to me, Jace. You who brought me back from despair. From fear and helplessness. It was you who made me believe I *deserved* more."

She wet her lips, her words rough. "I let you walk out of my life once, I'm not willin' to do it again."

"But Faith—"

She pressed a finger to my lips, and I swore I could feel the earth shift. The world spinning. "The only thing I need to know is whether you love me for me or out of obligation. If you love me because you ache for me or if this was always about Joseph stealing me away."

The branches whipped and the trees howled.

My hands found her precious face. I tilted her face up to me. "Do I love you?"

I blinked, savoring every curve and line of her face. "You are the one who taught me what that really means. You are the one who showed me what it was to believe in it."

I squeezed her cheeks in emphasis. "You are *love*, Faith. You are my heart. You are my beauty. My world doesn't know how to exist without you."

Tears streaked down her face. "Then let me be yours. Forever. Don't leave me, because I need you more than I've ever needed anything in my life. Tell me you'll stay . . . because I don't wanna go on dreamin' without you."

I glanced down at Bailey, who was completely wrapped around Faith's leg as she grinned up at me. "Will you stay, Jacie?"

I stood there, wondering if this was real. If this was possible. If I could ever be good enough.

Her words from so long ago filtered through my mind.

*"It doesn't matter what anyone says, Jace. It's what you believe. What you see in yourself. If you want it badly enough, you can have it."*

"I believe in us." It came out without question. Without hesitation.

A tremble of a smile moved across her lips. "You became my dream. Tell me you'll live it with me. *Let's dream again.*"

"Always. I'll fight for you. Love you. And I promise that I won't ever walk away."

Faith choked out soggy laughter. "Good. Then I'm goin' to need help painting that sign."

I shifted that way, squinting as I peered at the outline.

*Broadshire Blooms Bed & Breakfast*

She inched up and whispered in my ear. "Come stay at the BBB. Well . . . almost."

I laughed.

Laughed, and then I was rushing to hug her tight, hope billowing over.

Spilling out on the land.

Dream after dream after dream.

A family.

I wanted it, and I'd never stop fighting for it. I drove my fingers in all that lush, long hair, and I kissed her like she was my last breath.

That was exactly what she was.

My last breath.

Every breath until the very end.

Bailey tugged at my pant leg, and I ripped myself away, my heart pressing so damned full.

She was lifting a full gallon of paint, her little arms straining as she curved all the way back so she could show me what she had.

"You got to paint my room *aww* pink and tuck me in every night and *sway* the bad dragons. But not Mack. Mack is a good dragon."

Her eyes shone with this pleading kind of awe.

Magic.

I dropped to my knees in front of her, and I looked up at her mother, who was gazing down at us, her fingers running through my hair, before I turned my attention back to Bailey.

The little girl I would forever love as my own. Never think of her as anything else.

When I opened my mouth, I made a promise I would keep for both of them.

"I'll slay all your dragons, and I promise, I will never leave."

I sat on the edge of Faith's bed, the sound of her moving around in the bathroom after taking a shower soothing me while I held the letter she'd given me to read.

Torn.

Torn between hatred and devotion.

Swallowing down the years of resentment and anger, I turned the letter over and over in my hands, not sure if I wanted to listen to a thing he might want to say.

Finally, I forced myself just to read it.


*Jace,*

*If you have this letter, it means I got what was coming to me. You taught me about karma at a young age. I should have believed its truth. I didn't. But that didn't mean I didn't respect you.*

*Well, respect and envy are a very fine line, aren't they? I wanted to be you, and I hated you for it because I could never be that good. My heart never beat the same way as yours. Your soul ached to do good, and mine sought wickedness and greed.*

*Steven wanted me to prove my loyalty to him, and in turn, I broke the greatest trust I should have shared with someone. I put those drugs in your backpack and made the anonymous call that I'd seen someone breaking into the plantation.*

*I stole from you, but I'm the one who lost.*

*I lost everything. But it was always yours, anyway.*

*Take them. Love them. Don't ever regret finally turning me away. It was what I needed. What they needed. It was time.*

*I know you'll show Bailey what a real man is like. You'll teach her devotion and loyalty. You'll fill her with strength. Most of all, you'll fill that house with love. After all, it was always your ghost that lived there.*

*Goodbye, my brother. That was what you were. If I could change one thing, I would have been a better one.*

*Joseph*

Grief nearly cut me in two, and I squeezed my eyes closed after I'd read his final words. Part of me wanted to hate him. But hating him would solve nothing. It would never change the path we'd been set on.

The loss.

The lessons.

The love.

Love.

It creaked open the bathroom door, standing in the frame, her gorgeous face filling my eyes. I blinked at her, my throat growing thick, that feeling rising high.

So high.

I wanted to ride on it forever.

Faith slowly walked out, her hips a slow sway, the girl so sexy and she never knew it.

I knew she'd given me time. Privacy to read through the letter that had been left for me.

She came to a stop right in front of me, and I widened my knees, dragging her closer to me.

She set her hand on my face, her thumb running along the hollow beneath my eye.

"Are you okay?" she whispered her concern.

I let the letter flutter to the floor.

As wilted as one of the rose petals that fell.

Making space for something new to bloom.

I set both my hands on the outsides of her thighs, staring up at those chocolate eyes.

Emotion flooded fast.

A furious beat through my veins.

"Are you standing in front of me?" I let a grin quirk up at the corner of my mouth.

Faith smiled.

Smiled and that feeling swept me away, and I gripped her around the waist, spinning her around until she was pinned to the bed.

I gazed down at her.

At my love.

My life.

My hope.

My beauty.

She ran those fingers through my hair. "I guess that's my answer then."

I tugged at the towel she had wrapped around her body, revealing every soft, luscious curve. "You're my answer."

Her fingertips fluttered, hovering over the wound healing high on my chest near my shoulder before her hand traveled to my heart, her palm pressing flat against the beat.

I spread my hand over hers. "Beauty."

Faith didn't look away from my eyes as she pushed down my pajama bottoms, neither of us breaking our stare as I twisted the rest of the way out of them, as I crawled between her thighs.

"Beast," she whispered.

I pressed into the sweet warmth of her body. I loved her and cherished her, every shift of my hips as I rocked into her filled with devotion.

With loyalty.

I'd known the second I met her this girl was more.

Forever more, she'd be my everything.

# epilogue

*S*pring cast its warmth across the blue, blue sky, the trees green

and lush where they stretched across the narrow lane.

A shadowy hedge of protection that lifted up to shield the rambling plantation that rose behind me.

Now, it was completely restored.

Magnificent in its beauty.

But there was nothing quite as beautiful as the sight laid out in front of me.

The lawn shimmered with dew and the rose gardens were in a full, fragrant bloom.

Splashes of pink and purple colored the entire side of the yard, and rows of white chairs were setup in neat lines.

In them, sat our family and our friends.

Bailey was running down the aisle ahead of me, tossin' those petals in the air as if they might float all the way to the heavens that stretched overhead.

Heads turned as I slowly walked down the steps from the side porch on my father's arm.

But it was the man at the end of it all that stole my breath.

A shiver raced my spine, and that energy flashed through the air.

A thunderbolt.

Intense and potent.

Just like the man.

More gorgeous than ever. Tall and wide and wearing a suit that made my mouth water.

Those eyes were fixated on me.

The color of a brand-new, shiny penny.

A coppered shimmer that ranged between red and brown and orange.

Something vibrated through the air that I could taste.

The same feeling I'd felt the first time I'd ever seen him.

An omen.

A premonition.

It was the knowledge that nothing would ever be the same.

Because I was stepping into forever.

My daddy smiled down at me as we hit the white runner, and we watched as Bailey danced the rest of the way down the aisle and right into Jace's arms.

The man who adored her.

Loved her to the ends of the earth.

Filled her with hope and joy and the truest kind of devotion.

Her daddy.

He hugged her, kissed her cheek, and then shifted her onto his hip as the two of them grinned our way as we slowly approached.

The gentlest breeze blew through.

A whip of the wind. The sweet smell of roses riding on the air.

As if our dreams were swirling all around us.

Wrapping around us and holding us close.

My heart was nearly explodin' by the time we made it to the end, and my daddy kissed my cheek, whispered in my ear, "I'm so glad he proved me wrong."

He gave me an encouraging smile before he stepped away, and then I turned to face Jace and Bailey.

Emotion thrummed.

And Jace and I just stared.

Lost to the other.

To the culmination of this moment.

To us.

The way it was always supposed to be.

Finally, Jace slowly set Bailey on her feet beside him. She clung to his leg, grinning up at us as Jace touched my face and then touched my swollen belly.

*Benton.*

Our family was right here.

All of us present for this moment when our dreams became a reality.

Because this . . . my family . . . this place?

It was the completion of belief. Of love and hope and faith.

Jace wrapped his arm around my waist and I took Bailey's hand as we turned to the minister, who started the ceremony.

And we stood there.

Our hands intertwined as we promised our lives.

"I will love Faith Linbrock for the rest of my life. Cherish her. Respect her. Protect her. I will never take for granted the love she has given me. I will never forget the devotion I have for her as I stand here this day. And I will never, ever stop dreaming with her."

The minister turned to me, and I repeated my own. "I will love Jace Jacobs for the rest of my life. I will respect him. Adore him. Believe in him. I will never forsake the love he has shown me. I will never forget the way I feel standing here today, at his side, promising him forever. And I will never, ever stop dreaming with him."

The minister looked between Jace and I. "I now pronounce you husband and wife. Kiss your bride."

And oh, Jace did, right there in front of our friends and family. He kissed me in a way that he'd never kissed me before.

With the most devoted kind of passion.

With joy.

With belief.

That kiss?

I felt it like a signature across my soul.

Because this man had always been the greatest confession of my heart.

# the end

Thank you for reading MORE OF ! Did you love

getting to know Faith and Jace? Please consider leaving a review!

I invite you to sign up for mobile updates to receive short,
but sweet updates on all my latest releases.
Text "aljackson" to 33222
(US Only)
or
Sign up for my newsletter
http://smarturl.it./NewsFromALJackson

Watch for the next in *Confessions of the Heart* novel, *All of Me*,
coming Early 2019!

Want to know when it's live?
Sign up here: http://smarturl.it/liveonamzn

# More from A.L. Jackson

<u>*Hollywood Chronicles*, a collaboration with USA Today Bestselling</u>
<u>Author Rebecca Shea</u>
*One Wild Night*
*One Wild Ride*

# ABOUT THE AUTHOR

A.L. Jackson is the New York Times & USA Today Bestselling author of contemporary romance. She writes emotional, sexy, heart-filled stories about boys who usually like to be a little bit bad.

Her bestselling series include THE REGRET SERIES, CLOSER TO YOU, BLEEDING STARS, and FIGHT FOR ME.

Watch for the latest in her new series, CONFESSIONS OF THE HEART, coming Early 2019!

If she's not writing, you can find her hanging out by the pool with her family, sipping cocktails with her friends, or of course with her nose buried in a book.

Be sure not to miss new releases and sales from A.L. Jackson - Sign up to receive her newsletter http://smarturl.it/NewsFromALJackson or text "aljackson" to 33222 to receive short but sweet updates on all the important news.

**Connect with A.L. Jackson online:**

Page **http://smarturl.it/ALJacksonPage**
Newsletter **http://smarturl.it/NewsFromALJackson**
Angels **http://smarturl.it/AmysAngelsRock**
Amazon **http://smarturl.it/ALJacksonAmzn**
Book Bub **http://smarturl.it/ALJacksonBookbub**
Text "aljackson" to 33222 to receive short but sweet updates on all the important news.

Made in the USA
Columbia, SC
20 September 2018